NOTE ON THE AUTHOR

Eva Dolan was shortlisted for the CWA Dagger for unpublished authors when only a teenager. The four previous novels in her Zigic and Ferreira series have been published to widespread critical acclaim: *Tell No Tales* and *After You Die* were shortlisted for the Theakston Crime Novel of the Year Award and *After You Die* was also longlisted for the CWA Gold Dagger. In 2018 *Long Way Home* won the *Grand Prix Des Lectrices*. Dolan's first stand-alone thriller, *This is How It Ends*, was longlisted for the 2019 Theakston Old Peculier Crime Novel of the Year. She lives in Cambridge.

@eva_dolan

D0043214

ALSO BY EVA DOLAN

DI Zigic and DS Ferreira series
Long Way Home
Tell No Tales
After You Die
Watch Her Disappear

This is How It Ends

BETWEEN TWO EVILS

EVA DOLAN

R A V E N BOOKS

LONDON · OXFORD · NEW YORK · NEW DELHI · SYDNEY

RAVEN BOOKS
Bloomsbury Publishing Plc
50 Bedford Square, London, WC1B 3DP, UK

BLOOMSBURY, RAVEN BOOKS and the Raven Books logo
are trademarks of Bloomsbury Publishing Plc

This edition published 2020
First published in Great Britain 2020

A catalogue record for this book is available from the British Library

ISBN: HB: 978-1-4088-8644-1; TPB: 978-1-4088-8645-8; PB: 978-1-4088-8641-0;
eBook: 978-1-4088-8642-7

2 4 6 8 10 9 7 5 3 1

Typeset by Integra Software Services Pvt. Ltd.
Printed and bound in Great Britain by CPI Group (UK) Ltd, Croydon CR0 4YY

To find out more about our authors and books visit www.bloomsbury.com
and sign up for our newsletters

Day One

TUESDAY AUGUST 7ᵗʰ, 2018

CHAPTER ONE

'So this is where you're hiding,' Adams said, coming down the brown brick steps in front of Thorpe Road Police Station, a cigarette already hanging from his mouth.

'Just getting some sun.' Ferreira closed her eyes for a moment and tilted her face up: twenty-five degrees at 10 a.m., basking weather. Bikini-on-beach-drinking-rum-cocktails weather. Which is exactly where she'd been a week ago, Adams beside her then too, their first holiday together and they hadn't killed each other, so she guessed there was something to be said for him. He'd come back from St Kitts with a deep tan and a more relaxed air, and that was certainly helping too.

'You know Riggott's going to start docking your pay if you keep this up,' he said, lighting up.

'Where else am I supposed to smoke?'

'Crazy thought, but you could quit,' he suggested, exhaling a lungful.

Ferreira flicked an eyebrow up at him. 'I'll quit when you do.'

'Well, maybe cut down from thirty a day.'

'I don't smoke that much.'

'You're coming out here that often.'

She took another deep drag, her eyes straying to the station's broad, brutalist façade and the greyed-glass windows of what had been the Hate Crimes Unit on the first floor.

'You can't sulk about it for ever, Mel.'

Ferreira straightened up and away from the wall. 'I'm not *sulking*.'

'You know what I mean.' He tried a smile but she wasn't softening, not after having had this conversation with him repeatedly

3

and always with the same conclusion during the six months since the Hate Crimes Unit had been mothballed. 'They clung on for longer than anyone expected,' he said. And even her partner Zigic agreed on that point when she'd talked to him about it.

They'd had a good run, Zigic insisted. Being back in CID didn't mean they stopped investigating the hate-based offences that had consumed their professional lives for the last seven years; it just meant they did more for everyone else too. Now they had access to more resources when they needed them, a bigger team to draw on, more local knowledge and expertise. It meant that the burden didn't always have to fall just on them.

But she felt the burden on her when they were sent to another violent incident in New England, another dispute between neighbours or a drink-fuelled brawl that spilled onto the road or into the parts of the city where the citizens the council were actually bothered about lived. The way Ferreira saw it, they'd been taken off hate crimes and put on anything that involved a foreign accent, deployed more to save the cost of translators than anything else.

Their caseload had quadrupled and yet she no longer felt like they were helping people. Just keeping the peace. And if she wanted that she would have stayed in uniform.

'I'm not happy,' she said, almost at a whisper, almost without meaning to.

'I know.' He reached for her hand and she pulled away as his fingertips grazed her knuckle, checking to see if anyone around them had noticed.

'Not here, okay.' A moment of pain tightened his eyes and she pretended not to see it, tossed her head, already feeling guilty. 'Can I bum a fag?'

Adams sucked the last breath out of his own cigarette, dropped the butt into the bin. 'No, come on, we should get back up there.'

They headed into reception and through the stairwell doors, where a couple of guys from anti-terror were coming down, all swagger and growl as they talked about the cricket, making even that seem like a life-or-death matter. Part of her thought it was ridiculous, but part wondered how she'd fare with them. Maybe what she needed was more of a challenge?

'How do you fancy going out for dinner tonight?' Adams asked, as he held the door open for her.

'It's Tuesday.'

'Yeah, so?'

'What's the point of going out for dinner when we've got the whole rest of the week to put up with?'

He rolled his eyes at her. 'You are the worst fucking Catholic I've ever met.'

'What's my particular brand of indoctrination got to do with dinner?'

'Because you should know to take all the pleasures you can get whenever they're offered.' He gave her a cheeky wink and headed for his office, pulling his mobile out of his pocket.

She watched him pass between the rows of desks, saw Parr straighten in his seat as he approached, the new kids at their shared station in the corner looking extra focused for a few seconds, trying to make a good impression on the DCI. She saw his stride falter as he answered the phone, his free hand tightening into a fist and all the tension she'd holidayed out of his body returning in a rush.

He battered on the window of Zigic's neighbouring office and gestured for him to come out as he ended the call, then shouted back across his shoulder, 'Mel, Bobby, Colleen, in with me.'

Zigic emerged from his office, giving Ferreira a questioning look.

At the desks around them, a shiver of interest had raised eyes from screens, the rest of the floor scenting something in the offing and wondering if it would pull them in too. Despite the weather and the general tendency for things to get fractious in summer heat, it was quiet on the day shift; a dozen cases rumbling along, not quite enough to keep a team of a sixteen detectives as busy as they'd like. Everyone eager for some fresh hell to sink their attention into.

5

'We've got a call,' Zigic said to her. 'We need to get going.'

'I'm pretty sure this is bad news. We should probably ...'

Zigic glanced at his watch, grimaced. 'Okay.'

They filed in, Adams closing the door behind them. His face was hollowed out with concern, mouth a sick line.

'What is it?' DS Colleen Murray asked, taking one of the free seats at his desk, her eyes fixed on him. 'What's happened?'

'I've just had a call from a mate at the prison,' he said, dropping heavily into his chair. 'Walton's been released. Friday gone, they let him out.'

There was a moment of silence as they digested the news. A case that had consumed Adams and Murray for the better part of eighteen months, one which Hate Crimes had been pulled into in the weeks before they were shut down; CID's most prolific serial rapist had strayed into their territory when he was suspected of murdering a trans woman as she took her morning run around Ferry Meadows Country Park, a case that had led them to tying Walton to several more attacks on local trans women. They'd built an airtight case, which saw him sent down for life. A case built almost entirely on forensic evidence.

Which was where the problem lay.

In March a technician at the forensic lab had been exposed by a BBC documentary investigating instances of bribery and corruption at laboratories in the Midlands. As they were looking for blood alcohol tests bent to slip driving offences, they uncovered a more interesting story: a leading expert in DNA analysis who had faked their credentials through a twenty-year career, opening up two decades of convictions across the Midlands to new scrutiny. Detective Chief Superintendent Riggott had kicked into gear the morning after the documentary aired, instructing DC Bobby Wahlia to start a comprehensive review of every potentially affected case, in the hope that with some, at least, they could give the Crown Prosecution Service a second line of attack. There had been a slew of appeals already, the majority ending in overturned convictions, but this was the first to hit their team.

They'd argued the appeal and lost.

'We knew it was coming,' Wahlia said at last, his voice toneless, but the defeat written all over his face.

Ferreira imagined she looked just as beaten as he did, saw it on Zigic too, the grim resignation. Murray wasn't taking it quite so calmly; her shoulders squared with anger, face and neck flushed such a deep red Ferreira was sure she could see the rage glowing through her off-white blouse. But Colleen had been closer to the case for longer, had shepherded more of the victims through complaints which went nowhere, had to sit with them and explain why their particular attack didn't meet the CPS's standards for prosecution. Then, finally, she got to tell each and every one of those women that Lee Walton was finally going down. Not for what he did to them, but for something, at least.

Murray was hunched over now, fists between her thighs. 'Right, what are we going to do about this? We're not going to let this piece of shit back out on the streets to do whatever the hell he likes, are we?'

'There isn't much we can do,' Zigic said softly. 'We threw everything we had at Walton, there's nothing left we can use. It was all on the forensics.'

'Don't you think I know that?' Murray snapped, twisting in her chair to face him. 'What do you suggest then, we sit around and wait for him to do it again?'

'We're not waiting,' Adams said, drawing himself up where he sat. He pointed at Wahlia. 'Clear everything else off your plate, yeah? I want you totally focused on Walton, go back through every case file we have on him, every stalled investigation, every dropped charge, every withdrawn complaint. Burrow into this fucker's history and find something we can nail him for.'

Wahlia was on his feet and out of the office instantly.

Murray watched him go, turned back to Adams.

'Is that it?' she asked, incredulous. 'That's what we're doing?'

'It's what we can do right now,' he told her, and Ferreira heard the familiar conciliatory tone he hardly ever used at work.

She caught Zigic's eye, nodded towards the door. They slipped out, leaving Adams to try and talk Murray down from the peak of her rage.

CHAPTER TWO

They drove out of the city in silence, skirting the suburbs and endless housing estates, making fast progress on the parkway that snaked through the blocky landscape of warehousing and big-box megastores, heading into the bustle of the sprawling Eastern Industrial Estate, with its scent of green waste and rubble dust and epoxy. Then the city fell away with an abruptness that always struck Zigic as slightly unreal and ahead the fenland unfolded, wild and flat, and near lawless, all the way to the Wash. The sky was vast and cloudless, heat shimmering up off the road, haze in the distance, the light wind stirring up the threat of dirt storms as the fields lay parched from the rainless weeks. Crops were wilting, standing unharvested, vegetation yellowing, fruit dying on the stem. The shortage of seasonal labour was beginning to tell now. Hardly any sign of activity in the fields they passed. People who went home for Easter had decided against returning, heading for more welcoming options instead.

Peterborough felt quieter, Zigic thought. As if it had become a smaller city during this last eighteen months. Shops were closing, pubs were closing, companies relocating or just folding. Everyone seemed to be retreating indoors, the crimes they were investigating becoming smaller and quieter but no less devastating. More domestic violence, more fights among friends and frauds among families. Something in the air, he thought, something emerging but not yet defined.

They had been in and out of the various East European stores around the city and the suburbs, trying to stop a spree of violent armed robberies, and everyone they talked to reported the same thing: business was down. There was less footfall, fewer new people arriving. He could sense the fear, the uncertainty.

Eventually they'd caught the gang responsible, when one of them met the end of a baseball bat wielded by a shop owner who'd decided to stand his ground. It was risky and something they had explicitly warned against. The man was stabbed in the shoulder but he was a hero now. On the front page of the local paper, smiling with his bandaged wound on show.

The shops could go about their business with one threat removed, but the greater one remained.

Zigic slowed as they entered a small village of houses built close to the road and ramshackle farm buildings, a warning sign flashing his speed at him.

In the passenger seat next to him, Ferreira muttered something under her breath.

'What?'

'This place,' she said, throwing her chin up towards a row of old white-painted council houses. 'This is where we used to live. Before my parents took us to Peterborough.'

'And you're not feeling the nostalgia?'

She snorted. 'I don't even drive through here if I can help it.'

He waited for her to say more but she fell silent again. She'd been doing that more and more lately, and he was beginning to wonder if it was only the move out of Hate Crimes that was preying on her mind. He wasn't happy about it either but the decision was taken many levels above them, and there was no point fighting it at the time, even less brooding on it now that it was over and done with.

Their job hadn't changed. Not really. Even though the trappings and the setting were different. He wondered why she couldn't see that.

Was it Adams? he thought. Was there trouble between them? It was a question he couldn't ask her, a line he shouldn't ever cross. But with each passing week, with every one of these pregnant silences, it became more difficult not to broach the issue.

Zigic tightened his fingers around the wheel and accelerated out of the village towards and through the next, near identical one, catching sight of the bank of wind turbines standing sentry-still at the edge of Long Fleet, blades all stopped at different angles. Beneath them the village sat huddled around a central green, a few narrow lanes radiating away from it. A pub and a shop, a tiny primary school that he remembered visiting years ago as a newly recruited constable to talk to the children about stranger danger.

It was a pretty village. Barely heard of beyond the immediate ten-mile radius back then.

But now Long Fleet was synonymous with the Immigration Removal Centre that sat at its northern edge. The site had previously been an RAF base and would have passed for one still, with its long rows of barracks-style structures set around drab courtyards and the one grand building, all red brick and long windows and peaked gables fronting the road. Some effort had been made to hide it with screen planting, but it was too substantial to fully obscure. As they passed the village's welcome sign, the sunlight glinted on the barbed wire and flashed off the signs held up by the small band of forlorn protestors stationed across the road from its main gates.

Zigic held his breath for a Ferreira tirade but when he glanced over, he saw her attention was fixed on her mobile phone.

A moment later he spotted the coroner's distinctive vanilla-coloured Alvis coming the other way. She flashed her lights and he put his hand up, glad to know she'd done her part already and they could get started.

The place they wanted was on the edge of the village green, with a bus stop nearby and the pub opposite, the shop less than 100 metres away. It was the middle house in a row of Victorian workers' cottages, built low and listing away from the road, the ground around them eroded by the vicious winds that blew across the fens, leaving the houses standing like teeth in receding gums. But it looked neat and well maintained, wooden shutters drawn in the windows, a copper fisherman's lamp next to the front door and a boot brush set beside the low, worn step where a uniformed officer was currently standing, squinting into the sun and sweating profusely.

'This us?' Ferreira pocketed her phone and climbed out of the car, immediately pointing at the red Golf parked across the lane behind the forensics van. 'Kate's back? I thought she had another week's sabbatical yet?'

'No, back today,' Zigic told her. 'You've still got your holiday head on.'

He popped open the boot of the car and grabbed a couple of overalls, as she dragged her long dark hair up into a ponytail.

'I thought she was done, you know.' Ferreira stepped into her suit. 'She took it so hard.'

Zigic remembered sitting with Kate Jenkins in her office the day after the story about the corrupt lab broke, seeing just how devastated she was. There was no blame attached to her but watching so many of the cases she'd worked on slip away made the job seem pointless, she'd said, looking out at her own lab. He'd told her he felt the same way but that it was no reason to leave. They all had ones that got away, the lack of evidence and the absconders and the juries blinded by tricky lawyers and handsome defendants. It happened. Far too often. But they came intermittently, he'd realised, and you had time to process the rage and disappointment and the weighty burden of guilt you felt for the victims who'd been through so much only to see a case fail.

So many cases potentially compromised all at once had been overwhelming.

'Guess she just needed a bit of time to deal with it,' he said.

They headed for the front door, signed in with the uniform on guard and entered a flagstone-floored, white-painted hallway with monochrome cycling prints hung on one wall and an old bike wheel strung with small lights on the other.

'You actually like that, don't you?' Ferreira asked, catching his admiring glance.

'It's different.'

Voices led them through into the living room, Kate Jenkins and two of her assistants almost indistinguishable from each other in their coveralls and masks as they presided over the room.

Jenkins spread her arms wide.

11

'My two favourite detectives.'

'So good to see you back,' Zigic said, matching the smile he saw crinkling her eyes above her mask.

'The guy they had covering for you was a nightmare,' Ferreira told her.

'Yeah, I heard he was a bit of a dick,' Jenkins said and pointed at the figure peering into a copper bin next to the leather chesterfield. 'Elliot was keeping me up to date.'

'Got a condom in here,' he said.

'How could I *resist* coming back to this?' Jenkins asked.

'It's been used.'

She nodded. 'Great stuff.'

Another assistant was filming the body laid out in the smashed remnants of a dark-wood coffee table: Josh Ainsworth. A man of medium build with brown hair and a short beard, dressed in lounge pants and a heavily bloodstained T-shirt. From the state of his skin and the pungent aroma, even Zigic could tell he'd been dead at least a couple of days.

Zigic looked around the room as Ferreira asked Jenkins how her holiday went, taking in the teal walls and abstract art and the open top of a pizza box protruding from underneath the body. There was a wine bottle toppled on the floor near the sofa, a wine glass next to it, somehow still standing and half full, already marked out for further attention. He wondered where the other one was. If there was another one. The condom suggested company but didn't guarantee it, he thought, involuntarily wrinkling his nose.

'Actually, you know what,' Jenkins said abruptly. 'This is going to go way faster if you're not in here distracting me with holiday talk and gossip.'

'We'll get out of your way for a bit then.' Zigic gestured to Ferreira. 'You two can catch up later.'

'Drinks?' she asked over her shoulder, as he was hustling her out.

'Lots of them,' Jenkins said enthusiastically.

Outside in the lane they peeled off their suits and Zigic felt how sticky his bare arms had become in a matter of minutes. He tried to figure the heat into a time of death, eager to fix even a vague point for the crime, but stopped himself. There was plenty to do before the post-mortem gave them the information and other, better, ways to make an educated guess.

'I really missed her,' Ferreira said, with a crooked smile.

He was surprised how pleased he was to see that smile again. Realised how long it had been since he saw her anything but grimly or bitterly amused.

'She's one of the good ones, Kate.'

A silver Corsa came around the green ahead of them and pulled into the lane, trailed by a patrol car. DC Zachary Parr arriving with the extra bodies to set about the door-to-door.

'You want me to deal with that?' Ferreira asked.

'Thanks, Mel.'

She met Parr as he climbed out of his car and spoke briefly to him and the uniforms, peering at the tablet he had in his hand, dividing up the houses and setting them to work. It wouldn't be a long job canvassing the immediate vicinity but the green was likely a magnet for the village's dog walkers, judging by the sign reminding owners of the maximum fine for not clearing up after their pets. The area was relatively well lit for the sticks, enough street lights that anyone coming along after dark might have been seen and seen well enough to make a positive identification. With the late sunset they had a good chance of potential sightings. So they would ask around and put notes through the doors of any empty houses, hope that someone had seen something useful.

Small, tight-knit villages like this, there was always a dedicated observer or two. The kind who diligently recorded the number plates of unfamiliar vehicles and profiled any strangers they saw hanging about.

Zigic headed slowly down the lane, searching for security cameras on the line of cottages; rural crime was on the rise, as always, but with little to no CCTV in these parts lots of people resorted to independent measures. He rounded the green, scrutinising each façade and the eaves of every garage, hoping for a camera pointed across to Joshua Ainsworth's house. But there was nothing.

Of course they wouldn't be that lucky, he thought, returning to number 6.

Through the fine nets at the neighbouring cottage's front window, he could see an elderly man peering out, his cat sat on the windowsill, watching them more brazenly but with less interest.

Maybe they had CCTV after all.

CHAPTER THREE

The village shop was a flimsy-looking 1970s addition to what Ferreira guessed had probably been a picture-perfect cottage before they stuck the big white box on the side of it. The windows were plastered with neon stars advertising local cleaners and dog-sitting services, a twice-weekly Pilates class in the village hall and a painter and decorator boasting of his DBS clearance.

On the path out front, trays of fruit and veg wilted in the heat, the ripe, sweet smell of the bananas attracting a persistent swarm of small black flies and a wasp, which buzzed at her when she got too close. She swiped at it but gave the ground. You couldn't always be the hero.

The door stood open, shielded by a plastic strip curtain, which slithered unpleasantly around her as she went inside.

Behind the short wooden counter, a grey-haired man with a sunburned face sat reading a Maeve Binchy novel. He glanced up as she entered, nodded a greeting tinged with curiosity.

Always the same in these places, she thought. Remembering the shop in the village they'd lived in when she was a kid, almost indistinguishable from this, with the same truncated shelves scantily stocked with tinned goods and packets of instant mash and tea bags, all extravagantly marked up, because if you found yourself short so far from civilisation, well, that was your bad luck. She remembered how closely she'd been watched when she went in, the sense that they knew this little brown-skinned girl had come from the caravan site and consequently was not to be trusted. She'd watched other kids shoplift with impunity while the eyes of the owner stayed locked on her, suspicious of everything about her right down to the integrity of the coins she used to pay for her chocolate bars.

But she wasn't that girl any more, she reminded herself. She was a detective sergeant in a silk blouse and tailored trousers and very smart brogues, who didn't take shit from anyone.

She went to the fridge at the back of the store, grabbed a couple of bottles of water. Next to it a freezer hummed unsteadily, half full of ice cream and lollies. The sight of the rockets caused her to stop for a second, remembering a trip to the coast: the whole family stuffed into a borrowed car, eating one as her brothers wriggled and fought beside her, Paolo trying to keep Joe and Tom in line with pinches and small-fisted punches, her parents oblivious in the front, singing along to the radio like they'd forgotten they even had kids.

'Right, I've told you,' the shopkeeper shouted. 'You're not welcome in here.'

There was scuffling noise and swearing, the sound of cans scattering hard across the floor.

Ferreira rushed to the front of the store, saw him trying to hustle out an ungainly young guy with fluffy bleached-blond hair and wide holes punched in his earlobes. His hand was tight around the man's skinny upper arm and the young guy, off-balance in a pair of bright green flip-flops, lunged for purchase and cleared a nearby shelf of boxed instant rice as he grabbed for some anchor and missed.

'We only want to get some milk,' he protested, twisting his arm free.

Livid red fingerprints sprang up on his freckled skin.

'I told you this was a waste of time,' the woman with him said sharply, drawing him away. She shot the shopkeeper a fiery look, then turned to Ferreira. 'I hope you like giving your money to a fascist pig.'

The shopkeeper watched them go, hands on his hips in a defiant posture but Ferreira could see how shaken he was by the encounter, his mouth in a slack line and his cheeks spotted with colour.

'Sorry about that,' he said, eyeing the mess they'd made as he went back around the counter. 'Protestors from the Fleet.'

'Yeah, I think I saw them on the way in,' she said, feeling his desperation to talk now and knowing he needed little prompting.

'Most of them are no trouble,' he told her. 'Old women by and large, teacher types, you know what I mean? Come in for an iced tea and a bit of fruit, inoffensive lot. I've got no issue with them quietly going about their business. Peaceful protest ... I might not agree with them but they've got every right to stand there with their signs if they think it's helping.' He jabbed a finger towards the door. 'But those two ...'

'Not so inoffensive?'

'I can't prove it,' he said, dropping his tone conspiratorially, leaning across the counter. 'But someone's been leafleting the village for months. Really nasty stuff. Going on about what the staff are up to in there. Must be lies, mustn't it? You don't get away with that in prisons. Not in this country. There are rules.' He straightened again. 'We all know one of that lot's responsible, but smart money's on them two. They're bloody militants, you've only got to look at them.'

She murmured agreement, keeping him going so he'd be receptive when she asked about Ainsworth. 'What are they saying's going on there?'

'Bullying and that.' He nodded at her. '*Worse*.'

'It happens in the best-run prisons,' she told him.

'Maybe it does,' he conceded. 'But nigh on half the staff live in the village. They're good people and they're having their reputations dragged through the dirt with out-and-out lies. Lucky we know better than to believe it, but what if we didn't? That's how lives get ruined.'

He frowned deeply, lost in a brief introspection.

'Anyway ... you'll be able to judge the place for yourself soon enough, from what I hear.' A satisfied smile lifted his face momentarily and he inclined his head towards the door. 'Josh Ainsworth works there.' The smile dropped off his face. 'Worked. Sorry.'

Ferreira's turn to nod.

'You can always smell a copper, right?'

He tapped his nose. 'Always.'

Strange thing to be proud of, she thought. A boast she'd only ever heard come out of the mouths of criminals before.

'Was Ainsworth a guard?'

'Doctor,' the man said. 'What a waste of a good brain.'

'Who told you he was dead?' Ferreira asked, reaching into her pocket for some change.

'Old Mr Edwards, from next door. He's right shook up.'

Not too shook up to come over here and spread the news though, Ferreira thought.

She handed him the money for the waters and a card in case he heard anything that she might be interested in.

When she went back out onto the street, she saw the couple who had been thrown out of the shop had started walking away, towards the edge of the village and the protest at Long Fleet's gates they were going to rejoin. They'd stopped and were looking towards Joshua Ainsworth's cottage, too far away for her to read their expressions, but something about the man's hunched posture and the stiffness of woman's back made her think they might know something interesting too.

Chapter Four

Ferreira was sitting on the bonnet of his car, rolling a cigarette, when Zigic emerged from number 4, and it took him a few minutes further to extricate himself from Ainsworth's neighbour and his accomplice of a cat, which kept winding between his feet in a figure of eight. He assured the man that they would be in touch if there was anything else they needed from him. Explained once more the numbers on the card he'd handed over and that he didn't need to worry about the email address if he wasn't very good with his computer, just ring.

He half expected to be physically dragged back inside but made it up the short front path and through the freshly painted gate, feeling a twinge of sadness in his chest for the nice old man with the sharp eyes but the faltering hearing.

'Any good gossip from the shop?' he asked Ferreira as he sat down next to her.

'Ainsworth's a doctor at the detention centre.' She handed over his water. 'Half the village work up there, apparently. And we've got an ongoing protest situation that's verging on harassment of workers. Leaflet campaigns, public shaming. Probably not a million miles off the mark though, given what we know about how those places operate.'

Roughly the same as he'd just been told.

There was irritation in Ferreira's voice but an unmistakable edge of excitement too. He could see it lifting her as she lit her cigarette, could almost hear the cogs turning behind her sunglasses.

He was already envisioning the pressure he was going to come under from Riggott and all the many layers above and beyond him. Pressures Ferreira only felt at one reserve, protected from them by her rank because he had never been the kind of DI who passed his beatings down the chain of command. As bad as they'd been on other cases, he knew the potential here was significantly worse.

Long Fleet was operated by Securitect. The same company who were angling to provide Cambridgeshire Constabulary's emergency call services, their increasing roster of civilian support staff and, for all he knew, the sandwiches in the vending machines that had replaced their canteen a few months ago.

If Joshua Ainsworth's murder touched at all on his job at Long Fleet, they were going to be tiptoeing around landmines trying to investigate it.

It looked personal though. No sign of forced entry, Ainsworth killed in his living room as he ate his dinner, judging by the pizza box and the spilled bottle of red wine. Perhaps killed by the person he'd shared the meal with or why hadn't they tried to intervene? Or reported his murder right away.

'I think we need to speak to the protestors,' Ferreira said. 'There were a couple of them kicking off in the shop when I went in. I dunno,' she shrugged. 'They had that air, you know?'

'It looks like a fairly peaceful protest,' Zigic said hopefully.

'Then we can disregard them quickly.'

'We can't just pull them all in for questioning, not without grounds.'

'Isn't the harassment grounds enough?'

'It would be if we knew who was behind it,' he told her.

'We'll never find out if we don't speak to them.'

He sighed, hearing the tease in her voice.

'How about we take their number plates?' she suggested. 'Get their names, check if there are any known agitators involved, and then we can approach and see what kind of reaction we get?'

'Set Parr on it.'

She called the DC over and passed on Zigic's fresh orders, told him to be discreet.

Zigic gestured at the empty cottage with its curtains all drawn, wanting to change the subject. 'Nobody in at eight. Holiday let.'

'Here?' Ferreira asked, incredulous. 'Who'd come on holiday here?'

'It's pretty, I guess. Quiet.'

'Not this weekend.'

'No.' He picked at his shirt, already starting to stick to his back. 'And someone *was* staying there, so we'll need to track them down.'

'Number four was chatty then.' Ferreira glanced at the house. 'He's still in the window.'

'I got the impression he's a bit lonely.' The old cat and the interior like a time capsule; he brushed the thought aside. 'Ainsworth's been away on holiday too. Just got back Wednesday. But he'd been off work a few weeks before that too. Pottering around the house, his neighbour said.'

'Lost his job, do you think?'

Zigic shrugged. 'Or he'd banked a load of holiday time and decided to take it while the weather was good.'

'Did he hear anything?'

'No, nothing out of the ordinary but his hearing isn't up to much, so that doesn't mean they didn't hear something on the other side,' Zigic said. 'Ainsworth was a considerate neighbour, he reckoned. No loud music, no midnight DIY sessions. Not much in the way of visitors.'

'Girlfriend?' Ferreira asked. 'Boyfriend?'

'A woman occasionally, couldn't give me a description beyond "very elegant-looking, she is". Said he went out on his bike a lot in the evenings. It sounds like he was a bit of a loner.'

'Not much to do of an evening in a place like this,' Ferreira said. 'Maybe we should ask at the pub.'

'Bit early for drinks,' he warned.

They waited as an ambulance arrived to take away Joshua Ainsworth's body, and a few minutes later one of Jenkins's

21

assistants gave them the all clear to enter the house. They found her still in the living room, standing over the remains of the table, making notes. With Ainsworth's body gone Zigic picked out the glimmer of the second wine glass, which must have shattered under the weight of him as he fell. He winced at the thought, even though a few shards of glass in the back was a minor injury compared to the extensive damage that had been done to his face and head.

Automatically he and Ferreira had moved closer to the table, both picking their way carefully through the room, avoiding the areas that Jenkins and her team had marked up on the floor, pieces of evidence corralled and colour-coded, numbered and logged.

'Okay, so ...' Jenkins said, in business mode now, voice lower and more stern, eyes focused. 'This is *very* preliminary and prepare yourself for a change when we've done the real heavy lifting.

'We won't hold you to anything,' Zigic assured her.

'So, early thinking on the murder weapon is this table leg right here.'

Jenkins pointed to a piece of dark wood, lying where it had been dropped a metre from the table. It was fairly slim but substantial enough, Zigic thought, knowing how fragile the human skull was, especially around the temple.

'Multiple blows,' she said. 'Front on.'

'Once he was down?' Ferreira asked.

'You'll need to wait for the PM for that. But – and don't you dare quote me – judging by the severity of his injuries, I'm guessing he was put down in the initial scuffle.' Jenkins took half a step forward, making a shoving motion with her free hand. 'That's when the table broke – looked smart enough but it was not well made. Then once he's down, your killer retrieved the leg and beat him to death with it.'

'Our assailant didn't want him getting to his feet again,' Zigic said, turning towards the spray of blood across the carpet and up the sofa. 'They made a decision to put him down for good.'

'Frenzied?' Ferreira asked.

22

'In the grey area,' Jenkins said.

Zigic looked at the pizza box, still *in situ*, one slice left in it. 'They're in the middle of a meal and suddenly this happens?'

'Bit more than an argument over the last slice of pizza, surely?' Ferreira said. 'The neighbour mentioned a woman visiting. Does this look like something a woman could do? It would have taken a lot of strength to put him through the table.'

'We found a pair of knickers down between the sofa cushions,' Jenkins told them. 'Might have been there months but combined with the used condom in the bin and the lipstick on the wine glass, I'd say you're definitely looking for a female dinner companion.'

'Fingerprints off her glass?'

'And DNA, yes. Likely from the condom too. Find her and you'll have no problem proving she was here if she tries to deny it.'

Zigic's eyes had drifted back to the table leg, imagining the heft of it against his own palm, the force required to swing it over and over again, hitting bone so hard the wood was dented. 'Do we *really* think a woman could have done this, though?'

'Isn't he chivalrous?' Jenkins said, looking at Ferreira.

'Or a little bit sexist?'

'I'm only saying, because Ainsworth must have fallen with a fair degree of force to break the table.'

'We could get hold of a replica,' Ferreira suggested. 'Then I'll throw you at it and we can see if it breaks.'

They laughed at him and he shook his head. 'Alright, forget it. The dinner companion is our prime suspect then.'

'Any fibres?' Ferreira asked, glancing around herself at the light-coloured carpet. 'Footprints?'

'We have a few footprints, which the killer has obviously tried to scuff away,' Jenkins said, indicating the locations she'd marked out. 'We probably won't get a complete impression but I'll be able to give you an idea of size, for what it's worth.' She cocked her head. 'I can't really give you anything more right now, sorry.'

'What about his phone?' Ferreira asked.

'No sign,' Jenkins said regretfully. 'No tablet or laptop either. We found chargers but not the devices that correspond to them, so either this was a particularly violent robbery or your killer knows there's incriminating information on them and has had them away.'

Ferreira swore under her breath.

'We did find his wallet though.'

'Intact?'

'Cards and cash, yes,' she said. 'Kind of undermines the robbery theory but tech's easier to fence than cards and higher value, so ...'

'You've been a great help, Kate,' Zigic said. 'Is it okay if we have a look around the rest of the house?'

She nodded. 'If you're careful. We can't find any sign of activity beyond the living room though.'

Ferreira went upstairs, he stayed down. Headed into the kitchen that bore the traces of an initial survey by the forensics' team, but beyond that it was clean and tidy and told him nothing about Josh Ainsworth, except that he kept his juicer on the worktop and a lot of fruit and veg in his fridge.

He stood in the middle of the room looking out at the back garden, which was pretty but overgrown and yellowing around the edges from the heatwave. Somewhere beyond its far boundary, across a few fields, Long Fleet stood behind high walls and spiked wire. He wondered if Ainsworth had moved here with the job or if it had been a convenient option when he needed one.

Ferreira shouted to him from upstairs and he went to find her. She was standing in the doorway of a cramped box room, which had been turned into an office containing a small white desk under the window and a large leather chair. Shelves fitted in wherever they would go, filled with box files and binders, stacks of books and pots of pens.

'Look at this.'

She directed him in, to a blue box file opened out across the desk.

'Is this how you found it?' he asked.

24

'It's all been photographed already, don't worry,' she said. 'I saw this one on the shelf and thought it might be interesting. Seriously, look at it.'

He went to the desk. Inside the box file were dozens of leaflets about the Immigration Removal Centre: photographs of women on the covers, presumably inmates, the dates of their incarceration, pleas for their release. One about the suicide rate in Long Fleet, another that was fronted with a list of abuses, an image of a guard with his face fuzzed out. Maybe a stock photo, but possibly not.

'Why was Ainsworth collecting these?' Zigic asked.

She shrugged. 'Maybe he was getting ready to bring harassment charges. This is how you go about it, right? Collect the evidence, build your case, then contact a solicitor.'

'But he'd have to know who was responsible for them.'

'Maybe it wasn't the protestors then,' she said, leaning against the door. 'Maybe he was going to put the harassment on Long Fleet somehow.'

'Mel, come on,' he said, incredulous. 'There are theories and then there's just mad speculation.'

'It's not mad speculation to suggest he might have held Long Fleet responsible for drawing down this harassment on him, is it?'

Zigic murmured without agreeing.

'He was off work, wasn't he?' she said. 'And we don't know why.'

Ferreira came over to the desk and carefully removed a leaflet that looked different to all the others, more ersatz in style, deliberately punky, and when she opened it he saw that this one wasn't decrying the general regime at Long Fleet, it was directly accusing the medical staff of collusion, addressing Ainsworth by name.

'"You took a Hippocratic oath, Dr Ainsworth. And now you're cleaning up after the rapists and murderers of an immoral immigration system that criminalises victims."'

'You think this might be the kind of thing that you'd need a holiday from?' Ferreira asked.

Zigic sifted through the box, found another one in the same distinctive style. A flyer this time.

'"How many abortions have you performed in there, Dr Ainsworth? How many suicides have you covered up? The blood of innocent women is on your hands."'

He let out a slow and careful breath, seeing his fears about the impact of this case beginning to solidify.

'It might not be relevant,' he said hopefully.

'Or it might be why he wound up with his head smashed to bits on his living room floor.'

CHAPTER FIVE

'Are they here?' Zigic asked as he pulled onto the verge behind a line of cars belonging to the people protesting outside Long Fleet's gates. 'The couple from the shop, do you see them?'

'No,' Ferreira said.

He took out his phone, glanced at the list DC Parr had made of the protestors' vehicles. 'That tallies, we've got a car missing since Parr was here.'

'Must have noticed him and got spooked.'

'None of them have got records,' Zigic told her.

'They should be happy to help us, then,' she said drily.

He wasn't so sure.

From the car they looked like a collection of respectable middle-aged ladies, churchgoers and garden centre aficionados, dressed in leggings and linen shirts, with sun hats and glasses to protect them from the midday heat and dust from the road, as they kept up their vigil for the women on the other side of the gates. But as he climbed out of the car and felt their attention turn towards Ferreira and him, he started to get that familiar prickling sensation that comes before trouble.

They would know their rights, he guessed. Wouldn't be scared into complying, wouldn't allow themselves to be rounded up without justification or tricked into acting in a rash and illegal manner that would justify taking them into the station.

He needed them to *want* to help, but watching their mouths set into hard lines and their fingers closing tighter around the handles of their placards, he doubted their willingness to aid the police. Even for something as serious as murder.

All they could see were coppers. No better than the ones who'd raided homes and businesses and sent the women inside them through that gateway with no warning or argument brooked.

'We've got permission from the landowner to be here,' a voice said as they approached.

'We're not here to move you on,' Ferreira told them.

A stout woman at the front of the group drew herself up taller. 'I'd like to see you try, young lady.'

Zigic saw Ferreira's shoulders stiffen automatically then relax again. Knew she'd had to make a conscious effort to do that, show them an open face and a neutral attitude, when she would be desperate to snap back. She was getting better at hiding her temper, he thought. But it was still there and he hoped she could keep it under wraps for a few more minutes.

Ferreira reached into her bag and brought out her ID.

'I'm DS Ferreira, this is DI Zigic, we're investigating a murder in the village.'

'Zigic,' the stout woman said, coming towards him. 'That's a Serbian name, isn't it?'

It wasn't the part of the sentence he expected anyone to fasten on. Usually murder blew away any other concerns, but he didn't feel he could ignore her question when they needed help.

'It is.'

'So your family were asylum seekers?'

'My grandparents were, yes,' he admitted, feeling her eyes burning through her tinted glasses. 'A long time ago.'

'And how would you feel if your grandmother was locked up in that gulag?'

'We're investigating the murder of Dr Joshua Ainsworth,' Ferreira said firmly, trying to draw the rest of the crowd away from the developing scene.

The woman took another step towards him. 'Your grandmother fled oppression in her homeland so you could be born into stability and safety. Why shouldn't other women have that right?'

'My grandparents were very lucky to be given asylum,' he conceded, thinking of the bombed-out remains of their village,

28

the livestock stolen and slaughtered, their brothers and cousins executed in the mountainous forests they'd played in as boys. He forced the thoughts away, said, 'We could debate this issue in detail, but right now I need to find who murdered Dr Ainsworth.'

'Well, you won't find them here,' the woman said fiercely. 'This is a peaceful protest.'

'Have any of you spoken to Dr Ainsworth?' Ferreira asked, inclining her body away from the woman, directing her words to the more receptive faces.

There were murmurs but no direct responses.

'Whatever the rights and wrongs of the regime here, Dr Ainsworth wasn't a guard, he wasn't an oppressor,' she said. 'He wanted the same thing you do, to try and keep those women in there as safe and well as possible. He wasn't your enemy.'

Still no reply, but Zigic noticed the collective shape of the group changing, heads going down, shoulders rounding, as the defiance bled out of them in the face of this death.

'Dr Ainsworth has been brutally murdered,' he said. 'Nobody deserves to die how he died. Let alone someone who dedicated their life to helping others.'

'That is very sad,' the woman said, managing to sound genuinely contrite. 'But if you think any of us were capable, never mind willing, you are very much mistaken.'

'Someone had been harassing Dr Ainsworth.' Ferreira swept the crowd and Zigic followed her gaze, looking for a reaction, a moment of fear. But they were all too well hidden behind their hats and glasses. 'We're already aware of your leafleting campaign in the village.'

'It isn't illegal to inform people about what's going on in their community,' the woman said. 'And speaking the truth isn't harassment. It's the responsibility of every right-thinking woman and man who cares what happens to their fellow human beings.'

Zigic tried to picture her slamming that table leg into Josh Ainsworth's face, found the image came to him quickly and not entirely unconvincingly. She was perhaps fifty, strongly built and with a low centre of gravity, easy enough to see this fervour converting into fury and the violence she wouldn't be able to stop until she'd fully exorcised it.

'We're not interested in your leaflet campaign,' Ferreira said, an edge coming into her voice. 'And we can see that you're good people fighting for something you believe in. But there's a chance that the person who murdered Josh Ainsworth has passed through this group. And if when we find them they claim an allegiance with you, that's going to seriously damage your cause.'

Another murmur circled the crowd and Zigic heard the word 'blackmail' pitched low but strong. Couldn't see who'd said it.

The mood was shifting again, hardening.

'If anyone at the periphery of your movement has suggested a more direct kind of protest, we need to know about it,' Ferreira said, taking a box of cards from her pocket and beginning to hand them out. 'If there's been any threat of violence made towards Long Fleet staff, even jokingly, we need to know who made it.'

The women didn't want the cards, but they were nice middle-class ladies who'd had good manners drilled into them from an early age and they couldn't refuse Ferreira's polite requests or ignore how she thanked them, even under these circumstances.

'I know there are people working in there who are no good,' she said. 'But Dr Ainsworth was not one of them.'

Zigic glanced over the road towards the security hut at the main gate, saw that the guard was watching them, arms folded, chin thrown up. This was beyond his territory, but it might not stop him investigating and passing back what he saw.

Zigic would have liked to walk in there without giving the management warning, but that wasn't an option any more.

'Please,' Ferreira said earnestly. 'Ask your compatriots to contact us if they can think of anything. Anyone who made them uncomfortable, anyone who didn't seem to share your principles. We really don't want this to mar the important work you're doing here.'

A soft snort went up from within the crowd and Ferreira ignored it. Maybe she heard how thickly she was laying it on too, Zigic thought. But of the available options she'd taken the right tack.

In the car, a few minutes later, with Long Fleet falling away behind them, he found himself thinking of his grandparents again, remembering going through his grandfather's effects after he died and discovering the small booklet of common English phrases he'd been given on arrival here. It was creased and careworn, stained with the oil from his hands and, Zigic imagined, the nervous sweat that came over him when he was called on to speak at any length in his adopted language. His grandmother had been fluent, did the speaking for both of them most of the time, but his grandfather had always been a man adrift in a foreign country.

Would he pass a citizenship test now? Zigic wondered. If they hadn't died would they be fearing for their homes once again, seeing out their old age in the same terror they began their married life in? His chest ached at the thought of his grandfather trying to convince some dispassionate official of his need to stay in broken English, or his grandmother being taken through the gates of Long Fleet under the gaze of that same guard.

CHAPTER SIX

'I hate doing this,' Ferreira groaned, as they turned down the long driveway onto Wansford Marina, the water opening up ahead of them, sunlight glinting off it in shards so vicious that Zigic felt every one pierce his shades.

'Nobody enjoys it and it never gets any easier.'

They could have sent someone else to inform Joshua Ainsworth's parents of his death, but Zigic thought it was important for a senior officer to speak to them, so they would know it was being taken seriously and that everything that could be done for him would be done. He remembered being sent out as a young DC to make the dreaded death knock and how completely unprepared he'd been for it, too inexperienced to provide the requisite level of comfort and reassurance, too raw to protect himself from the force of their grief. It wasn't fair on anyone involved, sending a constable to do an inspector's job.

The Ainsworth house sat at the centre of the development, one of around two dozen houses sited facing the modest lake. It was a three-storey clapperboard place painted in a Scandinavian shade of dirty blue, with a neat little pathway running up the centre of a manicured lawn, still lush despite the heat.

For a moment after he switched off the engine, they both sat, gathering whatever inner resources they had.

'Come on,' he said, finally, getting out of the car.

He led the way, knocking on the brilliant white front door, feeling Ferreira behind him, reluctance radiating off her.

The door was opened by a petite, deeply tanned woman in a pair of shorts and a man's shirt, one hand still in a floral gardening glove, clutching its twin. She wore a polite smile, tinged with mistrust. They wouldn't get cold callers here, Zigic imagined. Not with the security on the gate.

'Yes, can I help you?' she enquired.

A beat later she noticed his ID and the smile froze on her face.

'Mrs Ainsworth?' She nodded too heavily, and he could see that she was already fearing the worst, was playing the scenarios through in her head as he introduced Ferreira and himself. 'Do you think we could come in, please?'

She led them silently through the house, her gait uncertain, her neck stiff, to a large room at the back, where a wide set of doors stood open on a balcony overlooking the garden. There were a few pots out there, in the process of being planted with jewel-coloured flowers from plastic trays.

She went out and dropped her gloves near the pots, came back with her fingers knitted together in front of her.

'I'm sorry, what did you say this was about?' she asked. 'There hasn't been another break-in, has there?'

'I think you should sit down, Mrs Ainsworth,' Zigic said, gently ushering her towards a long, low sofa scattered with cushions. 'Is your husband at home?'

'He's in his office.' She gestured vaguely and Ferreira followed her hand towards the doorway, going to find Joshua Ainsworth's father.

Mrs Ainsworth sat with her ankles crossed and her hands in her lap, head turned towards the view, tears already welling in her eyes.

People always knew. Long before you told them, they knew what had happened. From your mere presence in their homes, your discomfort and deference, the weight you carried visibly around on your shoulders, a burden they knew they would soon take from you. They would take most of it, but the part that was left couldn't be passed on to anyone else. That you kept forever.

Ferreira returned with Mr Ainsworth and Zigic could see that he knew already as well. That his reaction was going to be different to his wife's. Where she had retreated instantly to numbness, he was unbearably raw.

'It's Greg, isn't it?' he demanded. 'Something's happened to Greg and the boys?'

'No, sir,' Zigic said. 'We're here about Josh.'

Was he imagining it, or was that a very slight flicker of relief he saw pass over Mr Ainsworth's face as he crossed the room and sat down next to his wife, taking her hand in his own big paw.

'What's happened?' Mr Ainsworth asked, glaring at Zigic as if daring him to actually say it. 'Has Josh had an accident?'

'I'm very sorry to tell you that Josh was found dead in his home this morning.'

Mrs Ainsworth sobbed into her hand, looking at her husband who wasn't looking back at her, but instead had fixed his attention on the floor between his feet, his face reddened with the effort of keeping in whatever reaction was rising up through him. A muffled cry broke out of him and his wife drew her arms around his shoulders, burying her face in the back of his neck.

Zigic glanced at Ferreira and saw that she had turned away to retrieve a box of tissues from a nearby table. She placed it carefully on the arm of the sofa, as the Ainsworths talked to one another in choked undertones, saying Josh's name, cursing whatever twist of fate had brought them to this. In the background through the open doors, the sound of a summer day continued, as if this tragedy wasn't occurring; birdsong and laughter, the thwack and splash of somebody hitting golf balls into the water.

Eventually Mr Ainsworth wiped his eyes across his forearm and asked Zigic how Josh had died. 'Not those bloody stairs? I told him that cottage was a death trap.'

'No, Mr Ainsworth, I'm afraid Josh was murdered.'

His mother gasped. 'Why? Who would want to hurt Josh? He was always such a sweet boy. He was a doctor, for God's sake.'

'It's too early in the investigation for us to speculate,' Zigic said, perching on the edge of a denim blue armchair, feeling more comfortable now he could return to being a detective, and slightly ashamed of himself for noticing the change. 'We know Josh spent the evening at home with a woman. Presumably his girlfriend. Would you be able to tell us about her?'

'Josh didn't have a girlfriend,' his mother said, reaching for a tissue and blowing her nose.

'He was too young to settle down,' Mr Ainsworth said. 'I was always telling him that. "You're a good-looking lad, you want to play the field."' His voice broke. '"Plenty of time for all that marriage stuff."'

'Josh's neighbour reported seeing the same woman visiting on a regular basis. He was under the impression this was Josh's girlfriend. Did he ever mention her to you?'

'No.' Mrs Ainsworth tugged another tissue out of the box but just held it between her fingers, stretching it slowly, until it tore up the centre. 'I assumed he was dating but he didn't mention anyone special. Josh always kept that sort of thing to himself. I think he enjoyed the secrecy. He was like that when he was a little boy – hiding his toys away from his brother and playing with them on his own. Once Greg found them Josh wasn't interested any more.'

'Would he have discussed his relationships with his brother?' Ferreira asked.

'Maybe.' Mrs Ainsworth straightened sharply, grabbed her husband's arm. 'We need to tell Greg about this.' She looked at Zigic. 'You haven't contacted him yet, have you?'

'No, Mrs Ainsworth.'

'I think it'll be easier coming from us,' she said.

Zigic nodded. 'Do you have a recent photo of Josh, please?'

'I'll find one.' Mrs Ainsworth got up, shaky on her feet, and went over to a set of shelves where the family photos were lined up. Ferreira followed her and they began to speak softly, Ferreira asking who was who and saying how handsome the Ainsworth boys were, how happy Greg's children looked, very mischievous.

Mr Ainsworth slumped back on the sofa, his face drawn, eyes heavy. He'd aged ten years in as many minutes, and Zigic knew that some of the effect was temporary, but the man seemed to be staring into a void with the full knowledge that he wouldn't be able to ever completely pull back from it.

'Was it to do with his job?' he asked, barely moving his lips.

'We're not sure yet,' Zigic told him, surprised at the assumption. 'Did Josh feel unsafe there?'

'He can't have been safe, can he? Working in a prison. With that sort of people.'

'It's an immigration removal centre,' Zigic said. 'The women in there aren't criminals in the usual sense, they've just violated their visas.'

'And what about the people they associate with?' Ainsworth asked, fixing a beady eye on Zigic. 'You know as well as I do, lots of them are trafficked over here by real criminals. Now *those* people are dangerous. That's what you want to be looking into. Someone getting at Josh to get to one of them.'

'Had Josh been approached by anyone like that?'

'Josh wouldn't tell me if he was,' Ainsworth said, his voice thick with a peculiar blend of anger and regret. 'I never wanted him to go and work there. All that money for university, all those bloody textbooks at three hundred quid a pop, and for what? To work somewhere like that. He could have done anything, he was so bright. Naturally gifted, he never had to work at it. He could have done research or brain surgery or anything, but he wasn't ambitious.'

Mr Ainsworth looked around his cavernous, double-height living room, the gargantuan sofa and armchairs, the twelve-seater dining table and the striking chandelier hanging over it, all crystal and chrome. He'd been an ambitious man, Zigic imagined. Worked hard, wanted the best for his son, couldn't understand how intelligence wasn't always allied to aspiration.

'Did Josh mention the protest at Long Fleet to you?' Zigic asked. 'There's an ongoing leaflet campaign in the village.'

'I know about the protest, yes,' Mr Ainsworth said. 'We saw them sometimes when we went to visit Josh. Were they getting at him?'

'We found some leaflets in his house, it looks like he was saving them for some reason.'

Mr Ainsworth appeared perplexed. 'Some people will protest anything, won't they?'

'Whoever is responsible was targeting Josh very directly.'

'Saying what?'

'That he had blood on his hands.'

Anger flared across Mr Ainsworth's face. 'That's complete nonsense.'

'We're regarding it as part of a harassment campaign right now,' Zigic said. 'We don't think it's necessarily linked to his murder, but we need to keep in mind the possibility. Especially as it was obviously bothering him enough to keep the threatening material. Perhaps he mentioned pressing charges?'

A brief shake of the head from Mr Ainsworth.

'Had you seen much of Josh lately?' Zigic asked. 'We understand he'd been on holiday recently?'

Another shake. 'No, to be honest, this is the first I'm hearing of holiday time.'

Across the room Mrs Ainsworth was slipping a photograph from a frame and handing it to Ferreira. She promised they would return it as soon as they could, thanking his mother, who stood staring at all the other images, reaching out to straighten a couple of them.

'How did he die?' Mr Ainsworth asked in an undertone.

'It looked like there was a fight,' Zigic said, reluctant to go into the painful details.

'Josh never was a scrapper.' He frowned regretfully, knocking his knuckles together. 'I should have tried to toughen him up. I never thought he'd need it.'

They left the couple with assurances that they would keep them updated, the offer of a family support officer declined. Zigic tried to impress the value of their presence, especially during the difficult process of identifying Josh's body, but Mr Ainsworth waved it away and his wife didn't object. Ferreira seemed uncomfortable with their stoicism too, offered to go along with them if they'd like, directing the suggestion more towards Mrs Ainsworth. Another polite refusal.

In the car, pulling off the driveway, Ferreira said, 'They don't seem like they were very close.'

'Did you tell your parents about every boyfriend you had?' Zigic asked.

'The important ones,' she replied, but the vagueness of her tone made him doubt that.

'Have they met Billy?'

She turned away and stared out of the window. 'I'm not sure he's important yet.'

But he clearly was, Zigic thought, which meant she had another reason for keeping him away from her family. Embarrassed about him or them, scared they wouldn't get along and she'd find herself caught in the middle.

He wondered if that was the case with Josh Ainsworth and his mystery woman. Whether there was something about her he feared his parents wouldn't like.

CHAPTER SEVEN

By 2 p.m. the first round of information from the door to door enquiries in Long Fleet had come in. It was mostly retirees and stay-at-home parents in to speak to the officers and they had nothing to report. A few knew Ainsworth by sight, none called him a friend. No one had seen anyone suspicious hanging around the village over the weekend, just the usual walkers drawn by the nature reserve nearby. The other residents of the row of cottages on the green were all out at work, bar the neighbour Zigic had already spoken to, and all they could hope for was a phone call when they returned home this evening. Fourteen cottages tucked so close together, the odds were good, they thought.

Ferreira had set DC Weller the task of going through recent crime reports in the village and the ones surrounding it, looking for anything that might suggest a pattern of returning offenders drawn to the frequently empty homes. There had been a spate of shed break-ins, a few thefts of vehicles, but nothing jumped out as a possibility. Ainsworth's car was an eight-year-old Renault Clio with rust around the rims and a radio still boasting a cassette player, and his bike, which looked expensive, remained safe and sound in the small shed behind his kitchen.

Despite the absence of his mobile phone and laptop, burglary didn't look like a motive.

Zigic wouldn't rule it out, but Ferreira doubted anyone would be killed over them.

She added the information they had to the murder board, placing it up there more to rule out the possibility than as a spur to further action.

At the top of the board, a copy of the photograph Josh's mother had given them showed him beaming delightedly at something off camera. He had a quirkily attractive face, with heavy brown brows and small, clever eyes, a shadow of stubble across his cheeks only broken by the thick comma of a old scar at his jaw-line, a souvenir from his younger brother's hot temper and a long-gone metal coffee table. His mother had smiled sadly as she told the story, but all Ferreira could think of was the table leg that had been used to kill him.

'Maybe the killer took his phone and all that to make it *look* like a burglary,' DC Parr suggested, standing watching her as she recapped her pen. Inexplicably he was still wearing his jacket, despite the heat in the office, but had weakened enough to loosen his bright orange tie slightly, allowing the sweat on his neck some extra space to gather. 'Did they nick his wallet?'

'Nope, it was still at the house.' Ferreira took a mouthful of tepid coffee from the mug on her desk. 'Did you get in touch with the pizza delivery place?'

Parr nodded. 'Driver would have been wearing gloves but he's giving us prints for elimination on the box. Couple of other staff members coming in tomorrow as well.'

'You get any pushback from them on it?'

'No, they were happy to cooperate,' he said. 'I'm as surprised as you are.'

She made a note of it but her eye kept drifting to the part of the board where she'd stuck up images of the leaflets that Joshua Ainsworth had hoarded in his bedroom office, feeling her gut inexorably drawing her back to them.

The box file was on her desk now, the leaflets and fliers already dusted for fingerprints, and she wasn't entirely surprised to find that while the more professional and considered leaflets had yielded prints, those angry black-and-white fliers showed only Ainsworth's. Whoever produced them had been scrupulous when they handled them, wore gloves to keep their identity hidden. Meaning they were either in the system already or paranoid about protecting themselves from charges of harassment down the line.

Jenkins had managed to lift DNA samples from two fliers, though, and Ferreira was praying it wasn't just a matter of Ainsworth sneezing while holding them.

She tucked in her earbuds and went back to the briefing she was compiling on Long Fleet Immigration Removal Centre. Zigic had suggested putting a package together so they could be confident that the whole team was up to speed on what was happening there, giving them some background on the protest and the ongoing harassment campaign. She'd started with the basics, intending to keep things brief – Long Fleet Immigration Removal Centre opened in 2008 and held up to 300 women and children at any time, awaiting decisions on their asylum status or deportation. It employed 150 staff, had processed 35,000 cases to date – but quickly she realised more was needed than the Wikipedia version.

It was a time-consuming job to undertake during the first, vital hours of a murder investigation and the fact that Zigic had insisted she do it now suggested he considered it a significant avenue of enquiry.

They'd already checked out the women they'd spoken to outside Long Fleet's gates and they all came back clean. No criminal activity in any of their histories, at least none that had escalated to the point of police involvement, but he'd scented something there and she agreed. The serious agitators, the dangerous kind, wouldn't be hanging around the gates with placards, she suspected. They wouldn't be satisfied with peaceful protest.

She'd found the group behind the leaflet campaign quickly enough – Asylum Assist's website was printed on the back pages of each sheet, their Twitter handles and the Facebook group they'd launched to try and disseminate their message of lobbying local politicians and press, anyone who might be able to raise the profile of the cause and that of the women inside Long Fleet.

The website contained interviews with released women and testimonies from those still inside passed to their family members and friends or their legal representatives. All told tales of lives upended, of jobs and homes lost when they were taken in, of raids in the middle of the night. One woman had been arrested when she was a witness to a street robbery of a pensioner; she'd gone to help and the attending PC had reported her to immigration officers. Several had been caught as they went to A & E for emergency treatment, their overstayed visas ensuring that they were treated by Josh Ainsworth and the rest of the medical team in Long Fleet instead of their local NHS hospital.

It made for emotional reading but didn't help locate Ainsworth's murderer.

Ferreira added it to the file anyway.

Added as well the multiple news reports that had followed in the wake of a whistleblower who had exposed the myriad failings at Long Fleet two years ago. The abuses that the shopkeeper in the village she'd spoken to denied had ever happened.

But there they were, in black and white, with video footage too. Guards were fired, apologies were made and assurances given that important lessons had been learned. The former governor was released by mutual consent and the management brought in someone new. This was the man Zigic was currently trying to convince to allow them inside the centre so they could interview Ainsworth's colleagues.

They knew Ainsworth was working at Long Fleet two years ago, so apparently he wasn't implicated in the abuses, but she wondered about the whistleblower. Their identity had been protected but surely the staff members who were fired had some idea who exposed them. How could you possibly keep that secret in such a closely contained environment?

She leaned back and stretched her shoulders, music still blaring in her ears, watching the office go about its business, soundtracked by the Dead Weather. Adams and Murray were standing at the board where their attempted murder case was plotted out, Murray doing the talking, making sure the importance of her words were impressed on the collection of DCs and PCs watching her. Adams seemed content to let her take the lead and Ferreira liked that about him, that he respected Murray's years and her instincts.

The case was getting under his skin though. A violent altercation outside a nightclub that left a young man in a coma; they knew who was responsible within hours – George Batty, 24, Peterborough born and bred, nothing more serious than a couple of speeding fines on his records. Batty fled the country immediately, caught a lorry to Dover and then on to Calais. Knowing who your man was but not being able to grab him and bring him to justice was the greatest frustration of being a copper, and Adams wasn't taking it well. He seemed particularly annoyed because Batty was hardly a seasoned criminal who he'd expect to give him the runaround. Just some gobshite who'd run and made it further than he should have.

Ferreira finished the report and emailed it to the rest of the team.

She went back to Asylum Assist's Facebook page and scanned down the posts, reading links to news items and blogs on other groups' sites, calls for donations to legal defence funds and signatures for petitions, an occasional interview with a sympathetic politician or a live chat with a high-profile celebrity campaigner. They were a more significant force than the group outside the gate appeared, but there was nothing to suggest direct or violent action here.

Of course it wouldn't be visible, she thought.

These people spoke openly because they were hopeful their tactics could provoke change.

The private groups were where the radicals lurked.

Ferreira look up as DC Keri Bloom approached her desk, wearing a broad smile, which revealed the workings of her near invisible braces.

'Ma'am, I've got something I think you'll want to see.'

Ferreira pulled her earbuds out and followed Bloom to her desk, noticing a new photo of her pet ferret tucked up close to the monitor. It was wearing a tiny black beret and didn't look particularly happy about it. Obviously red was better suited to its colouring, Ferreira was shocked to find herself thinking.

'This is the listing for the holiday cottage next door to Joshua Ainsworth,' Bloom said, turning the screen towards Ferreira.

The images showed the cottage in its full picturesque glory, all cream-painted furniture and sheepskin rugs on the stripped pine flooring. The owners had written a breathlessly positive description of Long Fleet's manifold charms, describing a rural idyll perfect for nature lovers and fans of Norman churches, a description so tempting she had to check that it was the same place that she'd spent the better part of the morning in. No mention of the sprawling Immigration Removal Centre.

'And this –' Bloom scrolled down, 'is the review from the couple who stayed there at the weekend.'

'We couldn't in all good conscience recommend this beautiful cottage to others due to the shocking noise levels from the neighbours. We understand that this is beyond the control of the owners but our otherwise tranquil weekend was irretrievable, marred by the inconsiderate behaviour on Saturday night. It sounded like there was a war going on. One just doesn't expect that from a country cottage getaway.'

Ferreira straightened away from the desk.

'Good work, Keri.'

'Should I get in touch with the letting agency and try and get the guests' contact details? Or I could email them direct through the site,' she suggested. 'They have an enquiries form here. I think they'll pick that message up pretty quick, don't you?'

'Do both,' Ferreira told her, already heading for Zigic's office. 'Push the site, though. We need to speak to those guests asap.'

The phone was already in her hand. 'Yes, ma'am.'

Zigic was slamming his own receiver down as she went in.

'Long Fleet?'

'They won't see us until tomorrow,' he said irritably. 'One of their medical staff gets murdered and they're already putting roadblocks up.'

She told him about the guests at the holiday cottage and his expression became slightly less furious, even if it didn't soften completely.

'Are we sure they're talking about the murder and not Josh's lady visitor?'

Ferreira grinned at him. 'Either way, we've got potential witnesses and a potential time of death until the PM can confirm. Makes things easier, doesn't it? Narrows us down to Saturday night for questioning.'

'Very tentatively,' he said. 'Best we stick to what we actually know for now.'

Ferreira shrugged.

'Thanks for putting the stuff on Long Fleet together by the way.' He gestured at his computer. 'What do you think about the group? Asylum Assist?'

'I doubt they're behind the harassment,' Ferreira told him. 'But they probably have an idea who is.'

'The Paggetts?' he asked. They had been identified as the couple who had deserted the gates of Long Fleet this morning at the first sign of a police presence.

'You've looked at their records, right?'

'Do we really think people like this escalate to murder, though?' he asked, his face twisting at the thought of where this could lead, the trouble they were pushing up against. 'There's no lunatic fringe in these movements, is there?'

'All movements attract extremists. They don't necessarily believe in the cause, they just see an opportunity to cause havoc and they take it.'

CHAPTER EIGHT

'Idyllic,' Ferreira said, as they got out of the car, shouting to make herself heard over the incessant roar of the traffic on the A1 ten metres away from them. The house itself was even closer to the road, a ceaseless stream of lorries and cars thundering past the sash windows, so close that you could probably reach out and touch them.

The old farmhouse would have been idyllic once, Zigic thought, as they went to the back door, before the motorway was built. Tolerable even then maybe, when few people had cars and freight was moved largely by train. But now with the road widened and the constant activity, it must be torture. Never quiet, never still, the slipstream of vehicles rattling the windows and the fumes insidiously penetrating the gaps around the frames, seeping through the putty, the unpredictable semaphore of headlights flashing across the glass at night.

It was a substantial building though, with a large concrete yard bordered by outbuildings in various states of disrepair. Maybe that would be enough to compensate for the deficits of the location.

'Over there,' Ferreira said, gesturing towards the least dilapidated barn, which had its wooden roller door pushed back, revealing a workshop inside that was somehow gloomy enough, despite the sun, that they needed the network of strip lights hung slackly from the rafters. 'That's Paggett. He was the one in the shop this morning.'

Damien Paggett was hunched over a long workbench, his face hidden behind a protective face mask as he carefully spray-painted what looked like a door from a kitchen cabinet. Four more of them were lined up on the bench ahead of him, primed and waiting for the same midnight-blue topcoat. Music was playing at full blast, a band Zigic didn't recognise, thrashy and raw.

Across the barn at another workstation was his wife, Michaela, stood with her back turned to them as she searched through plastic tubs on a set of shelves.

Was this what had made them bolt from the Long Fleet demonstration this morning? An urgent job that needed finishing? It hardly made sense to show their faces for an hour and then leave.

Their police records were a much more feasible motivation.

Public order offences, trespass, vandalism, harassment and libel.

Both of them barely thirty-five and already with a long history of active involvement in the anti-capitalist movement, mostly focused on environmental issues, but recently they'd shifted towards anti-fascist groups and found themselves under the watchful eye of the anti-terror police.

'Not major players,' the specialist that DS Zigic had consulted said. 'But we're aware of them.'

Michaela Paggett turned away from the shelves and nodded as if she'd been expecting their visit.

'What do you want?' she asked, punching her hands into the pocket of her dungarees, looking like a surly teenager, an impression only enhanced by her heavy eye make-up and the stubby plaits in her black, teal-streaked hair.

Damien stopped working, straightened from the bench. Well over six foot and clearly uncomfortable about it from the set stoop of his narrow shoulders, he cut an awkward figure, but his was a job with a lot of heavy lifting involved and Zigic thought he would have been easily capable of overpowering Josh Ainsworth.

'We're not taking any new orders right now,' he said, shoving his face mask up onto the top of his head, revealing a slim face with a pierced nose. 'I can give you a few recommendations if you let me know what you're after.'

'You can tell us why you did a runner from Long Fleet this morning,' Zigic said, in no mood to indulge him.

'We didn't "do a runner",' Michaela told him. 'We had work to be getting on with, so we put in a couple of hours, showed our faces and came home. We can't be there all day, every day, we have to earn a living.'

'It's important we help them to keep the numbers up,' Damien said affably. 'The minute they drop it starts to look like we've deserted those women in there.'

'Nothing to do with all the police in the village then?' Ferreira asked.

'We've got nothing to hide,' Michaela said fiercely. 'We're talking to you now, aren't we?'

'You know about the murder then?'

'Someone called us, yeah. One of the doctors from the prison.' A hint of pleasure flicked the edges of Michaela's mouth up. 'Shame, that.'

'Josh Ainsworth was trying to do right by those women you claim to care about,' Ferreira said. 'He was actively helping them, rather than standing around on the road with signs achieving nothing.'

'We are achieving something,' Michaela shot back at her. 'We're raising awareness of what's going on in Long Fleet.'

'Will awareness change the law?'

'Are you suggesting a more direct approach might be better?' she asked. 'Because that sounds an awful lot like incitement.'

'From the look of your record you wouldn't need much inciting,' Ferreira said, and Zigic could see that she was already getting to Michaela Paggett. 'I'm surprised someone with your experience is satisfied with making placards and flyers.'

'We don't make flyers,' Damien said. 'It isn't the nineties.'

'So what do you do?'

'We stand around with our signs,' Michaela answered, her tone saccharine. 'Just like you said.'

'What's this got to do with some doctor getting murdered, anyway?' Damien asked, taking a rag from his pocket and wiping the sweat off his face.

'Dr Ainsworth was the victim of a targeted harassment campaign,' Zigic said, watching them both for a reaction.

'Nothing to do with us.' Michaela leaned nonchalantly against the workbench. 'You'll want to talk to Asylum Assist if you think he was murdered with a leaflet.'

'Ruby Garrick,' Damien added. 'She's the one who puts the leaflets together.'

'And she was *very* close to Dr Ainsworth,' Michaela said in a teasing tone, her face lit so bright with insinuation that Zigic didn't want to give her the satisfaction of asking what she meant. He didn't need to, though. 'We saw her coming out of his house a few weeks ago. She looked like she'd had a very pleasurable evening.'

'And how do you know where Dr Ainsworth lives?' Ferreira asked icily.

Michaela blinked, pushed herself away from the workbench while she scrambled for an answer. 'Well … he was seeing her out to her car, I figure that means that it was his house.'

'Just hanging around outside, were you?'

'We'd been to the pub for something to eat,' Damien said smoothly, looking to Zigic. 'They do a really good midweek barbeque in the summer. All you can eat for fifteen pounds a head.'

The idea of two environmental protestors driving half an hour to go to an all-you-can-eat barbeque struck Zigic as implausible verging on ridiculous.

'The pub isn't anywhere near Dr Ainsworth's house,' Ferreira said.

'We decided to go and walk some of the food off.' Damien shrugged as if it was the most natural combination of circumstances in the world. 'It's a pretty little village. We like to get away from this noise now and again.'

He was the one to watch, Zigic thought.

'And there she was,' Michaela said, some of the malice gone but desperation showing now as she tried to draw them away to another suspect. 'Ruby Garrick coming out of the enemy's house.'

'I take it she'll be getting a visit as well, will she?' Damien asked, some defiance coming into his voice. 'She was eager to get away from Long Fleet this morning. Asked us to give her a lift home.'

'And she doesn't have a job she needed to get back to.' Michaela folded her arms. 'She lives in that big block of flats near the sewage works. I'm sure she'll be in.'

It was a desperate ploy, which said more about the Paggetts than the potential guilt of Ruby Garrick, but there was clearly little love lost between them – despite their generosity in giving her a lift – and Zigic wondered what the woman would have to say about these two.

'Where were you two between 6 p.m. on Saturday August 4th and 1 a.m. Sunday August 5th?' Ferreira asked.

Zigic hadn't wanted to get to this just yet, would have preferred to wait until after the post-mortem when they had a more solid time of death, but watching the Paggetts share a momentary look of panic, he was glad Ferreira had put them on the spot.

She had her notebook open, waiting expectantly for them to provide their alibis.

'We went to a barbecue at a friend's house,' Damien said.

'You two are *big* fans of charred meat,' Ferreira said sarcastically. 'This friend have a name? And other friends who were also there? Just so we don't think you're lying.'

An unpleasant look crossed Michaela Paggett's face and now she looked a harder, nastier woman than she had before. Easy to imagine her cutting her way through barbed-wire fences and slashing tyres and smashing the windows of people she considered enemies of progressive values.

In a reluctant monotone, she read out names and numbers from her phone as Ferreira wrote them down, a dozen people who she claimed could vouch for them from 6 p.m. until the early hours of the next morning. Zigic watched her husband as she spoke, seeing how hard he was working at keeping his face blank, hardly blinking even with the sweat running out of his hair and into his eyes, barely breathing until Ferreira snapped her notebook closed, and then one big breath heaved his chest and he tried to pass it off as a cough.

'Dusty as hell in here.'

Michaela smiled at them. 'If there's anything else we can do ...'

'Oh, we'll be in touch,' Ferreira told her, matching the flint in her gaze.

Chapter Nine

'You like them for it?' Ferreira asked, as he pulled onto the slip road that took them over the motorway and back into the city centre.

'They're edgy,' Zigic said. 'But they could have a cannabis factory hidden in their barns and they're worried we'll be back with a search warrant.'

'They're not stoners,' Ferreira said. 'There's not a single possession offence on either of their records. People like that, getting picked up for every other public order breach going, they'll have had weed on them one time at least.'

'Alibis seem too good not to be true. You might get a couple of people to lie for you in the first instance but not that many. Not when it's murder.'

Ferreira murmured what sounded like agreement. 'He's the brains, we can agree that at least?'

'Do you believe them about this Garrick woman and Ainsworth?'

'He was with someone,' Ferreira said. 'But they were too desperate to pass the buck. We should definitely talk to her, right? If she was that eager to get away from Long Fleet just because Parr started nosing around.'

Zigic glanced at the time. Half past four. If they were quick and the traffic was kind to them, they could get to Ruby Garrick before he needed to be back at Thorpe Wood Station for the press statement. He put his foot down and overtook a long line of cars on the parkway, thinking about how often the Paggetts might have been hanging around on the village green and the huge coincidence that they happened to see Josh Ainsworth coming out of his house that one time.

Had they been watching him for a while? It would be easy enough to follow him home when he left work. Why would they do that? For a leaflet campaign or the sake of some nasty fliers? Just so they would know where he was if they ever wanted to get to him?

'How many of the others knew where Ainsworth lived, do you think?'

'It's a small village,' Ferreira said. 'If the leaflet campaigns are general, maybe none of the others know but if it is targeted at him, then obviously some of them will.'

'Unless the Paggetts are responsible for those fliers?'

'Yeah. But it seems small-time for their records.'

They arrived at the block of flats where Ruby Garrick lived, a recent development overlooking the parkway, sat at the edge of the Eastern Industrial Estate. The view to the south was across the River Nene and to the west it was the greenery of the embankment. It was relatively upmarket, solidly aimed at young professionals when it had been built, and as they got out of the car, he saw suited men and women coming home, early knock-offs but they all looked slightly fried around the edges, one woman walking barefoot across the car park, her high heels in her hand, their day's punishment suffered and survived.

Zigic wasn't sure where he'd expected the Long Fleet protestors to live but so far he'd found himself vaguely surprised.

It was stupid to expect them all to live in off-grid eco houses or rural communes, he realised. Some dated utopian ideal. These were ordinary people with ordinary lives who just happened to be dedicating large portions of their time to a fight that was not their own but which mattered deeply to them all the same.

Ruby Garrick let them in with little question and a warmer welcome than they'd received at the Paggetts. She was in her fifties, with grey-threaded black hair worn in braids, which reached her jawline and a small diamond stud in one of her slim, high brows. A line of finely inked script showed from the cuff of her white cotton kaftan.

'I've heard about Josh,' she said, showing them into a living room crammed with bookshelves and Ercol furniture, old film posters framed on the walls. They sat down when she offered and accepted the rose lemonade she insisted on fetching for them with a comment about the heat and what a long day they must have had.

When she returned she sank onto a floor cushion near the coffee table, where her laptop lay closed as if she'd been working before they buzzed. Zigic wondered what was on it, guessed the Asylum Assist network was fully consumed with talk of Ainsworth's murder right now.

'I can't believe it,' she said, drawing her knees up to her body. 'Was it a robbery?'

'Too early to say,' Zigic told her.

It was a natural assumption, the one people made because they'd rather believe in the bad faith of strangers than the bad actions of friends and family and lovers. With Ainsworth's devices missing, possibly as an act of misdirection, he reminded himself that she was a suspect, despite her nice manners and slightly absent air.

'You knew Josh quite well, we understand.'

'I didn't expect to become quite so friendly with him,' she said, her gaze going misty. 'We all have this idea that the staff at Long Fleet are scum. After what came out about the abuses in the place, it's difficult not to think that.'

'But they cleaned house,' Ferreira said.

'And replaced them with more of the same, most likely.' Ruby Garrick took a sip of her lemonade. The drink in her glass was discernibly less pink than the ones she'd brought for them, and Zigic wondered if she'd put something in it. 'Josh was different though, he genuinely cared about the women in there. He hated what the place was, what it represented, but he knew that somebody needed to make sure there was a safe space for the women to go into and tell what was happening to them. It took quite a toll on him.'

'But he stayed?' Zigic asked.

'For a few years, yes,' she said. 'Eventually it got to him, though. He resigned a couple of months ago.'

Zigic glanced at Ferreira.

'Are you sure about that?' she asked. 'We heard he was taking some holiday time.'

'I'm quite sure,' Ruby said, a little scorn in her voice as if she was used to being underestimated and didn't appreciate it. 'I tried to talk him out of it because those women need all the allies they can get. But ... when someone is so unhappy, you have to respect what they want.'

'It sounds like you were very close,' Zigic suggested softly.

She turned to him, wearing an unreadable smile. 'Detective Inspector, he was young enough to be my son.'

Ainsworth wasn't, not by some way, and it wasn't what Zigic had been getting at, but the fact that she'd interpreted the comment that way was interesting. Taking the same insinuation that the Paggetts had made. Perhaps she'd heard it all before. Perhaps she enjoyed the thought. Judging by the gentle smile lingering around her eyes, he suspected as much.

'You were a regular visitor to Josh's house.'

'I wouldn't say regular.' She touched her throat and quickly withdrew her hand. 'I'd been there a few times for coffee, he made me dinner once – he was a very good cook, doctors so often are, don't you find?'

Neither of them replied, no frame of reference to judge on.

'We talked,' she said. 'He was a very kind and gentle soul. The first time I approached him was when he was leaving work, oh, some time last summer, and I was in a filthy mood and I saw him coming out of the gates on his bike, and I stepped in front of him and I just started shouting at him. Telling him he should be ashamed of himself working in there, that he was taking blood money, that he was propping up a fascist apparatus that treated women's bodies as disposable.' She inclined her head towards

Ferreira. 'All of those things are true. But he didn't argue with me. He took a flier and promised me he would read it.'

Ruby rearranged herself on the floor cushion, stared into the tabletop like she was reliving the moment.

'That evening he emailed me,' she said. 'I don't know what I was expecting. An argument, maybe. A defence of Long Fleet at least. But he agreed with me. It went on from there, we talked about the politics of the centre and what was wrong with the immigration policy behind it. Then we started talking about other things too. I'm a history teacher and we discovered that we shared an interest in twentieth-century social history and some things like that. Eventually we decided to get together for a coffee and chat.'

'But it never went any further?' Ferreira asked and Zigic heard the mistrust in the question.

'No, believe it or not, it is possible for a man and woman to spend time together without jumping into bed.'

'Was Josh seeing someone?'

'I believe so,' she said slowly, a trace of annoyance in her voice. 'But I never asked. I thought it was his business and he'd tell me if he wanted to. All I can assume is that it wasn't a very serious relationship.'

Was that hope? Pointless now.

'These leaflets,' Ferreira started, reaching for her glass. 'How many of them do you put out?'

The sudden swerve seemed to catch Ruby unawares and she frowned at the question, looking quizzically at Ferreira. 'As many as we need to. About once a month we produce a new one and deliver them around the village.'

'To all the houses?'

She nodded. 'Even Josh's?'

'I don't deliver them,' Ruby said, an evasion Ferreira fastened on immediately.

'Do the rest of the protestors know about your friendship with Josh?'

Her mouth made a thoughtful moue. 'I didn't think it was something I needed to share with them.'

'Why?'

'He was part of my private life, not my protest activities.'

'How would they have felt if they knew?' Ferreira asked.

'I don't know.'

Zigic took his phone out, found a photograph of the flier they'd found in Josh Ainsworth's office, the one accusing him of having blood on his hands.

'Do you recognise this, Ms Garrick?'

She glanced at the screen. 'It isn't one of mine. Asylum Assist is dedicated to raising awareness, not harassing people.'

'But you knew Josh had been sent this?' Zigic asked.

'I did. He'd shown me it.'

'Did he think it was one of yours?'

She gave him a cold look. 'Josh knew better than that.'

'Did he ask if you knew the person behind it?'

'No.'

'And do you?'

'No.' Even colder this time. 'I don't condone this kind of activity. It harms our cause if people can point to something like this and write us off as hysterical cranks. *This* undermines all the hard work we're doing.'

She climbed to her feet, her movements quick and nimble, and picked up her empty glass. 'Would either of you like another?'

They both declined, sat in silence until she returned from the break she obviously felt she needed. They were getting close to something, Zigic thought.

'Why did you leave the protest this morning?' he asked.

She sighed. 'One of the others – Michaela Paggett – she told me she'd seen you at Josh's house. She said there was a forensics van there. Well, it doesn't take a genius to work out that something terrible had happened. I was upset. I wanted to be on my own.'

It was a feasible extrapolation but something about the ease with which she claimed to have made it unsettled Zigic. They could have been there for any number of crimes that weren't fatal.

'You just assumed he was dead?'

'I assumed whatever happened was very serious. I tried calling him but there was no answer.' She lowered her eyes. 'Maybe I should have gone round there.'

Ferreira leaned forward. 'Were you at Josh's house on Saturday evening, Ms Garrick?'

'No, I was here.'

'Can anyone corroborate?'

'Only my Netflix account,' she said, with an odd glimmer of self-deprecating humour that struck Zigic as misplaced. 'I'm sorry, are you asking me if I have an alibi for Josh's murder?'

'It's purely a routine question,' Zigic told her.

'Did Josh ever mention anyone in particular he was having trouble with?' Ferreira asked.

'No, apart from those fliers, I don't think he was having trouble at all. He was stressed at work, but ... he resigned. His life should have been getting better finally.' Her voice thickened and she apologised as the emotion hit her. 'I'm sorry, is that all? Please, I just need some time to sit with this and process it.'

Zigic stood, Ferreira following his lead.

'You've been very helpful, Ms Garrick, thank you for talking to us.' He handed her a card and told her they would see themselves out.

In the car downstairs, looking up at the balcony of her apartment, seeing her move to close the sliding door, he wondered at that sudden swell of sadness. It looked genuine but it felt very conveniently timed too.

'Mel, make sure we get hold of the CCTV for her building. I want to be absolutely sure she was here Saturday night.'

CHAPTER TEN

Zigic dashed straight into his office when they got back to Thorpe Road Station. The press pack was already set up on the front steps, the press officer waiting with the statement she'd prepared. She left the room as he changed into his suit and Ferreira watched her knock on Adams's door and go in, heard Lee Walton's name mentioned before the door closed again.

Once the woman had left Ferreira went in there herself, found him ploughing through paperwork, three empty coffee cups on his desk and an unlit cigarette balanced on the packet; the reward he would allow himself when he'd done enough work to justify the break. She smiled to herself as she noticed it. For all his mouth and brio he had a streak of self-discipline that was oddly sweet to see. Sometimes she wondered how much of his attitude was a pose, a defence mechanism against the horrors of the job and the stresses it brought. He'd been another man while they were on holiday, quieter and more thoughtful, less biting in his humour, less cynical in his observations. Someone she didn't like more, exactly, just differently.

He looked up as she entered.

'Alright?' he asked. 'Developments I need to know about?'

'The case is moving along,' she said. 'I'm sure Ziggy will have a full and detailed report for you before the end of shift.'

He huffed lightly. 'I do not need another full and detailed report right now.'

'But you did need a briefing from the press officer?'

Adams lifted his eyes from his work again. 'This is what happens when Ziggy leaves the hacks waiting downstairs, they start getting restless and asking about embarrassments like our freshly released serial rapist. "Are we going to apologise to Walton for wrecking his good name?"' Disgust flashed in his dark brown eyes. '"Do we have any leads on who was *actually* responsible for the crimes we fitted him up for?" Oh, yeah, we fitted him up now.'

'Christ.' She threw herself into a chair opposite him. 'What did you say?'

'I said to tell them they're working for a dying media and they should retrain as anal-bleaching technicians.'

Ferreira laughed, letting the tension break.

It had been a long day and now that she was in here with him, she felt the weight of the hours on her. The accumulation of other people's grief, their lies and evasions and the constant ticking away of her brain, playing with what they'd been told, trying to slot together the incomplete pieces into something coherent. It was too early in the process but her gut wouldn't accept that, kept telling her to look closer at the Paggetts, that they should have pushed Ruby Garrick harder.

The first day was always like this. Information overload but very little of it actively useful. Day one was where your suspicions were raised, she thought. After that a murder investigation took on its own peculiar momentum. Maybe another twenty-four hours before you found the killer, maybe a month or a year or never, and the terrible thing was you didn't know which it would be, so you carried this nervous energy, this unwieldy burden, with no idea if you'd ever be able to set it aside again.

And sometimes, like with Lee Walton, even when you thought you'd freed yourself, the case came back at you.

'We're going to get him, Mel,' Adams said, but it sounded more like he was reassuring himself than her.

'I know.' She stood up. 'Back to your paperwork then.'

In the main office she detected the same slump in energy as she felt in herself, saw more sugary drinks on desks and junk food wrappers as people tried to drag themselves over the hump. On an ordinary day the room would be beginning to thin out by now, but Ainsworth's murder was in its first flush of activity, and even Adams and Murray's case seemed to have developed during the afternoon, judging by the new photographs stuck to the board.

At the furthest corner of the room, with his back turned and his earphones in, DC Bobby Wahlia was diligently focused on his review of their files on Lee Walton, pausing occasionally to take a bite of the tuna sandwich sitting by his keyboard and stinking up the room. His normally perfectly styled hair had sunk during the day, sitting flat against his skull, except for one tuft at the front that he had a habit of playing with while he was thinking.

Ferreira looked away, struck by a sudden sadness she didn't want to examine right then.

'Okay, update me, people,' she said, going to over to Josh Ainsworth's board. 'Keri, where are we at with the couple from the holiday let next door?'

'I'm still waiting for a call back,' Bloom said. 'But I've tracked down the woman's social media and it looks like they're out walking, so could be awhile.'

'She's posting photos but she can't be arsed to check her messages?'

'People don't always check their messages,' Bloom said with a helpless shrug. 'I guess maybe they're just trying to enjoy the scenery or something.'

'Zach.' Parr put down the doughnut he was eating and momentarily Ferreira wondered how he could eat such crap all the time but was still rail thin, especially when he boasted of never exercising. 'We need to get hold of the CCTV from Ruby Garrick's building. She claims she was home the night Ainsworth died but she's got no alibi and a totally blatant crush on him, so –'

'You think she was his pizza buddy?'

Bloom let out a small giggle. 'Is that what they called it in your day?'

He pulled a face at her.

'And I want someone to talk to the postie who found Ainsworth's body,' Ferreira said.

'He's not got any priors,' Parr reminded her.

'Nobody has priors until they do,' Ferreira told him. 'What did he tell the first response?'

Parr clicked around on his keyboard, finding the statement. 'He said he noticed the door wasn't fully closed and thought he should check everything was alright.'

'So, public-spirited or opportunistic, do we think?' Ferreira asked.

'I'll get onto him again.' Parr's face twisted nervously. 'But ...'

'But what?'

'I'm supposed to be taking my kids to the cinema tonight. I promised them ages ago.'

Ferreira knew she should tell him to rearrange it, that the case came first, that the initial twenty-four hours were eat when you can, sleep when you're dead territory. But she also knew his kids had taken the divorce badly and had only recently started to forgive him for it. He was on probation there and his eyes said he feared a return to the bad old days of sullen visits to McDonald's and flat-out refusals to see him.

'Alright, but first thing tomorrow. Even if you have to stalk him while he's doing his rounds,' she said. 'Get in his face and see what the real story is there.'

'Yes, boss.' The relief washed over him. 'I'll try for the CCTV though, right? I've got time before I need to go.'

'Someone else can go and pick it up if necessary.' She looked at DC Weller, spinning a pen around between his fingers. 'Rob, anything you want to share?'

'Not much to report, boss,' he said. 'We've had a couple of calls from people in the village who were out during the initial canvassing, but mostly they were fishing for gossip. All of them mentioned the protest at Long Fleet and the leaflet campaign. One of them got pretty arsey about it, said we should be doing more to protect the village from them.'

'The protest has been peaceful, as far as we know,' Ferreira said. 'Unless you've been told otherwise?'

'No, it's just the leaflets. He seemed to think they constituted harassment.'

'Does he work at Long Fleet?'

'I asked, he said not.' Weller was swivelling back and forth in his chair slightly, knees spread. 'Thought it might be significant though, if there's a feeling in the village that Long Fleet is bringing hassle to their doors.'

Ferreira heard what he was saying but read another story in his body language. He'd been slacking today and had nothing to justify his time. She fought down the urge to tell him as much, knew she should have stayed on him and made sure he had tasks in front of him. Some officers you could trust to work off their own common sense, but DC Weller was not one of them.

'Right then, you need to call in Ainsworth's financials and phone records,' she said, giving him the job he should have done off his own bat.

He glanced at Parr. 'It's nearly six.'

'Just get them,' she said, going to answer the phone, which was ringing on her desk. Reception calling. 'What is it?'

'Gentleman down here to see you, a Mr Ainsworth.'

CHAPTER ELEVEN

'Sir, this is Greg Ainsworth, Josh's brother,' Ferreira said as Zigic walked back into the reception area, with his thumb stuck in the knot of his tie, trying to wrench it off.

Greg and Josh Ainsworth looked alike, same pale skin and brown hair and small eyes, his framed in heavy black glasses and the purplish smudges of early fatherhood. Greg kept one hand on a double buggy, two small boys strapped into it, wearing matching dungarees and striped T-shirts. One was soundly asleep, the other talking quietly to the stuffed blue elephant he was dancing on his lap.

'Mr Ainsworth.' Zigic held out his hand. 'We're very sorry for your loss. It must have been a terrible shock.'

Greg nodded. 'Thank you. Yes, yes it is. He's always been such a sensible person.'

Zigic wondered at the train of thought between the two statements. As if only wild living and bad decisions could get a person murdered.

'We should go upstairs and talk,' Ferreira said.

Zigic helped Greg to manoeuvre the buggy through the door and into the lift, asking about the boys, how old they were and what were their names, smiling at them when they looked at him. Greg returned the questions, a reflex politeness, but it was good to get him talking. His voice was flat and he seemed overwhelmed by the strangeness of the surroundings, eyes on everything until they were settled in the muted colours and soft upholstery of the family room.

Shock, Zigic thought. The grief would be in there, gathering, waiting for the numb, stunned feeling to wear off before it hit him full force.

The moment that the door closed one of the boys began to grizzle and Greg lifted him into his lap, where the boy started playing with the flap of his shirt pocket.

'Mum and Dad have just got back from identifying Josh's body,' he said.

'How are they doing?' Ferreira asked.

'Not good. I'd have done it if they'd told me. I just wish I could have spared them it.' He grimaced. 'Dad said it was bad. I don't know what I thought had happened to Josh, but I didn't think it was going to be so violent.'

Zigic was surprised his parents went into detail, wondered why they hadn't protected him from the truth after they protected him from the ordeal of actually seeing his brother's body.

'We need to ask you a few questions,' he said. 'If you're up to it?'

'I want to help,' Greg told them, visibly steeling himself to the task.

'How much did Josh tell you about his job?' Ferreira asked.

'Which one?'

'Did he have more than one?'

'He was working pretty much full-time at this detention centre near his house,' Greg said, a vague disgust wrinkling the skin around his nose. 'But he was doing shifts at a private hospital in town as well, the GP surgery there. Only three or four times a month, but I think he needed a break from the other place, to be honest.'

'Greg left Long Fleet about two months ago,' Zigic said. 'Did he tell you about that?'

'Yes, sorry, of course. He resigned. He didn't want Mum and Dad to know, so I've got a bit too used to lying about it, I suppose.' Greg rubbed his eye behind his glasses, almost knocking them off his nose. 'I'm not thinking straight right now.'

'That's completely understandable,' Ferreira said gently, but Zigic could see a hint of mistrust in how she shifted in the armchair. 'What did Josh tell you about the circumstances around his resignation?'

The little boy on Ainsworth's lap started to squirm and he lifted him up and sat him down again on the other thigh, told him to be good and they could go for ice cream later.

Greg sighed. 'I know he hadn't been happy there for a while. He didn't agree with the place in the larger sense, its existence, you know? Our grandmother was from Ukraine and Josh was always very aware that she might have ended up in there if she was seeking asylum now. But he also knew someone needed to be in there looking after those poor women.' He frowned, watching his son walk the stuffed blue elephant along the arm of the sofa. 'Josh was trying to do good in a bad place. But I suppose it just got too much for him in the end. Five years is a long time to fight your conscience.'

'Is that what he told you?'

'Not in so many words, no. He didn't have to say it.'

'Why exactly did he think Long Fleet was a bad place?' Zigic asked, wanting to see how much Josh had confided in his brother.

Greg pushed his hand back through his hair. 'Josh saw the problems at Long Fleet right from day one. Bullying, harassment, abuse. Most of it low level but some of it not. He spent the first two years he was there taking complaints to his boss and he kept getting them thrown back at him. Insufficient evidence, the women are liars, they're trying to entrap staff members. He was banging his head against a brick wall.' Greg looked at his sons, as if wondering how much of this they might be taking in. 'He was about ready to quit, but a new governor came in and then the abuse accusations were being taken seriously. People being sacked left, right and centre. People he'd seen acting like animals for years finally getting their marching orders. It was like a weight lifting off his shoulders.'

Zigic thought of Josh Ainsworth's cosy chats with Ruby Garrick and all the information she'd disseminated through her leaflet campaign. Information which had come from somewhere. Maybe from Josh himself, using her to get the word out when his previous boss has been brushing it all under the carpet. But the timings didn't work out, he realised.

Unless their relationship went back further than she'd claimed.

Josh Ainsworth had obviously been fighting the system there almost from the moment he took the job.

'His former colleagues can't have been happy about Josh's involvement in their sackings,' Zigic said.

'No,' Greg rubbed his jawline. 'I wouldn't have thought so.'

'Did Josh mention anyone in particular?'

'Probably, but this was two years ago and I've not got the best of memories.'

'It would be a great help if you could try and remember,' Zigic told him.

A terrible light came into Greg's eyes. 'Do you think one of them killed Josh?'

They hadn't, Zigic thought. Not until right then but he could see the potential line of enquiry emerging in front of them. The logic of it. An explanation for the brutality of Josh's murder. It was a raging, wild attack. The action of someone accustomed to violence and practised in its uses.

'Josh had been off work for a while,' Zigic said. 'Do you know what he was doing with his time?'

'He went away for a bit.' Greg stooped to retrieve the toy his son dropped. 'Cycling holiday.'

'Where did he go?'

'Uganda,' Greg said. 'I went last year and I think he was a bit jealous that I got there first. Great rides. The scenery's spectacular.'

'Did you speak to him while he was away?'

'A few times, yes. He wanted to see the boys, so we FaceTimed.' Greg looked thoughtful for a moment. 'I think he just needed to get right away from Long Fleet for a while. Get outside and clear his head, you know. He always said he felt best when he was on his bike.'

'When did he get back?'

'Last week,' Greg said. 'Wednesday. I picked him up from the airport.'

'How did he seem?'

'Like a new man,' he said brightly. 'The break obviously did him good. We talked on the way home about what he was going to do, jobwise. He said he was going to start looking for a locum role, just while he worked out what he wanted to do next.'

The sadness rose up and broke over Greg like a wave and Zigic could see the reality of it hitting him full on.

He thought about the short space between Josh Ainsworth's homecoming and his murder. If that was significant or not. Was someone waiting for him to return? *Their* plan already made. Or was it less premeditated than that?

Ferreira was asking Greg Ainsworth about the leaflet campaign now, showing him the flier, getting nothing new. She asked about the protestors and Greg only knew the minimum about that too, didn't recognise Ruby Garrick's name or have any idea about the extent of his brother's relationship to her.

'Josh had company the evening he died,' Zigic said. 'A woman. Do you have any idea who that might have been?'

'Josh wasn't seeing anyone to the best of my knowledge,' Greg told them. 'Not properly anyway. I mean, he was *seeing* women, but not really dating them.'

'Any exes we should talk to?' Ferreira asked.

Greg blew out a thoughtful breath. 'There's not been anyone he was serious about for – Christ – a few years, I think.' His face darkened. 'Portia.'

They waited for more but nothing came.

'Does she have a surname?'

'Josh never introduced her to any of us. Mum always made such a big fuss about whether he was dating and when he was going to find a wife and settle down and have kids. He got sick of the conversation and just stopped taking anyone home. I don't really know much about her, except that he said she was a wild woman.'

'Was he suggesting she'd been aggressive towards him?' Zigic asked.

Greg frowned. 'Not that kind of wild.'

'Oh.'

Ferreira shot Zigic a pitying look. 'How long ago did they split up?'

'To be honest, I'm not sure they did entirely split up,' he said uncomfortably. 'She got married a few years ago. Not long after they called it off. But Josh was still seeing her.' Greg turned to Ferreira. 'Josh wasn't that sort of bloke – you need to understand that – he wouldn't mess around with a married woman. It was just *her*. She came after him, he said. I told him not to get involved and he promised he wouldn't, but then he started dropping little hints, and I realised they were still seeing each other on the side.'

Zigic tried not to be judgemental about it, told himself it was immaterial what he felt about the couple's behaviour.

'Is there anything you can tell us about her?' Ferreira asked.

'He met her at work.'

'Long Fleet?'

'No, at the hospital,' he said. 'She's a surgeon of something or other.'

The kids were getting restless and there was no more to say, so they finished up, Zigic assuring him they'd keep him updated, even though they both knew a murder investigation moved too quickly and too erratically for them to do it.

Back in the main office Ferreira added the name Portia to the persons-of-interest column on the board.

Zigic looked at the clock, pushing around towards seven. 'We'll talk to her tomorrow.'

'You sure?' Ferreira asked. 'We get her at home, she's on the back foot right away.'

'If we get her at work, she has less reason to lie,' he countered.

He drove home through the tail end of the rush hour traffic, unbothered by the slowness of the journey and the long line of cars, which held him up at the edge of the Bretton suburb, knowing what was waiting for him when he got in.

Not quite the silent treatment but very nearly.

Days of it now but it felt like weeks because they never argued. Not seriously or at any length. They'd always been the kind of couple to air their grievances early and fast, to try to stay honest with one another because they'd both grown up with parents who nursed their grudges and petty jealousies, portioning them out and playing the kind of vicious mind games that could tear the security blanket from even the most well-adjusted children. They'd seen and suffered enough of that not to want to inflict it on their own kids.

Zigic slowed as he entered the village, coming up behind two women on horses who ambled along past the row of stone-built cottages and the primary school before they reached a paddock where a couple more animals stood with their heads poking over the fence, watching the traffic going by. The dog walkers were out in force enjoying the evening sun and the beer garden at the Prince of Wales was already full. The temptation to stop in for a cold beer tugged at him, but he resisted. Turning into the lane he saw people dotting the allotments opposite his house and that exerted a pull on him too. He'd wanted an allotment ever since they moved in eight years ago, but knew it was a pleasure that would have to wait until he retired, no chance of his having the energy for it while he was still working.

He pulled onto the gravel driveway, catching a glimpse of the back garden through the side gate as he locked the car. Anna was out there on a wooden lounger, Emily playing in the shade of a large parasol. The blinds were all drawn in the front windows, an attempt to keep the house cool, but it felt painfully symbolic as he let himself in. The rooms were close and quiet, the boys moving around upstairs. He went out to the garden.

'You've had a long day,' Anna said, eyes unreadable behind her sunglasses as he bent to kiss Emily. 'I've already fed the boys.'

'Did you eat?' he asked.

She nodded slightly. 'There's salad in the fridge for you.'

He hadn't expected a rapprochement when he got home but he'd been tentatively hopeful of a thaw. He'd read too much into her initiating sex this morning, he realised now. It was satisfaction, not intimacy, she'd wanted. The chill between them remained in place and would do until he gave ground.

Something he couldn't imagine doing.

Not on this.

He went back into the house, headed upstairs to shower off the long day in the field and the stuffy hours he'd spent in the office trying to find some shape in the case developing in front of him. A task made all the harder because at any given moment, a quarter of his brain was working out how to contain and absorb the fallout from an ostensibly minor act of violence against his family.

Minor on paper. Dealt with in an instant. Apologies and embarrassment; genuine, heartfelt regret.

It wasn't enough though.

Because 'sorries' didn't free anyone except the person giving them out.

Zigic ran the shower cold over his body, gritting his teeth against the shock of it, stood there until it drained all the heat from his skin. The rest of it, deep in his muscles and bones, was going to take more cooling though. Wouldn't go anywhere until this was settled one way or another.

Dressed, he lingered in the doorway to the boys' room for a moment, watching them playing with their Lego. A new pirate ship kit that Milan was acting the foreman with, trying to sort the pieces into some order before they started building it, while Stefan held a dinky pirate figure in each hand, making them argue over who ate the last yoghurt in his gruffest pirate voice.

Zigic went and sat on the floor with them, letting Stefan's pirates fight it out across his shoulders while he helped Milan separate the light-brown pieces from the beige ones. Every now and again Milan would bend lower over his work and his dark curled hair would part, revealing a small bald patch on his crown.

CHAPTER TWELVE

The flat smelled close and stuffy, old cigarette smoke heavy on the air, a vague hint of dirty washing from the pile in the bathroom. They'd flown home from St Kitts on Friday and spent the weekend crashed out at Billy's place, recovering from the flight and the epic session that had taken them from Thursday night in the bar on the beach to Friday morning breakfasting on Bloody Marys at the airport. Somehow it seemed logical to deal with the punishingly early start by pulling an all-nighter. She couldn't remember whose idea that was but neither of them had the common sense to disagree.

Then staying at his seemed preferable to coming home and dealing with the mess she knew she'd left here.

She opened the windows throughout the flat, letting in what scant breeze trickled up Priestgate, carrying traffic fumes and engine sounds, an occasional warning call from the station as a high-speed train passed through without stopping. The washing went in the machine, the sweetly rotting contents of the fruit bowl went into the bin and she showered thinking about what to make for dinner.

Looking at the near bare shelves in the fridge, she decided Billy was right about going out to eat. Or ordering in.

This place was starting to feel less like home, she realised, as she stared out of the kitchen window at the workers trudging towards their cars and the bus stops on Bourges Boulevard. When she'd signed the rental agreement three years ago, she'd wanted to be in the city centre, with the constant thrum of activity around her. But somehow, gradually, the traffic noise had started to grate on her, and the grim utilitarianism that filled her view only increased the sense of isolation she was feeling here. It was an ugly building to draw up to every night after work, still looked like the office block it had been, cold and impersonal. She'd ignored it – or maybe just hadn't noticed – when she'd been single, out drinking, coming back in the early hours with nothing in mind but a shower and her bed.

Billy had raised the option of her moving in with him while they were away, but it felt too soon.

Their 'relationship' had been an on-and-off thing, way more off than on, for almost a decade. Never serious or exclusive, never more than a series of spur-of-the-moment encounters based entirely on physical attraction. She couldn't deny the change that had occurred in the last eighteen months though, even if she wasn't quite ready to discuss it properly with him or make that one big step he was pushing her towards.

She shook the thought away, put a pot of espresso on the hob and ate a few handfuls of granola from the jar while she waited for the coffee to come bubbling up, remembering that last night in the bar on the beach. The pair of them drunkenly stringing along an ageing Dutch couple who they were sure wanted to swap partners for the night. Her pretending fascination at the husband's stories of spearfishing and skydiving, distracted by his grey chest hair and very blue eyes, while Billy flattered and flirted with the wife in a voice too low for her to hear. Another few drinks and they might have talked themselves into it. They were an attractive couple and now that she thought about it, the husband wasn't much older than Billy anyway, had a good, hard body and a filthy look.

When the coffee was ready she took it into the living room, put on some music and opened her laptop, throwing back one shot while it booted up and pouring a second as she typed 'Joshua Ainsworth' into Google.

It wasn't a common name but she scrolled through a few people who weren't her dead man: a professional photographer and a long-deceased soldier, people who blinked in and out of their own online presence.

On Facebook she found an account Josh had started in his teens but not touched since he graduated from med school. It was tame stuff: lots of photographs of bikes and off-road rides, views from fell paths and moments where he stopped to capture the dappled sunshine hitting forest trails.

She kept scrolling, until she got back to his first post, a shot of the vaulted metal ceiling of a train station, taken from an elevated walkway.

'*Okay, let's do this.*'

The message of a man psyching himself up to suicide, she thought darkly. But the dates were right for it to be him heading off to university.

His friend list was just under three hundred people and she wondered at how easy it was not to notice his lack of activity for the last fifteen years. If anyone had reached out to him when he fell silent.

As she clicked onto the friend list, a moth settled at the centre of her screen, the backlight glowing through its delicately patterned wings. It had fallen dark outside without her noticing.

She got up and went to close the windows, wondering what was keeping Billy so long at the station. In the bedroom she paused to grab her mobile, found a message two hours old, saying he was delayed but was on his way. She texted him as she tugged on the bedroom window, stopped without knowing why she was doing it and looked up.

Across the street, half hidden in a recessed doorway, she saw a figure turned towards her. Couldn't see his face but could feel him staring at her.

As she stepped back, he stepped forward into the light spilling from a window above him.

Lee Walton.

For a second she couldn't move. Part of her wanted to turn the light off and make herself invisible to him, but part thought she should go down there and challenge him. Her pulse was beating in her neck, eyes wide and unblinking, as she waited to see what he would do.

What felt like an eternity passed and she was sure she could see the expression in his eyes, fierce and flat at the same time, that dead intensity she remembered from the interview room, the moment when she had been toe to toe with him and felt herself being flayed down to the bone.

A car came around the corner, breaking her gaze, and she registered the shape and sheen of Billy's Audi turning into the space under the building.

Now Walton was moving away into the city centre, hands in pockets, taking his time. Heading for the isolated grey tunnel next to Barclays bank and whatever woman was unlucky enough to be walking home alone at half past nine on a quiet Tuesday night.

She flicked the light switch with shaking fingers.

Had Billy seen him?

He must have. He drove right past him. Four or five metres away.

And if he hadn't and she told him about it, what was he going to do? Tear off after him and hand him a caution for loitering?

She heard the front door slam home hard and knew that the questions were moot, that he'd seen Walton.

The Billy she'd left at the station was not the one in front of her. His face was ashen under his tan, hair pulled about at strange angles, while a disconcerting wildness sent his eyes wandering around the flat. He threw his jacket down onto the sofa, the flutter of a newspaper underneath it.

'You want a drink?' he asked. 'I need a drink.'

She followed him into the kitchen, pulling down the blinds as he poured a hefty slug of rum into a glass and sank it.

'Sadie Ryan,' he said. 'You remember her?'

Ferreira nodded; the moon-faced, black-haired young woman Lee Walton had dragged off the path on Orton Mere and raped. Who Colleen Murray gently coaxed into bringing charges, only to see her refuse to cooperate mere days after making her official statement, scared off by a visit from Walton.

'She took an overdose,' he said.

'Shit. Is she okay? What happened?'

'Walton was back on his manor this morning. Someone saw him, sent her a photo. All kicks off on Facebook, people saying she was lying about being raped, that she must have been if he's out.' Tension wrinkled his forehead and he took another drink to try and wash it away. 'Her mum got home from work tonight and found her passed out in her bed, fucking vodka and Tramadol cocktail. She called me from A & E.' He rubbed his face, stared into nothing. 'She's going to pull through but her mum's terrified she'll try again and she won't find her in time. And, you know, she's going to, isn't she?'

Ferreira slipped her arms around him, held on to him, feeling his chest swell against hers with each breath he took. Deep ones, slow ones, trying to calm himself but failing. He buried his face in her neck and she stroked the back of his head, saying the usual words they brought out in these situations.

It didn't work with another copper though. He'd said them, too. Knew how hollow they were.

'We've got to do something about him,' he said, drawing back slightly from her, arms still locked around her waist.

'We are doing something,' Ferreira said firmly. 'Bobby's working on it.'

'You didn't see that girl,' he groaned. 'She's looking at a fifty–fifty chance of brain damage. Her mum's in fucking bits. Bobby going through the files isn't anything like enough. Col was right, we can't just wait around for him to do it again.'

'What can we do?' she asked. 'Seriously? We don't have a lot of options here.'

He looked helpless. 'Fucking *something*.'

She said nothing because there was no answer now, just like there hadn't been this morning in his office. She guided him into the living room and sat him down, moving his jacket and the newspaper underneath it.

The front page held a splash on prisoner releases imminent in the city as a result of the compromised forensic results. She scanned it quickly: no mention of Walton, but plenty about the failings of the police to keep people safe, about the abuses of justice, innocent individuals sent down on corrupted evidence.

'They don't mention him,' she said.

'Page four,' he said wearily.

She turned to it, straight into a photograph of Walton looking like a model citizen with his girlfriend and son. An old photograph that didn't show the marks on the girlfriend's arms, which Ferreira had seen when she interviewed her or the shadow of trauma visible behind her son's eyes.

Miscarriage of justice, the headline said.

'"I'm scared for my safety,"' Billy quoted, spitting out the words. '"The police have branded me a predator and even being exonerated by the courts won't clean away that stain. There are scary people out there who aren't above vigilante justice."'

Ferreira swore softly, feeling the anger rising in her chest.

'Anything we do now, we'll be accused of harassment,' he said.

'You don't know that.'

A humourless smile twisted his mouth. 'Oh, I do know that. Because I called the boss from A & E and he told me in no uncertain terms that we're to steer clear of Walton.'

Ferreira dropped, stunned, onto the sofa next to him. 'Why would he say that?'

'There's legal action in the offing.' He shook his head, the disbelief written across his face. 'Fucked-up system, yeah? Walton is suing for false imprisonment.'

'But he won't get anywhere.'

'Probably not.'

She stared at the photograph. 'So, what does that mean for the investigation?'

'Nothing, we have to keep going,' he said, determination squaring his shoulders, even though she could hear the hesitancy in his voice. 'We don't need to talk to Walton to dig something up on him.'

Instinctively she glanced away, towards the window, thanking the God she didn't believe in that he hadn't seen Walton on the street outside. The mood he was in he might have beaten him to death right there on the pavement. Or more likely, found himself laid out.

One thing she knew for certain, she couldn't tell him what she'd seen.

Day Two

WEDNESDAY AUGUST 8TH

CHAPTER THIRTEEN

Zigic called the morning briefing for eight, evidently wanting to get a jump on the case. He didn't look as perky today, Ferreira thought, looked like he'd hardly slept in fact. His hooded green eyes were deeply shadowed and drooping, his beard unkempt, cheeks slack above it. Maybe it was only the sweltering heat wilting him, but the careless way he'd dressed this morning and the distracted approach he took to the coffee machine, spilling half a scalding cup over his hand, suggested there was something bigger at work in his life.

Or perhaps he was just as rattled by Walton's release as Billy.

She watched from her desk as the rest of the team arrived, checking her emails and rolling a cigarette she was already desperate to get lit. Parr was eating a two-bag breakfast he'd picked up from Greggs, today's sunflower-yellow tie placed carefully over his right shoulder as he tucked into an eclair, his chin thrust forward as he took delicate bites to preserve the parts of his shirt the double-napkin arrangement didn't cover. In the corner of the room the new kids, Keri Bloom and Rob Weller, were watching and quietly mocking him.

They seemed ridiculously young to Ferreira, almost children. Maybe it was because they'd known each other so long, through school together, then training, then uniform and now, sharing a desk and the same stupid in-jokes they should have grown out of.

She spun slowly in her chair to see what was going on with Adams and DS Colleen Murray, who had already been sequestered in his office when Ferreira arrived. He'd left her bed at first light, said he was going home to change, even though he kept clothes at her place. She suspected he'd gone back to the hospital to check on Sadie Ryan.

She'd spent half the night awake, thinking about Walton and what he wanted: was it an attempt at intimidation or something more serious? There was no guarantee she'd see him out there, only luck that she did, and as the dark hours ticked by, she started to realise that whatever he was planning, it must go further than standing around in doorways.

By the time she'd dozed and dithered and worried, she was ready to tell Billy about it. But she woke to find his side of the bed empty and now, seeing how agitated he was, pacing around his desk while he talked to Murray, she began to weigh up again the cost of telling him. What he could achieve against how much trouble he could get himself in.

They emerged from the office, Murray taking her seat at the desk opposite Ferreira's, Adams staying at the back of the room, leaning against the wall with his arms folded and his face set hard, no more than an observer in Zigic's case.

When she and Zigic had moved back to CID, Ferreira was worried Adams would pull rank over Zigic just to wind him up, not considering how it might make her position between them uncomfortable. They'd had a fractious relationship before the establishment of the Hate Crimes unit separated them – like two troublesome schoolboys sent to opposite corners of the classroom by the teacher. But so far Adams was using his chief inspector powers lightly and Ferreira was quietly grateful for it. Would have hated having to pick sides.

'Okay, everyone, let's get started.' Zigic was standing at the board, visibly pulled together now and ready to go. He tapped the photograph with his knuckle. 'Joshua Ainsworth, thirty-four years old. Single, lived alone in Long Fleet. Doctor at the immigration removal centre in his village. Murdered sometime on Saturday evening after an altercation in his home. Today we're going to fill in the blanks in this man's life.'

Quickly he précised the progress they'd made yesterday and outlined the new avenues of enquiry it had opened up – making sure everyone understood how important it was to pursue these lines while they were hot. He divvied up the day's tasks, took the few questions that followed, got his nods and 'yes, sir's, then clapped his hands together.

'Crack on then.' He gestured at Ferreira. 'Mel, let's go.'

Downstairs she lit up and dawdled the short distance to his car, taking deep draws because she couldn't smoke once she was inside. Wahlia arrived as she was scrubbing out the butt, late and dropped off in a strange vehicle.

'That'll be the fiancée, then,' she said, catching a flash of platinum hair and big sunglasses before the SUV pulled away.

She got into the car and waited as Zigic shared a quick conversation, personal-looking rather than professional with Bobby, ending with a slap on the shoulder. Wahlia put a hand up to her before he went inside and she waved back, thinking how distant he felt to her now.

That was what bugged her about Bloom and Weller, she realised uncomfortably. They were just like she and Bobby used to be. And she couldn't pinpoint any one moment when they stopped being like that. Could blame it on the move from Hate Crimes, when they were no longer sharing a desk and shit-talking each other all day. Or on things getting serious between her and Adams, keeping her home in the evenings like an old married woman. But if she was honest with herself it started before that. Fewer nights out together, tickets for gigs bought and not used, jokes misfiring. She couldn't even blame his new woman because their friendship had survived numerous partners in the past and there was no reason this one should be any different.

Except that he was getting ready to marry her, Ferreira reminded herself.

Maybe it was just a natural ending. It didn't feel natural though.

She dragged her attention back to the moment, seeing that they were almost at the village.

In the distance Long Fleet Immigration Removal Centre sprawled squatly against the horizon. Sections were shielded by dense screen planting, which only drew more attention to the spread of the place, and let anyone driving by know that it was somewhere that should be hidden. As the road looped around she saw the red-brick and grey-clad buildings clustered at its centre, the site's former incarnation as an RAF base clear from the utilitarian architecture. A few niceties had been added: brightly planted flower beds and a vegetable patch ostentatiously located within easy view of the road.

The perimeter was cordoned off by dark green security fencing, solid up to three metres high and then more mesh, topped with spikes. The panels had been sprayed with the names of women, presumably inmates, and entreaties to free them underneath with the dates of their deaths sprayed in different-coloured paint.

'I watched that documentary you sent over,' Zigic said. 'Didn't make for a good night's sleep.'

She'd found it late yesterday evening, after Billy collapsed exhausted on the sofa and she found she couldn't sleep. Restless and over-caffeinated she went back to her laptop and starting looking more thoroughly into Asylum Assist, searching for some clue left behind by Ruby Garrick or the Paggetts.

The documentary was barely fifteen minutes long, more of a short film, shot inside Long Fleet with a hidden camera, with the images often juddery and erratic. It had been put together by Asylum Assist, voiced over by Ruby Garrick, and it struck Ferreira as odd that she hadn't mentioned it during the interview.

Whoever was wearing the camera had access everywhere, from the women's small grey cells where there was scant trace of personal items or softening touches, to the kitchen where they worked, cooking for each other, and the facilities they cleaned for a pound a day. The hallways all looked the same, white walls and the ceilings too low and the lights blue-tinged, the doors not quite prison-like but unmistakably penal, especially when it came to who had control over them. The camera's bearer had stood behind guards opening those doors onto women sleeping or dressing, who scrambled to cover themselves but never quickly enough. They had sat in the staff rec area and captured the dehumanising language they used about the women, the racist nicknames they gave them and the impressions they tossed between themselves to vicious laughter.

The voice of the man wearing the camera had been obscured in the edit but it was definitely a man. He spoke infrequently, only when necessary, and Ferreira had wondered while she watched if that was because he had nothing left to say or if he wanted to minimise his chances of being identified when it went public.

'It was Ainsworth, wasn't it?' she said. 'Someone smuggled a camera in to get that footage and handed it over to Garrick. Who else could it have been?'

'She claims they only met last year and this must have been filmed a few years ago,' Zigic reminded her. 'There was an anonymous whistle-blower, remember. That's who provided the footage for the Channel 4 news exposé, that's who gave testimonies about what they'd witnessed. It's highly likely whoever they were, they were in contact with Ruby Garrick because her group are outside the gate every day, and she's the one pushing local politicians and press to do something. She'd be the first port of call for any member of staff wanting to get the truth out.'

'I still think it could have been Ainsworth,' she said firmly.

'I doubt he'd have kept his job after exposing the place to that level of embarrassment.'

'He was working there when it was filmed,' she said, pressing because she could feel his desperation to let it go, and she was worried that he'd rather keep the focus away from Long Fleet. She understood the pressure he would be under from Riggott and above, but that only made it more important that she kept up the pressure from below. 'Look, we know he was close to Ruby Garrick. Doesn't that prick your instincts even a little bit?'

'Mel, this is such a delicate investigation we can't go off half-cocked wherever our instincts lead us.' He tapped his fingers against the steering wheel, chewing on his bottom lip. 'And think about it, okay, what *doesn't* that footage show?'

'It doesn't show Josh Ainsworth.'

'It doesn't show any of the medical facilities,' Zigic said. 'It doesn't show any kind of health-based interaction with any women. Whoever was wearing that camera was wandering around the halls, they were on night shifts following guards on surprise inspections. Does that sound like part of a doctor's work schedule?'

Grudgingly she admitted that it didn't. 'Unless he went out of his way to be in those places to get the footage he needed.'

'You're grasping at straws now,' he said, as they drew up to the main gate. 'The most logical explanation is that a guard filmed it and Ainsworth's connection to Ruby Garrick is incidental.'

'Because coincidences are suspect. So it's "incidental".' She eyed the security guard coming out of the hut towards them. 'Tell you something, I bet his former co-workers would have known if it was Josh exposing them.'

Chapter Fourteen

They were directed to the Visitors Centre at the front of the complex where a middle-aged woman in a navy suit was waiting for them. She checked their IDs again before she would take them inside.

'Welcome to Long Fleet,' she said, shaking their hands. 'I'm Catherine Field, the liaison officer. You should direct any enquiries through me in future.' She smiled as if it was a helpful suggestion, but Zigic could hear the machinery churning behind it. 'Please, follow me.'

It was a large room, set up like the reception area of any medium-sized office or university. Cafe tables and chairs, stools at a curved counter, several vending machines along one wall and bright abstract prints on another. Another woman sat at the counter, bent over some paperwork, ID clipped to her jacket. She looked like a solicitor, Zigic thought. He couldn't imagine many other people getting access.

'If you wouldn't mind waiting for a moment,' Field said, directing them to a table before going over to the solicitor. 'I'll take you through now, Ms Hussein.'

'Quicker than usual,' the woman said, eyeing Zigic and Ferreira and smiling faintly as if suddenly understanding. 'Are you police?'

Zigic nodded.

'We should go through now,' Field said.

The woman took a business card from her pocket, handed it to Zigic. 'In case you need to know anything they're not prepared to tell you.'

Field's face showed the briefest flicker of annoyance.

'If you wouldn't mind waiting,' she told them again and this time the solicitor went with her through a set of airlocked double doors and away.

Ferreira's eyebrows went up. 'So much for introducing a new regime of greater transparency.'

'Let's play nice, hey, Mel?'

'I'm just saying.' She made a circuit of the room while he sat and waited, looking through the heavily reinforced glass doors to the corridor beyond, thinking of the footage he'd watched this morning unfolding between those walls. 'Do you think they know yet?'

'Almost definitely,' Zigic said. 'If there's other staff living in the village, word will have got around.'

'So we should prepare to be fed a line.'

'Play nice and keep an open mind,' he said.

Field came back and headed back outside. 'This way, please.'

She led them along the front of the building, footsteps brisk in a pair of sensible court shoes that rang against the paving, and to a smaller block landscaped with evergreens and with a water feature running next to its door. They were doing everything they could to make it not look like a prison, but there was no ignoring the gates and high fences, the cameras positioned at regular intervals and the key points wherever they went.

They passed through a nondescript reception area and into a suite of bland offices, via an airlock manned by a sturdy woman in a grey uniform. Field led them to a door at the end of the corridor, which was standing open ready for them.

The brushed steel nameplate read JAMES HAMMOND, GOVERNOR.

Field popped her head around the door, 'Visitors for you, sir.'

Hammond was younger than Zigic was expecting, barely forty, smartly suited, clean-shaven and with blond hair carefully styled in a deep parting. He carried a vague air of ex-military in his bearing and the precisely calibrated strength of his handshake, and Zigic wondered if that was how he'd come to have such a senior position at his age. Military into private sector security was a well-trodden path.

He gestured for them to sit as Field closed the door and retreated to a seat behind them.

'Terrible news about Ainsworth,' he said in a clipped voice. 'I'm sure by now you've heard that he wasn't working with us any more, so I'm not certain how much I can tell you. We're more than happy to cooperate with our brothers and sisters in blue however we can, though.'

'Perhaps you could fill in some of the details for us,' Zigic suggested. 'Like when exactly Mr Ainsworth left?'

Hammond glanced over Zigic to Field and she piped up from behind Zigic's back.

'June 1st this year.'

A little over two months before his murder.

'And what was the reason for him leaving?'

'Stress.' Hammond frowned, turning away to the window beside them, which overlooked a vegetable garden containing rows of canes and plastic cloches, nobody tending to them today. 'As I'm sure you can imagine this environment takes a lot out of even the strongest of us. It's pretty relentless, pretty thankless work, and not everyone's cut out for it. Not long term anyway.'

'How long did Mr Ainsworth last before it got too much for him?'

'Five years,' Hammond said, a hint of admiration in his voice. 'Longer than anyone expected.'

'You didn't think it would suit him?'

'Joshua was an outdoorsy type, a keen off-road cyclist. We chatted a bit about that when I came on board. The way he talked about being out in the woods, the kind of trails he rode, I didn't think he'd deal well with being cooped up all day.'

Zigic saw Ferreira's fingers flexing above the armrest, a sure sign that she was holding in some comment, making an effort to play nice as requested.

Hammond was looking at her too now. 'Our staff are locked up just as surely as our clients are, Sergeant.'

'And they get to go home to their families at the end of their shift,' she said coldly.

'As a police officer I'm sure you can appreciate the importance of maintaining the rule of law.' His tone was dry, bordering on sarcastic and Ferreira straightened in her chair. 'When you encounter a lawbreaker, you do your damnedest to lock them up. When we see someone flouting immigration law, we do the same. For as long as necessary to ascertain their right to remain. And then we release them or deport them as the law demands.' He folded his arms on his desk. 'This isn't a gulag, Sergeant Ferreira.'

Zigic spoke before she could.

'We need to talk to the other medical staff. Anyone who worked closely with Mr Ainsworth in the weeks leading up to him quitting.'

Hammond nodded curtly. 'Of course. Catherine will set you up in an office along the hall. Our medical day shift is rather depleted at the moment, but they're both in this morning so it shouldn't be any problem having them come in for a quick chat.'

He stood, letting them know this interview was over.

They were put in a disused office three doors down from Hammond's, half the size, no window and with nothing but a desk and four mismatched chairs around it.

'Was that what playing nice looks like?' Zigic asked, once they were alone.

'He's full of shit.'

'People frequently are, Mel. That doesn't mean you have to pull it out and feed it back to them.'

Field returned a few minutes later with a youngish guy in chinos and a white linen shirt folded back to his elbows. He was blandly good-looking, blue-eyed and lightly stubbled. Attractive enough that Zigic noticed Ferreira giving him a once-over. Her type, he thought, before he caught himself. Since she'd started dating Adams, he wasn't sure what her type was.

'Dr Sutherland,' Field said.

'Patrick.' He shook Zigic's hand as the introductions were made, reached across the desk for Ferreira's, both of them holding on for a second longer than necessary. 'Sorry to be meeting you under such sad circumstances. Josh was a lovely bloke. Really great doctor. We're all a bit shell-shocked right now.'

Field retreated from the room and shut the door behind her as they took their seats.

'How well did you know Josh?' Ferreira asked.

'Fairly well, I think.' Sutherland frowned. 'I mean, I thought I did, but then he went off with stress like that, just out of nowhere. I had no idea it was all getting on top of him. He seemed fine, Considering.'

'Considering what?'

'This isn't the easiest place to be a doctor. He'd have been better off in a GP's post somewhere. We all would, I suppose, but someone has to do the job, don't they?'

Zigic sat back, watching Ferreira nodding as she watched Sutherland, wondering if she knew how obvious she was being.

'Did he ever tell you why he came to work here?' she asked.

'No, but I know he moved around a fair bit before he settled down here. That's why I was surprised he left. People who locum for years, generally when they find somewhere they're content, they stick with it to the end.' He closed his eyes for a moment. 'That was a bad choice of words, sorry.' He took a fast, deep breath. 'I think there was an ideological component to it for him. I know there is for me. And the way he dealt with patients, you could see he was trying to let them know someone cared about them. That he understood what they'd gone through and he was always going to be incredibly careful not to make them uncomfortable.'

'You must have a lot of challenging cases in here,' Ferreira said.

'A lot of the physical complaints are fairly minor,' he told her. 'But what underpins them can be quite heavy. We see a lot of self-harm for instance. So we swab the area and give them a few stitches, but as for what's causing it … we can't really do anything. That can be hugely challenging. Josh suffered a lot with the frustration of it.' He shrugged lightly. 'I suppose stress and frustration are interchangeable, aren't they? But nobody says they're quitting over frustration.'

His gaze drifted away into the corner of the room as his voice faded into silence. His expression was queasy, as if he was already regretting what he'd said.

'Did you two stay in touch after he left?' Ferreira asked.

'I kept meaning to call him,' Sutherland said regretfully. 'Swing by and drag him out to the pub or something, just check up on him. But they were struggling to get another doc in to cover his shifts, so I ended up doing most of them.' He rubbed the back of his neck. 'Honestly, I don't feel like I've been out of this place for the last couple of months.'

'When was the last time you saw him?'

'I hadn't talked to him since the day he left.' Sutherland looked between the two of them. 'Sorry, I don't feel like I'm being much help here.'

'It's fine,' Ferreira told him. 'You can only tell us what you know.'

He smiled at her, looking relieved at her reassurance.

'How long have you worked here, Patrick?'

He glanced up at the suspended ceiling. 'Oh, six years, just over. Josh started not long after me.'

'So you both survived the purge.'

Zigic felt a chill come across the table from Ferreira, wondered if he'd misjudged her attention towards the man. Had she seen something that intrigued her more than an attractive doctor with half decent dress sense?

Sutherland's face hardened. 'We did. And we'd both been calling for action for quite some time before the board finally decided to drag the old governor out and bring in someone who wouldn't keep looking the other way on the abuses we were dealing with in the medical bay on a near daily basis.'

'It didn't occur to you to bypass the governor and come to us?' Ferreira asked.

He pressed his lips together. 'I'm legally forbidden to discuss this. I'm very sorry. I really want to help you however I can but, you have to understand, this isn't a hospital. It isn't even a regular prison. Different rules apply here. I'm sorry.'

Ferreira settled back in her chair for a moment, seemingly satisfied that she'd got to the root of the problem, but they were a
long way off it yet, Zigic thought, and Sutherland apparently saw
that too.

'What I *can* say is I really don't think any of that could have
anything to do with Josh's death. It was two years ago. The staff
who were sacked will all have moved on.' He tucked his hands
between his thighs, shoulders curling around protectively. 'At the
time – heat of the moment – I wouldn't have been surprised if
some of them got nasty, but now? No, it doesn't make any sense,
does it?'

'Did Josh give statements against anyone in particular?'

A fearful look crossed Sutherland's face. 'I can't comment on
that. I'm sorry.'

'I'm sure you understand the importance of these questions, Dr
Sutherland.' Zigic tried to keep the frustration out of his voice.
'Somebody has brutally murdered your friend. If you have any
information you are bound by law to tell us. Who did Josh
report?'

Sutherland couldn't meet his eyes.

'Dr Sutherland, this isn't just about Josh any more,' Ferreira
said softly. 'If someone you two reported has gone after Josh,
there's every chance they'll be coming for you next.'

Sutherland pressed his lips together tightly, whitening the skin
around them.

'Is there anything you can tell us?' Zigic asked, trying to contain the desperation he felt.

'I wish I could.' He turned to Ferreira again, leaning across the
desk towards her. 'Truly, I really wish I could help you.'

Then he stood up and left the room, slumped and sheepish,
drained of the easy confidence he'd walked in with.

'Still believe he left with stress?' Ferreira asked.

CHAPTER FIFTEEN

Five minutes later the door opened again and a doughy middle-aged woman in a set of blue scrubs came in. She cast a wary look at each of them, peering out from under the ash-blonde wedge of her fringe, green eyes quick and searching, before she turned back towards Field for guidance or permission.

'This is Ruth Garner,' Field said, waving her towards a seat. 'Detective Inspector Zigic and Sergeant Ferreira. They just have a few questions for you. Anything you need I'm just along the hall.'

The door closed and Zigic noticed Ruth Garner's head cock towards it as if she was listening for Field's retreating footsteps. When she realised they were both watching her, she crossed her arms defensively over her stomach, swallowed hard.

'Is it true?' she asked. 'Was Josh really murdered?'

'I'm afraid so,' DI Zigic said regretfully. 'How well did you know him?'

'We'd worked together for four years, so fairly well, I suppose.'

'And what did you think about him resigning?'

'I didn't – I don't know,' she stammered, seemingly caught off guard by the question. 'It was a bit of a shock. I thought he liked working here. As much as you can like it.'

'How did he seem to you in the weeks before he left?'

'I wasn't here then,' she said, looking between them, not sure who to settle her attention on. 'I had to take some time off. My mother-in-law was diagnosed with a very aggressive cancer in April. We weren't sure how long she had but she was adamant she wanted to die in her own home, so I took some time off to look after her.'

Zigic offered their condolences and she thanked him automatically, almost dismissively.

She shook her head clear. 'What was I saying? Yes. No, I wasn't here when Josh left. I came back a few weeks ago and he'd already left. Stress, apparently. It does get to you. I think it's worse when you live in the village too. You're never fully away from the place, not really.'

'Do you live in Long Fleet?' Zigic asked.

She nodded.

'How much do you know about the protestors here?'

'Not much. They seem dedicated.'

'Have you seen the leaflets they're putting out?'

She nodded again but she looked confused by the shift in conversation. 'Sorry, do you think they're behind this?'

'It's far too early to speculate,' he said, as he brought out his phone and opened the photograph of the black-and-white flier Josh Ainsworth had been sent. 'Do you recognise this?'

Ruth peered at the screen and then sat back in her chair. 'Not that one exactly but I've been sent similar ones. I didn't know Josh was getting them too.'

'He never mentioned it?' She shook her head. 'We found a large collection. It seems like he was saving them for some reason. Did he ever complain about being bothered by the protestors?'

'No. We all try not to interact with them, to be honest with you. It's not worth the hassle, is it?' Ruth thrust out her bottom lip for a second. 'They can be quite verbal when you're coming and going though. I'd be happier if they were moved on but they have the right to be there, I suppose. Not much we can do about it.'

Zigic found the Paggetts' latest mugshots and showed them to Ruth Garner. 'These two? Are they verbal?'

'I couldn't tell you who's doing the shouting,' she said, still looking at the images. 'I keep my head down and get past them as quick as I can.'

'Have these two ever approached you beyond work?'

'They've never come up to me, but I've seen them in the village pub a few times.' She pushed his phone back across the table. 'I was a bit nervous when I saw them, in case they started having a go at me while I was with my family. But they were no trouble to be fair to them, they just sat there and ate their dinner.' She tapped the table. 'Actually, now that you mention it, I *did* see them near my house awhile ago too. There's a public footpath at the end of my garden – it's a lovely walk, I see quite a lot of hikers and walking groups going by at the weekends – but it was a bit of a shock seeing them there.' Ruth frowned. 'Should I be worried about them?'

'You should be vigilant, Ms Garner, but I don't think you need to be particularly concerned about them.' Zigic slipped his phone away again, thinking of the Paggetts hanging around outside Josh Ainsworth's house, walking along the back of Ruth Garner's place. Tried to think of an innocent explanation but couldn't come up with one he even half believed.

'How did Josh get along with the other members of staff?' Ferreira asked.

'Fine.' Ruth Garner shrugged, a little too casually. 'We don't have a huge amount of contact with the other staff in the medical bay. Just the guards when they bring someone in for treatment. We're quite self-contained.'

'But Josh knew enough about the wider staff to know when they were abusing inmates,' Ferreira reminded her. 'Did you know what was happening, Ruth?'

Ruth let out a murmur pitched somewhere between confusion and discomfort. A trapped animal sound.

'You were working here then,' Ferreira said. 'You must have known.'

Zigic could see the thoughts passing behind Ruth's eyes. Was she remembering events she didn't want to discuss or trying to decide if they were important enough to defy her apparently iron-clad NDA?

'Dr Sutherland told us things got very nasty,' Ferreira said, dropping her voice, so Ruth would understand that she knew the risks of speaking openly, too.

'It was a long time ago.' Ruth toyed nervously with her ID badge. 'Mr Hammond took a zero tolerance approach when he arrived. He sacked most of the guards, brought in more women to do the job. This isn't the same place it was back then. The women are safe now.'

Ferreira straightened in the chair next to him. 'Hammond sacked these guards based on *your* testimony?'

'My testimony, yes,' she said slowly. 'And Josh's and Patrick's, we'd all seen things happening we knew were wrong. We had to speak out.'

'And now Josh is dead,' Ferreira said and let the weight of the words hang for a few seconds. 'If Josh's death has anything to do with those reports, then you could be in danger as well. You need to tell us who the guards were.'

'I can't,' she said, her voice cracking.

Ferreira leaned across the table. 'Josh was your friend,' she said fiercely. 'You owe it to him to help us.'

Under the table Zigic nudged her leg, signalling for her to rein it in.

'He died a horrible death.'

Again he nudged her but all she did was shift away from him slightly in her chair.

'I can't give you the names,' Ruth said, virtually mouthing the words. 'Please, I can't afford to lose this job.'

'What can you give us?' Ferreira asked, desperation edging into her voice. 'We need to speak to these people.'

The door opened and Field came in. A palpable relief washed over Ruth Garner, her face lifting immediately, her shoulders easing down from around her ears.

'I'm sorry,' she said, with a regretful little shrug and a show of her upturned palms. 'I didn't see Josh outside of work. He has a brother, maybe he could tell you more about his social life.'

Ferreira snapped her notebook closed and Zigic stood up.

'Well, thank you anyway,' he said tersely. 'We appreciate your taking time out to talk to us.'

CHAPTER SIXTEEN

A security guard escorted them out to their car and Zigic half listened as Ferreira tried to engage him in conversation, getting nowhere. The man had a dull, dead-eyed look, and a neck as thick as Zigic's thigh. Seemed the type who would take his orders without deviation.

'Well, it's immaterial now, isn't it?' Ferreira said, with grim satisfaction, when they were back in their car.

'What is?'

'Whether Josh Ainsworth was the anonymous whistle-blower from the film or not. We know he was informing the governor about his colleagues' behaviour, and my guess is *they* knew he was the one doing the informing that got them sacked.'

'Sutherland and Ruth Garner were equally responsible,' Zigic reminded her.

'Ainsworth cost people their jobs,' she said, animated now, hands turning in the air. 'He probably cost them their relationships too because how do you explain that to your other half?' She pointed at him. '*That* is a very good motive for murder.'

'But we don't have any suspects,' he said, still half hoping this line of enquiry would fizzle out. He'd driven in through the gate, praying they would leave with nothing, desperate not to have a political hot potato in his hands.

Now it was becoming increasingly likely that Joshua Ainsworth's murder had something to do with his job and the regime change at Long Fleet. Whether the blame lay with the protestors harassing him or one of these former colleagues who'd be lining up to pay him back for telling the truth about them, he didn't know.

There were still other possibilities, he reassured himself.

Like the woman who'd been at Josh Ainsworth's house the night he died. She hadn't come forward as a witness or to rule herself out of enquiries, as he'd requested during yesterday's public appeal.

Or the ex-girlfriend his brother mentioned.

Or maybe it wasn't this job that had brought a killer to his door, maybe something had happened at the private hospital where he did his GP shifts. A symptom wrongly interpreted, a misdiagnosis, an avoidable death …

There were plenty of less politically sensitive possibilities.

'You think if we approach Sutherland and Garner off-site we'll get any further?' Ferreira asked, dragging his thoughts back through Long Fleet's gates.

'You saw how scared they are,' Zigic said. 'Ruth Garner was downright terrified.'

Ferreira swore. 'Two more minutes and we'd have got a name out of her.'

'No, she wasn't going to do that,' Zigic said, remembering the relief on Garner's face when the door opened and saved her from herself. 'She said more than she meant to. But it's a start.'

'So we're going to pursue this?' Ferreira said.

'Do you actually need me to say it?' She nodded. 'Yes, we're going to pursue this. But you need to accept that it's going to be a slog because Hammond won't make this easy for us.'

Ferreira waved the warning away. 'We don't need him.'

Zigic slowed as he passed through a village. The one Ferreira had grown up in. She scrunched down in her seat and he decided to look for a different route into Long Fleet next time.

Did she know she was doing it? he wondered. He knew she'd had a tough time of it growing up, but he'd never really thought about how visceral the memories still were for her. Never considered the possibility that she hadn't fully dealt with the emotional fallout. He'd always assumed her anger was a coping mechanism. Didn't regard it as healthy, but thought it must be working or why would she hold on to it so closely?

'Are you scared?' she asked.

'What of?'

'What's going to happen now?' she said. 'To your family. If we hard Brexit. If they might get deported.'

He glanced over at her. Saw how tightly she held herself.

'You're really worried about getting sent back to Portugal?'

'Of course I am.' She turned away, stared out of the window. 'You go to a place like Long Fleet, you have to see how insecure we are here. None of those women expected to end up there. Half of them probably believed they were here legally, then suddenly their paperwork isn't quite right or they get a speeding fine, and there's a knock on the door and bang, they're locked up, looking at getting deported over nothing.'

'I really don't think it's going to come to that.'

She made a derisive sound. 'Have you been reading the news at all?'

Zigic didn't answer, kept his eyes on the road, accelerated to overtake a slow-moving lorry. He didn't want to talk about it. Didn't want to even think about it. He *wasn't* reading the news. Wasn't watching it either. Tuned out every conversation about Brexit he heard for the sake of his stress level and his sanity.

'Your grandparents were asylum seekers, right?' she asked. 'What's going to happen to your grandmother if things go bad?'

'She's technically stateless,' he told her. 'I don't think she can be deported. There's no country there to send her back to any more.'

Ferreira remained tactfully silent, but he could guess what she was thinking because he'd thought it himself already. That that might not matter, if the mood of the country kept shifting, if the government decided to play hardball. His ninety-year-old grandmother being thrown out of the country she'd called home for seven decades, returned to wherever was closest to the place her bombed-out-of-existence village once stood.

'You won't get deported, Mel,' he said finally.

'Yeah? They're deporting doctors and scientists. So I really doubt that being a copper is going to be much help.' She sighed. 'Did you ever think you'd have to consider shit like this?'

He didn't answer because it was a question that didn't seem to need a reply, but the longer they drove on in silence, the more difficult it became not to speak.

'Anna wants to change the boys' names,' he said.

Ferreira twisted fast in her seat. 'What? Why the hell would she want that?'

'In fairness it was Milan who suggested it,' he said, feeling immediately guilty for putting Anna in a bad light. 'Are you seriously going to tell me you didn't wish you had an English name when you were at school?' he asked. 'Because I sure as hell thought about it. You wouldn't believe how difficult Dushan is to pronounce. Apparently.'

'Did something happen?' she asked. 'With your kids?'

'The last week of term, this girl and her little gang … attacked Milan. They gave it all the usual shit about him being a dirty Pole because they're ten and they think all Europeans are Poles. They pulled a handful of his hair out.'

'Fucking bitches,' she spat. 'What did you do?'

'What could we do?' he asked, feeling the hopelessness afresh. 'They're kids.'

'Batter their parents? That's where they got it from.'

'The main girl's parents were totally mortified,' he said, remembering their expressions of nauseated shock. 'They blamed the grandparents, they'd been babysitting a lot lately and they were coming out with shit like that all the time.'

'Probably don't leave the kid with them then,' she muttered.

'So Milan thinks if he has an English name, it won't happen again.'

Ferreira shook her head. 'Shit, Ziggy. You can't let him do that. If he changes his name those bastards win. It'll be like erasing his whole history.'

'I know,' he said quietly.

'Anna must get that.'

'She's scared for them. Milan goes up to secondary school in September and she's convinced it'll be even worse there.'

'She's probably right,' Ferreira admitted. 'The reported incidents in schools have gone through the roof the last few months.' She winced. 'But their *names*. What are you going to do?'

'I don't know.'

'You could kill the girls who attacked him?'

Zigic laughed. 'That's not funny.'

'It was always my plan B at school,' she said, and he wasn't entirely sure it was a joke.

Was this what he was condemning his children to? A lifetime of scars, deep and wide and never fully healing, of constant self-defence in the face of offhand comments and dirty looks.

Did he want his kids to end up carrying the burden of rage Mel couldn't rid herself of?

Milan would take it worst, he knew. He took everything to heart, nurtured his pains in private, shielded them for days or weeks before he and Anna managed to coax them out into the open. Stefan – he was a fighter, but that was no comfort. Fighters were only tough until they met someone tougher. And what about Emily? Too young to know what was going on, although he was sure she was picking up on the frosty mood between her parents already, saw how watchful she had become, although her language skills were still all a babble.

'There must be a better way to deal with it,' Ferreira said.

For a second he considered telling her Anna's plan but stopped himself. Because what if Mel agreed with her? If the two most important women in his life both told him he was wrong, then what option would he have but to give in?

CHAPTER SEVENTEEN

They found Josh Ainsworth's ex-girlfriend on the website of the private hospital in Peterborough where he did occasional weekend shifts. She was listed as a head and neck consultant, specialising in reconstruction surgeries after major trauma and disease. She was highly regarded, had published multiple papers and developed a new procedure for rebuilding damaged ears.

'Portia Collingwood.' Ferreira turned her phone towards Zigic as he unbuckled his seatbelt.

It was a professional shot, showed a fine-boned, pale-skinned woman with auburn hair pulled back into a severe ponytail. She wore a pin-tucked blue shirt that looked vaguely puritan to Ferreira. She thought about how Josh's brother had described her – 'a wild woman' – and wondered if that was true or just boy talk.

'Is she what you were expecting?'

'I don't know,' Zigic said. 'What were you expecting?'

'She doesn't look like the Domino's and quickie type to me.'

'Come on, Mel. It's her work photo. What do you look like on the station website?'

'Like a kick-ass bitch, obviously.'

He shook his head at her. 'And yet look at you now.'

'What?'

'This,' he gestured towards her blouse. 'The corporate ice queen in a Scandi thriller get-up.'

'I like nice clothes,' she said sternly, but she knew what he meant and wondered how long he'd been thinking it without saying anything.

She had changed her appearance since they'd moved into CID. The skinny jeans and baggy jumpers she'd worn in Hate Crimes felt wrong suddenly, her leather jackets and parkas somehow unprofessional. They were still the right clothes for out on the street but in the office, surrounded by a much larger team who all plumped for suits, that was where she'd felt out of place.

'You do look smart,' Zigic said, in the tentative voice of someone immediately regretting an ill-conceived attempt at humour.

'I'm more comfortable like this,' she told him.

'Yeah, you want to be comfortable at work.' He looked down at his jeans and the white cotton shirt she guessed he'd picked because they were going into Long Fleet today and thought he should smarten up. 'I should probably wear my suits more.'

'You've made this conversation weird,' Ferreira told him and got out of the car.

The hospital sat in a slight hollow, surrounded by greenery, carefully tended flower beds and a broad arc of grass, and beyond it a dense stand of trees, which extended for acres into open countryside. It was at the edge of Peterborough but felt entirely removed from it, except for the faint hum of the traffic on Bretton parkway.

As they walked in, entering a reception area that wouldn't have looked amiss in a boutique hotel, with a main desk where the staff all wore smiles and relaxed airs, Ferreira thought how jarring the transition must have been for Ainsworth; Long Fleet during the week, this place on the weekends. Privilege to penitentiary from shift to shift. Wouldn't it have been tempting to stay here?

They waited behind people paying bills and making appointments and when they finally got to the front of the queue, the man behind the desk told them they would have to speak to someone in HR. He gave them directions and said he'd call ahead for them.

Laura from HR met them, already showing signs of grief, her eyes puffy and her nose pink through her make-up.

'Are you here about Josh?' she asked and didn't wait for a reply. 'We're all in shock. I'm sorry. You just don't expect something like that to happen to someone you know.'

They followed her into her office and sat down as she searched her desk for the box of tissues that had somehow ended up on the windowsill behind her, next to a line of succulents dusted in glitter and a framed photograph of her and a group of friends on what looked a pretty sedate hen party.

She dabbed at her eyes.

'I'm sorry,' she said. 'Sorry, I keep thinking I'm done but I'm not.'

Unprompted she launched into a speech about what a valued member of staff Josh had been, so polite and considerate, excellent with the patients, always ready to help out when they were stuck for cover at weekends. Everybody loved him.

'It must be hard for you,' Zigic said, trying to tactfully bring the woman's reminiscences to a halt now that they had circled back to where she started. 'We'll try to keep this brief. We'd like to talk to Portia Collingwood, we believe she's here today.'

Laura blinked at them. 'Why would you need to speak to Mrs Collingwood?'

'We just have some questions for her,' Zigic said evenly. 'She is in today?'

'Let me check,' she said, her mouth set in a prim line, as she tapped at her keyboard, long pearlescent nails skipping around. 'She was in this morning, but she works at City Hospital on Wednesday afternoons. You'll have to speak to them, sorry.'

Ferreira watched her knit her fingers together on the desk, closing herself off from further questions. It was a strange reaction, especially for someone who had been so emotional when they walked in.

'Did Dr Ainsworth and Mrs Collingwood work together very often?' she asked.

'I don't believe their departments crossed over at all,' Laura said, inclining her head at an awkward angle. 'To the best of my knowledge they don't know one another.'

'And you'd know that? Working in the HR department.' Laura didn't answer, must have heard the insinuation Ferreira was trying to keep out of her tone. 'That would be part of your remit, yes? Staff relations?'

The tilt of Laura's head became slightly more painful-looking. 'I'm afraid I don't know what you mean.'

Zigic cleared his throat. 'Have there been any complaints recently about Dr Ainsworth?'

Laura bristled visibly. 'What kind of complaints?'

'From patients,' Zigic said. 'Anyone who didn't feel he'd done his job as well as they'd like.'

'Josh was an excellent doctor and we provide the very highest-quality health care here,' Laura said, sharply, drawing herself up higher in her seat. 'We have been rated good in all inspection criteria for the past six years. Our reports are in the public domain if you wish to read them for yourself.' She pursed her lips, took a moment. 'I am frankly amazed that you might think Josh brought this on himself somehow.'

Ferreira glanced over at Zigic, meeting his eye and seeing that he thought they were done here.

'Thank you very much for your help,' she said, as they both rose from their chairs. 'We'll be in touch if there's anything else.'

Outside in the car, Zigic looked thoughtfully towards the hospital's glass façade.

'Is it me or does every woman we speak to about Josh Ainsworth seem to have some degree of a crush on him?'

'No, it's absolutely not you,' Ferreira said. 'I suppose he must have just been one of those guys.'

'Nice, you mean?'

She smiled at him. 'Sure, *nice*.'

'Not nice then?' he asked.

'Nice guys have long-term girlfriends or very contented wives,' she told him. 'Like you do. Men who inspire crushes in every woman who brushes past them are … well, they're a breed apart and in my experience they generally know it.'

There was a faint trace of a blush underneath his beard and that only made her smile deepen. He really was a sweet little boy trapped in the body of a forty-something Slavic manbear, she thought.

'What does that mean for our case?' he asked.

'It means there are probably a load more women in his phone that we need to be talking to.'

Chapter Eighteen

The office was in a spasm of activity when they returned. The team working on Adams and Murray's attempted murder gathered around as Murray briefed them on a new development in their missing suspect George Batty's whereabouts. Colleen's blood was up, her movements sharp and jerky as she paced in front of the board, detailing the discovery of a friend of the missing man who had a holiday place in southern France, which they now believed he was heading for.

As Ferreira dumped her lunch on the desk, Murray despatched two DCs to go and bring in the man so she could question him.

At the other end of the open-plan office, their own investigation was proceeding more quietly but Ferreira was pleased to see DC Weller concentrating on the task he'd been given for the day, his screen displaying Josh Ainsworth's financial records, a pad next to him full of notes.

He was the kind of officer who preferred to be out in the field, she knew, but he needed to get used to this kind of careful, methodical work if he was ever going to become a worthwhile and competent detective. Because that was what underpinned every epic showdown in the interview room, every cat-and-mouse game you played with a suspect: the accumulation of information which you threw at them, one piece after another, until their protestations of innocence broke down in the face of an undeniable reality.

Zigic disappeared into his office, going to chase up Kate Jenkins and the forensics report they were in desperate need of. Despite what he'd promised as they left Long Fleet, she could tell he was still hoping for a more personal, less politically delicate explanation for Ainsworth's murder, and he was banking on something from forensics to allow him to lead the investigation in that direction.

She understood the pressure he was under, guessed DCS Riggott had already spoken to him about it, even if he'd chosen to keep the discussion to himself for the time being. She wondered what decision she would make in his position, if she would ever be able to play that game, the one which got you to inspector and beyond. Deep down she suspected she wouldn't.

Ferreira unpeeled the lid of her quinoa salad and began trawling for information on Portia Collingwood as she ate. Wanting to get a feel for the woman before they went to speak to her at City Hospital. Ferreira had called from the car, found out that Collingwood was in surgery right now and would be for another hour at least.

No criminal record, but she hadn't really been expecting one.

A patchy social media presence that was entirely professional on Twitter, focusing on her work as an advisor and occasional speaker, the charities she worked with encouraging girls to go into the medical sector and research roles, concentrating on trying to level the playing field for those from traditionally under-represented backgrounds. Maybe that was one thing she had in common with Josh Ainsworth, a social conscience.

Her Instagram presence was very different. So personally revealing that Ferreira was surprised she didn't have it set to private. But it was easy to kid yourself that no one was interested, she supposed, that you weren't worth spying on. Or perhaps Collingwood had an exhibitionist streak, like almost everyone else who used the site.

Her photos were aspirational, intimate and posted in flurries. The places she took her young daughter, the romantic dinners she shared with her husband, the antique shop finds and blowsy bouquets she bought 'just because'.

From the outside the Collingwoods looked like a model family, the kind you could use to sell upmarket SUVs or ethically sourced knitwear.

Was she really still seeing Ainsworth on the side, Ferreira wondered, spearing another piece of chicken from her salad.

The last series of photos Collingwood had posted were from a Sunday afternoon trip to a local stately home. A picnic in a wicker basket, a plaid rug on the grass, her husband grinning boyishly as a tame deer came and took an apple right out of his hand.

Could Portia Collingwood have murdered Josh Ainsworth on Saturday night and then gone home to her family as if nothing had happened? Found the picnic basket in the utility room and placidly made up their sandwiches, cutting the crusts off and wrapping them in parchment paper. Could she have gone out the next morning and given nothing away?

You'd have to be a psychopath, Ferreira thought. But Collingwood was a trauma surgeon, well accustomed to managing risk and stress, to keeping her hands steady while her heart and mind were racing.

'I spoke to the postie,' DC Parr said, coming straight over to her desk. He smelled faintly of weed and seemed to notice her catch the scent. 'He's got back problems apparently. It's medicinal. I didn't think it was worth making anything of it.'

'Not unless he did rob Ainsworth,' Ferreira commented. 'But you don't think so, do you?'

'I'd be surprised,' Parr said, thrusting his hands into the pockets of his slightly dated grey suit trousers. 'He's ex-army, pretty upstanding sort of bloke, and his husband's a coder so they're not short of money. I can't see any reason why he'd pinch a couple of hundred quid's worth of tech.' He shrugged. 'Difficult to know for sure. But my gut says no.'

Ferreira considered it for a moment. Parr had been about long enough to know when he was being sold a line, but he also had a hard-wired deference to anyone he thought was 'the right kind of person'. A blind spot she doubted he'd ever get over.

'Alright, not much else we can do,' she admitted.

He headed for his desk and she called him back.

'Zach, I need you to see what the situation with Ainsworth's holiday was. The brother said he was cycling in Uganda. Just check he was where was supposed to be for me, okay? Rob's going through his financials, he should have phone records coming through too. Check everything lines up, yeah?'

Parr half turned on his heel. 'Anything else, boss?'

'Keep an eye on the tip line for me?'

'Sure thing.'

'Keri, what's happening with the couple from the cottage next door?' she asked.

Bloom hunched her shoulders defensively. 'Still no word, Sergeant.'

'What the hell are they doing?' Ferreira threw herself into her seat. 'Who goes this long without looking at their phone?'

'Maybe they did it,' Weller piped up, not lifting his eyes from his screen, and Ferreira caught the hitch of a smirk across his cheek.

Zigic came out of his office, stretched his neck with a crunch she heard across the room. He glanced at the board as he passed it, not enough progress made in the last hour or so to require any more attention.

'Portia Collingwood's out of surgery,' he said.

Ferreira grabbed her bag. 'Hit her while she's shattered, right?'

'It's not always a fight, Mel.'

CHAPTER NINETEEN

They found Portia Collingwood sitting in the corner of the cafeteria at City Hospital, looking less polished than she did in the photograph that was stuck up in the suspects list on Josh Ainsworth's board. She'd been in surgery three hours by Zigic's reckoning and he guessed she was probably even more tired than she looked, as she toyed with a slice of chocolate cake, probing at it with the tines of her fork but not actually cutting any off to eat.

A guilty conscience or a stomach full of grief, he wondered.

She stood sharply as they reached her table, and they didn't even have a chance to introduce themselves before she spoke.

'I think this is a conversation we should have in my office.'

It was a conversation for an interview room, Zigic thought, but he decided to let her feel in control for a while, was curious what she would admit to while she still believed she was driving proceedings.

They followed her along the corridors, up a stairwell and into a quieter area of consulting rooms and empty waiting areas, to her office. She opened the door and ushered them in, closing it behind them with a deliberation and slowness that he read as an act of acceptance. Or maybe just preparation.

Her office was small and drab and grey, one window but she had the blinds drawn at it and the sill was lined with textbooks. There were files piled up on her desk, more on the cabinets, but she'd made space on the shelves for a series of awards and framed photographs of her with the local MP and one where she was curtseying to a minor royal, more showing her with groups of teenaged girls in school uniforms. There were thank-you cards dotted around and on her desk a gift-wrapped box he guessed was from another happy patient.

Portia Collingwood unbuttoned the jacket of her smart grey linen suit jacket and sat down. She wore a small gold cross and a saints medal high in the neck of her white silk blouse.

'I was intending to visit you after my shift today,' she said, as if this interruption was an unreasonable breach of some agreement they had already made. 'I'm sure you can appreciate how difficult it is for me to get away.'

'You didn't have a chance any other time between Saturday night and now?' Ferreira asked.

'I didn't know what had happened to Josh until I saw the news this morning,' Portia Collingwood said icily. She shifted her gaze back to Zigic. 'I'm not an idiot, Inspector, and I'm sure you aren't either. I'm not going to try and deny being at Josh's house on Saturday evening.'

'That's a good start,' he said, knowing the denial would come next.

'I have no reason to try and mislead you because, obviously, I'm not responsible for what happened to him.'

'For his murder,' Ferreira said.

Portia swallowed, dipped her head for a moment. 'Yes, for that.'

'Why were you at Josh's house?' Zigic asked.

She shot him an incredulous look. 'For sex, of course.'

'It isn't the only option,' he commented.

'Please, can we dispense with the play of ignorance.' She put her hands up, impatient already, and they'd hardly begun. She was nervous, he realised. And guilty or innocent she was right to be. 'Josh and I had a relationship several years ago that neither of us wanted to pursue into marriage. I *am* married now, but we continued to see each other occasionally because we enjoyed sleeping together.'

Was this bluntness a ploy, he wondered. It was a surprisingly common one. Be brutally honest about the things you knew the police would already know in the hope that they would believe everything else you told them.

'I am quite prepared to cooperate with you in any way I can,' she said, showing him a perfectly open face. 'But I would greatly appreciate it if we could proceed with some discretion. I have my family to think of.'

'Was your husband aware of your relationship with Josh?' Ferreira asked, tapping her pen against her notepad.

'He was not. And I'd prefer to keep it that way.'

Zigic nodded, although it was a naïve wish on her part. She might think her husband was unaware of her affair but in his experience people were never as adept at hiding infidelity as they thought they were. Just because Mr Collingwood hadn't confronted her it didn't mean he knew nothing about it.

But they could come back to that.

'Tell us what happened on Saturday night.'

'I arrived at Josh's place around six,' she said. 'We had a glass of wine, we had sex. Josh ordered a pizza and when it arrived we ate it. I had another small glass of wine and I left.'

'At what time?'

'Around nine.'

'Where did your husband think you were?' Ferreira asked, needle in her tone.

'My husband,' Portia said, staring back at her, 'is away in Berlin for work, so I didn't need to concoct some story for him.'

'Who was looking after your daughter?'

A flash of a cold smile. 'We have an au pair. I told her I'd been called in for an emergency consult.'

'Is that your usual cover story?'

'It is,' she said, lifting her chin defiantly. 'An advantage of our chronic underfunding here. I can be needed at the drop of a hat.'

'So, you're a good liar,' Ferreira commented.

'I'm not misleading you,' Portia said firmly. 'I may not be the perfect, faithful wife but that doesn't make me a murderer.' She touched the cross around her neck. 'I loved Josh. We just couldn't live together. I needed somebody more predictable and dependable. That's what Alistair gives me.'

'You don't seem particularly upset about his murder.'

Ferreira was pushing her harder now and Zigic knew he was soon going to have to pull her back or take this conversation into the station. He was already regretting giving Portia Collingwood so much leeway.

He didn't have her pegged for a killer, that was the problem. She was barely eight stone, he guessed, her wrists so slim he doubted she was physically capable of wielding the table leg that killed Josh Ainsworth.

But looks could be deceptive and rage could make you strong enough to do amazing and terrible things.

'I'm not going to cry just to make you believe me,' Portia said flatly. 'I'm heartbroken about Josh. When I saw the news this morning, I felt like somebody had cracked my back open and filled my body up with ice water. I still feel like that. I couldn't cry then and there because I was giving my daughter her breakfast and how would I explain myself to her? I just changed channels on the TV.' Her small, pale hand was curled into a fist, the bones of her knuckles a starker white, painfully prominent. 'I haven't cried since and I'm not even sure I'm going to because if I do I might never stop, so I think the best option is never letting it start in the first place.'

She sounded genuine, Zigic thought. Barely supressed emotion vibrating her throat, her pulse visibly beating there. The kind of reactions you couldn't fake.

But guilty people felt them too, he reminded himself.

'Did you see anyone hanging around Josh's house when you left?' he asked.

He watched her carefully for signs of relief as he changed the subject, saw none. She only shook her head.

'Nobody who jumped out at me as a potential murderer, anyway. There was an old man walking his dog on the green but he could hardly bend over to clean up after his dog, so I doubt he'd be able to get the better of Josh.'

'Had Josh mentioned being worried about anyone to you?'

'No.'

'Did you know about his work situation?'

Her eyes narrowed as if she suspected him of trying to catch her out. 'He'd quit his job at Long Fleet, is that what you mean? Of course I knew about it. I was encouraging him to start a GP practice of his own, but he was talking about going away for a few months to do some charity work.'

'And you didn't like that idea?' Ferreira asked.

Another cold look. 'Yes, I murdered him because he was going to go abroad for a couple of months and deprive me of my extramarital sex. What world do you live in?'

'One where murderers tell whatever lies they need to so we don't charge them.'

Zigic drew Collingwood's attention back to him. 'What about the protests at Long Fleet?'

'What about them?'

'Did you discuss them with Josh?'

'I knew he'd had some leaflets through his door but he wasn't concerned about them. Why would he be worried about them?' She shook her head, looking perplexed. 'I'm sorry but I suppose I assumed this was a burglary gone wrong. Are you saying you think Josh was killed because of his job at Long Fleet?'

'It's too early to say yet,' Zigic told her, the words slipping thoughtlessly off his tongue, sounding like the stock answer they were. 'Now, we need you to come in and provide us with fingerprints and a DNA sample, Mrs Collingwood.'

She picked up her phone and thumbed at the screen. 'My last appointment this evening is at seven, would that be doable your end?'

Like she was fixing a house viewing or a check-up with the hygienist.

'That will be fine,' he said.

A few minutes later, as they were crossing the seemingly endless car park, Ferreira finally snapped.

'What the hell was that?' she demanded. 'Why aren't we hauling her in?'

'Does she seem like a flight risk to you?' Zigic asked, pausing to look along the lines of cars.

Ferreira turned around and stalked back over to him.

'If she cleaned toilets for a living you'd have taken her in.'

'That's what you think this is about?' he asked, incredulous. 'You think I'm class-struck?'

'You're acting like you are.'

'She thinks she's in control,' he explained. 'The more leeway we give her, the more confident she feels, the more likely she'll end up contradicting herself.'

'So you accept that she's our prime suspect right now?'

'She always was.' He finally spotted his car, half hidden by a van. 'We just didn't have a name for her before.'

Chapter Twenty

DC Keri Bloom sprang out of her chair as Ferreira walked in.

'I've just got off the phone with the couple from the holiday let,' she said excitedly. 'They *did* see someone at Dr Ainsworth's house on Saturday evening. A woman.' She consulted her pad. 'She arrived around half six, that's when they saw her. Petite, slim, redhead, fortyish, the wife said; her husband thought she was in her late twenties.'

'This woman,' Ferreira told her, plucking the photo of Portia Collingwood from the board and moving it to the top of the suspects list.

'Oh.' Bloom's face dropped. 'I thought I'd made some progress.'

'You did,' Ferreira said. 'We've got corroboration for the time she arrived. What we need now is to find out if she left at nine o'clock like she claims she did.'

'They didn't see her leave.' She gestured back towards her desk. 'Should I try them again?'

'Keri.'

'Yes, Sergeant?'

'What did they say about the fight?'

Bloom cringed and Ferreira remembered that feeling, embarrassment that in your desperation to reveal one piece of information to a senior officer, you'd completely blanked out the rest.

'It was just before midnight,' she said. 'Apparently they'd gone to bed early because they wanted to be up for a dawn walk. But they were woken by the sound of raised voices and something smashing next door.'

'Male or female voices?'

'Neither of them would commit.'

'Did they see anything?'

'Nothing.' Bloom shrugged apologetically. 'I did wonder why they didn't go and have a look to see if everything was okay.'

'People don't,' Ferreira said. 'That's what they keep us for.'

'I suppose I wouldn't, if I was older.'

'But you'd call the police, wouldn't you?' Ferreira asked, getting a nod. 'So why do you think they didn't bother?'

Bloom considered it for a second. 'Because they had plans for the next day and they probably didn't want to disrupt their schedule talking to us?'

'Never underestimate the potential for selfishness when you're struggling to find witnesses.' Ferreira went over to the coffee machine and poured herself a cup. 'Next we need to pull the CCTV for the streets around the Collingwoods' house. See what time she got home and we'll take it from there.'

'Yes, Sergeant.'

They'd stopped at the house – a Tudorbethan mini-mansion with tiny windows and a black-and-white wooden façade – on the way back from City Hospital, wanting to speak to Portia Collingwood's au pair about her movements on Saturday night, hoping she hadn't straightened out her story with the young woman already.

After the interview in her office, Ferreira wouldn't put anything past Portia Collingwood. She was too held together, too upright and stone-faced. Nobody who exerted that level of self-control could maintain it for ever and in her experience, they were the people who exploded the most extravagantly at the first sign of a crack. She couldn't help but wonder just why the doctor felt the need to be so contained. What was lurking in there she didn't trust herself to let out?

The au pair backed her up.

'Mrs Collingwood was called into work at six o'clock on Saturday evening,' she'd said, as she folded towels in the pristine white laundry room behind the equally pristine black kitchen.

The young woman had returned to the room as soon as she'd let them in, hurried back to her work as if she didn't have a second to spare in her day, not even to speak to the police.

'Mrs Collingwood often has to go to work in the evening,' she'd told them. 'She is a very important surgeon.'

Ferreira had studied her for any hint of malice or insinuation as Zigic asked the questions, knowing that there could be no secrets in a household where somebody else washed your sheets, but she saw no sign that the au pair was lying. Not when she said that Mrs Collingwood was a good employer, very fair, or when she maintained that she returned home from 'work' at half past nine.

You might lie for a good employer, Ferreira thought as she marked up the times of Portia Collingwood's alibi on the board under her photograph. If your other positions had been bad enough, if your au pair friends shared their horror stories … a safe placement, well paid and with a well-tempered boss might be worth misleading the police to protect.

Somehow Ferreira doubted that she was a well-tempered boss though.

But there it was, until they managed to prove otherwise – Portia Collingwood away from the crime scene by nine o'clock.

'Zach,' she called.

Parr glanced up from his screen. 'Boss?'

'Where are you with Ruby Garrick's alibi?'

'Checking out the footage now,' he said.

Ferreira went over to his desk, watched across his shoulder as the images on the screen moved by at 6x speed, long stretches of nothing as the doorway into Ruby Garrick's building remained undisturbed, then a blur of a figure at which point he would slow it down and go back to be sure that it wasn't her.

He was at 6:24 p.m. on the Saturday evening, long shadows coming into shot before their owners did, crisp in the late sun.

'I can narrow down the time frame if Collingwood was at his place until nine, right?' he said hopefully.

'No, you need to do the whole evening,' Ferreira explained. 'Just because Collingwood didn't mention anyone else hanging around Ainsworth's house doesn't mean Ruby Garrick wasn't there.'

'Gets jealous when she sees him with a younger woman?' Parr asked, leaning forward as he slowed the image down, leaning back when he realised it wasn't her. 'That makes sense.'

'Let's just be thorough here, okay.'

Ferreira returned to her own desk, finding that the PM results had come in while she was away. As she opened the file Zigic emerged from his office and went over to the board.

'Listen up,' he said. 'PM results are in and we're looking at blunt force trauma, as expected. More tests to be run and they might show something interesting, but for now this is the cause of death on Josh Ainsworth.' He reached into the file he'd brought with him and stuck up a photo of the death wounds. 'At least ten distinct blows all on the right side of his head, concentrated on the temple, eye and cheek area. One or two would likely have proved fatal.'

'Overkill,' Weller murmured.

Ferreira had the same image open on her screen and she realised how little she'd taken on board at the crime scene. Now, beyond the shock of the violence, she could see the telltale signs of a body that had lain for days, the discoloration of Ainsworth's skin, the dark tracery of blood going bad in the veins of his face and neck.

'What about his broken nose?' she asked. 'It says here the break is inconsistent with the murder weapon. So, a first punch to put him down?'

'But he didn't fight back at that point?' Parr said, perplexed. 'Why didn't he try and defend himself then, before it escalated?'

'Shock?' Bloom offered.

'Or it was a sweet shot and he didn't get a chance,' Weller suggested, a hint of admiration in his voice.

'Approximate time of death late Saturday night early Sunday morning,' Ferreira read out loud. 'That matches what we're getting anyway.'

Zigic had tacked another photo up on the board – the table leg.

'This is our murder weapon.'

121

'Heat of the moment, then,' Parr piped up, rubbing his eyes with his knuckles.

'It's manslaughter, right?' Weller asked.

'We'll worry about that when we find who did it,' Zigic said impatiently.

He wasn't impressed with Weller either, Ferreira thought. Had probably noticed, the same as she had, that he was quick with his commentary and slow to offer anything useful.

'We have defence wounds,' Zigic went on, adding a photograph of Ainsworth's hands, his broken fingers bent sickly out of alignment. 'Nothing that suggests he managed to get any blows of his own in, so don't expect to see injuries on his murderer. This was him putting his hands up and getting them broken, nothing more.'

One more photo went up, of the underside of Ainsworth's fingers and palms. 'These wounds are another matter.'

Ferreira found it in the file, magnified it on screen.

'These are old,' she said, looking at the line of parallel holes stabbed into Ainsworth's skin across his palm. Four on his left hand, five on his right; a ruler next to them gave spacing at 2.5 cm, the holes themselves barely 3 mm.

'They were made several days before his death,' Zigic said. 'The coroner won't commit to a cause, but they're distinctive and we need to keep these marks in mind.' He tapped the photograph. 'Any thoughts?'

Weller blew out a noisy breath, lips smacking against each other.

'Ainsworth was a cyclist, wasn't he?' Bloom asked. 'Maybe they're from some kind of bike maintenance? Could he have done it on the spokes or the chain perhaps?'

Zigic frowned and Ferreira could see him wanting to be encouraging even as he was going to shoot her theory down. 'Good thought, but I don't think you'd see multiple wounds on both hands under those circumstances.'

'Torture?' Weller asked.

Parr let out a derisory snort of laughter, more for the hopeful tone Weller had used than the suggestion, Ferreira thought. They did see instances of torture, very occasionally, but it was usually in the context of sexual or domestic violence, or carried out to obtain financial details during robberies.

'I doubt he was tortured several days before his death without reporting it, do you?' Zigic asked, letting Weller see the scorn before he shifted slightly to take the whole team in again. 'We work with the facts we have, we don't start indulging in fantastical thinking. There are enough leads here to keep you busy.'

'If the wounds are several days old, does that mean they might have happened while he was on holiday?' Bloom asked.

Zigic looked at the timeline on the board.

'It's a distinct possibility,' he said. 'Mel, call the brother and see if Josh's hands were bandaged when he picked him up from the airport. He'd have probably mentioned it but we should make sure.'

With a final glance at the board and a few words of encouragement, he retreated to his office again and Ferreira called Greg Ainsworth's number, wondering why Zigic was so fixated on the odd little marks on Josh's hands.

They were strange, but they would likely have a banal explanation.

Greg answered fast, the bright and bouncy sound of cartoons playing in the background, and the first question he asked her was whether they'd arrested anyone yet.

'We're making progress,' she told him. 'But we're very early in the investigation.'

She asked him about the wounds and he told her that Josh had been fine when he collected him from the airport, no signs of injuries of any kind. The only complaint he had was an infected bite on his backside, which had sent the boys into fits of laughter.

His voice thickened as he recalled it and Ferreira was about to say her thank-yous and goodbyes when he asked, 'Have you talked to Portia yet?'

'We have.'

'What did you think of her?'

Ferreira paused a moment, choosing her words carefully, because she wasn't expecting him to press her on the matter and wasn't sure why he would.

'She seems to be holding her grief very close to herself.'

'Was Josh still seeing her?'

'They were casually involved, yes,' Ferreira told him.

'Even though she's married?'

'Yes.'

'Then it must have been her husband, mustn't it?' Greg said.

'It best not to leap to conclusions,' Ferreira warned, sure that he wasn't the kind of man to go around to the Collingwoods' house and kick off, but grief could stir the vengeful spirit in even the most placid people. 'Mr Collingwood's alibi looks very strong right now.'

'What about hers?'

'Why would you think she was responsible?'

'She had a temper,' Greg said. 'I don't think she was ever seriously violent with Josh, but he described her as "fiery".'

'Fiery doesn't necessarily mean violent.'

'She was possessive though, isn't that usually a red flag in situations like this?'

Ferreira supressed the sigh she felt rising in her chest. His story had changed, subtly but definitely since they last spoke to him, taking on fresh aspects at a pace she didn't quite trust. Usually the worst version of a person came out in the initial interview, as grieving friends and family members transferred their irrational anger towards the victim onto another, still available, target. This felt like Greg grinding an old axe.

'I can assure you that we are pursuing every avenue of enquiry,' she said, clicking into the familiar assurances they always used, the ones that were superficially comforting but gave nothing away. 'Thank you for your help, Mr Ainsworth.'

She ended the call before he could pry any further, went back to the post-mortem results and began a thorough readthrough.

She tried to keep her attention on the job at hand but she kept drifting back to the conversation with Portia Collingwood, remembering her chilly demeanour and her air of self-assurance, wondering how she and Josh Ainsworth fitted together as a couple. If their relationship was really as free and easy as she suggested.

Without his side of the story, she could say just about anything.

CHAPTER TWENTY-ONE

Joshua Ainsworth's clothes were laid out on one of the long steel-topped tables in the lab, ragged-looking even though they were largely undamaged, sad and forlorn under the pitiless lights. Lightweight grey yoga pants and a T-shirt with a Soviet-era cycle race on the front. There was blood on the T-shirt, long dried and darkened to that specific reddish-brown you'd never mistake for anything else.

The clothes looked small for a man of his size. Five foot eleven, according to the post-mortem report, 76 kilos of what must have been lean muscle, the build of a dedicated cyclist.

Zigic had written off Portia Collingwood as his killer because of the size disparity he'd perceived. Had half disregarded Ruby Garrick for the same reason and probably any other woman they might come across during the investigation. In his head it was already shaping up into a man's crime but now he wasn't so sure.

A sudden push, a bad fall, a weapon to multiply the force of the killer's rage: yes, a woman could have been responsible under those circumstances, he thought, looking at the narrow chest of the T-shirt and the span of the trouser thigh.

'Sorry for the delay,' Kate Jenkins said, shuffling out of her office. 'I think every single thing in here has been moved while I was away. In fact, I'm starting to think they did it just to annoy me.'

The small office she used, little more than a cupboard, still bore the previous occupant's uncomfortably Gothic taste in art and a virtually dead spider plant in a wicker hanger over the desk, untouched by sunlight. Zigic could see that Kate had started bringing her own personal possessions back in, photos of her kids on the drawers of the filing cabinets and a few postcards on the corkboard, but she'd either run out of steam or time, and there was a transitional air to the room, caught between two owners for now.

'You've got the post-mortem report, right?' she asked.

'Blunt force trauma,' Ferreira said. 'Lots of it.'

'More than enough,' Jenkins agreed. 'But, sadly, very little in the way of wrestling in the lead-up, so we've managed to recover some fibres from his clothes, but I suspect they're going to be from his lady friend's clothing rather than the killer's.'

A tray of samples sat on the other work table, all bagged up and labelled in her careful handwriting.

'Light pink cotton–linen blend on his T-shirt.' She cocked her head. 'Ninety-nine per cent chance that's from womenswear.'

'We're not ruling her out as the killer,' Ferreira said, leaning against the counter and shooting Zigic a meaningful look. 'Portia Collingwood will be in later to give us fingerprints and a DNA sample.'

'She's cooperating then?' Jenkins asked.

'She's worked out it's the smart play.'

'Well, I've got fingerprints on the wine glass and the pizza box,' Jenkins told them. 'DNA from the condom and the knickers, but if she's not denying being there ...'

'Yep, not something we can use against her,' Ferreira said. 'We'll ask for the pink knitwear though. If she wants to maintain the line that she left before he was killed, she'll have to hand that over for analysis. Maybe we'll find some blood on it.'

'Any signs of a second visitor?' Zigic asked.

'We've got bloody footprints on the carpet and out into the hallway,' Jenkins said, swiping through photos on her tablet to find the right ones. 'Some effort was made to disguise them.'

'But not to clean them up?' Zigic studied the image she put in front of him, could see that it wouldn't tell them anything solid.

'No,' Jenkins said. 'It looks like the killer saw that they were tracking blood through the house and then maybe realised that their footprints could be incriminating, so they went back and swiped their foot over them until all we're left with is these smears.'

'Their shoes must have left some kind of pattern though,' Ferreira said, reaching over Zigic's arm to enlarge the photo. 'Anything we can use for matching at all?'

'Give me a little bit more time for that, okay? We're not talking huge quantities of blood here. It was more from Ainsworth's broken nose than from the head injury – he died too quickly to bleed much.'

'Okay.'

Jenkins went on. 'After your killer did their cover-up job, we've got them wiping the rest of the blood off their shoes on a jute mat at the front door. We recovered some black flakes from it that are likely off the soles of the shoes.' She kept talking as she went into her office and returned with a bottle of apple juice. 'I'm really dehydrated, sorry. So, these flakes would suggest a shoe in not great condition or they wouldn't have degraded like that at the first bit of scuffing.'

Zigic nodded, wondering how useful that was. If the killer took Joshua Ainsworth's devices and disposed of them, then the chances of recovering the shoes or clothing they wore were close to zero, he imagined.

'We don't have a foot size or anything?' Ferreira asked.

'No, we do.' Jenkins took another sip of her drink. 'Size nine. We found a fairly crisp print under Ainsworth's leg that the killer missed.'

'Burying the lede there, Kate,' Ferreira grumbled.

'That's not the lede,' she said, heading over to a wooden counter under the window where the blinds were drawn, blocking out the sun. Three of the fliers they'd recovered from Josh Ainsworth's house were lined up there, the evidence of Kate's attention still dusting them.

Zigic felt his shoulders slump when he saw them. Was hoping for something more. Ferreira was leaning over them already, the excitement obvious on her face.

'Okay,' he asked, trying to hide his disappointment. 'What have you got?'

'The only fingerprints we could find belonged to Ainsworth, okay?' Jenkins told them. 'Whoever made these up was scrupulous to keep themselves unidentifiable. We've got traces of chalk, so I'm guessing common or garden latex gloves, but ... I got this.'

She produced a plastic tube and Zigic peered at the contents; a very fine hair, barely three centimetres long, virtually translucent.

'Peroxided to within an inch of its life,' Jenkins said. 'I can only assume that's why they never saw it stuck in the fold of the flier.'

'Damien Paggett,' Ferreira said, relishing each syllable. 'I knew it.'

'Helpful?' Jenkins asked hopefully.

'We'll definitely be hitting them with this,' Ferreira told her, but immediately her face dropped. 'You can't get DNA from that with the dye, can you?'

'We might be able to, but it'll take a bit more time and cost a bit more money.' Jenkins looked to Zigic, knowing that budget would be a concern that fell squarely on his shoulders.

'Let's wait on that for now,' he said.

Ferreira let out a small huff.

'It was inside a *flier*, Mel. It wasn't in Josh Ainsworth's dead mouth. I can't justify expensive forensic procedures just to find out whether Damien Paggett was definitely responsible for sending him some offensive notes.'

'Threatening notes,' she said.

'Insulting notes,' he countered.

Jenkins looked between the two of them, a trace of a smile on her face, and he felt how ridiculous this was, more like a negotiation with one of his boys rather than a discussion on a potential line of enquiry in a murder investigation. Wasn't sure if that was his fault or Ferreira's, or maybe it was just the long day spent arguing against each other's theories that had finally reduced them to this.

'I'll send you everything I've got so far,' Jenkins said, tactfully breaking into the moment. 'Anything else you need, just give me a shout.'

Zigic thanked her and they left, Ferreira going on ahead, the annoyance square across her shoulders and audible as she went, heavy-footed down the stairs. On the landing she stopped.

'I think we should bring the Paggetts in,' she said. 'Put a scare into them.'

'We don't have anything on them,' he told her, trying and failing to keep the exasperation out of his voice. 'Yes, the fliers are problematic but as Ainsworth didn't make any kind of report about them, he clearly didn't feel he was being harassed.'

'He kept them, though. They were obviously a source of concern. And we know the Paggetts were hanging around in the village.'

'We need more than that.'

'And if I get more?'

He sighed. 'Then, yes, okay. But don't start obsessing about them, please.'

'They both have records for intimidation and trespass and criminal damage,' she said firmly. 'They're the only people we've identified so far who have the kind of mindset that could ramp up to murder.'

'Lots of people's first crime is murder.'

'No, the first crime we hear about is murder.' She stood between him and the door, blocking his route to the office, not ready to give up yet. 'You know as well as I do that violent behaviour doesn't emerge out of nowhere; it's built up to over years and the only reason anyone believes otherwise is because they don't see all the shit we do.'

Voices rose up the stairwell, footsteps underneath them.

'The Paggetts have been engaging in criminal activity for over a decade,' Ferreira insisted. 'They have systematically targeted companies and groups and individuals who offend their sense of morality. Is it so unbelievable that the fliers they sent to Ainsworth were opening gambits in a longer game?'

Two uniformed officers came up the stairs and Ferreira grudgingly stepped aside to let them through the door, stepped smartly back in front of it before Zigic could go through as well. She didn't want to have this conversation in front of the rest of the team, he realised.

'They'd been hanging around Ainsworth's house,' she said. 'We've got them down the end of Ruth Garner's back garden. Doesn't that concern you at all?'

It did, but he was reluctant to admit that when she had such a fiery look in her eye.

'Why do you think they were doing that?'

He didn't reply.

'Intimidation?' she asked. 'Worrying if it's that, right? Scouting out their households for some reason? Even more worrying, given that we have a bludgeoned corpse on our hands. Or maybe they're looking to move to a quieter village. Do we think that's feasible?'

'Mel –'

'And weren't they eager to distract us with another suspect?'

'Mel – I already said, yes, alright? But don't let yourself get derailed by this. We have enough else to do.'

'I won't get derailed,' she said stiffly.

He reached for the door and she moved away, heading back to the stairs they'd just come down.

'Where are you going now?' he asked.

'To see Kate.'

'Do not tell her to run that test,' he warned, trying to make it sound like a joke.

'I need to sort out a time for drinks.' She rolled her eyes at him. 'Jesus, you don't trust me at all, do you?'

He didn't. Not when she had the bit between her teeth.

Chapter Twenty-Two

Zigic kept one eye on Ferreira's desk as he got on with the paperwork that had accumulated during the day, waiting for her to come back up from forensics, sure he'd be able to read the guilt on her face if she did go ahead and order the test.

Who arranged drinks in person rather than over text? She had a phone. Her calendar was on it.

He took a sip of his coffee, recoiled when he realised it was actually tea. He'd been trying to cut down on caffeine but was hating every moment of it. There was something in the station's pipes he was sure. Something that made the water taste faintly stale and metallic, left a nasty tang that only the strongest, blackest coffee could cover.

When he glanced up from his screen a few minutes later, he saw DCS Riggott standing by Ainsworth's board with Parr, absorbed in a conversation that was clearly unrelated to the case. Parr laughing at whatever Riggott was saying.

Riggott's presence always seemed to sharpen up activity on the floor. The youngest officers wanting to impress him, the longest-serving ones either traumatised by working under him or so thoroughly drilled by his management that the mere sound of his voice would send a bolt up their spine and kick them into a higher gear.

Zigic felt it himself, a clench of muscle memory that went right back to his time as a newly minted detective constable under the then DI Riggott's wing. He remembered the pride he'd felt when Riggott singled him out for some task on a case, how he'd wanted his approval more than that of any other DIs, how he'd work longer hours, go into more dangerous situations, all for the gift of Riggott's brief and bluff approval.

It had been Riggott who encouraged him to take the sergeant's exam, who pushed him on to inspector level when he was just getting comfortable in that role, telling him he was too good to settle at some middling rank. Riggott who'd handed him the Hate Crimes Unit to manage. Insisting his ethnicity had nothing to do with the promotion, pointing out that a dozen other detective inspectors had applied, officers with similar backgrounds to his, ones prepared to move from the other end of the country to be involved in their pioneering experiment.

A failed experiment, Zigic thought glumly.

But Riggott had been supportive while it lasted, managed them with a light touch by his standards, trusting them to get the job done.

Since they'd returned to CID, Riggott's presence had become more overt and Zigic wasn't sure if it had been always like this for the rest of the team or if it was something to do with Riggott's impending retirement. As his career came to a close, he seemed to find himself drawn back to the floor more frequently, sitting in on briefings, dogging the footsteps of his DIs. More than once Zigic had come out of interview rooms to find Riggott had been watching on a monitor, wanting to offer tips on technique.

It was retirement, he decided.

It was only natural that an officer who'd sacrificed so much to the job couldn't bring himself to let go.

His age was beginning to show on him, decades of sixteen-hour days and sleepless nights, all the drinking and stress and the pincer of pressures that only increased as you moved up the ladder. Fifty-eight but he looked ten years older, the beginning of a stoop visible at his shoulders despite his expensive suit habit, the hint of a bald patch at the crown of his otherwise full head of grey hair. He'd always been slim but now he looked thin, the threat of power going out of his body, the suggestion of muscles wasting under that summer-weight wool tailoring.

Zigic left his desk and went out onto the floor.

Riggott and Parr were discussing golf, he quickly gathered, the bets they'd each been placing on the Women's Open and how, miraculously, neither of them had lost money yet.

'There you are, Ziggy.' Riggott turned on his heel, spread his arms wide. 'Thought your backside was welded to that chair.' He pointed at Parr. 'Swedish women for the team championships. Mark my words, that's where the smart money'll be laid.'

Parr grinned at him. 'I'll take that tip. Thank you, sir.'

'Right, so, what's going on with your dead one?' Riggott asked, taking a step back as if he needed to do that to appreciate the scope of the board.

'We've got plenty of leads but very little forensic evidence,' Zigic said. 'Prime suspect right now is the woman he spent the evening of his death with.'

Riggott chucked his chin up at Portia Collingwood's photograph. 'Aye, she's got trouble written all over her.'

'We're checking her alibi right now. Hers and her husband's.'

'The husband?' Riggott's thin grey eyebrows went up but his attention shifted swiftly to the Paggetts. 'What about these two? Sure, they're a rare-looking pair.'

'They were harassing Josh Ainsworth in the months before his murder,' Ferreira said, coming up behind Zigic. 'And I ran into them in the shop opposite his house on the morning his body was discovered.'

Zigic willed her away to her desk but she wasn't going anywhere, not now Riggott's gaze was fully turned onto her, his interest piqued.

'Back to the scene of the crime, aye?'

'Briefly, yeah. They did a runner as soon as we got near the protest though.' She nodded towards the board. 'They're involved in the demonstration against Long Fleet Immigration Removal Centre.'

Riggott's face darkened.

'We've got sightings of them near the homes of other Long Fleet staff members, too,' Ferreira said quickly, seeing the wariness that entered Riggott's eyes at the mention of the centre. She stood up straighter. 'The Paggetts are career protestors. Direct action frequently tipping into outright criminality. Both have multiple convictions relating to their political activities.'

'Anti-terror have anything on them?' he asked Zigic.

'Nothing that would suggest they're capable of murder.'

Ferreira shot him an angry look but this wasn't the time to back her up. Riggott was getting nervous already.

'These firebrands have alibis?'

'We're still running them down,' Zigic told him, knowing it hadn't been done yet but not about to admit it. 'They gave us a dozen names though, so we're expecting them to hold.'

Riggott nodded. 'So, the mistress is your most likely candidate.'

'Still early days.'

'Not that early, son.' He nodded towards the door. 'Come and have a drink, tell me all about this Portia Collingwood.'

Riggott walked away from the board without a backward glance and Zigic followed, giving Ferreira a helpless shrug as she glowered at him.

They headed along the corridor and past the empty desk where Riggott's PA had already left for the day. Gone six now and Zigic often wondered how the DCS managed to keep her busy for a full shift anyway. Just how much work could be involved in organising his meetings with the higher-ups and whatever local businesses and dignitaries came to him looking for support or reassurances or whatever was within his remit to bestow?

A set of golf clubs sat in the corner of the office, so he guessed that had to be organised too.

Riggott went to the shelf where his glory days were recorded in gilt frames and commendations, took a bottle of whiskey from the collection standing on a brass tray and a couple of lead crystal glasses. He didn't offer, just poured Zigic a measure that was stiffer than he'd want in a spirit of his own choosing, let alone one he didn't actually enjoy.

'Now, what's the situation with Long Fleet?' Riggott asked, dispensing with any attempt at preamble.

'They don't want us in there,' Zigic said. 'They've been cooperative, up to a point, but I'm not sure how much further we could get if and when we need to talk to their staff again.'

'Seems like your man had enough else around his arse.'

'The protest isn't something we can ignore.' Zigic took a small sip of his whiskey. 'Honestly, I'm not convinced anyone involved in it's a genuine threat but ...'

'But Mel's gotten all riled up about it.'

'She's being thorough,' Zigic said carefully. 'I think we all know this has got the potential to be a troublesome case and we need to work every angle.'

'Troublesome, aye.' Riggott swirled his drink around in the glass. 'You always catch 'em, don't you, Ziggy?'

'It still looks personal to me.'

'Ainsworth's boss doesn't think so,' Riggott said. 'And *his* bosses are shitting bricks over the negative publicity potential.'

They'd been in touch then, Zigic thought. Securitect bringing their muscle to bear on Riggott or his superiors; the ones they were already in close contact with via the contracts they held with the local council and constabulary, the tenders they likely had ongoing to outsources services he could only guess at.

'The press don't seem very interested,' he said. 'I don't think they've got too much to worry about.'

'Best you make an arrest before they catch on. Last thing you want is for this to go national.'

Zigic nodded his understanding, decided to leave it at that. Let Riggott feel the message had been delivered and assimilated, no need for him to jump on their backs about it. The last thing he *actually* wanted was Riggott micromanaging them up to an arrest.

The Long Fleet machinery being spooked enough to exert their influence at this stage was interesting though. Maybe it was purely the fear of bad press and the effects of that on their share price. Or maybe they were withholding damaging information themselves, hoping that without it the case would develop in a less embarrassing direction.

Riggott sank his drink and poured a second one with a heavier hand.

'You see that bastard Walton in the paper last night? Shooting his mouth off about his false conviction? Waste of fucking skin. I had my way he'd be hauled out onto the fens in the middle of the night and shot in the fucking face.'

Zigic hadn't seen it, avoided the local paper as much as possible.

'He's after suing us,' Riggott snarled. 'Grand way to deal with a rapist, aye? Apologise to them and chuck them a wedge of fucking cash.'

'He won't get anywhere with it,' Zigic said.

'Bet your arse on it?' Riggott shook his head. 'Mad old world we're living in, son. Wouldn't surprise me if he had the lot of us through court.'

This was why Riggott had pulled him into the office, Zigic suspected. Not the Ainsworth case, which he'd shown little interest in until two days in. Lee Walton's release was preying on him, just like it was on the rest of them.

'I'll tell you something for nothing,' Riggott pointed at him, 'I'll not retire while that fucking beast is loose.'

'We'll get him,' Zigic said, the words feeling and sounding hollow, but it was the mantra they were all clinging to.

'Oh, aye, because youse had such an easy run with him the first time.'

These weren't Riggott's first drinks of the afternoon Zigic was beginning to suspect. It was easy to forget that Lee Walton had been Riggott's collar too, a stain on his clear-up rate and conscience. Riggott was still a DCI the first time Walton was arrested, for an aggravated sexual assault he walked away from, literally whistling down the station steps, the victim abruptly deciding she couldn't confidently identify him.

'And now we've got the lawyers telling us to steer clear of the bastard. "Don't give him any more ammunition",' he quoted, in a high and squeaky voice. 'I know what ammunition I'd like to give him. Both barrels up the shitter.'

Zigic watched the play of dark and malicious thoughts across Riggott's face, how they knocked a few years off him, bringing out the man he used to be.

'Does this mean we have to stop the cold case review?' Zigic asked.

'Catch yourself on, son.' Riggott grinned viciously. '*We're* the fucking law here.'

Chapter Twenty-Three

She didn't see him until it was too late.

One hand full of shopping, the other thumbing her phone – answering a text from Billy wanting to know where she was – her whole body unbalanced by the effort of keeping her gym bag from slipping off her shoulder and taking her handbag with it. Walking through an underground car park full of shadows and hiding places with her wits split between petty distractions.

So distracted she walked straight into Lee Walton.

'You should look where you're going,' he said. 'Never know who you'll bump into otherwise.'

Ferreira took a step back. Involuntarily. Her lizard brain telling her to run while her copper's brain said stand your ground, Sergeant.

'What the fuck do you want?' she asked, her voice coming out at a whisper, pitched between fear and anger. A voice she hardly recognised as her own.

He closed the gap between them. He'd bulked up during his six months inside, arms thick in a short-sleeved shirt, all cord and veins. He looked like he could twist her head right off her shoulders.

She slipped her phone away. Thinking she might only get one shot at him.

'Well?'

Still he didn't answer. Just stared at her with that unwavering gaze filled with contempt and hunger and a strange kind of boredom, which only made her more desperate to turn and flee. She'd seen it in the interview room and then in court, where he'd made more of an effort to hide it, needing the jury to see an ordinary man smeared by the police and a parade of hysterical, lying women. Ferreira had waited and watched for it, seeing him turning it on and off like there was a switch marked psychopath just behind his ear.

But it wasn't turning off now.

It was intensifying.

She thought of the wine bottle in her shopping bag, how quickly she could get it out and smash it across the side of his face. Whether that would be enough to put him down.

She thought of Billy, upstairs in her flat, and whether she could get him here without Walton noticing her texting. If she even wanted to do that.

No. She wasn't going to give Walton the satisfaction of calling for help like so many women had done before, while he drank in their terror, secure in the knowledge that nobody was coming to save them.

'Where's Dani?'

So that was it. The girlfriend.

'She doesn't want anything to do with you,' Ferreira said sharply.

'She'll come crawling back the minute I tell her to.'

Not a trace of doubt in his voice or his face. Even though she'd given evidence against him. Finally retracted the alibi, which had kept him safe for so long, then disappeared with his son under a new name to a distant city.

'You got into her head,' he said, jabbing a finger in her face.

'Yeah, I did.' She dredged some bravado from the pit of her churning stomach. 'And it was easy. Because you got her so fucked up she didn't know how to think for herself any more. She was just waiting for someone to tell her what to do.'

'I want my son back.'

'Tell it to Fathers for Justice,' she said. 'They've probably got a Spiderman costume that'll fit you.'

He grabbed her around the bicep, fingers digging in hard.

'You're going to call her and tell her to get back here with my boy.'

Ferreira shook her head. She could hear her heartbeat thundering in her ears, so loud she was sure he could hear it too.

'Never going to happen.'

His jaw clenched. He dragged her towards him, so close now that she could smell the rage in his sweat, feel the heat burning off his overblown muscles.

'If you don't call her ...'

'What?' She threw her chin up at him.

Walton smiled at her, brought his face to hers. 'You know what.'

She didn't breathe. Didn't blink.

'Not here, though,' he said. 'It'll be somewhere more private for you.'

He took a deep inhale, like he was sucking her fear down into his lungs, wanting to hold that part of her.

A car horn honked behind her and Walton didn't even flinch. He just released her arm and ambled away, hands shoved into his pockets.

The horn sounded again and she started to move out of the vehicle's path, on automatic, one numb footstep after another into the back lobby and then the lift, and she was shaking, teeth clenched, vision filmy. When she tried to fit her key in the lock, it kept skidding away from the hole.

And all the while she had the smell of him in her nostrils, could taste the reek of him.

Billy opened the door and she forced her way past him, kicking the door shut and dropping her bags.

'What's wrong?' he asked, face tight with worry. 'You look like you're about to pass out.'

'I'm fine,' she said, voice wobbling. 'It's nothing. I'm fine.'

'Mel, you're freaking me out right now.' He took hold of her hands and she fought down the urge to snatch them free, the adrenaline still pumping through her veins, making her shudder even at his touch. 'What happened?'

She took a deep breath.

'Walton was downstairs.'

He pulled away from her, reaching for the door. She moved fast to block him off, threw her full weight at the fake walnut ply, slamming it shut again.

'Please don't go down there.'

'My God, what did he do to you?' Billy's hands were on her shoulders, eyes searching hers. 'Did he hurt you?'

'Just *leave* it.' She grabbed the front of his shirt. 'Walton's gone, alright? I saw him off.'

He let out a groan of frustration, deep and guttural, as he dragged her into a hug, arms tight around her shoulders. 'Shit, Mel. Come on, I've got you.'

They stood like that for a minute, neither speaking, and she felt the fear beginning to dissipate, her body slowly accepting that she was safe now, that she had escaped, that there was nobody here to fight. She rubbed her face against his neck, breathed in the familiar scent of him, the stale cigarettes and faded aftershave; inhaled him, exhaled Walton. Kept doing it until she felt ready to speak again.

'Can you get me a drink?'

She held on to his hand as they went into the kitchen, watched him close the blinds before he took a bottle of rum from the cupboard, the good dark stuff, twenty years old. He poured two glasses and drew her back through into the living room, sat her on the sofa and lowered himself carefully next to her.

'Is this the first time he's approached you?'

She nodded, knowing that telling him about Walton being outside the night before would only make things worse.

'Okay, you need to tell me exactly what he said.'

'I handled it.'

It was a lie but she couldn't admit that she got lucky, that she didn't know what would have happened next if that car hadn't come along.

'Mel, you need to tell me, please.'

'He wants to know where his girlfriend and son are,' she said. 'Is that it?'

She nodded, her hand going to the place where he'd gripped her arm. 'For a second there I thought about telling him.'

'You can't do that.'

'I'd never do it,' she snapped. 'For God's sake, what do you think I am?'

He apologised, lowering his eyes.

'That's what Walton does,' she said quietly, back in the moment. 'That's how he got away with what he did for so long. He gets up close to you and he just bludgeons you with his presence. He's – shit, I don't even know how to explain it – he has this force field around him almost.' Her fingers gripped her glass. 'And once you're inside it, you're not the one in control any more. You feel like he could make you do anything.'

Billy slipped his hand into hers, stroked her knuckles.

'If *I* felt like that, what the hell did all those other women feel like?' She took a mouthful of rum, held it on her tongue, letting its fire burn away that admission of weakness.

'It's okay to feel like that.' Billy kissed the side of her head. 'Honestly, of all the fucking animals I've encountered in this job, Walton's the only one who really got to me. The only time I've ever felt like I was going to lose it during an interview was when you walked in on us and I saw how he looked at you. I wanted to tear his throat out with my bare hands.'

She wished she could say something funny – tell him it was every girl's dream to watch her man tear out a throat for her – just to drain the intensity from the moment, but found she couldn't. Instead she screwed her body up small and laid her head against his chest.

'What do you want to do about this?' he asked finally.

'I don't know,' she admitted. 'I'm not sure there's anything we can do. Riggott's already warned you off approaching Walton.'

'That was before.'

She straightened away from him. 'But this doesn't change anything, does it? Walton hasn't done anything illegal. We can't charge him with being in a car park.'

'It's harassment,' Billy said.

'No, it isn't. Not yet. Not one time. And even if it was, we both know how bad harassment needs to get before a case gets anywhere near a courtroom.' She went for another drink and found her glass empty. 'People are stalked for years and it ends, at best, with a three-month prison sentence.'

'We can't wait until he actually attacks you,' Billy moaned. 'Because that's what we'd be doing. It's what we *are* doing already, waiting for him to attack someone so we can arrest him.' He gripped her hand tighter. 'I'm not going to let that person be you.'

'He's not going to do that,' she said, trying to sound like she believed it. 'He's only just out of prison, even Walton isn't stupid enough to go after a police officer.'

'He thinks he's untouchable.'

That was how it felt. Down there in the parking garage, with people walking by on the path just beyond the low wall. They would have been close enough to hear a scream but how many would stop and investigate? Who would actually do something? No one, she knew, thinking of the night Josh Ainsworth was murdered, the neighbours only a thin wall away, hearing violence and deciding to stay put, finish their drinks, maybe turn the sound on the television up and pretend to themselves that it was nothing.

She thought of Walton dragging his victims off the footpaths he'd snatched them from. But never very far. Within earshot of anyone passing. As if he enjoyed the possibility of being caught or, more disturbingly, watching the passers-by pretending they didn't know what was going on a few metres away from them.

'It'll be somewhere more private for you.'

A shudder wracked her body at the memory of his words and for a moment she thought she was going to be sick, felt the swell of fear once again, cold and tumbling at her centre.

'I just need to be more careful,' she said, the words sounding inadequate.

He shook his head at her. 'That isn't a solution, Mel. You're not coming home alone again. Sorry, but that's non-negotiable.'

'Alright,' she said. 'We'll leave work together from now on, okay?'

'Maybe you should come to mine for the duration.'

She wanted to protest, tell him she wouldn't be forced out of her home by a piece of shit like Walton, that she could handle herself. But she heard the fear in his voice and felt it still churning within her, bodily terror at the thought of running into Walton again. Or worse, not seeing him until it was too late.

'I'm not asking you to move in permanently, if that's what's worrying you,' he said, smiling like it was a shared joke, rather than a reproach buried in humour.

They'd had the conversation before, often enough that she knew he was beginning to see her repeated refusals to give up her flat as a lack of commitment to him rather than a need for her own space. Now wasn't the time to repeat that discussion and it wasn't what she was thinking.

She didn't want to be the kind of woman who ran away.

But she knew that was the kind of thinking that would get her hurt – or worse.

Ferreira hauled herself up from the sofa. 'I'll go and pack a bag.'

DAY THREE

THURSDAY AUGUST 9TH

CHAPTER TWENTY-FOUR

When she saw the number pop up on her screen, Ferreira immediately left her desk, excusing herself from the conversation she was having with Colleen Murray about a blind date Colleen had been on the night before; a set-up by a mutual friend that had somehow resulted in her attending a lecture at Peterborough museum by a visiting professor of early modern English jewellery design.

'Couldn't work myself into the mood for it after that,' she said.

By the time Ferreira was in the stairwell, she realised she wasn't ready to answer the call, didn't know what to say to Evelyn Goddard, whether it was her place to apologise or not. Even though she was sure that's what Goddard was ringing her for.

As the leader of a local trans rights group, Goddard had been instrumental in bringing Walton to justice, had provided them with the forensic evidence that had helped secure his conviction and that had ultimately led to the same conviction being quashed. She'd also been responsible for convincing one of Walton's victims to talk to Ferreira about her attack; a conversation that had proved so traumatic that Goddard blamed Ferreira for the victim's suicide a few days later.

Ferreira felt that she owed Goddard something, but wasn't sure what she could offer her that could possibly help.

Instead she let the call ring out and rolled a cigarette.

Within two breaths Billy was taking her lighter out of her hand to spark his own fag up.

'Is this my life now?' she asked. 'You freaking out every time you don't have eyes on me?'

'The fucking ego on you. I just needed a fag, alright?'

She told herself to let it go. But last night had taken so much winding down from that neither of them slept more than a couple of fitful hours, kept awake by circular conversations that kept slamming up against the hopelessness of the situation and urgent, unsatisfying sex that only made them both more frustrated.

It was as if Walton had forced his way between them disturbing their usual rhythm, making it impossible to fully concentrate on one another.

'Did Colleen tell you about her date?' Ferreira asked.

'Yeah, I'm thinking of getting her a metal detector for Christmas.'

She smiled.

'Makes you glad you're not on the market any more, doesn't it?' He sounded nostalgic rather than regretful.

She gave him a dead-eyed look. 'That wasn't how my dates went.'

'And I thought you came to me spotless,' he said, faking outrage.

'About as innocent as you were.'

He flicked ash off his cigarette. 'Any movement with your murder?'

'I'm not sure yet,' she admitted. 'We've got suspects but nothing concrete tying anyone to the scene and they all seem to have pretty decent alibis.'

'I hate it when suspects do that,' he said, with a flicker of a grin. 'This is what I love about all the pubs closing and TV getting so good, everyone stays at home and nobody has an alibi any more. You could fit up anyone you wanted.'

'What about your boy Batty?' she asked.

'Idiot just used his credit card in Marseilles. I'm waiting on a call from the local *gendarmerie*. Hopefully, they'll get their arses into gear and pick him up before he hops a ferry to Morocco or something.'

'What's he going to do in Morocco?' Ferreira asked. 'Bloody Peterborough boy.'

'Hey, I'm surprised he made it as far as Marseilles. His mum reckoned he never left the country before. Only got a passport so he could open an online gambling account.'

'Bolting from an attempted murder charge really does broaden the horizons, doesn't it?'

'He'll have some interesting stories for his cellmates, anyway.' Billy dropped his cigarette butt and crushed it dead. 'You coming back in?'

'Got a call to make.'

Once he was gone she dialled her voicemail and braced herself.

Evelyn Goddard laughed in her ear, a sound throaty and dark and utterly without humour.

'It doesn't surprise me one little bit that you aren't brave enough to actually answer your phone to me, Sergeant Ferreira.' Goddard took a deep, shuddering breath and Ferreira could imagine the tightness at her jaw and the imperious way she would be holding herself for this. Even at this distance it made her feel small. 'My God, the things we went through for you. What we've *lost*. I let you into our community. We stripped ourselves bare so you could put that animal in prison where he belonged.'

She wanted to stop now. Delete the message, never know what else Goddard had to say to her, but she kept listening, every word stinging.

'And what did you do?' Goddard asked. 'After I gave you his victims? After I gave you the bloody *evidence* of what he did to Jasmine. You still managed to screw everything up.'

It wasn't me, Ferreira thought. But it was a weak and unconvincing statement. Because it might not have been specifically *her*, but it was very much *them*.

Goddard took another deep breath, sighed it out. And when she spoke again she sounded weak and saddened rather than angry. 'I hope you understand this – the next woman he attacks, every moment of hell he puts her through, it will be your fault.'

For a long moment she listened to the silence, the reverberation of Goddard's words rattling around in her head, feeling every drop of poison in them seeping through her ear. She couldn't blame the woman for her fury and indignation, even though it was misdirected.

And at the back of Ferreira's mind was the thought that the next woman Lee Walton raped or killed might be her.

She deleted Goddard's message, pulled herself together and went back upstairs.

Zigic was standing at the board, marker pen in hand.

'That's Alistair Collingwood out, then.' He drew a black line across the photo they'd lifted from Collingwood's LinkedIn account.

'What's this now?' Ferreira asked.

'His alibi's rock solid. Flew out of Stanstead the Friday morning, live-tweeted a series of seminars about 3D-printing techniques for two days straight then shows up in a bunch of group shots taken by one of his colleagues in a cabaret bar at two a.m. Sunday morning.'

During the morning they'd crossed out Ruby Garrick too. Parr went through the CCTV on her building three times but there was no sign of her leaving at any point during the Saturday evening Josh Ainsworth was murdered. The fire escape was a possibility but the door was alarmed and sent a report directly to the property management company, which said it hadn't been breached.

Ferreira stood next to Zigic, seeing their options narrowing down.

Portia Collingwood was still in the frame.

The Paggetts were very much a possibility.

Parr was busy checking their alibis, going through the long list of people who'd attended the same barbecue on the Saturday evening. He seemed pretty content to be welded to his seat, had already worked his way through an entire McDonald's breakfast and a couple of doughnuts from the big bag he'd arrived with this morning, 'for the office'. Somehow he could eat in the spaces between asking questions, by taking quick bites, hardly chewing. Maybe that was why he was good at this stuff, she thought, because he listened more than he talked, mouth always otherwise occupied.

A few minutes after she sat down at her desk again, she heard Parr's voice lift with a sudden surge of excitement.

'Could you bear with me for a moment, sir?' he said into the handset, gesturing furiously to Ferreira. 'I'm just going to pass you over to my sergeant.'

He hit the hold button.

'Boss, we've got a defector,' he said. 'Michaela Paggett's brother-in-law, Ian Carver, I think you'll want to hear what he's saying.'

'Send him over.' She picked up the call. 'Mr Carver, thank you for waiting.'

'No problem, I'm happy to help,' he said pleasantly. 'Should I just tell you what I told the other officer?'

'If you would, please.'

'Well, like I was saying, Damien and Michaela were pretty wasted so I'm not sure how seriously you want to take this. And frankly, they're always full of plans for what they're going to do to "tear down the system".' She heard the air quotes he threw around the words, the hint of contempt. 'If they spent half as much time actually working as they do complaining about every tiny thing that's going on in the world, they'd probably be a lot happier and better off.'

Ferreira sat back, decided to let him run on unprompted, getting a sense of the man as he talked.

'They'd cornered one of our neighbours, young guy, he was wearing a Corbyn T-shirt so I suppose Damien thought he'd found a soulmate.' In the background a photocopier whirred softly into life. 'Damien starts talking to him about the importance of grass-roots movements and how change has to come from the bottom, all of the usual crap. And, I mean, I'd had a couple of beers so I was in a baiting mood, if I'm honest. I started asking him if he really thought that was going to change anything. At Long Fleet, right, because he'd been talking – at painful length – about what they're doing there. And suddenly Damien gets this look in his eyes, all faraway like, and says, "The best form of protest is spectacle," and I'm like, what do you mean, and he goes, "If you want people to stand up and take notice, you need to do something too big for them to ignore." And *then* Michaela comes over and says, "Long Fleet are kidnapping women, they're snatching them from their beds at night. How do you think they'd like it to happen to them?"'

Ferreira straightened in her chair again, making eye contact with Parr who just nodded at her, a look of satisfaction on his face.

Carver kept going. 'Michaela says, "Imagine if we treated one of their staff like they've treated the inmates." And I laughed at her because it was just so ridiculous. She wasn't very happy about that. But Damien was mouthing off again, saying they could record the whole thing, put it online, show people the reality of locking up innocent civilians.'

'Is this the kind of thing they usually talk about?' Ferreira asked, trying to keep the excitement out of her voice.

'No, not really. I just put it down to the drink, but then I saw about that doctor getting murdered on the news, and I was wondering if it was important when you called me.' A drawer slid open and closed his end, and Ferreira pictured him in some office, this man who'd got saddled with the Paggetts as in-laws. 'I don't know if they're actually capable of kidnapping but they've done some serious stuff, haven't they? In the past. I mean, they can say it's not like being criminals because it's political activism, but they've committed crimes.'

Haven't they just, Ferreira thought.

All that preparation, all those trespass charges and the accusations of intimidation.

This was the logical next step.

A spectacle.

'What time did Damien and Michaela leave your house, Mr Carver?'

'Around eight.'

Ferreira glanced at the board: the Paggetts claimed they'd been there into the early hours of Sunday morning.

'Eight in the evening?'

'It was an afternoon barbecue,' he said. 'We're all boring olds, Sergeant. None of us can manage all-night parties any more.'

'Would you be prepared to come in and make an official statement about what you've just told me?' Ferreira asked, looking at the photos of the Paggetts on the board.

'If you need me to, sure. I could come on my lunch hour, I'm only five minutes away.'

She thanked him and passed him back to Parr.

'Get the name of that neighbour,' she told him. 'We need to be sure this isn't just some family drama.'

But she didn't think it was that, despite the relish in Carver's tone and the way his words tumbled out. And even if it *was* some long-held grudge at play, that hardly mattered. As long as what he'd said was true.

Ferreira went into Zigic's office and told him what Carver had told her.

'An attempted kidnapping gone wrong?' he asked, not quite incredulously but she could sense the resistance in him, the annoyance too maybe, that the case was heading in a direction he'd wanted to avoid. 'That's your theory?'

'I feel like I keep saying this,' she told him. 'But the Paggetts have been hanging around Long Fleet staff members' houses for some reason. This could be it.'

'It seems a very half-arsed attempt.'

'They get drunk and wound up and go off half-cocked,' she said, playing the scene out in her head. 'They knock on the door, overpower Ainsworth. He puts up a fight and gets knocked out. Nobody's saying they're criminal geniuses.'

'He gets knocked out isn't the end of it though, is it?' Zigic said, putting up a staying hand. 'If they went after him without thinking it through, why would one of them then beat his head in?'

'How many murders are committed to cover up other crimes?' she asked. 'We see it all the time. They tried to kidnap him and failed and he knew who they were so they killed him.'

155

Zigic sighed. 'We're going to need more than drunken party talk.'

'What, like a concerted harassment campaign in the run-up?'

'Witnesses,' he said firmly. 'Forensic evidence.'

'They've already lied to us about their alibi,' she told him. 'They said they were still at the Carvers' house when Josh Ainsworth was murdered, but they left at eight p.m.'

'And why would they lie about the time unless they knew when he was murdered?' Zigic asked, as she was poised to say the same thing.

'Exactly.'

'Okay, pull them in.'

CHAPTER TWENTY-FIVE

It was a smaller protest outside the Long Fleet gates that morning. Smaller and more subdued. Placards leaned on rather than waved, a couple of the older women sitting on the ground with a banner spread across their thighs. The heat was punishing as midday approached and Ferreira found herself wondering at their dedication. Could think of very little that would impel her to spend her days standing by the side of a dusty road in thirty-degree heat, getting more abuse than support from the passing drivers.

They stirred as she pulled up, two patrol cars behind her.

The Paggetts looked nervously at one another, stepped away from the rest of the group, who noticed the move and stiffened their postures in preparation. All except Ruby Garrick. She folded her arms, watching the Paggetts as their conversation became more heated.

'Damien and Michaela Paggett,' Ferreira said, striding across the road. 'I'd like you to come with us.'

'We don't have to go anywhere with you,' Michaela snapped.

'What's this about?' Damien asked nervously, still trying to act the innocent man.

'What do you think it's about?' Ferreira said. 'When you lie to the police, you get pulled in. You should know that by now.'

'We haven't lied,' he said, but there was little force in his voice.

Ferreira read them their rights, seeing Damien's shoulders slump as Michaela's firmed for action. When PC Green approached her, Michaela dropped to the ground, making her body a dead weight. Green just sighed and went to get hold of her under the arms, while PC Barnes hitched his belt up and steeled himself, grunting as he lifted her feet.

'This is harassment,' Michaela shouted. 'This is what they do to us when we stand up for our principles.' She kept shouting as she was carried awkwardly across the road. 'The police are tools of Securitect, doing their dirty work trying to silence us. But we won't be silenced, we know the truth and –'

The slammed door of the patrol car cut her off, but she kept going, mouthing angry words through the rear window, pointing at Ferreira, her face red with rage.

Damien went with less resistance, head down, trudging between the two officers and let himself be put in the back of the other vehicle.

Nobody spoke up for them, Ferreira noted with interest. Most of the group didn't even look in their direction as they were led away. It was a subtle but encouraging sign, she thought. If their own comrades were uncertain about them, then maybe she was on the right track.

'Sergeant Ferreira, could I speak to you, please?' Ruby Garrick stood at the edge of the group, toying with a long beaded necklace.

'Of course.'

They crossed the road and got into Ferreira's car, watched all the time by the few protestors now left on the verge.

'Are you sure you're happy to do this in front of them?' Ferreira asked.

'We all know what the Paggetts are,' Ruby said, her disapproval clear. 'Unfortunately, you don't get to choose your allies.'

A lorry went past them, moving too fast for the uneven rural road, its slipstream shaking the car. Ruby shuddered but Ferreira thought she would have done it anyway, her unease rising from something completely different.

'Do you really think they killed Josh?'

'We've uncovered some inconsistencies in their stories,' Ferreira told her. 'Innocent people don't usually lie to the police.'

'Unless they're scared of you,' Ruby said.

'Did they seem afraid?'

Ruby looked away into a recently cut field where a flock of crows were picking about in the stubble.

In her rear-view mirror Ferreira saw a figure emerge from the guard hut at Long Fleet's main gate, checking the credentials of the driver of a silver Lexus before letting it in. The guard came out once again, stood looking out across the road at the protestors.

Would this arrest be reported to the governor, she wondered. She couldn't believe they were as hands-off with the protest as they appeared to be. Suspected some degree of monitoring would be in place. For security if nothing else.

'I wasn't sure if I should say anything,' Ruby began, smoothing her hand across the thigh of her cargo pants. 'But if they are involved, then I think I owe it to Josh to do everything I can to help you.'

'What do you want to tell me, Ms Garrick?'

'There has been a lot of talk among our group over the last couple of days about what happened to Josh.'

'It's only natural for people to speculate,' Ferreira said gently. 'A murder is a big thing to process.'

'It is.' She blinked slowly, shook her head.

The grief was still thick around her, an almost tangible thing, and Ferreira resisted the urge to press her.

'I thought we were better than this,' Ruby said. 'We are supposed to be decent people. But the way some … elements in our group have talked about Josh's death has been very disappointing.' She bit her lip. 'God, that's an understatement. I'm trying to be nice and they don't deserve my consideration. They've been *vile*, Sergeant Ferreira. I'm beginning to wonder about the kind of people I'm associating with.' She twisted in the seat, facing Ferreira full on. 'We talk so much about decency and morality and the right way to do things, and I always believed that we were good people.'

'All groups attract a less than perfect element.'

'They're revelling in Josh's death,' she said in a strangled voice. 'Not just the Paggetts. We're a group of around two hundred people and half of them think Josh's death is a good thing for our cause. They don't feel any sympathy for him or his family. They've called him collateral damage.'

The smell of harvest dust from the nearby field and Ruby's citrus perfume were making Ferreira's nose prickle. She turned on the air conditioning.

'I need to see these conversations,' she said, as softly as she could, not wanting to spook Ruby.

'I've taken screenshots for you.'

She wasn't expecting that. Was primed for a negotiation, had her most compelling arguments lined up and ready to go.

But, as helpful as it was, she realised it wasn't enough.

'Screenshots are really useful,' she said. 'But I need to see everything.'

Ruby Garrick shook her head. 'Absolutely not, that would be a gross breach of the trust that the group has placed in me.' She took her mobile out. 'I have the screenshots here, I'm prepared to give you them. Why isn't that enough?'

'Because I need to see how those conversations develop,' Ferreira told her.

'I can keep you updated,' Ruby said.

Ferreira took a breath, seeing the agitation in Ruby's eyes, the sense of some great moral battle taking place behind them.

'Time is of the essence here, okay. Now we've taken the Paggetts in, we're going to see a reaction to that, and I need to be able to view it developing in real time.' Ferreira held her gaze, needing Ruby Garrick to understand how vital this was. 'Now, I can get a warrant for your devices, but that will take me awhile. And during that delay somebody might write something or – more likely – delete something that could prove vital in catching Josh's killer.'

'But I thought the Paggetts killed Josh,' Ruby said. 'Aren't you sure?'

'I think you know what the Paggetts are.' Ferreira curled one hand around the steering wheel. 'They've been saying some worrying things, haven't they?'

'They're all bluster.' She waved her hand dismissively but her face told a different story.

'All big talk?'

'Exactly.'

'About kidnapping a member of the Long Fleet staff?'

Ruby gasped, pressed her fingertips to her mouth. 'If I knew about that I would have told you when you came to my home.'

Her eyes were full of tears.

'You're the only person who cared enough about Josh to help me,' Ferreira said. 'And I'm sorry I have to ask you to compromise your principles. I truly am. But sometimes we have to make these sacrifices for the people we care about.'

'Poor boy,' Ruby muttered, shaking her head. 'That poor, poor boy.'

'I need you to give me access to the group, okay?'

With a trembling hand Ruby opened her phone's case and keyed in her code.

'For Josh,' she said.

CHAPTER TWENTY-SIX

Ferreira was prowling up and down the rows of desks, to the board and back, pausing occasionally to look across Parr's shoulder as he typed up the witness statement about the Paggetts' kidnapping plans, then over Keri Bloom's shoulder as she reviewed the CCTV footage from around Portia Collingwood's house.

She didn't linger very long there, Zigic noticed from his office window.

Collingwood wasn't out of the frame as far as he was concerned, but there was no denying the increased likelihood that it was the Paggetts who had something to do with Josh Ainsworth's death.

The problem was, as certain as Ferreira was, he couldn't quite shake the feeling that they were innocent. They were angry and nasty and had a long history of criminality, but somehow he couldn't buy the idea of such an inept kidnapping.

Hanging around the village when they were so distinctive-looking, running a harassment campaign targeting Long Fleet staff ... they were putting themselves so thoroughly in the frame for any act of violence against Josh Ainsworth that they couldn't possibly have been planning to go any further.

Even explaining how it would all work at a barbecue. What kind of kidnapper did that?

Then going out – that very same night – and doing it.

No. Nobody was that stupid.

They were smart enough to insist on having solicitors called before they would speak anyway. Both were stuck down in the cells right now, waiting for them to arrive. Usually a brief stint on a hard bench, behind a heavy door sharpened a suspect's mind.

The Paggetts had been there before though; they'd been locked up plenty of times, both with several short stretches inside to their names, and he doubted that an hour in detention would rattle either of them.

Zigic went out and made himself a cup of tea, saw that Ferreira was back at her desk, focused now as she tapped away.

'Something interesting?' he asked.

'Ruby Garrick has just opened up their private Facebook group for me.'

'I thought Asylum Assist was a campaign group,' he said curiously. 'What are they going to achieve if what they're doing is private?'

'No, this is a different one. Anglia Migration Support,' she said.

They'd already gone through the screenshots Garrick gave her, found a lot of unpleasant chatter in the aftermath of Josh Ainsworth's death, far too much gloating for a bunch of moral guardians, Zigic had thought, but nothing they could actually use against the Paggetts. And none of it pre-dating the murder.

He pulled up a spare chair.

'I could just send you this,' she said, shuffling aside slightly so he could see the screen.

She was scrolling so fast he couldn't see how she was taking any of it on board, but maybe it was an age thing. He'd found his ability to deal with the blare of information from social media wasn't as sharp as hers, mainly because he never used it.

He glanced away as Bobby Wahlia passed behind him going into Adams's office with a file in his hand. He'd been in and out of there all morning, blinds drawn at the internal window, no noise escaping, as if their conversation was so delicate that it could only be conducted in hushed tones.

Something was coming, Zigic thought. No other explanation for it. The office was radiating a kind of contained energy, almost pulsing with it.

'Shit,' Ferreira exclaimed.

'What?' His attention snapped back to the screen.

She pointed to a comment with Michaela Paggett's name next to it.

'That,' she said.

He read the comment, then went through the rest of the conversation. 'Did Ruby Garrick mention this?'

'No.' Ferreira frowned. 'I suppose she might not have seen it.'

'She's the admin, right?'

'Doesn't mean she's monitoring every single conversation in the group. And it's pretty well buried in there.'

Zigic stood up. 'Let's see what Mrs Paggett's got to say about this.'

'Her solicitor arrived about twenty minutes ago,' Ferreira told him. 'That's plenty of time, isn't it?'

They went to the interview room where Michaela sat slumped next to a middle-aged man in a black suit and a blue shirt, his thin greying hair plastered to his ruddy scalp with perspiration. Michaela eyed them as they entered, didn't shift or straighten in her seat, made none of the usual attempts to appear pulled together or upright. She was more comfortable in these rooms than most people, remaining unfazed by the process of setting up the recording equipment and stating her name, when she was prompted, in a flat and emotionless voice.

'On the evening of Dr Ainsworth's murder, you attended a barbecue at your sister's house, is that correct, Mrs Paggett?' Ferreira asked.

'Yes.'

'And you told Detective Inspector Zigic and myself that you and your husband were there until the early hours of Sunday morning, didn't you?'

'I don't think I gave you an exact time,' Michaela said, pulling a confused face at them. 'I believe I told you it was a late one, but as I didn't take particular note of the time myself, I wouldn't have given you a time.'

She was contradicting herself already and Zigic realised that underneath the surly demeanour and the supposedly relaxed body language she was worried.

'Would you like to tell us what time you left now?' Ferreira asked pleasantly. 'Make a stab at it?'

'Late,' Michaela said shortly.

'You seem to be having trouble remembering your precise whereabouts for the evening in question,' Ferreira said. 'Fortunately, we have two witnesses from the party who can say with certainty that you and Mr Paggett left the barbecue around eight p.m.'

'No, it was later than that.'

'Our witnesses also state that you'd been drinking quite heavily, so perhaps it's only to be expected that you can't remember the details of your movements on the night Josh Ainsworth was murdered.'

'We weren't drunk,' Michaela said defiantly. 'I was driving, so I only had two small glasses of wine.'

'Then you'd say your memory of the evening is clear?'

Michaela nodded, a flicker of suspicion in her eyes. 'I didn't take note of the exact time we left because I had no reason to. But I wasn't drunk.'

'That's good,' Ferreira said brightly. 'You'll be able to explain these comments you made then.'

Michaela stiffened, rose incrementally in her seat for a moment before catching herself and visibly forcing herself to relax again.

Ferreira took out the neighbour's statement. 'I quote, "Michaela said, 'Long Fleet are snatching innocent women out of their beds at night, how do you think they'd like it if we did that to one of them?'"'

Michaela let out a high peel of laughter, so sudden and unexpected that her solicitor started slightly in the chair next to her.

'That's it?' she asked, incredulous. 'I make an offhand comment at a party and you drag us in here like dogs.'

'You and Damien expounded at length to this gentleman about the need for direct action against staff members from Long Fleet Immigration Removal Centre,' Ferreira said. 'It was hardly an offhand comment, more of a manifesto.'

'A statement of intent,' Zigic suggested.

Michaela turned to him. 'It speaks.'

Ferreira was reading from the statement again. 'Damien said, "If you want to effect change you have to do something too big for people to ignore." Well, we're paying attention now, Michaela. You've got what you wanted.'

'We did not go anywhere near that doctor,' Michaela said, overenunciating each word, sitting up straight now with her forearms on the table.

'Come on, "that doctor"? You know his name,' Ferreira said smoothly. 'Josh Ainsworth. You knew where he lived. You knew what he looked like. You were posting targeted hate mail directly through his front door.'

'That wasn't us,' Michaela snapped. 'I told you already, those fliers are nothing to do with Damien and me.'

'Then how did one of Damien's hairs get stuck to one of them?' Ferreira asked.

Michaela's face coloured and Zigic knew that look well enough: the expression of a wife who had told her husband to do something the right way a dozen times only to still see him screw it up.

'Well?' Ferreira asked. 'How did it get there?'

She didn't answer, only ground her jaw and stared hard at Ferreira like she was willing her to disappear.

'There's two options I can see – either Damien's hair got in the pamphlet when he was making them up. And we know that isn't possible because you've just told us he isn't responsible for them. Or it happened when Damien was inside Josh Ainsworth's house.'

'No.'

'When was he there?' Ferreira asked.

'No, this is rubbish.'

'The pamphlet was in Josh's office. That's upstairs in his house – which you'll probably know already but just for the benefit of the tape. So, did Damien go up there before or after he killed Josh?'

'Neither of us has been inside his house.'

'Or maybe you killed Josh and Damien was so repulsed that he ran off upstairs looking for somewhere to be sick and just happened onto Josh's office and *that's* how his hair got there.'

'For fuck's sake,' Michaela shouted. 'We made the fliers, okay. Jesus, what are you on? We made some fliers and stuck them through his letter box. It isn't illegal and it doesn't mean we killed him. Because, obviously, we didn't.'

'Obviously?' Ferreira asked. 'We've got you and Damien planning to kidnap a member of Long Fleet staff four hours before Josh was killed.'

'That was just *talk*.'

'You've got a weird concept of small talk,' Ferreira said. 'You plan a lot of kidnappings in front of strangers?'

'Do you understand the difference between *saying* something and *meaning* it?' Michaela asked, her hands cutting down hard on the table as she spoke. 'We'd never do something like that.'

'It was just a fantasy?'

'Not a fantasy, just … some stupid thing Damien said one time.'

Ferreira cocked her head, smiled slightly at Michaela. 'One time?'

Michaela didn't answer.

'We've been having a look through your conversations in the Immigration Action group.'

'That's a private group,' Michaela said tersely. 'Have you hacked it?'

'We were given access,' Ferreira told her. 'And it seems like you and Damien have been working on this kidnapping plot for quite some time.'

'I don't know what you mean.' She swallowed hard.

'From June 12th of this year,' Ferreira said. 'Here you are suggesting kidnapping a member of Long Fleet staff and then negotiating a prisoner swap for a woman who was on hunger strike.'

'That was a *joke*,' Michaela said, throwing her hands up.

'You joke about people on hunger strike?' Ferreira asked, getting a scowl in response. 'In the same conversation you outline the challenges of taking a member of the security personnel, and eventually decide that one of the office or medical staff would be easier to snatch. And I quote – "a lot of the guards are ex-forces and filth, they're going to put up a fight. A doctor or a secretary will be a better option."'

Michaela's hands curled into fists on the tabletop and she flattened them out carefully and deliberately.

'It was just talk,' she said, her voice low and raw. 'We were angry about what was happening in there and we were dealing with it by joking. Gallows humour, right? You understand that?'

Zigic folded his hands on the table. 'You need to think very carefully about what you're going to do next, Mrs Paggett.'

Her eyes widened. 'Oh, and here comes the paternalistic routine, encouraging me to confess and apologise and take my punishment.'

'We all know you've been here before,' Zigic said. 'You obviously understand how it works. So why don't you take some time to consider what's going to be best for you now? Talk to your solicitor, weigh up your options.' He stood and pushed his chair back under the table. 'In the meantime, we're going to speak to Damien, see if he's a bit more forthcoming.'

CHAPTER TWENTY-SEVEN

Damien Paggett was far less composed than his wife. Had drunk two full bottles of water while he waited with his solicitor in the interview room next door and crushed the plastic down into semi-collapsed discs. Zigic read agitation or anger in the action.

Seeing how Damien's eyes fixed on the camera set high in the corner as Ferreira prepared the tapes, he decided it was most likely fear at work.

Damien picked at the front of his T-shirt, the pink cotton sweaty and sticking to his skin, even though the room was relatively cool. Zigic wondered how he'd managed to survive a decade of protests and arrests, how he'd managed to keep it together when they cut their way through fences and snuck up on people's houses to vandalise their cars and throw blood on their front doors.

Had Michaela been the driving force? Did she wind him up and set him off, or was it simply that without her at his shoulder he couldn't properly function? There was always a boss in any criminal partnership, always a sidekick. And usually, when you isolated the latter from the person who provided the brains and the backbone, they cracked.

Ferreira led again, asked the same questions they'd run through with Michaela Paggett about the specifics of their alibi and the conversation with the neighbour at the barbecue.

He gave the same answers. Not word for word but close enough that Zigic suspected they had decided to get their stories straight in readiness for this eventuality.

The kidnapping plan was a joke, he insisted. Just talk. Like you talk about selling everything up and going travelling around the world. Something you would never do.

'Plenty of people sell up and go travelling,' Ferreira said. 'Less actually go through with a kidnapping but the ones who manage it tend to spend a good while on the planning. Just like you have.'

Damien buried his face in his hands and rubbed it until his cheeks were red. He was already jittery, his knees jiggling under the table and his gaze flitting around the room. Every answer he gave was addressed to the walls or the ceiling or the centre of the table between them.

'We've got your DNA inside Josh Ainsworth's house, Damien,' Ferreira reminded him.

'I'm not denying that we're the ones who made the fliers.'

'But you were so scrupulous with them,' Ferreira said, playing up her confusion. 'I mean, you didn't leave a single fingerprint anywhere on them, so we know you were wearing gloves – why would you do that?'

'Because you have my fingerprints on record,' he admitted, squirming in his chair.

'And why would you suppose we'd ever fingerprint the fliers?'

He shrugged one narrow shoulder. 'I just thought I should be careful.'

'There's nothing illegal about putting fliers through someone's door,' Ferreira said. 'So, why would we be checking them for fingerprints?'

He didn't answer.

'The only explanation I can see is that you were planning to do something much more serious to Josh Ainsworth, and you didn't want the fliers to tie back to you.'

'No,' he said determinedly. 'That isn't what happened. We were worried about being sued for libel.'

Ferreira laughed. 'Libel? Come on, Damien. You two broke into a fur farm and released a hundred mink. You're telling me you had the confidence to do that but you were worried about a libel charge?'

'We were younger then,' he said, eyes fixed on one of the crushed bottles. 'We were stupid.'

'You're hardly smart now. You've been seen hanging around Josh Ainsworth's house, you've made threats, you've harassed him. And now we've got evidence of you planning to kidnap a member of Long Fleet staff just hours before he was murdered.' Ferreira tapped her fingertips against the table. 'What happened, Damien? You got all drunk and pumped up and decided to take a stand?'

'No.'

'You thought a doctor would be easier to take down, we know that. But when you got to Josh's house, you found out he was stronger than you were expecting.' Ferreira's voice was soft with regret and understanding, pitched just right. 'He put up a fight, things got messy and he falls and hits his head. Is that it?'

'No,' Damien said, finally looking at her. 'None of that happened. I'm not a violent person. I believe in direct action but that doesn't include violence. If we act like that we're no better than they are.'

'You think Josh Ainsworth was a bad person?' Ferreira asked.

'I know he was,' Damien said sternly.

'Because he worked in Long Fleet? He was a doctor, Damien. Those women need medical care and he was in there trying to help them. Josh Ainsworth was not your enemy, he was your ally. And if you'd taken the time to actually speak to him instead of bombarding him with hate mail, you would have found that out for yourself.'

A wry smile lit his face briefly. 'Ruby tell you all that, did she?'

'She was his friend,' Ferreira said, opening her hands up wide. 'I'd say she knew him better than you did.'

He nodded to himself. 'Yeah, okay, right.'

Zigic could see how desperate he was to be prompted and guessed Ferreira could too and that was why she sat back in her chair and made a show of picking something non-existent off her trouser leg.

'Have you talked to any of the women who left Long Fleet?' Damien glanced at Zigic and then back to Ferreira, the skin around his eyes tight, nostrils lifted by disgust. 'No? You didn't think that might be important? You just talked to a bunch of people who all thought Ainsworth was God's gift.'

'Is this your defence?' Ferreira asked flatly. 'You're going to tell us Josh Ainsworth was a piece of shit and he deserved everything you did to him?'

'We didn't touch him,' Damien said. 'But he did deserve what he got and fair play to whoever did it. You've seen the fliers we sent him, where do you think we got that stuff from? Do you think we just made it up?'

'Yes.'

'Ainsworth was not a good guy.'

Ferreira rolled her eyes theatrically and Zigic felt the same impulse, seeing where this was going. Damien Paggett trying to draw them away onto someone else just like Michaela had when they first went to speak to them in their workshop and she directed them to Ruby Garrick.

'Long Fleet made a big song and dance about clearing out all their abusive staff members, but they didn't get all of them.' Damien Paggett wet his lips. 'Ainsworth was just as guilty, but he got the accusations in first so he looked clean.'

Ferreira groaned. 'This is rubbish, Damien.'

'No, you look into it and you'll see I'm right.'

'Where did you get this from?' Ferreira asked wearily. 'We need names.'

'It's all online.'

'Oh, it's online, is it? Well then, it must be true.'

'Just because people maintain their anonymity, it doesn't mean they're lying,' he said hotly. 'They're scared.'

'Great, online and anonymous.' Ferreira smoothed her hand back over her hair and turned to Zigic. 'Do you want to listen to any more of this?'

'I don't think he's got anything sensible to say,' Zigic told her and gestured for her to end the interview.

They had Damien Paggett taken back down to the cells and returned to the office.

'Are we giving any credence to that?' Ferreira asked, taking out her tobacco and beginning to roll a cigarette.

'It seems unlikely, doesn't it?' Zigic perched on the corner of her desk, remembering the sly expression that had crossed Damien Paggett's face as he spoke. 'He was going to tell us that whatever. It's like he'd worked out a way of shifting attention off him and Michaela, and he was going to run with it regardless of how stupid it was.'

'The governor purged Long Fleet two years ago. I don't think Ainsworth would have survived that if he was guilty.'

'He's got no evidence,' Zigic said. 'If he'd really seen an accusation coming from a reliable source, he would have given us their details.'

'I'm pretty sure Michaela would have mentioned it too.'

'There's no way he knows about it and she doesn't, if it's true.'

'We need to stay on them.' Ferreira was looking at the private Facebook group, still open on her screen. 'My guess is it went down how we think. It's too much of a coincidence that they'd identified a doctor as a good potential target and then Josh is killed.'

'But we haven't got enough to hold them.'

'No,' she admitted irritably. 'And without forensics we're not going to be able to charge them, are we?'

He blew out a frustrated sigh. 'We need a witness.'

'I'll send their photos over to the couple from the holiday let, see if they saw them. It'll give us a stick to beat them with if nothing else.' She snatched up her lighter. 'After I've smoked this.'

She left the office and he sat there for a moment, looking at the conversation on her screen, thinking of the lack of forensic evidence at the scene and Damien Paggett's careful use of latex gloves when he was just making fliers. Had they gone into the house prepared? Covered up to make sure they left nothing of themselves behind?

'Ziggy.' Adams gestured at him from his office door. 'Need the benefit of your experience here.'

Chapter Twenty-Eight

Adams all but hauled Zigic inside, fizzing with energy as he closed the door and went back around his desk, where a case file was spread out around his lunch. Crime scene photos and an image of the victim: a round-faced teenaged girl with dark brown hair in a high ponytail, the grey and white of a school uniform.

Bobby Wahlia saw Zigic looking at it. 'Tessa Darby. Murdered in '98.'

He remembered the case, or rather her murder. Back in '98 he hadn't signed on yet, was just out of university and taking a gap year, doing field work out on the fens to get some money together so he could start his adult life on the right footing. He'd been living in a shared house in Wisbech with three Polish guys. Grafting hard and drinking too much, getting into fights he gradually started to win, getting hardened when he didn't need to be but wanting it all the same. To prove what kind of man he was.

Tessa Darby had been a few years younger than him, a student at the city tech college, and her murder was so high profile in Peterborough it even came to dominate the conversation of the migrant workers isolated on the outskirts. What they would like to do to the man who killed her. How he should suffer. How the English didn't punish the beasts in their midst properly.

A beautiful girl, they'd all said sadly. As if it doubled the tragedy. Such a waste.

'Sit down,' Adams said impatiently.

He drew a chair up to the desk.

'Why are you looking at this case?' Zigic asked Wahlia. 'It's closed. Someone confessed. One of her friends or something. He went down for it.'

'Yeah,' Adams answered, before Bobby could. 'And you know who another one of her friends was? Lee Walton.'

Zigic took a deep breath, trying to dampen the agitation he felt stirring in his gut.

'Right, okay. So she knew Walton. But someone still confessed.'

'Fuck me, Ziggy, you know as well as I do how easy it is to get a confession out of someone.'

Zigic laughed, humourlessly. 'If it's that easy why do you have two open murders on the boards out there? Just pick a suspect and make them confess.' He swore under his breath, started to stand up.

'There's more to this,' Wahlia said.

Zigic stopped. Bobby wasn't stupid and he didn't have the handicap of ego that Adams carried. If he'd seen some possibility in this case, then Zigic needed to listen.

'First thing I went looking for was Walton's victim type,' Wahlia said. 'Maybe that's an imperfect method but we all know he doesn't deviate from that type. At least not in the cases we're aware of.' He crossed his legs, curled his hand around his ankle, thumb tapping the heel of his red suede trainers. 'And I'm not a psychiatrist or a profiler or anything flash like that, but even I know a serial predator with a type has a original victim who defined his choices.'

'Tessa Darby could be Sadie Ryan's sister,' Adams said. 'She's in intensive care, by the way. In case you hadn't heard. Overdosed after she found out Walton was on the street.' He gestured at Zigic. 'Just so you appreciate the stakes here.'

'I appreciate the stakes,' Zigic said coldly. 'You're not the only person who worked that case. It's not your special preserve to care about it.'

Adams just nodded at him, a look in his eye that was almost admiring, and Zigic silently cursed himself for rising to the bait.

'Can I go on now?' Wahlia asked. 'So, we're not only looking at Walton's victim type but she was also strangled –'

'Which we know he's a fan of too,' Adams interjected.

'Was she raped?' Zigic asked.

Wahlia shook his head. 'No sign of sexual activity.'

'This is likely to be Walton's first victim,' Adams said quickly, because he knew this deviation from Walton's MO was a stumbling block almost as big as the fact that another man had confessed to the crime. 'We see this a lot when serial predators start out. First time, they can't perform or they don't even totally understand that the aggressive impulse they're feeling is sexual. So we just get murder from him this time.'

'Say you're right about all of that,' Zigic said, looking at Tessa Darby's photograph. 'You still have a confession, which you're prepared to disregard just because we need to send Walton down again. And I get it, we do need that. But I don't think this is the case.'

Adams turned to Wahlia. 'Give us a minute will you, mate.'

'Sure.'

As Bobby closed the door behind him, Adams leaned across the desk, elbows on his paperwork.

'You want to know what the full stakes are here, Ziggy?' he asked, with a studied calm. 'Walton was outside Mel's flat last night. He was waiting for her when she came home.'

The news hit him like a blow.

All day she'd been carrying that and going on with work like usual, and he hadn't even seen it.

'Is she okay?'

'She's fine. He didn't do anything, he just wants to know where his girlfriend and kid are and he thinks Mel can tell him.'

'You need to go to Riggott with this right now.'

Adams threw his hands up. 'And what do you think he's going to do about it? Walton hasn't committed an offence. Even if he goes back there every night for a year, it's only going to be considered stalking and you know how that goes.' He stabbed his finger at Zigic. 'No, we need to deal with him.'

'By pinning a murder on him?' Zigic asked, incredulous. 'Are you listening to yourself? This is insanity. Someone *confessed*. And even if you're right and Walton did kill that girl, and we can prove it, how long's that going to take? Meanwhile he's out there stalking Mel. We need to tell Riggott.'

'And what if it was your wife he was coming after?' Adams growled. 'Wouldn't you want to take care of the problem yourself?'

For a surreal moment Zigic thought he was proposing a more radical solution. Half expected him to take a couple of balaclavas out of his desk drawer.

Adams wasn't shy of violence. A few years back he'd shot a suspect dead as the man held a gun to Zigic's head, and the killing didn't seem to faze Adams one bit. He holidayed on his forced leave, strutted back into work like the hero the whole station thought he was. And Zigic was grateful for his cold-bloodedness in the instant, but he knew that if it had happened the other way around, he wouldn't have been able to brush off the guilt so quickly.

If he'd do that for a fellow officer he didn't much like, how far would Adams go to protect his girlfriend?

Zigic moved towards the door. 'I'm talking to Riggott.'

Adams darted over and dragged him back, stronger than he looked, propelled by the fear and anger so intensely drawn on his face that Zigic didn't fight him.

'Mel's staying at mine. She won't be on her own,' Adams said. 'I can protect her.'

Could he?

'Let's give it a few days, alright?' Adams moved into negotiating mode and Zigic realised then just how desperate he was. 'See if there's any play in this Tessa Darby case. You know Bobby's got good instincts. This could be all we need.'

Zigic felt himself softening slightly. Because he knew Adams was right, that they weren't going to stop Walton with a friendly warning. He'd been attacking women with impunity for years. Been in and out of the interview rooms, always ready with an alibi, delivered in such a way as to make it clear to them that not only was it a lie, but that he knew they knew it and they couldn't do a thing to get his girlfriend to retract it. And now he'd escaped prison he would be feeling invincible.

'Alright,' he said. 'Give me the file.'

CHAPTER TWENTY-NINE

Ferreira was beginning to feel a twinge of guilt about the tedious nature of the work she was dumping on Parr and Bloom, as a day largely spent on the soul-sapping, eyeball-drying work of watching CCTV footage had now become two days, only broken by an occasional stint sifting through phone records or credit card statements.

As she watched them from across the office, she thought it might be a good idea to take them out to the pub at the end of shift. Colleen as well, who was taking an afternoon tea break and swiping through profile pics on Tinder, doing it so slowly that Ferreira suspected she was actually giving each one full consideration. A few drinks would do her good, a bit of karaoke, which Colleen harboured a not-so-secret love for. As well as a set of lungs that could sandblast the paint off a boat.

But as she was mentally running through the options of where to go, she realised she wouldn't be doing anything tonight but waiting for Billy and heading home with him. As much as she hated the idea of having even a single evening of her life dictated by Lee Walton, she knew that for now the wisest course of action was the most paranoid one.

She'd agreed a safe and sedate catch-up with Kate Jenkins at her house next weekend, promised she'd bring dessert. Hadn't told Billy yet that it would be a couples thing. Or that he'd be making the dessert. This was more uncharted territory for them but Kate's husband was a nice enough bloke, funny and smart and a big boxing fan, so she figured they would have something to chat about.

Parr got up from his chair and began to execute a series of side stretches with a perfectly straight face, seemingly unaware of the smiles he was raising from the surrounding desks. With a small, satisfied grunt he sat down again.

Ferreira shook her head and went back to Michaela Paggett's last arrest report: a caution she'd taken for assaulting a demonstrator outside her local polling station during the recent council elections. It was little more than a shove and when Ferreira checked out the guy she'd injured, she found a similar history of agitating in his record.

'What about this one?' Colleen asked abruptly, turning her phone to Ferreira.

She leaned over her desk and looked at the photograph of a bloke that might have been lifted from an erectile dysfunction advert. All teeth and hair and leathery tan.

'He looks like someone who murders rich older women for their life insurance.'

'Joke's on him then,' Colleen said. 'I'm brassic.'

A text vibrated Ferreira's phone and she saw that the couple from the holiday let next door to Josh Ainsworth had finally picked up the message she'd sent them an hour ago – the Paggetts' photographs and a query about whether they'd seen them.

They'd hadn't. *Sorry. Wish we could be more helpful.*

She swore under her breath.

She was thinking about running a second set of door-to-doors in Long Fleet with their photos, see if they could build a pattern of loitering for the Paggetts. It would be thin and barely even circumstantial but it would be something. And, she figured, some of the locals who said they'd seen nothing might actually remember these two, as distinctive as they looked.

'Him?' Colleen asked, brandishing her phone at Ferreira again.

This one's teeth were a slightly more natural colour, but there was a hardness around his eyes and a shallowness to his smile that she didn't like.

'He's a bit EDL, Col.'

Murray sighed and picked up her Poldark mug. 'This one?'

'You know my feelings on Poldark.'

'This job's warped you,' Murray said, tossing her phone aside.

'No, I was definitely warped before I got here,' Ferreira told her.

'How did you manage to date when you don't trust anyone?' Murray asked, exasperated. 'They can't all be pieces of shit.'

Ferreira just shrugged, wasn't about to admit that she'd always been on high alert, always prepared for the man she was with to snap and reveal some side of himself he'd managed to hide through drinks in the pub and the journey back to his place or her own.

She returned to Michaela Paggett's arrest record, more of the same stuff, going back twelve years, and as she read it she kept thinking about what Murray had said and realised she was pushing away an instinct she didn't want to admit to.

Damien Paggett's accusation about Josh Ainsworth was playing on her mind, had been from the moment he tossed it at them across the interview-room table.

She didn't believe it.

Knew exactly what Paggett was trying to do.

But some small part of her was wondering ...

Everything she'd seen about Long Fleet suggested that the house clearing by the new governor had been deep and wide-ranging, the abuse problem so thoroughly entrenched that the only proper way to deal with it was sacking everyone who was implicated. Ainsworth had been a key informer according to the other medical staff, whose own testimonies backed him up.

If Ainsworth was anything but an absolute paragon of virtue, he wouldn't have survived that purge, would he? His own accusations would have triggered counter-accusations if he was guilty. And the governor would have been forced to thoroughly investigate or risk sacking people on tainted evidence. Opening the company up to wrongful dismissal suits and tribunals that might go embarrassingly public.

The problem was they couldn't get access to any of the reports around the purge, couldn't speak to any of the sacked employees because they simply didn't know who they were.

For a few minutes she debated contacting the other doctor, Sutherland, or the nurse, Ruth Garner, who had worked alongside Ainsworth. But she remembered how spooked they had both been during the initial interviews at Long Fleet and doubted that they would be any more forthcoming now.

She could speak to Damien Paggett again, but that felt like an admission of defeat. She wouldn't even consider talking to Michaela about the accusation, knew she would spin out whatever story she could think of to try and muddy Ainsworth's name and raise the prospect of other suspects.

There *were* other suspects though.

All of those sacked staff members with grudges against Ainsworth. Two years was a long time to seethe without taking any action, but not unheard of. A smart person would wait, she thought. Let their victim amass other enemies.

She looked at the board where Ruby Garrick's photo had been struck through. She hadn't left her flat on the night of Ainsworth's murder, had no opportunity as well as no motive.

Portia Collingwood too. Home by half past nine just as she claimed.

Ferreira knew they were only half investigating this murder. Focusing on the suspects they had identified easily, the ones they could actually get to and question. They needed the Long Fleet management to lower their guard and start helping to find whoever murdered their highly valued and well-liked doctor.

So, why *weren't* they helping? They should have turned over a list of ex-employees without being asked, committed themselves to cooperating with the investigation because, after all, they were all colleagues. 'Brothers and sisters in blue,' the governor had called them, and then offered the very thinnest assistance he could.

He would keep stonewalling them until they found a way to break through and force him to help, she realised.

Paggett's accusation against Josh Ainsworth might be all the force they needed.

It didn't need to be true and they didn't need to believe it. Just as long as they appeared to when they spoke to the governor.

CHAPTER THIRTY

'Can I have everyone's attention, please?'

Zigic looked up from the report he was typing, the insistent pitch of Ferreira's voice sending a bolt of anxiety through him.

'*Everyone*, please,' she said again.

He went into the main office as the last few officers on the floor spun around to face Ferreira where she was standing, in front of the big screen. As he got closer he saw a Twitter stream open, couldn't read any individual message because she was blocking it off with her body.

'We need to identify this Twitter user,' she said, stepping aside. 'PcthirtyOne, based in Peterborough and clearly either a serving or ex-officer, judging by his familiarity with procedure.'

'Knowing procedure doesn't mean they're actual police,' DC Lear said, from the far corner of the room. 'They might be a groupie or some sad obsessive.'

'No,' Ferreira said firmly. 'We've got the same ID used across several platforms, going back six years, during which they posted images from inside the station.' Lear opened his mouth to offer another explanation but Ferreira didn't give him a chance. 'Not from common areas. This isn't a visitor or a suspect. We're looking at a copper.'

'What have they done?' Rob Weller asked, a hint of defensiveness in his tone.

'We've got them tweeting at the official account about Josh Ainsworth's death, Rob.' Ferreira took a step towards his desk. 'Which you were supposed to be keeping an eye on, weren't you?'

'Sorry, boss.'

'PcthirtyOne has been offering us advice on how to investigate Joshua Ainsworth's death,' Ferreira said. 'Which is pretty big of him, I think we can all agree.'

'How do you know it's a man?' Lear asked.

'Because nobody asked for his opinion but he's giving it anyway,' Ferreira snapped. 'He seems to think we should be talking to Ainsworth's patients and asking them about his "bedside manner".'

'Armchair psychologist,' Murray said gruffly. 'You know how social media brings them out.'

'No, this guy knows something about Ainsworth. He knew Ainsworth worked at Long Fleet before we'd even gone public with his murder.' Ferreira gestured at the screen behind her. 'Tuesday afternoon, 2:14, we've got a tweet advising us to "ask the ladies of Long Fleet how warm his hands were".'

Zigic saw the implications ripple through the room.

'He must work at Long Fleet then,' Keri Bloom said. 'Who do we know who quit the force to go and work there?'

Her question was met with an awkward silence but Zigic noticed the look of approval Ferreira shot her.

'Somebody knows who he is.' Ferreira's gaze moved slowly around the room and he followed it, searching for the same thing she was, a twitch of discomfort, an attempt at hiding it. 'I want you all to take twenty minutes –'

A few low groans.

'This is a murder investigation, in case any of you have forgotten that,' she said fiercely. 'So you can put aside whatever it is you're doing and look through his Twitter feed and see if there's anything you recognise.' A few seconds passed and nobody moved. 'Now, people.'

Slowly, the room turned its back on her and Zigic gestured her into his office, watching some of the confidence morph into defiance as she walked in. He closed the door behind her, not wanting anyone to overhear this conversation.

'Why didn't you run that past me before you did it?'

She looked stunned. 'Since when did I have to do that?'

'We discussed Damien Paggett's accusation and decided there was no merit in it,' he reminded her. 'Now you've announced to a room full of officers – some of whom you know can't be trusted to keep their mouths shut – that we're considering the possibility that Josh Ainsworth is a sexual predator.' He heard his voice rising, forced himself to bring it back down. 'Mel, for Christ's sake, if one of them leaks this to the press ...'

'Someone's tweeting this stuff at the force's Twitter account,' she said, a hand flying out towards the screen in the other room. 'It's already in the public domain. It's been public for three days.'

He rubbed his beard, anticipating the hassle this would bring them from Riggott. The pressure Long Fleet would hand down.

'If you want to give anyone a bollocking, it should be Weller,' she said. 'I *told* him to stay on top of social. I swear to God I don't know how he ever made it out of uniform.'

She was right but it was a deflection he wasn't going to fall for.

He pressed his hands together, feeling like he needed to say this as slowly and calmly as possible, because he knew why she was so agitated and why she was fixating on the accusation against Josh Ainsworth now.

Walton was in her head. All of that emotion couldn't stay strapped down. Especially not in her. She needed to let it out somewhere and she'd transferred it onto Josh Ainsworth.

'The Paggetts are lying to protect themselves,' he said firmly. 'We know that. It's been their approach since the first time we spoke to them. And now it looks like they've picked up this accusation from Twitter and tried to use it to throw us off their scent.'

She crossed her arms.

'We have absolutely no reason to believe Josh Ainsworth was abusive to the women in his care,' he said. 'Okay? This is just standard online speculation. But at least we know where the Paggetts picked it up from so it was definitely worth digging into.'

Ferreira gave him a quick, tight smile. 'Great pep talk. The thing is, I *don't* believe the accusation and I'm *not* buying any of this crap from the Paggetts.'

He eyed her warily, knowing she would never give up a hunch so quickly.

'But I figured that if we can convince Long Fleet's governor that we believe it, we might be able to scare up some names from him.'

'What names?' Zigic asked, feeling a stirring of interest, his anxiety falling away now he could see the sly way her mind was turning.

'The staff members who got fired over Ainsworth's abuse reports.' She leaned back against the wall, a little too casually. 'I mean, where are we right now? We've ruled out everyone bar the Paggetts.'

'They're our prime suspects for a reason, Mel,' he said, but he knew where she was going with this and that she was right.

They couldn't keep fighting shy of Long Fleet's influence. And Riggott's discomfort about the investigation moving closer to it couldn't be allowed to knock a whole line of enquiry out of play. A couple of days ago when their other suspects were still looking like strong possibilities, it had been easy for him to take the steer from Riggott.

Now he had to follow his gut and his experience.

Both were pointing to Long Fleet.

CHAPTER THIRTY-ONE

DC Keri Bloom found their man.

While the rest of the office was scrolling through PcthirtyOne's Twitter feed as Ferreira had instructed them to, Bloom was on the phone to the station's human resource department, asking which former officers had requested references to Long Fleet Immigration Removal Centre.

A piece of detective work that Zigic admired even as he was wondering why Ferreira hadn't taken that route herself. She was off her A-game, he thought. Understandably with Lee Walton circling her.

He would have to talk to her about it. Couldn't let this secret fester away between them, keep pretending he believed she was fine when she obviously wasn't.

'Do you remember him?' Ferreira asked, as he turned into the car park of the big-box superstore where former PC Jack Saunders was now working.

'Not really.'

'Me neither,' she admitted.

'How old is he?'

'Twenty-seven. So he'd have been in after we both moved upstairs. No reason to notice him unless he was a dick.'

Thorpe Wood had provided him with a glowing reference when Long Fleet came calling because they'd never had any trouble with him and they wanted to help him onwards in his career after he left as a result of stress.

Another one with stress, Zigic thought.

He wondered what kind of reference Long Fleet had provided Jack Saunders with when he left. Maybe they hadn't given him one at all and he'd excused the break in employment some way, falling back on his excellent, if undistinguished, record in the police force to get him a job flogging DIY supplies.

In the store huge banners and stands everywhere advertised their summer sale, garden furniture and outdoor ovens arranged inside the main door, astroturf displays and pallets stacked high with charcoal.

At the information desk they flashed their credentials and asked where they could find Saunders, were told he was working in the kitchen design centre.

Up the stairs to a mezzanine level under the blast of air conditioning.

'That's him,' Zigic said, pointing to a rangy guy with dark brown hair in an undercut and a prominent Adam's apple. He wore a shirt and tie, rather than the uniform the other staff sported, but he still looked like a copper. Still held himself that way, rigid-spined and wide-stanced.

Zigic remembered him now. Not from work but from the hidden camera footage recorded inside Long Fleet. Jack Saunders strutting down an over-lit corridor, casting a conspiratorial glance back across his shoulder before opening the door of a cell without warning onto a woman standing in her underwear. He remembered the woman scrambling to cover herself with a sheet and how Jack Saunders had apologised, sincerely and at length, then made a grotesquely racist comment to the person with him as he was closing the door.

Saunders was showing an interested young couple the inside of a range cooker, opening each door in turn, a lot of flourish in his movements.

'You could cook dinner for twelve in this one,' he said. 'It's the ideal model if you enjoy entertaining.'

'Not cheap,' the man said.

'Quality never is,' Saunders told him. He turned to the woman, smiled. 'Does he do much of the cooking?'

She matched his smile. 'Only in the microwave.'

Saunders turned back to the man. 'You should always let the lady have her way.'

'Jack Saunders,' Ferreira said, letting him hear the official in her voice. 'We'd like a word.'

Saunders apologised to the couple, said he wouldn't be a minute, why not check out the worktop options while they waited.

'Sergeant Ferreira,' he said, walking towards them and keeping going, trying to move them away from his customers.

They stayed put, forcing him to stop.

Reluctantly, he did.

'Sir.' He nodded curtly to Zigic. 'I don't suppose you're here to buy a new kitchen.'

'Drop the shit, Saunders,' Ferreira snapped. 'You wanted our attention, now you've got it.'

'I don't know what you mean,' he said anxiously.

'See, this is why you never made it out of uniform. We've seen the tweets, we know it's you.'

'This is a bit of a comedown from Long Fleet, isn't it?' Zigic said. 'Why did you leave? You seemed to be enjoying yourself there.'

Saunders glanced nervously around them. 'I resigned.'

'After Josh Ainsworth reported you to the governor?' Zigic could see the ire rising in him. 'Sounds more like you were sacked.'

'Purged,' Ferreira said.

Saunders tucked his hands into the small of his back, reverting to his training posture.

'I was let go with no recourse to legal advice, no tribunal, no nothing,' he said, anger and self-pity mingling in his voice. 'All on the say-so of Ainsworth and Sutherland.'

'And that unfortunate undercover footage,' Zigic reminded him. 'And the testimony of the women involved.'

'But only Ainsworth's been murdered,' Ferreira said.

Saunders shuffled where he stood, gaze dropping to the toes of his shiny brogues for a nervous moment before he looked back at them, a new resolve in his eyes.

'It's no secret I didn't like Ainsworth much. We didn't get on and he said some hurtful and untrue things about me, but I'm sorry about what happened to him.'

As hard as he was trying to keep it together, Zigic could still see the old wounds were troubling Saunders.

'And what exactly about his allegations were untrue?' Ferreira asked.

He looked around them again, wanting to be sure there was no audience.

'Alright, so I said some things that I shouldn't have. But it was just banter.'

'It was hate speech,' Ferreira told him. 'As an ex-copper you know the distinction, so don't come the fucking innocent with us.'

'I wasn't abusive,' he said angrily. 'I wasn't like some of them. I didn't force myself on anyone. I didn't hurt anyone. I just made a few comments where I shouldn't have.' He was directing all of this to Zigic, picking him for the sympathetic ear. 'Christ, you can't say *anything* any more without someone jumping down your throat.'

'You weren't just saying "anything",' Ferreira reminded him. 'You were using grossly offensive racial slurs and threatening language towards highly vulnerable women in your care.' She stabbed a finger at him. 'And we saw you bursting into those women's rooms, Saunders. We know exactly what you are.'

Saunders took half a step towards her and Zigic saw what Ainsworth must have seen in him. How thin the veneer of decency was, how warped and cracked.

Easy to imagine this man snapping. Picking up a table leg and battering Joshua to death with it.

'I never abused anyone,' he growled. 'Why the hell would I want to touch one of *them*?'

Zigic watched him realise what he'd said a split second after the words left his mouth, saw annoyance but no shame. He could have punched him but instead caught hold of Ferreira's arm as she made for the man, spitting a Portuguese curse at him.

Saunders's face flushed and he moved away from her, pointedly averting his eyes.

'Maybe my behaviour was less than perfect but I'm not dangerous,' he said, speaking more slowly now, guarding himself against further accusations. 'Unlike Saint Joshua. You're looking for who killed him? You might want to start with the woman he attacked.'

Ferreira snorted. 'This is seriously how you want to defend yourself?'

'I've done nothing wrong,' he said firmly. 'I don't need to defend myself.'

'Ainsworth cost you your job. You really do need to defend yourself, Saunders.'

'Where were you Saturday evening?' Zigic asked.

'Works' bowling night. People can vouch for me if you need that. But I'm telling you, I never touched Ainsworth.'

'We do need that.'

Ferreira took down the names he gave, their numbers. The temporary lull should have taken the wind out of his sails, but Zigic heard him becoming more irritated with each string of numbers he read from his phone, and he knew Ferreira heard it too because she kept asking him to repeat them, reading them back to him with mistakes he was sure she wasn't making.

'Did they tell you why Ainsworth quit?' Saunders asked, as he slipped his phone into his pocket. 'Probably gave you the old "resigned with stress" line, right?'

'The same as you gave when you left Thorpe Wood,' Ferreira said.

'I *was* stressed,' he insisted. 'How long's it been since you got your little hands dirty? You've got no idea what it's like for us lot on the front line.'

Ferreira just smirked at him, satisfied that she'd hit a sore spot.

Saunders visibly gathered himself, looked to Zigic again, still believing he was the receptive one. All boys together, Zigic thought. That was what Saunders was accustomed to and he couldn't envisage any man not wanting to play the game.

'You don't believe me about Ainsworth, fine.' He shrugged, wounded. 'Talk to the governor. Ask him about the "resignation".'

'Everyone we've spoken to says that same thing about Ainsworth,' Zigic said. 'Everyone apart from you. And you are not a reliable witness. You're a suspect.'

They started to walk away and Saunders followed them.

'I've still got mates at Long Fleet,' he said. 'Word is one of the girls accused Ainsworth of attacking her. Attempted rape, I heard. Nasty attack.'

'Who are they?' Zigic asked, rounding on him. 'We need names.'

'They won't talk to you,' Saunders said, taking a quick backwards step. 'They can't. The contracts we had to sign going in, they're serious stuff. NDAs, the lot. I shouldn't even be talking to you about this now. They could sue me.'

'Getting sued is the least of your worries right now,' Zigic told him.

CHAPTER THIRTY-TWO

'I don't like this,' Zigic said finally.

They hadn't spoken as they left the superstore, except to agree that they both needed a drink. Ferreira suspected he only suggested it in the first place because he wanted to have this conversation away from the office, felt it was something they needed to decide upon between themselves before they returned.

He pulled into the car park of a pub on the Oundle Road, quiet as five o'clock approached, too early for the post-work crowd, too late for anyone else. Only a few older couples taking advantage of the two-courses-for-a-tenner meal deal, sitting facing each other but saying very little, as she'd gone to the bar and ordered their drinks.

Now, outside in the beer garden, settled in the dappled shade of a big old maple tree, alone with the road noise and the birdsong, they could get down to business.

'He's lying, right?' she said, as she rolled a cigarette. 'He's got good reason to want us to think Ainsworth was a piece of shit. Just the same as the Paggetts.'

'And their accusation likely came from seeing his comments online.'

'Until they can provide us with another source for it, yeah, I think we have to assume so.' She lit up. 'I've been all through their group's posts and there's no hint of an insinuation that Ainsworth was a problem, and I think someone would have mentioned it if they'd heard anything.'

'Unless it was said and deleted by the admins,' Zigic suggested.

'Possible,' she admitted, thinking of Ruby Garrick's commitment to Ainsworth. She wouldn't have let something like that stand. 'But the news broke two days ago now. We'd be seeing more chatter online if it had been proper gossip doing the rounds.'

'So what, do we ignore it?'

'Can we?'

A pained look crossed his face. 'If we had a victim actually come forward, that would be one thing, but all we've got is an unsubstantiated accusation from a disgruntled ex-employee who had a massive problem with Ainsworth.'

'I could see if there's any mention of this elsewhere online,' she said, already knowing she was going to do it when she got home.

'But even if you find it, how do we know it isn't just more of the same originating with Saunders?' He shifted his weight, sending the rickety picnic table wobbling. 'Or someone else like him? He isn't the only person who lost their job because of Ainsworth.'

Ferreira took a deep drag on her rollie. 'I'd have expected a few more of them to come out of the woodwork by now, wouldn't you, especially after the TV coverage?'

'Unless they've all realised they're going to be suspects and they're smart enough to keep their heads down,' he said. 'Long Fleet have got them all under pain-of-death NDAs. They know they're probably not going to get named. The only way we find them is if they stick their heads above the parapet.'

Ferreira sighed. 'The thing is, say it's true – and I'm still not convinced –'

'Me neither,' he said.

'Say it is, where's this woman now? Chances are she's either still locked up in Long Fleet because if Ainsworth was sacked over it, then it was probably a recent thing and the likelihood is she won't have been processed yet.'

'Or she's been deported,' Zigic said, finishing her thought.

'Exactly. She's not a viable suspect.'

'Whereas Saunders and his compatriots are.'

She heard the doubt in his voice.

'They are. I know you think two years is a long time to wait to go after someone but we can't ignore the motive there.' She picked a small bug out of her rum and Coke. 'We have a whole bunch of people out there with good reason to want to damage Ainsworth, and we have literally no idea who they are. Doesn't that bother you?'

'Of course it does,' he said.

'And not just any people,' she went on. 'People who have a history of abusive behaviour. Bullies, right? People who don't like it when they don't get their own way. How do you think they felt when they were pulled up on their behaviour?'

'Still,' Zigic said slowly. 'Murdering Ainsworth for telling the truth?'

'For *revealing* the truth about them.'

His shoulders slumped. He looked defeated already, three days into the case, and she wondered just how much pressure Riggott was bringing to bear on him.

'We need to find out who they are,' she said firmly. 'We need to speak to every one of them or we're not doing our job properly.'

'You're right,' he admitted, toying with his beard.

'You look at the scene of the crime,' she went on, now she felt him coming around. 'No forensic evidence, no witnesses. What does that tell you? We're dealing with someone who had some idea of how to get away with murder. They were careful. Too careful for a spur-of-the-moment thing. Even if it superficially looks like one. This was a considered crime. Someone has spent time planning and watching and waiting for just the right opportunity.'

'When he'd had a girlfriend visiting we might blame it on?'

She nodded. 'If we were crappy coppers or she didn't have an alibi, we'd be charging her, wouldn't we?'

'Maybe.' He took another mouthful of red wine, kept hold of the glass, turning it around by the stem. 'You think Saunders is a possibility?'

'He'd be stupid to kill Ainsworth and then start baiting us, wouldn't he?'

'He's still furious,' Zigic said thoughtfully.

'He's lost status as far as he's concerned. Copper to prison guard to shop assistant. He really doesn't like that.' She crushed out her cigarette and immediately began to roll another one. 'Basically, we need to know who else was fired on Ainsworth's evidence. That's it. Job one, right?'

'So, we go back to Long Fleet with the accusation against Ainsworth.'

'Use that to open the door.'

'Act like we're concerned about other potential victims and lay the suggestion that we might go public with the theory?' He was looking more uncomfortable by the second but he was too much the professional not to go through with the plan, morally dubious as it was.

When people threw up roadblocks in front of you, you used whatever means necessary to go through them. He knew that just as well as she did. Except, she thought, Zigic was more the type to find a way around.

'The governor has to believe we'll bring scrutiny to his gates,' she said. 'He's terrified of negative publicity. That's his button.'

'So we hit it.'

'Hard as we can.'

Chapter Thirty-Three

It was gone six when they returned to Thorpe Wood Station; most of the day shift officers from the other teams had left already, only a few dotted around, finishing up paperwork that might take them another hour or two. Zigic had never got used to it, not even now, after so many years on the job, the sheer scale of information they had to process, collate and prepare for other people to take over. Continued to underestimate how long it would take him.

His team were still in place, although flagging after a frustrating day. So much slow and repetitive work and little to show for it. But the next phase threatened to be more combative than the last.

On the drive in from the pub Ferreira had kept up a near constant monologue about the Long Fleet staff and their capacity for murder, repeating herself and going off at tangents, so determined to prevent a silence developing that he began to worry that she was actually scared of going home.

Walton was there last night, was she expecting another showing tonight?

She was staying with Adams now though and he hoped that would deter Walton from approaching her again. Part of him, the most cynical and dispirited part, suspected Walton saw little threat in Adams. Men who attacked women were frequently comfortable using violence against men, too. And Adams would hardly be an intimidating prospect to someone like Walton. Three inches shorter, fifteen kilos lighter, and for all his attitude Zigic wasn't sure how useful Adams would be in a fight.

Violence was ever-present when you were in uniform, but once you moved into plain clothes the chances of being attacked were rare and you usually had enough backup in place to ensure the first punch thrown was also the last. You got out of the habit of defending yourself. Began to talk down aggressive suspects rather than steaming into them.

Zigic realised he hadn't been injured in the line of duty for four or five years now. Then immediately cursed himself for thinking that, as if he was jinxing himself. The last time it had happened Ferreira had pulled him out of harm's way, gone wading back into the fray with her face wild and her baton swinging.

She was well capable of taking care of herself, that was why he found this nervous air she was carrying so disconcerting.

Parr was looking expectantly at him. Bloom and Weller too.

'Alright, let's call it a day,' he said.

They gathered their things quickly, just in case he changed his mind, and hurried out of the office.

'Briefing at eight,' he shouted at their retreating backs.

'I think we broke them,' Ferreira said, opening and immediately closing a patisserie box that had appeared next to the coffee machine sometime during the afternoon.

'You should get off, too.'

She waved towards Adams's office. 'I'm going to wait for that one.'

'Are you ...'

She looked sharply at him, a warning in her eyes but he was going to say it.

He moved closer to her, aware of the few stray officers still in their seats nearby.

'Are you okay?' he asked, in a low voice. 'With all this Walton stuff?'

'He told you,' she said, nodding to herself.

'Of course he did. I don't know why you didn't tell me yourself.'

'It's under control.' Her jaw set hard and she reached for the coffee pot, pouring the last of it into her FC Porto mug. 'Nothing to worry about.'

He wanted to say more, tell her he was there for her if she wanted to talk about it, if she needed anything, but he'd waited too long, he realised, picked the wrong venue. She wouldn't talk here, not with the eavesdroppers at the surrounding desks, would hate the idea of looking weak in front of them.

And maybe she just didn't want to involve him, he thought, surprised to find himself wounded by the rejection.

Zigic drove home still thinking about Walton, experiencing a rising sense of anger that he had dared go to Ferreira's home. Out of prison a matter of days and his only thought was threatening her into revealing the whereabouts of his girlfriend and son. He'd put those thoughts aside since Adams had told him about it, but they had festered at the back of his mind and now he found himself even more determined to see Walton locked up again. If he was arrogant enough to go after a police officer, what wouldn't he do?

The house was empty when he got home.

He went into the rare quiet and stillness, feeling slightly adrift as he moved through the rooms. Anna had taken the children out for the day with her mother, to some model village she'd visited as a child and was sure they'd love. He'd half expected them to be back by now, texted her to check they were all okay and got a reply a few minutes later as he was stripping off in the bedroom. They'd stopped off for dinner, would be back in a few hours, she said.

He showered and dressed, went into the kitchen and drank a cold beer while he hunted for something to eat in the fridge. Finally, he gave up and ordered a takeaway, exploiting this rare opportunity to indulge without Anna judging him for it. While he waited he went out into the garden and watered the boys' little vegetable patch, finding the tomatoes ripening nicely but the lettuces wilting.

You could have made a salad from them, the virtuous voice in his head suggested, but it was too late for that now and it would be worse to waste the pizza he'd ordered. Especially since it had three different meats on.

When it arrived half an hour later, he realised he'd made the right call. He ate two-thirds of it and then carefully hid the evidence of his small culinary crime at the very bottom of the bin. Even under the rubbish the leftovers smelled amazing, and if he'd had a couple more beers, he might have been tempted to dig the box out again.

There was no more avoiding it, he thought, as he closed the bin lid. The job he should have done in the office but didn't, because it felt wrong to turn away from the investigation into Joshua Ainsworth's murder. Or if he was honest with himself, because he wanted this to be right so badly that he was deferring the possibility of finding out it wasn't.

He put a pot of coffee on and opened the file Adams had given him about Tessa Darby's murder.

DAY FOUR

FRIDAY AUGUST 10TH

CHAPTER THIRTY-FOUR

Zigic woke up on the sofa, head bent at an awkward angle against the arm, shoulders aching and his left foot numb. His phone was ringing on the coffee table, hidden under the case file he'd been reading.

As he unstuck his eyes, he saw Milan sitting on the floor in front of the television, cartoons playing muted with the subtitles running. He'd made himself a tray of breakfast: milk in a pebbled glass, yoghurt and toast and an almost-green banana. Next to the tray he had the prospectus from the school they were visiting this morning.

'It's not time for work yet, Dad.'

He was right. Barely half six but Adams was calling him, driving the last of the sleep-fuddle out of his brain.

'What's happened?' he asked.

'We should meet up before shift starts,' Adams said, the sound of a toaster popping up at his end. 'Half an hour long enough for you to get yourself together?'

'Where do you want to meet?'

'Sainsbury's caff near you.'

'You bringing Mel to this clandestine meeting?'

Adams swore. 'Yeah, you're right, better make it half seven. I'll get her off to her spin class first.'

'Does she know about this case?'

'I think she's got enough to stress about right now,' he said. 'See you in an hour.'

Adams rang off.

Zigic stood up and stretched the night out of his body, shoulders cracking, ribs complaining. 'You going to make me breakfast, bud?'

'There's no more bread,' Milan said gravely. 'But I can make coffee. You'll have to light the gas for me.'

'You watch your cartoons, I'll sort myself out.'

Milan turned back to the TV, reaching for his yoghurt. 'Are you coming with us later?'

'I've got to work,' he said, seeing Milan hunch over slightly, the disappointment shrinking him. 'You look around and then tell me all about it when I get home, okay?'

'Okay.' Milan opened his yoghurt and briefly examined the state of the spoon before tucking in.

Upstairs Anna was still asleep, hidden behind a silk eye-mask. At some point in the night she must have got up because Emily was lying next to her, corralled by a couple of pillows to stop her rolling off the bed.

By the time he'd showered Anna was awake, standing at her wardrobe trying to find just the right outfit for this morning's appointment with the headmistress of the school the boys would probably love and that they definitely couldn't afford to send them to.

'The appointment's at half past eleven,' she said, as he was putting on his shirt. 'It would be good for the boys if you were there.'

He bit his tongue, wouldn't say that she'd obviously made her decision and this was just a formality, wouldn't ask why she'd made an appointment that she knew his work would keep him from attending.

'I won't be able to get away,' he said.

She sighed lightly, as if this was just the kind of nonsense she expected from him.

'I want this to be something we're together on, Dushan.'

'And I don't want to disappoint the boys by taking them around a school we can't afford to send them to,' he told her, the words out before he could think better of it.

'They have a scholarship programme,' she said, gritting her teeth because she was probably tired of saying it.

That stupid lie they were still colluding in, even now, after weeks of disagreement, because neither of them was willing to openly discuss the ugly truth it was covering just yet.

Zigic watched her turn away and select a lightweight shirtdress that she always looked amazing in. He almost told her it was the right choice but stopped himself, said instead, 'Please don't make the boys any promises you'll regret breaking.'

When he got to Bretton the car park was all but deserted but everyone who was there seemed to be in the supermarket cafeteria. He ordered a bacon roll and coffee and went to join Adams at a table set against the far wall. There was nobody else around them, all the other early risers drawn to the sun-drenched tables alongside the picture window.

Adams was jittery. Tired-looking and over-caffeinated, fiddling with the cigarette packet left out on the table.

'So, what do you think?' he asked, as Zigic sat down.

He wanted to tell Adams there was nothing there. That Bobby was wrong, that he was just so desperate to make the kill on Walton that he was seeing discrepancies that didn't exist.

But he couldn't.

Last night he'd gone through the entire file twice, concentrating on the eyewitness reports and the statements from Tessa Darby's friends and family. There was nothing conclusive in any of it. Her killer – Cooper, the young man who confessed – was known to her, was said by a couple of her friends to be obsessed with her, but there was no hard evidence of that and a handwritten note suggested that the friends were not as close to Tessa as they made out. Not according to her family anyway.

'I think,' Zigic said slowly, 'that if it wasn't for the confession, Lee Walton would have been looked at a lot more carefully than he was.'

'They dropped the ball, right?' Adams's face lit up, the relief obvious. 'Tessa's boyfriend's in the frame until his mate Walton gives him an alibi. Then when they realise those two's story isn't going to crack, they just turn all their focus onto this stupid lad who confesses.'

'What about the boyfriend?' Zigic asked, stirring a couple of sugars into his coffee. 'It's way more likely Walton was covering for him than the other way around.'

'Boyfriend's dead. Army, got blown up in Iraq a few years back.' Adams dismissed him with a vague gesture. 'But the way I see it, soldier boy knows he's bang in the frame – he's the boyfriend, we *always* suspect the boyfriend – so he begs his mate to give him an alibi. Inadvertently alibiing Walton who actually killed her.'

Across the cafeteria a woman called out Zigic's number and he put a hand up. They fell silent as she came over and placed his breakfast on the table in front of him.

'There's nothing to tie this bloke Cooper to the murder at all,' Adams said.

'Except that he confessed.'

Adams shot him an awkward smile. 'Except that, yeah.'

'So why do you think he confessed if he didn't do it?' Zigic asked, genuinely curious, and started on his bacon butty.

'Two options. First one, coercion.'

Zigic swallowed hard, his food moving painfully down his throat. He took a mouthful of coffee.

'You accept that's an option, then?' he asked.

'Yeah, of course I do,' Adams said with a shrug. 'But let's come back to that. Or –'

'Because you understand what's going to happen if we find evidence of coercion?'

Adams glared at him. 'I understood it the second I read the fucking file, same as you did.'

Zigic nodded for him to continue.

'Second, better option: Cooper wasn't quite the full ticket and maybe he *was* obsessed with Tessa and maybe he somehow, in his confused, not particularly sharp mind, convinced himself he *did* kill her.' Adams was trying to sell the idea too hard because nobody who'd looked over the file would ever buy it. 'We don't know, maybe he'd thought about killing her before? Maybe all that got jumbled up in his head and then she's dead and he feels guilty and he can't tell reality from imagination any more.'

Zigic wiped his mouth on a paper napkin, pushed the empty plate aside.

'You just inhaled that butty, mate. Anna not feeding you?'

'We need to cut out this second option rubbish,' Zigic said firmly. 'Because if we're going to pursue this we need to be honest with ourselves about the potential consequences.'

All the jitteriness flooded back into Adams.

And Zigic could understand it. He'd felt the same surge of anxiety and adrenaline when he opened the file and saw DCS Riggott's name all over it. DCI Riggott back then. Leading an investigation that went high profile instantly, under pressure to get a fast and clean result before people started asking too many questions about the safety of women and girls in the city. Before they started drawing the conclusion that falling police numbers were endangering them and everyone else.

Riggott's reputation had always been that of an officer who knew how to get a conviction. Tough, they said. Sharp. Not above bending the rules when it was necessary.

But even twenty years ago the rules were strict enough that you could only bend them so far. Whatever Riggott might have been morally capable of, the station should have held him in check.

Theoretically.

'If Riggott finds out we're sniffing around one of his old cases ...'

'I know,' Adams said uneasily. 'But that doesn't mean we stop. We just need to tread carefully for a bit.' He straightened up where he sat, regathered himself. 'No point poking the bear until we have to, right?'

'We can only go so far before we start making noise,' Zigic pointed out. 'Not very far at all.'

'You'd be surprised how much you can achieve off-book.'

Zigic shook his head at Adams, wondered if it was bravado or naïveté. 'We've got a couple of days, tops, before someone leaks this to Riggott.'

'Better make them count then, Ziggy.'

CHAPTER THIRTY-FIVE

Back to Long Fleet.

No preamble this time. Minimal niceties.

Straight into the governor's office where the air conditioning was running full blast, creating a distracting background hum and rippling the fronds of the fern James Hammond had placed on the corner of his desk. Its leaves had been recently misted, the smell of damp soil in the air, along with the smoked fishiness of lapsang souchong, which always made Ferreira gag.

Hammond took it in a china cup and saucer, which sat on a dainty silver tray. The sparkling glass teapot next to them functioned like a stink bomb.

Ferreira chose the seat furthest away from it, noticing Zigic wrinkle his nose as he moved in to sit.

'So,' he said. 'Tell us about the woman who Joshua Ainsworth attacked.'

Hammond chewed on it for a few seconds, an over-deep frown wrinkling his chin and cutting a line between his fine blond eyebrows. He'd been expecting the question, Ferreira realised with a start.

'We didn't entirely believe the accusation.' Hammond reached out to straighten his pen and the notepad he'd ripped a page off and binned as they walked in. 'But given the potential for negative press, we thought it was better to err on the side of caution and suggest Josh resigned.'

'You need transparency for negative press,' Ferreira said.

'Why would Ainsworth agree to resign if he was being falsely accused?' Zigic asked, his attention fixed firmly on Hammond.

'I think he was coming naturally to the end of his time here,' Hammond said. 'It wasn't how any of us would have chosen to lose him, but we gave him a glowing reference and a respectable severance package.'

'Is that how you deal with all your accused sex offenders?' Ferreira asked. 'Burnish their CV and give them a bucket of cash?'

Hammond glared at her. 'As I said, Sergeant Ferreira, I didn't believe the accusation had merit.'

'Did you explain that to Ainsworth?'

He shook his head. 'That would just have complicated matters.'

'It must have been very confusing to him then,' Zigic suggested.

Hammond cupped his hands in front of him on the desk. 'He wasn't happy about the resignation request, no. He denied the accusation vehemently. He was absolutely mortified to have that said about him after everything that had happened here under the previous regime.' Hammond sighed. 'Perversely, I think that made it an easier decision for him. He'd given a lot to this place; as he saw it, he'd been instrumental in making our ladies safer, and then one of them made this accusation about him. I think, possibly, he felt there was a lack of gratitude from them. And, probably, from me, because he didn't receive immediate, unequivocal support.' For a moment he looked queasy. 'But when an accusation is made, I have to investigate it whether I believe it has merit or not.'

It didn't make sense, Ferreira thought. A spotless track record derailed by one accusation. An accusation that Hammond claimed he didn't trust.

'Had there been any other accusations against him in the past?'

'No, none. As I told you on your last visit, he was very well liked.'

Zigic scratched his beard. 'I'm sorry, Mr Hammond, but this doesn't make much sense. You believed Ainsworth was innocent and yet you sacked him –'

'Asked him to resign.'

'Semantics don't really figure here,' Zigic said. 'There must have been *something* to the woman's accusation.'

'Or maybe you wanted Ainsworth out for another reason,' Ferreira suggested.

Hammond dragged his hands off the desk into his lap, the small movements through his shoulders giving away how nervously he was twisting his fingers together.

'Fine,' he said bitterly. 'He's dead now so I don't suppose it matters. Frankly, I thought there may have been some merit to the accusation. We had very little evidence either way. It was simply her word against his, but Josh had been such a vocal accuser of other people over the preceding years that I began to wonder if he wasn't doing that to cover for his own bad behaviour.'

Ferreira nodded, more to herself than him. She heard the pretence drop out of his voice, replaced by a slightly ragged and exasperated edge.

'It isn't the most fair or rigorous way of dealing with an accusation,' he admitted. 'And if it had ever come out, we'd have probably been in trouble. But my gut told me to listen to this particular young woman.'

His gaze drifted into middle distance for a moment.

'We need to speak to the woman,' Zigic told him.

Hammond's attention snapped back onto him, his face shutting down, going back into professional mode. 'I'm not sure that's possible.'

'Is she still in the facility?'

'I'm afraid I can't give you that information.'

'You must understand how important it is that we speak to her,' Zigic said, frustrated. 'She's one of the few people who can give us a direct insight into Ainsworth's behaviour.'

'You can't seriously be suggesting she's a suspect.'

'I'm not suggesting that,' Zigic said. 'It's very hard to consider what her position might be until we know if she's still in here or not.'

Hammond reiterated his position, speaking slowly, and Ferreira half listened to his explanation of data protection and human rights, managed not to jump on him at that last one. She heard the stirring of fear under the arrogance in his voice, as if he realised he'd given too much away now for them to simply back down and forget about it.

Zigic went into politician mode, promising discretion and tact, that nothing he told them would be leaked to the press or used in official briefing statements. It was what Hammond wanted to hear but Ferreira doubted it was enough to assuage him.

Hammond was running a fiefdom here, backed by a board of directors who had likely not set foot in the place since the ground-breaking ceremony held for the trade papers. People whose main interest was the bottom line and secondary to that, what needed to be done to keep things running smoothly and their company's name out of the headlines.

He'd made a unilateral decision on Joshua Ainsworth's guilt. Just the same as he had with all the abusers and enablers he'd sacked when he started at Long Fleet.

She knew it was wrong but she couldn't help but feel envious of the power he had.

He saw guilt, he took action. And for all they knew, as long as he refused to hand over his files, there was ample evidence of that guilt.

The more defensive he became about Ainsworth the more convinced she was that the evidence on him must exist. Because how bad would it look if it came out now via a murder investigation?

Especially since he'd made Ainsworth's testimony the back-bone of the wave of firings he had initiated. It threw all of that into question. Opened them up to wrongful dismissal suits and civil action. Gave fuel to Long Fleet's critics, the ones who had consistently questioned the lack of transparency and oversight.

'You have to understand, Mr Hammond,' Zigic said blandly. 'We now have a former member of your staff making insinuations about Josh Ainsworth on social media. This is a man who was sacked as a result of Ainsworth's testimony against him.'

Hammond blanched.

'The sooner we close this case, the less damage you'll see done to your reputation here.'

'Ainsworth being murdered by a disgruntled ex-employee is way less embarrassing than a former inmate who you allowed to be abused by him seeking her revenge,' Ferreira suggested. 'But until we can investigate those former employees – the ones Ainsworth informed on – well, we have to assume this woman might be responsible.'

Hammond was stony-faced. 'I categorically cannot give you a list of former employees.'

'We'll find out who they are sooner or later,' Zigic warned him. 'And it's going to cause a lot more noise us digging around and making public appeals.'

Ferreira turned towards him. 'We could use that hidden camera footage – pick out all their faces, have it shown on the local news.'

'And the national,' Zigic agreed. 'Those men could be working anywhere, we'd need national coverage.'

Hammond's head was hanging now, the inevitability of it so clear that he couldn't deny it to himself any longer.

'We would rather do this discreetly,' Zigic said. 'Believe me, we're aware of how important the work you do here is.'

Ferreira just managed to stop herself scoffing at that.

'Nobody wants this to get ugly,' Zigic went on. 'If you can give us what we need, I promise to you we'll make every effort to do our job as quietly as possible.'

'Alright, Inspector,' Hammond said, the merest hint of ire in his tone. 'I'll get you the records. And, the other matter ... that's a little more complicated, but leave it with me.'

Zigic stood, held his hand out. 'Very much appreciated, Mr Hammond.'

CHAPTER THIRTY-SIX

'So Ainsworth attacked someone?' Keri Bloom asked, shocked and perplexed by the sudden revelation, just as Zigic had been when Hammond unburdened himself in his office. 'What does this mean for us?'

'It means we have a potential suspect if the woman's been released from Long Fleet,' Zigic told her. 'But we still don't know if she has been, so for now we're going to be concentrating on the former guards who were sacked as a result of Ainsworth informing on them.'

'How do we know he wasn't lying about all of that?' Rob Weller asked, tapping a pen against his desk. 'If he was at it, maybe he lied to cover for himself.'

'There's recorded evidence of abuses,' Ferreira said, giving him a look that could have stripped his skin from his flesh. 'You saw the footage. That isn't up for debate.'

'And it doesn't alter the fact that those employees have a strong motive for going after Ainsworth,' Zigic reminded him. 'They lost their jobs, they were outed as predators. These are people with an axe to grind and we need to track them down and question each and every one of them.'

Hammond had emailed them the list of former employees and it was up on the board now, twelve fresh names in the persons-of-interest column, printed in angry block capitals by Ferreira. Ten men, two women. All guards.

'You need to divide them up and get around to them today,' she said. 'Sooner we know where we are the sooner we can discount or dive deeper into this lot.'

'Alright,' Zigic said, clapping his hands. 'You know what to do. Get on it.'

He walked away from the board, heading for the door with his keys in his hand.

Ferreira caught up to him at the stairwell. 'Where are you going?'

'Family stuff. I'll be as quick as I can.'

It should have been family stuff, he thought, as he turned onto Thorpe Road, heading in the direction of the school where Anna would already have arrived with the boys done up in their smartest clothes, told to be on best behaviour; she believed in always being early for things. It would have been easy to slow and turn down the tree-lined driveway, call her and apologise for everything and ask her to wait for him before she went in to plead her case before the headmistress.

But he couldn't bring himself to do it. Knew he was going to fight this to the bitter end.

Because he couldn't stand ten or fifteen years of Anna's sanctimonious, superior parents rubbing his nose in his inability to pay for his children to have the kind of education he didn't even want for them. Every holiday he'd be reminded of it, every birthday, every new term when their money would fly into the school's bank account, he would have to deal with their smug faces, even if he didn't actually see them. He would know they were at home, delighting in their act of charity, congratulating themselves on the good sense of their investments and the efficacy of their tax planning.

He kept his eyes on the car in front of him as he passed the turning to the school, kept driving with the temptation to turn around gradually fading the further across the city he went, until he was pulling up outside a bungalow in Fletton and all that was left of it was a faint hint of regret buried deep in his chest.

Adams had already arrived, was standing talking to a woman with a pair of dachshunds on the small area of scrubby parkland at the centre of the development, under a tree that looked so dry Zigic half expected it to spontaneously combust. Adams was smiling and squatting down, fussing the animals while the woman talked. Even from a distance of twenty metres, Zigic could see she was flirting with him.

The address they wanted was a couple of doors along the road and Zigic eyed it from inside the car, knowing this estate was patrolled by a particularly attentive neighbourhood-watch scheme and that anyone lingering on the paths would soon come to their attention.

It was a 1960s bungalow, hard grey bricks and metal window frames that had been repainted a disconcerting shade of blue, in contrast to the brilliant white of the surrounding properties. The front garden was untended, had been a single gravelled parking space at some point in the past but was now mostly weeds, or more charitably an urban wildflower meadow, Zigic thought, given the preponderance of dandelions and thistles.

Finally Adams broke away and trotted over the road.

'Neighbourhood watch,' he said.

'Had you down as a wrong 'un, did she?'

'She clocked you right off, mate. Thought you were a dealer.'

'Racial profiling.'

'Or the stoner beard,' Adams suggested. 'How are you standing that in this weather anyway?'

Zigic ignored the comment.

'I didn't think Cooper would be out yet,' he said.

'Confessed and apologised profusely to the family.' Adams shrugged, as if that wasn't the single biggest reason they shouldn't be there. 'Makes life easier for us anyway, means we can get to him.'

Adams started towards Neal Cooper's place and everything in Zigic's body was screaming at him to drop back, get into his car and away from this mad scheme. He could still make the appointment at the school, slip into Anna's good graces again and extricate himself from the position he was poised to assume in Riggott's bad ones.

But he knew deep down that this was the only way.

Adams rang the doorbell, eyes on the toes of his shoes until the moment the lock clicked. Then his warrant card came out and the smile switched on, cold and unfriendly.

'Neal, we'd like a word. Don't mind, do you? That's great.' Adams barrelled in, hand going to Cooper's shoulder, walking him backwards into the hallway. Cooper stumbled over his feet, one arm bracing against the floral-papered wall. 'Let's head through into the living room, yeah?'

Zigic felt an immediate prickle of discomfort, watching how little resistance Cooper put up, not even so much as a question about what they wanted before he complied. He moved unsteadily, his whole body tilted to the left, shoulder hanging slightly too low, like it had been dislocated and never properly reset, his steps slow and uneven, each one seeming to require a degree of thought as he made it.

He was barely forty, younger than either of them, but he looked at least ten years older. Prison had been tough on him Zigic guessed, the way it could be on men who killed pretty girls. It only took a couple of bona fide tough guys to see something of their daughter in the victim, and he would have been marked for the duration.

Cooper's previously black hair was greyed now and cropped close to his skull, unevenly done, like a home-shave job made by an unsteady hand. His skin was pallid and deep wrinkles had settled between his brows and around his mouth, his forehead set in a permanent crease of concentration or contrition. He sat down in a chair next to the dead electric fire, hands tucked together between his knees, his whole body bent over to avoid looking at them.

Zigic looked around the living room, saw a woman's touch had been in evidence once but maybe not now. The decor was at least twenty years out of date, all burnt umber and ochre yellow, the sofa was old but the TV new, while a smell of air freshener did little to cover the scent of confined male body.

'You seen your mate Lee Walton lately?' Adams asked, taking a seat on the sofa opposite Cooper.

Cooper shook his head but he looked confused, Zigic thought. Whatever he was expecting from them it wasn't this.

'You know he went away?'

His knees started jiggling. 'I heard.'

'Didn't do his time though,' Adams said. 'Not like you did. Walton got lucky, in and out in less than six months. For what he did. All those women he hurt. That seem fair to you, Neal?'

'I dunno.'

'You did twelve years. While Lee gets away with murder.'

Cooper said nothing, kept looking at the carpet between his feet.

Adams was watching him carefully, unblinking.

'We're running a cold case review,' he said. 'You understand what that is, Neal? It means we're looking into old murders where the conviction is in dispute.'

'I didn't do anything,' Cooper said, risking a quick glance at him. Zigic saw the fear in his eyes.

'That's exactly what we were thinking,' Adams told him conspiratorially. 'But what we're wondering is why you confessed to Tessa's murder.'

Zigic rolled his eyes. Was this the best he had? Waltzing in and laying it all out to this man, who they knew next to nothing about. Who Adams had clearly assumed was an idiot underserving of finesse or guile.

'She was your friend, wasn't she, Neal?'

He nodded.

'And someone killed her.'

'I don't want to talk about Tessa any more.'

He started worrying at a patch of worn fabric on the arm of the chair. Zigic noticed the red skin around his nail beds, the chewed-up cuticles.

'Someone followed Tessa,' Adams said, moving to the edge of his seat. 'Someone watched her, waited until she was in an isolated spot. And when he was sure nobody else was around, he dragged her off the path, into the leaves and the dirt, and he strangled her.'

Zigic watched Cooper, waiting for some kind of reaction. One he couldn't control. Some trace of remembered pleasure or still-fresh guilt. But he saw nothing except an overwhelming desire for

Adams to stop talking in the way Cooper tucked his chin down into his chest and drew his heels closer in to the chair, his hands twitching like he wanted to cover his ears.

'It takes a long time to strangle someone, Neal.' Adams voice was low and dark. 'People don't realise that. They see it done on TV and think it's all over in a few seconds. But it takes two minutes, three maybe, if she's strong. Do you think Tessa was the kind of girl who fought back?'

Cooper was shaking now and Zigic thought of all the murderers he'd seen faced with the truth of their crimes, how none of them could entirely contain themselves when the memory of it was stirred afresh. A murder like Tessa Darby's, men who did something like that, you *always* caught a hint of satisfaction on their faces. Even the smartest killers couldn't hide that.

Cooper looked like he wanted to cry.

'Can you imagine it, Neal?' Adams asked, almost whispering. 'Pushing Tessa face down into the dirt and feeling her fighting for her life, minute after minute. And it *isn't* ending, she's still there, trying to save herself. Can you imagine what that would feel like? Knowing you could stop and she'd live but you don't, you keep going and still she's alive and kicking but it's getting weak. You can feel the life going out of her under you. How do you think that feels?'

A tear ran down Cooper's grey-stubbled cheek. 'I don't know,' he said, his creaky voice barely audible.

Adams glanced at Zigic, a split second of 'I told you so'.

'Why did you confess, Neal?'

He just shook his head, a low humming noise vibrating around his throat.

'Did someone threaten you?'

'I don't want to talk to you.' He looked up finally, eyes bloodshot and wet, his mouth contorted with pain. 'Leave me alone. Get out of my house. I don't have to talk to you.'

'Did Lee Walton threaten you, Neal?'

'Get out.'

Adams stood up but only moved in closer to Cooper. 'Did Walton kill Tessa?'

Cooper started humming again, louder now.

'If Walton killed Tessa and you covered for him, then every other crime he committed is your fault, Neal.'

Zigic grabbed Adams by the elbow, tried to pull him away, but he snatched his arm back and leaned down into Cooper's face, hands on the arms of the chair, mouth inches from his ear.

'That makes you an accessory,' he said. 'You understand what that means? It means you go back to prison.'

Cooper shot to his feet, shoving Adams away from him. Zigic braced himself to tackle the man but he made no further move, only stood panting in front of them as if he didn't know what to do next.

Slowly Zigic stepped between them. 'Neal, we're just trying to find out what really happened to Tessa, alright? I can see how upset you are right now. I saw that in the statements you gave to our colleagues all those years ago. She was your friend and you were obviously devastated about what happened to her.'

'I loved her,' Cooper said quietly, unable to meet Zigic's eye.

'If you loved her then you must want to see her killer punished.'

'It's too late.' He sat down again, stared at the dead electric fire. 'Leave me alone. I'm not saying anything else to you.'

Adams's mouth was open ready for another round but Zigic pushed him back once more.

'I'm leaving you my number, Neal. If you change your mind, call me.' He took out a card and left it stuck in the frame of a gilt mirror. 'The sooner you talk and the more you help us, the less likely it is you'll be charged with any further offences.'

He wasn't sure if Cooper even heard him.

CHAPTER THIRTY-SEVEN

It was impossible for Ferreira to concentrate with Colleen Murray sitting across the desk from her, speaking perfectly accented French. Her posture had shifted, becoming looser and more expressive, her free hand wheeling in the air as she berated the *gendarme* on the other end for something that remained absolutely opaque to Ferreira, other than the mention of a hotel.

Murray pouted as she listened to the person on the other end of the phone. Stayed silent for less than five seconds before she rolled her eyes violently and threw up her hand, letting off a string of invective that concluded with her slamming the phone down.

'*Putain!*'

Ferreira knew that one.

'Col, girl to girl, I have to tell you, you are sexy as all hell.'

She gave a throaty laugh. 'Maybe I'll try the French on my next date.'

'I guarantee that will get you out of any museum trips,' Ferreira said. 'Take it they lost Batty?'

'Yeah, dragged their arses and by the time they got to the hotel, he'd upped and checked out.' Her face clouded over again. 'What kind of idiots wait until eleven to pull someone out of a hotel? Bloody place has checkout at ten on its website.'

'Do they have any idea where he was heading?'

'They're looking into it, apparently. Not going to hold my breath though.' She took a sip of her tea. 'He'll be running out of money in the next couple of days. So it's a toss-up between him making a call home for more cash or winding up somewhere cheap and dodgy and getting himself knifed.'

'Or getting arrested trying to rob some more?'

Murray shook her head. 'Batty's not the robbing sort. Not got the balls for it.'

'He's up for attempted murder, Col.'

She sighed. 'They're all hard cases with their mates around. Take that away, he's just another little gobshite.'

Ferreira went back to work, still looking into the Paggetts, even though she felt the likelihood of them being responsible for Ainsworth's murder fading.

It wasn't necessarily a valid feeling, she knew that, kept reminding herself that just because a new and more promising line of enquiry had opened up it didn't mean this one was fully closed.

If she didn't find something compelling, she would be forced to release them in ninety minutes, and she didn't think she'd find anything in the contents of their mobiles, which the tech department had delivered late yesterday afternoon.

Both phones had been turned on around the time of Ainsworth's murder but not used. Which told her nothing. Especially as neither of them was a particularly heavy phone user. They seemed to be doing some kind of digital detox, judging by the pattern of usage, which was divided into strict half-hour blocks four times a day, both of them on the same schedule.

Within those blocks most of their activity was related to the various activism groups they belonged to, regular blogs and Michaela's habit of posting photographs of whatever custom trainers she was wearing that day.

Annoyingly they hadn't outlined their plans to kidnap Joshua Ainsworth in the notes app or recorded photos of his corpse for posterity.

Ferreira refreshed her email again, checking whether Hammond had come good on his promise to send over the file on the accusation against Ainsworth yet.

Still nothing.

'Thought you'd have taken the opportunity to get out of the office,' Murray said. 'Nice day like this, don't want to be sitting on your arse while the kids have all the fun with your suspects.'

'I overdid it at the gym this morning,' Ferreira told her. 'My arse needs the rest.'

'Mine needs some biscuits.' Murray opened her desk drawer and brought out a Tupperware container of homemade cookies, held it out to Ferreira. 'Dark chocolate and cardamom.'

'Thanks.' She took one and resisted the urge to shove it in her mouth whole. 'Damn it, these are good.'

Murray bobbed her head at the compliment, broke her own biscuit in half and dunked it quickly into her tea.

'Bit of a shocker with your man,' she said, speaking with her mouth full from behind her hand.

'I'm not shocked by anything any more.' Ferreira thought of the moment Hammond came clean about Josh Ainsworth and how inevitable it had felt. She'd become incapable of separating power from its abuses, mistrusted anyone who actively sought out jobs with the vulnerable. 'Everyone we talked to went on and on about what a good bloke Ainsworth was, right?' she said. 'And the more you hear that the more you think it has to be lies.'

'It's the job,' Murray told her.

The second time in two days she'd said it and Ferreira wondered which of them she was trying to convince.

Murray went back to her report and Ferreira blew out a sigh as she returned her attention to the Paggetts, still thinking about Ainsworth and how they'd been right about him all along. Wondered if they'd known he was a predator before Jack Saunders's tweets started popping up in the public domain.

She opened up the scans of the pamphlets, found the one she was looking for.

Initially she'd assumed it was about Ainsworth's work at Long Fleet, alluding to what they saw as the fundamental immorality of the place. But now she was wondering.

Did they know about the alleged attack? Would that have been motive enough for them to make the step from harassment to assault?

She called the tech department, asking them to find her a date for the flier.

'You've got their cloud data in the bundle,' the guy at the other end said wearily. 'Check the files and you'll see a time stamp on it.'

She thanked him and got a 'no problem' in return, the tone of a man who spent most of his day fielding stupid questions.

Ferreira had Michaela Paggett brought up from the cells. She looked crumpled but unbothered by her night in custody. Ferreira had expected no different, knew people accustomed to the cells rarely cracked in them.

'You've got to release us in the next twenty minutes,' Michaela said, once the tapes were set up, pointedly eyeing the clock on the wall above them. 'And I don't have to speak to you without my solicitor present so I hope you can get him here fast.'

'We can hold you for another forty-eight hours,' Ferreira told her. 'As I'm sure someone of your experience would know.'

'With cause.'

'Planning to kidnap Josh Ainsworth is cause.'

Michaela snorted. 'A joke at a party. That's not a plan.'

Ferreira ignored her, brought out a scan of the flier and pushed it across the table.

'I told you, I'm not going to speak to you without my solicitor.'

'I'm not questioning you, Michaela,' Ferreira said. 'But I'd like you to explain to me what you meant by this: "You act like your hands are clean but we know what you are."'

Michaela glanced at it, then back at Ferreira. She saw confidence rising in the woman's posture, realisation on her face.

'Damien told you then. About the accusation?'

'Is that what this is about?' Ferreira asked.

'Why should I tell you?'

'Why wouldn't you?' Ferreira countered. 'If you're innocent you should want to help us.'

A quick laugh utterly devoid of humour. 'I don't care who killed Ainsworth. We didn't do it but he had it coming.'

'Because he worked at Long Fleet? That's not reason enough to murder someone. Not even in your world.' Ferreira leaned on the table. 'What did Josh Ainsworth do?'

'I only know the same as Damien,' Michaela said dismissively. 'We heard Ainsworth was no better than the rest of the them.'

'From where?'

'Online.'

'When?'

Michaela looked at the flier. 'I can't remember. Awhile ago.'

'Like a month awhile or a few days awhile?'

'A month or so, I guess.'

Ferreira tapped the flier. 'You made this on June 28th. And I can't find any mention of Ainsworth as a potential abuser online before Tuesday.'

'Maybe you don't know where to look.'

'So tell me.'

'I can't remember where I heard it. Things get said.' Michaela shrugged, twisting away from the table slightly. 'Maybe I didn't see it online, maybe someone told me.'

'Who?'

'God, do you remember where every single piece of information in your head came from?' Michaela asked, exasperated.

'This isn't just any old piece of information,' Ferreira pressed. 'It's something you gave enough credence to to turn it into a special piece of hate mail.'

Michaela threw herself back in her seat, arms folded. 'Look, all I know is I *heard* that Ainsworth wasn't the good guy everyone thought he was. There was some rumour that he'd attacked a woman and that was why he wasn't at work any more.'

'This came from someone inside Long Fleet?' she asked.

'Piss off,' Michaela snapped. 'We don't have anything to do with anyone who works in Long Fleet.'

'Ruby Garrick did.'

'Well, she wasn't as fussy about the company she kept.'

'Did this gossip come from her?'

'No.'

'So you remember where it *didn't* come from?' Ferreira asked. 'How about if I we go through the entirety of your contacts list and everyone in your groups, and you can tell me the ones it didn't come from until we get to the person who actually told you?'

'If you think you can do that in –' Michaela checked the clock again. 'Eight minutes.'

'I'm pretty sure I can get through them all in the forty-eight extra hours I'm going to hold you and Damien for,' Ferreira said, giving her a saccharine smile. 'Alternatively, you could stop bullshitting me and go home today.'

'Typical,' Michaela muttered into her chest.

'Going to be hot again this weekend,' Ferreira told her. 'And you wouldn't believe how stuffy those cells get. No through draught. The *smell* when the drunk-and-disorderlies start coming in.'

'You think that bothers me?'

'No, you're impressively battle-hardened, Michaela. But I heard Damien isn't doing so well. Puked his guts up last night, didn't he?'

'You're scum,' Michaela spat.

'And your opinion is of zero interest to me.' Ferreira laced her fingers together on the table. 'You have one piece of information I want. Give it to me or go back down for the weekend. I'm sure you can tap out some words of support on the wall between your and Damien's cells.'

Michaela Paggett scowled at her.

'To my best recollection,' Michaela said, speaking slowly, like she was forcing out each word at some great personal cost. 'We were at an anti-austerity event in Manchester at the beginning of June and it was late in the day, and we went along to a pub with some people we didn't know and we got talking about Long Fleet.' She wet her lips. 'There was a woman there, older, red hair, not local.'

'Not local to Manchester or not local to here?'

'Either,' Michaela said. 'But she seemed to know a lot about what was going on in there. And she said she'd heard that there was a doctor in Long Fleet who was abusing his patients.'

Ferreira blinked at her. The story was vague and the source untraceable, but the Paggetts had clearly fastened on it because it chimed with what they already believed and allowed them to justify the harassment they'd already perpetrated against Josh Ainsworth.

'You do realise Ainsworth wasn't the only doctor working there?' Ferreira said.

'He's the one who doesn't work there any more.' Michaela shrugged. 'Stands to reason it's him.'

CHAPTER THIRTY-EIGHT

Zigic wanted to call Anna and ask how the interview at the school had gone. Something about the grimness of Neal Cooper's life had made him crave the sound of her voice, the chatter of the kids in the background.

Neal Cooper wasn't supposed to end up how he had, all bent up and beaten down, a convicted murderer whose neighbours would all know exactly who he was and what he was supposed to have done. His whole life had been derailed by a conviction, one that now looked increasingly suspect.

Would he have been a good father? A considerate husband? What had been stolen from him the second he made that false confession?

Because Zigic was almost completely certain now that it was false.

'Nine-fifty,' the young guy behind the counter said in a tone that suggested it wasn't the first time he'd said it.

Zigic apologised and tapped his card on the reader, then picked up his order and carried it out of Krispy Kreme and across the packed car park to where Adams was sitting smoking on a picnic bench with a charming view of the traffic snarled up at the Serpentine Green roundabout.

He was full of himself now. Bullish with the success of driving a weak man into revealing a lie he had been holding close to himself for twenty years. And doing it in a matter of minutes, with no evidence, just the force of his personality and a complete lack of proper process.

That none of this would stand up in a court of law didn't seem to faze him.

Zigic sat down opposite him, pushed his iced coffee across the table.

'Cheers, mate.' Adams flipped open the box of doughnuts. 'Where's my Nutty Chocolatta?'

'I refuse to say such stupid words to another adult,' Zigic told him, picking out a plain glazed ring. 'You want to go in and get one, be my guest.'

'God, you can be po-faced. We've just found the case we're going to take down Walton with, and you're begrudging me my choice of doughnut. How has Mel put up with you all these years?'

'She doesn't make infantile pastry orders,' Zigic said firmly. 'And we're still a long way from this being a case.'

'You will at least admit that Cooper didn't do it?'

'You want to take that thought to its logical end?' Zigic asked. 'Cooper didn't do it but he confessed anyway because someone exerted pressure on him. And the only person in a position to exert that kind of pressure on him was the officer who led the investigation and who carried out every single interview with him: Riggott.'

Adams sipped his coffee, trying to look unconcerned. But Zigic would bet that behind his sunglasses were the eyes of a very nervous man.

Just like there were behind his.

'Riggott isn't the only option,' Adams said. 'Who's to say Walton didn't bully him into it?'

'Is that why you kept banging on about him?'

Adams gave a shrug that looked more like a shudder. 'Makes sense.'

'No, if we're going to pursue this you can't keep doing that,' Zigic said, leaning across the table, aware of the family away to their right. 'Stop trying to find a way of wrecking Cooper's conviction without fucking over Riggott.'

'I just want to be certain before we do that.'

Adams was getting more uncomfortable by the second. Seeing his career advancement stalling, Zigic thought. All the backstabbing and arse kissing he'd put in over the years, the late-night drinking sessions with Riggott, listening to his stories and performatively absorbing his wisdom, all of that time and effort suddenly wasted if it turned out Riggott had coerced someone into a false confession.

Zigic dipped his doughnut into his coffee and waited for Adams to elaborate. Or finish mourning his lost future as DCS.

'We need something concrete,' Adams said slowly. 'If we're going to take that case apart, we need more than Cooper whispering about not doing it.'

'And?'

'There was a saliva sample lifted from Tessa's cardigan,' Adams said. 'It wasn't a match for Cooper, so they took the view that it wasn't relevant, and could have happened days before she was killed.'

'I'm already aware of that.' Zigic felt a chill across the back of his neck at the thought of what came next, if he let it. At how dangerous a proposition they were edging towards. 'But we can't run the test without cause and we can't get cause without running the test.'

'I mean, we can,' Adams said, swirling the ice around in his coffee, looking into that rather than at Zigic. 'Running a DNA test is no big ask. We'll just use a private lab. Get verification – or not – then see where we stand when we have full information.'

'And how do you intend to get hold of the sample?' he asked.

Adams gave him a grim smile. 'Me? You suddenly not a part of all this, Ziggy?'

'Do you have an idea or not?'

'I'll get it,' he said, a little of the bullishness returning. 'Wouldn't want you doing anything that made you uncomfortable. Christ, if you can't even order a doughnut with a funny name –'

'You have absolutely no integrity,' Zigic said, before he could stop himself, sick of how lightly Adams was dealing with this slow-moving catastrophe they were engineering for themselves.

'Integrity? Really? Does that seem like something important right now?' Adams demanded. 'Is integrity going to keep Walton out of Mel's face? No, it isn't. Integrity can go fuck itself.'

'This could get us both sacked.'

'Sacked?' Adams gave a bitter laugh. 'It could get us locked up.'

'And you're happy to risk that?'

'If you have a better plan I'd love to hear it.'

Miserably, Zigic took another doughnut from the box and tore it into pieces, dipping each into his coffee in turn, eating them without pleasure, the pastry sticking to the roof of his mouth, feeling each time he swallowed like he was going to choke.

He didn't have a better plan.

His only plan was to speak to Riggott before things went too far.

But in his gut, he knew that point had been passed the second they walked into Neal Cooper's home. The only way was onwards; find the evidence – however they came by it – then take it to Riggott. Present him with a fait accompli and hope the part of him that wanted justice for Tessa Darby would outweigh the part that wanted a smooth run through his last year before retirement.

Nobody wanted to go out like this, though. To leave under a cloud of failure, or worse, suspicion.

How many more reputational hits could their station take?

'If you want out you can go,' Adams said. 'It's not your fight anyway.'

The statement felt loaded. Zigic couldn't help but wonder why Ferreira hadn't said anything to him about Walton. All the silent car journeys the last couple of days, all the times she could have asked for his help or at least his advice.

Why didn't she trust him with this? After all the time they'd known each other.

Was it because she realised Walton was a problem you had to deal with by bending the rules to breaking point? That she didn't think he had the nerve or the sense of loyalty to do that? She knew Adams did though, trusted him to do whatever dirty work was necessary.

And she was right.

Assuming she knew what he was planning, Zigic thought.

'How much does Mel know about all this?'

'She doesn't,' Adams said firmly. 'And she's not going to.'

'If you think she likes being kept in the dark, then you don't know her very well.'

Adams cocked his head. 'Think I know her a bit better than you do, mate.'

'You don't think it might put her mind at ease knowing something's being done about Walton?'

'I dunno. Do you feel particularly zen right now?'

CHAPTER THIRTY-NINE

Ferreira didn't expect Patrick Sutherland to actually answer his phone, was poised to leave a message when his voice cut in with the kind of wary hello a call from an unknown number merited.

'Dr Sutherland, this is DS Ferreira, we spoke a couple of days ago.'

'Of course, yes. I remember,' he said, sounding vaguely harassed, but she supposed there were very few moments of respite in Long Fleet's medical bay. 'Is there something I can help with?'

'I was wondering if you could come into the station,' she said. 'There are some photographs I need you to look at. People who were hanging around Josh's house. We think they might be have been targeting other staff members.'

'Is this the couple you showed me before?' he asked.

'No, other people,' Ferreira said.

There were no other people, but she would find some images and pack a file thick with them, to distract him while she primed him for the real questions she wanted to ask. About Josh Ainsworth and the allegation against him and why exactly he'd kept so tight-lipped when they first questioned him.

Sutherland would cite the NDAs and contract she was sure.

But away from Long Fleet, under the jurisdiction of a higher law, she felt confident that she could bring Patrick Sutherland around.

'Is after my shift okay?' he asked. 'It'll be around seven. Or I could manage Saturday morning if that's easier for you. I don't want to keep you there late on my behalf.'

'I'm here until the day's done,' Ferreira told him. 'Seven's fine.'

'It's a date then.' He swore, apologised. 'I forgot who I was talking to there. Sorry. I'm going to hang up now and be embarrassed in private.'

He ended the call and Ferreira shook her head, smiling as she replaced the receiver. It never ceased to amaze her how flustered people got on the phone to a police officer. She'd lost count of the amount of people who had accidentally ended a call with 'love you, bye'.

Her mobile rang – Parr.

'Another one with a rock-solid alibi,' he said.

'Which one?' Ferreira asked, getting up and going over to the board where the names of three of the guards she'd despatched them to chase up were already crossed out.

One dead, one emigrated to New Zealand and a third mid-Caribbean cruise.

'His ex-wife was still at the address we have,' Parr told her. 'I couldn't get away from the woman. She's not bloody happy, not one bit.'

'Where is he?'

'Doing three years inside for beating up some old boy after a Luton Town match. *That's* when she decided to divorce him.'

'Not when he got sacked from Long Fleet?'

Ferreira struck through his name.

'No, that was all lies according to the ex.'

'Loyal to the last.'

'He was always a perfect gentleman apparently,' Parr said, voice deadpan. 'Anything more from the others?'

'Not yet.'

He hung up just as the email from James Hammond hit her inbox. Quickly she read through the scant details he'd sent over about the woman who had accused Joshua Ainsworth of attempted rape.

Hammond apologised for the limited information he could give her, blaming data protection rules. Said he hoped it was enough to find her. Ferreira imagined he meant the precise opposite, was giving them the minimum he could so as to look like he was helping the police but not actually assisting.

She opened the attachment to find the barest of bare minimums.

Nadia Afua Baidoo's last known address and that of the hostel they had delivered her to on her release. The dates of her stay at Long Fleet but nothing about the time she was there.

Nothing about her accusation against Joshua Ainsworth.

Ferreira called Hammond's office.

'Sorry, Mr Hammond is in meetings all afternoon and absolutely cannot be disturbed,' the woman on the other end said. She didn't ask for a name or offer to take a message, just put the phone down.

Acting on Hammond's orders, Ferreira guessed. He was smart enough to know his email would warrant an immediate follow-up.

They'd get nothing more from him.

She printed the photo of Nadia Afua Baidoo and stuck it up in the persons-of-interest column, feeling a slight twinge as she did it, but the woman had a motive, and the sympathy Ferreira felt for her didn't change that.

The photograph would have been taken when she was processed into Long Fleet, showed her stunned and fearful. She was nineteen but the shock had rendered her even younger-looking, clear-skinned and big-eyed, a ripple around her chin that suggested she'd been on the verge of tears.

Ferreira wondered if that was why Joshua Ainsworth had targeted her, the vulnerability radiating from her.

Nadia Afua Baidoo had been released from Long Fleet on June 16th, 2018 and spent her first night of freedom, after a full year locked up, at a hostel on Lincoln Road that was run by an inter-denominational charity and staffed largely by volunteers.

After that, nothing.

Ferreira ran all of the usual checks, finding no sign of recent activity on Baidoo's passport. No criminal record except for the immigration offence for which she'd been sent to Long Fleet. Caught overstaying in a raid on the restaurant in Cambridge where she'd been working. Ferreira remembered the raid. It has caused a minor stir in the press when it emerged that the owners had cooperated with the investigation in order to avoid the fines they should have been hit with, had called in all the affected staff on one shift to make it easier to round them up and ship them off.

She wondered why Hammond hadn't given them any information about the reasons why she was ultimately given leave to remain.

Overstayers weren't usually so lucky.

The hostel should be the next move, she thought, eyeing Zigic's empty office. Obviously the 'family stuff' that wouldn't take long had been more complicated than he anticipated but after two hours' absence she thought he might at least have texted her.

She went to the board and added a mark on the timeline of Joshua Ainsworth's murder to show the point where Nadia was released from Long Fleet.

Seven weeks between her freedom being granted and his murder.

Two weeks before Nadia was released, Ainsworth resigned.

Was she reading too much into it?

She knew how infrequently the victims of violence sought revenge.

Revenge was a fantasy, a coping mechanism, something people ran through in their heads to exorcise the demons of their trauma, a little of the pain fading away with each new method of torture and despatch.

Almost nobody carried it through into reality because mostly when you were confronted with the person who hurt you, the remembered terror renewed itself, and your body, which had been so sure and strong in those fantasies, started to shake and go numb, or else to freeze you to the spot. It would take an almost superhuman feat of will to overcome the muscle memory of being victimised, force yourself to move forwards and strike first when every atom in you cried 'run'.

Ferreira looked down and saw that her hands were in fists.

Her own body going back to the parking garage under her building, back into the all-encompassing burn and thrum of Lee Walton's personal space.

Was that how Nadia had felt when she saw Ainsworth?

Could she really have got past that lamp-stunned rabbit feeling and shoved him onto a table hard enough to break it? Then picked up one of the smashed legs and methodically struck his temple again and again until she exposed grey matter?

Maybe she was that kind of woman.

Maybe Long Fleet had hardened her.

Ferreira turned to Murray, sitting typing up a report, stabbing at the keyboard like it had offended her.

'Hey, Col, do you fancy a drive?'

CHAPTER FORTY

Haven House was at the northern end of Lincoln Road, beyond the rows of grand old houses carved up into bedsits, the beauty parlours and solicitors specialising in immigration law, the employment agencies and language schools, the B & Bs and hostels that seemed to spring up weekly and change their names once a year. Portuguese cafes and Polish delis, Turkish restaurants and endless takeaway places. Different ones to when Ferreira had lived there but in the same buildings with the same cramped flats above them.

It was always a disconcerting sensation, returning there, to the place she'd spent her teens and much of her twenties, seeing how everything and nothing had changed.

She slowed as she passed the white stucco front of her parents' pub, saw that the car park wasn't as busy as it should have been, fewer smokers outside too. Her mother's hand was evident in a chalkboard sign offering a full English breakfast and a beer for £4.95. There was no way they could do it for that price, Ferreira thought. Things must be getting desperate.

Why hadn't they said something, she wondered angrily. Asked for her help.

With a twinge of guilt she realised she hadn't been to visit them for weeks. Months maybe, if she was honest with herself. Made plans that got blown by work or she used work as excuse to blow them because she had other things she'd rather do with her scant free time. She could blame Billy but knew she'd only been lying to herself. He'd been dropping subtle hints about meeting them for a while now, long enough that she knew he'd probably go in there and introduce himself if she didn't arrange something soon.

The thought of it sent a ripple of unease across her shoulders.

'Alright, girl?' Murray asked.

'I'm good.'

She pulled up in front of Haven House, a double-fronted Edwardian villa with large bay windows edged in stone and a steep-pitched roof. It had an austere quality from the road despite the well-stuffed flower beds and the pillar-box-red front door, which had been recently reglossed. It wasn't until they were on the front step ringing for entry that Ferreira noticed the ghost of a swastika showing faintly through the paintwork.

They'd had trouble, she knew, more in the last twelve months than the previous ten years. Dog shit pushed through the letter box and windows smashed, spurious complaints anonymously called in about the place being used by sex workers and drug dealers, anything to cause them inconvenience. Helping refugees and asylum seekers drew as much hatred as it did admiration. Hence the new security measures.

'Sergeant Ferreira for Mr Daya,' she said to the intercom.

The door buzzed and they went into the Minton-tiled hallway where children's drawings had been framed on one wall. Boxes of food donated by local businesses sat underneath them, waiting to be taken into the kitchen where something aromatic was cooking, the scents of ginger and garlic filling the air.

Overhead a vacuum cleaner was running back and forth at speed, poppy music playing above it and somebody singing along.

Ferreira tried to imagine how it would feel to come here straight from Long Fleet, wondered if Nadia Baidoo had felt safe or if she kept expecting to be taken away again. Freedom became harder to believe in once you'd lost it. All the positive energy and soothing paint colours in the world couldn't rebuild innocence.

Adil Daya emerged from his office.

'Sergeant Ferreira.' He shook her hand warmly and turned to Murray.

'Colleen,' she said. 'Sergeant. Murray.'

She was flustered but he was used to it, Ferreira thought.

Adil Daya was a tall, lithe man, in his late fifties now, but he looked much the same as he had when Ferreira was a kid, still handsome and with a full head of wavy grey hair. She'd been friends with his son at school, the pair of them bonding over their strict parents and an unfashionable love of *Star Trek Deep Space Nine*.

He ushered them into his office, a small, windowless room painted brilliant white, with innocuous art on the walls and a series of boards covered in targets and lists. On his cluttered desk a stubby vase held a flower arrangement culled from the front garden, the marigolds fragrant in the confined space.

'How's Mo getting on in London?' Ferreira asked, as she sat down.

'Very well,' Mr Daya said. 'He's just had another baby. Three now. He wants to stop but his wife loves being pregnant. She'll fill the entire house if he lets her.'

'That's great, I'm so happy for him,' Ferreira said.

'I will tell him you asked after him.' Daya lowered himself into his seat. 'And you are well?'

'Never better,' Ferreira told him, beginning to feel vaguely absurd, having this catch-up, but sometimes you had to do the family chat first.

'But you have a problem?' he asked, tone shifting into the professional.

'We're looking for one of your former residents,' Ferreira told him. 'Nadia Afua Baidoo. We understand she was here briefly but we can't find her and we need to speak to her as a matter of urgency.'

'Is she in trouble?'

'No, we're just concerned for her safety right now,' Ferreira said.

'This doesn't surprise me,' Daya said, clasping his hands on his stomach. 'We hoped she would stay with us while she found her feet. To go from being locked up like that ... it's never an easy transition. Especially for such a young girl.'

'How long did she stay with you?'

'Only for one week. She was in a state of shock, I think. They so often are. It takes some time to acclimatise to freedom. And once that process has begun there is the larger issue of where to go and what to do with your life.' He shook his head. 'Sadly, there are very limited options and it is a great challenge to rebuild a life that has been ... shattered how Nadia's life was. It can be overwhelming to try and do that alone.'

'Did she speak to you about her time in Long Fleet?'

His eyes darkened. 'That place. We have many women come from there and always it is the same. The depression and the anger. For the first two days Nadia stayed in bed. She wouldn't eat, she hardly spoke.' He put one hand up. 'Please understand, she was a lovely young woman. Polite and considerate but the sadness was so deeply buried in her she seemed only half alive.'

Ferreira thought about the alleged attack by Josh Ainsworth and how it would only be natural that she was struggling when she was released.

'Surely she'd have been relieved to be out?' Murray asked.

'It is not that simple,' Daya told her regretfully, but said no more, as if he didn't have the words to explain.

'Do you know why she was given leave to remain?'

'No, she didn't want to talk about her circumstances, which is understandable and not uncommon.' He frowned, forehead crinkling. 'She was quite concerned about being taken in again. I remember she asked me whether her leave to remain could be revoked and under what conditions. I couldn't help without knowing more details but she didn't know the details herself.'

'Isn't that rather unusual?' Murray asked. 'People who stay out of trouble are usually left alone.'

'Regrettably, that is not always the case,' Daya said. 'And it is quite common to be confused about the law. The powers that be aren't always at pains to explain themselves, and often the ladies are so relieved to find they will be released that they don't always take on what they are being told.'

Ferreira could understand that, your mind blotting out everything apart from the news that you were free.

'What about her solicitor?' Murray asked. 'They must know the details.'

Daya nodded. 'They would, but I'm afraid I don't know who her solicitor is. As I said, she was not very forthcoming. I hoped she would tell us more as she became more comfortable and more confident. Helping the ladies rebuild trust in people is one of the main challenges we face here.'

Beyond his office door the hallway filled with the sound of women's voices, speaking a language Ferreira didn't recognise, a child with them singing in a wonky falsetto, a song from an advert.

'How did Nadia come to leave here?' she asked. 'She must have had somewhere to go.'

'She told me she wanted to go back to Cambridge,' Daya said, the thought of it still clearly troubling him. 'I'd asked her about her family there and she told me she had nobody, so it seemed strange that she would want to return but I supposed the familiar place might be good for her. And to put some distance between herself and Long Fleet.'

'Did she have money?' Ferreira asked. 'A phone?'

'We gave her some money for a bus ticket. And clothes – she arrived here with nothing.'

'So, she didn't have a phone?'

'We provided a phone for her – a local phone shop donates the out-of-date models and we put a pay-as-you-go SIM card in them,' he explained. 'Nadia was reluctant to take it because she said she had nobody to contact.'

Ferreira felt a stab of sympathy, trying to imagine being so alone in the world.

'Do you have a number for the phone?' she asked.

'I will find it.' Daya took a ledger from his desk and started flipping through the pages.

'Did Nadia mention friends she might go to stay with?' Murray asked, a hint of concern in her voice now. 'A boyfriend, perhaps?'

'No, she was very insular,' he said, hand hovering over the book. 'Although I did see her with a man a couple of days before she left.'

'Did he come here?' Ferreira asked.

'No, I saw them at the cafe across the road. I remember being happy that Nadia had gone out, even if it was only to have a coffee. I thought it was a positive sign.'

'Do you think she knew him?'

'I think so, yes. I watched them for a moment, because of course we have a problem with grooming gangs targeting our ladies, and I was concerned that he might be one of those men. But Nadia appeared to know him. And later, when she came back I asked her about him and she said he was a friend she'd run into.'

'Didn't that seem strange to you?' Murray asked. 'She said she had nobody but then this guy just happens to run into her?'

'Nadia seemed relieved,' he said, thoughtfully. 'Yes, that is what I remember. She seemed somewhat happier after meeting him and so I thought it could only be a good thing.'

Ferreira showed him a photograph of Josh Ainsworth. 'Is this him?'

'I didn't see his face,' Daya said. 'He had brown hair but I cannot say any more than that.' He turned another page in the book. 'Ah, here we are.'

He read out the number for Nadia's phone and Ferreira noted it down, while Murray typed it into her own mobile and dialled it.

She waited.

'Switched off,' Murray said irritably.

'This is very worrying.' Daya leaned forward, placed his palms flat on the table. 'She was in a highly vulnerable state when she left, but we are not a prison and I couldn't force her to stay here, as much as I think this was the best place for her.' He gave Ferreira a searching look. 'I think there is something you're not telling me, Melinda.'

She hesitated a beat too long, feeling caught out under his gaze, a teenager again visiting the Daya house and trying to remain on her best behaviour, be respectful the way Mo had been with her parents.

'Is this because of the doctor from Long Fleet who was killed?' he asked.

'We wanted to speak to Nadia for some background,' Ferreira said. 'But we're quite concerned for her well-being right now.'

A pained expression clenched his face. 'We should have tried harder to keep her here.'

'There was nothing you could have done,' Ferreira assured him. 'Nadia's a grown woman.'

'She's only a *girl*,' he said desperately. 'She's a vulnerable girl and we let her go out into the world with a few pounds and a change of clothes. We failed her.'

Ferreira tried to persuade him that he'd done the right thing but he was becoming smaller and older as he sat there. She wished they hadn't come here and unsettled this good man, but murder investigations created all kinds of emotional collateral damage. Often in the places you least expected. Just another one of the job's burdens.

He saw them to the door and Ferreira promised she would be in touch when she knew anything more, would tell him when they found her. Hoped it was a promise she could keep, but as she got into the car and pulled away, the uncomfortable sensation that had been growing in her stomach only hardened and settled in.

She had a terrible feeling they weren't going to find Nadia Baidoo.

CHAPTER FORTY-ONE

'This doesn't feel right,' Zigic said, as they crossed the gravelled car park into the garden centre, passing people coming out carrying net bags of bulbs and straggly perennials with sale stickers on. 'We shouldn't be approaching her at work.'

'It's not my first choice, but we're on a clock here, Ziggy.' Adams dropped back to let an elderly woman in a wheelchair through, her daughter thanking him. 'We'll be delicate, okay? You take the lead.'

A young guy in a green Aertex and an assistant manager's tag pointed them to Tessa Darby's mother, working in a distant corner among the piles of terracotta planters and lengths of willow fencing. She was sweeping the brick pathway with a stiff brush, gathering up the mess of a broken pot, the big pieces already in a wheelbarrow, just shards of blue-glazed ceramic and powder remaining.

Wendy Darby looked like her daughter, the woman she would have grown up into if it wasn't for Neal Cooper.

Or Lee Walton.

Zigic still wasn't entirely sure. The more the day wore on the more he felt he was being pulled along by Adams's desperate energy and his desire to make this about Walton rather than chasing actual facts. If this was an open case, if he had to justify his actions at the end of each shift, would he be here?

'Excuse me, Mrs Darby?'

She stopped brushing mid-stroke, her back stiffening, and turned around slowly. Alerted by the tone of his voice, Zigic thought, the combination of apology and insistence you could never fully shake off once you'd adopted it. She looked scared underneath the weariness and sadness.

'How can I help you today?' she said, looking between them, hoping that she was wrong.

But then Zigic made the introductions and her fingers tightened around the broom handle, and he wondered if this was how she'd found out about Tessa. Two strange men approaching her out of nowhere with the worst news a parent could hear.

'I'm very sorry to disturb you at work,' Zigic said.

'What's this about?'

'I wondered if we could talk to you about Tessa.'

She closed her eyes for a moment. 'What else is there to say?'

There was no delicate way to do this, despite what Adams had said, and now he saw why his senior officer stepped back and handed over the lead. This wasn't like going into Neal Cooper's house and rattling him. There were consequences for Mrs Darby that were going to hurt and that pain would be on him.

But she would want the right man to be punished, Zigic thought, and forced himself to press on.

'Do you remember one of Tessa's friends, Lee Walton?'

A flicker of panic passed over her face and he realised he didn't have to explain. That she was connecting the dots by herself. Maybe she had already wondered about him.

'They weren't friends exactly,' she said. 'I'm friends with his mum – me and Jackie have known each other for years. Tess had known him since she was little.' Her hands twisted around the broom handle. 'Why are you asking me about him? What's he got to do with anything?'

'He was released from prison recently,' Zigic said.

'Jackie told me all about it,' Mrs Darby said, a caustic edge coming into her voice. 'She always said he wasn't guilty.'

'And did you agree with her?' Adams asked.

'All mothers want to see the best in their sons.' Mrs Darby shook her head. 'But I followed the news. That many women don't just lie.'

'It was a lot more women than the ones he was charged over,' Adams said.

Zigic moved slightly, putting himself between them, pieces of broken pot crunching under his feet. But the damage was done, as it was always going to be.

Mrs Darby knew where they were going. Twenty years after her daughter's murder, eight after the man convicted of it was released from prison, why would anyone be asking about the case now?

'Neal Cooper killed my girl,' she said fiercely. 'He confessed.'

'We have reason to believe his confession may have been made under duress,' Adams said. 'We're carrying out a case review prompted by the discovery of new information that might have a bearing on how the original investigation was conducted.'

Zigic felt his pulse thudding in his neck, wanted to round on Adams and tell him to go, take his lies and hunches and complete lack of tact, and leave this to him.

A soft, keening noise came out of Mrs Darby and she let the broom drop, the sound like a gunshot in the walled confines of the garden centre.

'You've got no right to do this,' she said, her voice clogged, hand going to her throat. 'Cooper confessed. He killed my Tess. He was obsessed with her. Why do you want to make out he's innocent? Isn't it bad enough he only served twelve years? For my daughter's *life*. He's out and about, living it up, doing whatever the hell he wants. And my little girl is *dead*. Why are you defending him?'

Zigic put his hands out, wanting to calm her but seeing it was impossible.

'We just want to make sure the right man is punished, Mrs Darby.'

'No, you think I'm an idiot,' she snapped, darting towards him. 'You lot messed up and now Lee's out and you want to put him back inside. God knows, he deserves to be banged up and never see the light of day, but I will not let you use my little girl to do that.'

'You really think there's no chance he was responsible?' Adams asked. 'Knowing what you know about him now – what we all know he's capable of – don't you want us to at least investigate the possibility?' She looked at him, eyes brimming. 'Maybe we can save another mother from going through what you're suffering.'

Mrs Darby wiped her eyes on the back of her wrist.

'All we're asking is that you think about this for us,' Zigic said. 'If there's anything you can tell us about Walton, anything you didn't mention to the original investigation, it could make all the difference.'

He held out a card to her but she just stared at it.

'Neal Cooper murdered Tessa,' she said firmly. 'He confessed and I believe him. You weren't there. You don't know what kind of boy he was.' She glared at Adams. 'I don't even know who you are. If you come near me again, I'll be making a formal complaint of harassment against you.'

Wendy Darby stooped to pick up her broom and walked away from them.

Zigic watched her go, seeing a woman moving at speed because she didn't know how long she had before she was going to break down completely. And he thought of how quickly they had upended her life, shredded whatever tenuous acceptance she'd come to, ripping the old wounds open again.

He trudged back to his car, relieved that Adams had finally worked out how to keep his mouth shut for a couple of minutes. Zigic wanted to blame him for what had happened but they'd both done it, decided, without openly discussing it, that the ends justified the means.

Chapter Forty-Two

The satnav directed Ferreira through central Cambridge and down a series of residential streets until she entered a 1970s housing estate of neat detached properties, all two windows wide and standing a car's depth back from the path. Their driveways were mostly empty at this time of the afternoon, but somebody was home at the last known address they had for Nadia Afua Baidoo.

A fifty-something woman with a lot of grey-threaded black hair piled on top of her head answered the door. She wore an oversized T-shirt with a sequinned French slogan and shorts she'd cut down from a pair of jeans.

She eyed them suspiciously and didn't relax at the sight of their warrant cards as Ferreira made the introductions. She seemed reluctant to even give her name.

'We're looking for Nadia Baidoo,' Ferreira said. 'Does she live here?'

'I should think you people have a better idea than me where she is.'

'Please, Mrs Loewe, Nadia isn't in any trouble. We just need to speak to her.'

'About a crime?'

'She isn't a suspect,' Ferreira reassured her. 'Just a potential witness. She was released from an immigration removal centre a few weeks ago and nobody seems to know where she is now. As you can imagine, she's in a vulnerable position and we'd like to be sure that she's okay.'

Deborah Loewe put a shrewd eye on her. 'Well, which is it? You want to question her or you're concerned about her safety?'

'The two things are linked,' Ferreira said, seeing that the white lie had pricked Loewe. 'It's in relation to a murder investigation. Do you think we could come in, please?'

The woman directed Ferreira and Murray through the house to a boiling-hot kitchen overlooking a back garden strung with three lines of washing, sheets limp where they hung. The sliding doors were open but the breeze was so light it barely stirred the paperwork scattered across the small glass table – a series of sketches which looked like logo designs. There was a strong smell of weed but Loewe made no attempt to hide the ashtray it was coming from or the grinder that had prepared it.

They sat down at the table.

'When did you last see Nadia?' Ferreira asked.

'I haven't seen her since last summer,' she said. 'June time. She went out to work as usual in the morning, but she didn't come back. I started to get worried and called the restaurant. They were very cagey about it, insisted they couldn't tell me anything because I wasn't Nadia's family. So I went down there and made a bit of fuss.' She smiled at the memory of it, reaching for a pack of cigarettes. 'Finally, the manager admitted that they'd had an immigration raid and Nadia had been taken away.' She unpeeled the wrapper. 'But she's been released, obviously. Which rather begs the question of why she was taken in in the first place.'

There was an accusatory note in her voice and Ferreira felt the sting of it, hating that it was being directed at her rather than the people responsible.

'Nadia was given leave to remain in the country,' she explained. 'I'm afraid I can't say any more than that. She was released to a hostel in Peterborough but she only stayed a few days before telling them she was coming back to Cambridge. We were hoping she might have come here. Does she have any family she might have gone to?'

Loewe shook her head. 'It was just Nadia and her mother. But her mum died a couple of years ago. The rest of Nadia's family are back in Ghana.'

They knew she hadn't gone back there, no activity on her passport.

'Does she have any family over here?' Murray asked.

'From what I know of Nadia's family situation, I doubt very much that she'd make contact with any of them.' Loewe finally lit her cigarette. 'You do know why Nadia and her mum came to England?'

Ferreira shook her head.

'Nadia's mum – Lola – was gay. Which is not a good thing to be in Ghana. Especially when you're married to an abusive piece of shit.'

'She was given asylum because he was violent?'

'Violent hardly covers it,' Loewe said bitterly. 'One day he came home from work early and found Lola with her girlfriend. Not in bed, not really doing *anything*. They were just together in her kitchen and he put two and two together and dragged Lola out into the street and beat her into a coma.'

Ferreira swore. Murray shook her head angrily.

'As soon as she'd recovered well enough to walk, Lola grabbed Nadia and got on a plane. Luckily she'd been tucking some money away or she'd have been stuck there with him, and God alone knows what would have happened then.' She took a deep drag on her cigarette. 'Lola was given asylum on the grounds that her life would be in jeopardy if she returned. Nadia was here as a dependant.'

'But then she turned eighteen,' Ferreira said, seeing it all click together. 'And she wasn't a dependant any more so they were going to send her back.'

'That's what I presumed. Nadia wasn't facing the same danger as Lola was so there was no reason to let her stay here.' Loewe's mouth twisted in disgust. 'Except for the fact that she'd spent most of her life here and she was a good student and a hard worker. And that she'd been recently bereaved. None of that counted for anything.'

'Maybe that's why they let her stay,' Murray suggested, more to Ferreira than to Loewe.

'What happened to Lola?' Ferreira asked.

'Cancer,' she spat. 'She was dead within six weeks of them finding it.'

'That must have been hard on Nadia,' Murray said sympathetically.

Loewe sighed heavily. 'It pretty much obliterated her. Coming out of nowhere like that and then progressing so fast. She didn't have any time to adjust and she was trying so hard to stay strong and upbeat for Lola that when ... the end came, it was like there was nothing left of Nadia.'

'They were close then?'

'They were everything to each other,' Loewe said sadly. 'Nadia kept it together long enough to get through the funeral and then she collapsed. We got home and she crawled into bed and she didn't get up for months. Barely ate, I had to beg her to drink so she wouldn't dehydrate. She didn't speak, didn't bathe. I honestly thought she was willing herself to die.'

'Did you take her to see someone about it?' Ferreira asked. 'It sounds like she was dangerously depressed.'

'It wasn't depression, it was grief,' Loewe said fiercely. 'You can't medicate grief, you can't pray it away. You either survive it or you don't.'

'So you didn't get her any help?' Murray asked, doing nothing to hide her disapproval.

'Of course I got her help,' Loewe snapped. 'I had the doctor in to her, I even called her bloody priest, fat lot of good he did. She wouldn't speak to either of them. Just rolled over towards the wall and ignored them.'

'How long did this go on for?'

'Three months or so,' Loewe said. 'One morning I got up and found her in here eating a bowl of cereal. She wasn't right, though. Or better. Not really. She was just up and moving about and she could answer a question with a word or two.' Loewe scrubbed out her cigarette and reached for a half-smoked joint in the ashtray before she thought better of it. 'She'd got up because she had exams coming and she thought that if she missed them, she'd be wasting all the effort Lola put into her education. She'd missed so much school that when she got her results they were a lot weaker than she was expecting. That set her back a bit. But she found a job and she was going to retake her A-levels the next year.' Loewe smiled absently. 'I was so proud of how she started pulling it together again.'

'But then she was arrested?' Ferreira asked.

Loewe nodded.

Ferreira tried to imagine how it must have felt to Nadia, fighting slowly through her obliterating grief, working to do her mother's memory proud, be the girl she'd raised. Only to find herself spirited away to Long Fleet. Locked up, the last strands of stability she'd been clinging to snatched away.

How had she survived? Had she turned in on herself again?

Or had the grief numbed her so comprehensively that even Long Fleet's regime, its claustrophobia and threats, the assault by Joshua Ainsworth, couldn't get through?

Murray took over, breaking the silence that had fallen between them.

'How long had Nadia been living here?'

'She and Lola moved in five years ago,' Loewe said, her face clouding over. 'They'd been shunted around from pillar to post before that. Private rentals here are astronomical and not many landlords will take housing benefit. I don't usually, to be honest, but I liked Lola and I could see what a good mother she was.' She smiled, as if at the memory of them. 'Every child deserves a stable roof over their head and Lola worked hard to make sure she could provide that for Nadia. I tried to do right by Lola and look after Nadia when she passed.' She blinked quickly. 'I did my best.'

Another momentary silence and Ferreira could feel the pain radiating from the woman, something like shame too. She'd never mentioned visiting Nadia in Long Fleet or staying in contact with her, and Ferreira wondered if that guilt was biting now.

'Are there any friends we could contact?' Murray asked.

'They disappeared pretty fast when Nadia took to her bed,' Loewe said disapprovingly. 'Lives to get on with, exams and uni and gap years, all that stuff.'

'What about a boyfriend?'

'Not that I knew of. But Nadia was very … demure, I suppose. She wouldn't have brought anyone back here, I think. She wouldn't have thought it was proper.'

'What about her church?' Murray asked, picking up on the hint Ferreira was about to pursue. 'We'll need their details in case Nadia reached out to someone there.'

Loewe gave them the address, the name of the priest who she'd called to the house for Nadia.

Murray noted down the details.

'We're discussing her like she's dead,' Loewe muttered, looking away from them into the back garden. 'Do you really think she's in danger?'

'Anyone coming out of a facility is vulnerable,' Ferreira said, thinking of the gangs who preyed on young adults spat out by the care system and women released from prison into halfway houses. 'The fact is Nadia has been out for almost two months now and we have no idea where she is.'

'Maybe she went back to Ghana?'

'No, we have no record of her leaving the country.'

'Have you let her room out?' Murray asked.

Loewe nodded. 'I would have held it for her if I could, but ... it's been a year and my bank isn't quite as sentimental as I am.'

'Did you keep any of her things?'

'There wasn't much,' Loewe said. 'I boxed everything up and put it in the garage. You're welcome to have a look through it, if you think it'll help.'

She took them outside, heaving up the cranky metal door, and pointed them to the two modest cardboard boxes with Nadia's name written on them. On the shelves above and below were boxes from other former residents and Ferreira wondered why Loewe had kept them – if everyone had left under such unusual circumstances and if she was waiting for their returns too.

Murray started to go through the boxes as Ferreira stood with Loewe on the driveway. She asked about her other lodgers and how many she had in the house, finding that she let out two bedrooms and a bedsit in the converted loft and that none of her current tenants had been living here at the same time as Nadia.

'Do you have contact details for anyone who was?' Ferreira asked.

Loewe went to get her phone book, a slim item that seemed to belong to another century. But Ferreira was glad of it. Lately they'd started struggling with contact details, as people lost and changed their phones and didn't always back up their information.

She took down the names and numbers and email addresses of the two people who had shared the house with Nadia, hoping that one of them might have got to know her better than Deborah Loewe, maybe even well enough to be her first port of call when she left the hostel.

Nadia hadn't done that on a whim, she thought.

She had a solid destination in mind.

Murray came out of the garage.

'Nothing obvious, but maybe we should take it with us.' Loewe looked momentarily uncomfortable. 'We'll give you a receipt for it, ma'am. And if Nadia returns in the meantime, you can tell her we have her things.'

She nodded her reluctant agreement and Ferreira left Murray to deal with the paperwork while she checked her messages. Bloom reporting another potential suspect struck off the list – his alibi concrete. Nothing new from Weller or Parr yet and she hoped that meant they were both pursuing more promising leads.

Now that she knew more about Nadia Baidoo, she didn't want to see the young woman as a suspect, was praying a more likely one would emerge from the list of Long Fleet's sacked security guards.

She looked back at the house, wondering why Nadia had said she was coming back here when she had no intention of doing so.

Adil Daya had given her money for a bus to Cambridge but he didn't watch her get on it. She could have gone anywhere, Ferreira realised with a sinking feeling.

She dialled the number he'd given them for Nadia, held her breath until the tone sounded and an automated voice apologised, but the caller could not be reached.

CHAPTER FORTY-THREE

There was no sign of Ferreira when Zigic got back into the station. Murray gone too, along with the rest of the team, and he felt a moment of dislocation, checked his watch to be sure that the shift hadn't ended. Twenty past two and the only reason he could see for the empty desks was a list of names freshly printed on Joshua Ainsworth's board.

Sure enough he found the same list in his emails. The staff members fired from Long Fleet after the purge. A few were crossed out already and he assumed Ferreira had divvied them up and sent the others out to question them.

Maybe she was doing the same but he suspected it was the other name that was absorbing her attention.

Nadia Afua Baidoo – the woman Joshua Ainsworth had been accused of assaulting. Her photo was up on the board and sure enough when he checked Ferreira's computer, he found the message from James Hammond open on her screen. The details were thin but obviously enough to propel Ferreira into action and out of the station for a few hours.

She hadn't called to keep him updated but given how he'd spent the better part of his day, he wasn't surprised. She knew something was going on, would have noticed Adams's absence and realised they were together.

DC Keri Bloom came in as he returned to the board. 'I thought the others would be back by now,' she said.

'Nope, you're the first,' he said. 'Anything to report?'

'All of mine look fairly soundly alibi'd, sir.' She picked up the marker pen and struck through two more names, a man and woman. 'But everyone I spoke to told me the same thing.'

'That they were totally innocent?'

She pulled a face. 'They did say that, yes. But also that Jack Saunders took his dismissal very badly.'

Zigic remembered how ex-PC Saunders had acted when they spoke to him at the DIY store, the barely contained fury, the fierce insistence of innocence even as he openly admitted to multiple abuses.

'Apparently Saunders confronted Josh Ainsworth over the accusations,' Bloom said. 'Three of the people I spoke to live in Long Fleet and evidently they all use the local pub quite regularly – Ainsworth included. Saunders went there a few days after he was sacked and attacked Ainsworth. He didn't say anything, just went up to Ainsworth and punched him in the face.'

'He didn't mention that when we talked to him,' Zigic said.

'Maybe we should wait to have it corroborated by the others but I think it's true. They all took too much pleasure in telling me about it for it to be a lie. I got the feeling they saw it as just punishment for Ainsworth.'

Did it feel that way to Saunders though? he wondered. Or was it an unsatisfying revenge? The kind that only sharpened his focus and made him realise he would need to go further.

'Has anyone checked out Saunders's alibi yet?' Zigic asked.

'No, sir. Would you like me to make a start on it now?'

'If you would, Keri.'

'Of course.' She went to her desk, carefully positioned her linen jacket over the back of her seat and sat down to begin.

He heard Ferreira and Murray before he saw them, their raised voices coming up the stairwell, speaking over one another; Murray slower but persistent, Ferreira exasperated and angry. Their conversation came to an abrupt halt when they entered the office.

Each had a cardboard box in their arms, 'Nadia' written on the sides in swirling capitals.

'Did you find her?' he asked.

'No,' Murray said, putting the box down next to her desk. 'Her previous landlady gave us this lot.'

Ferreira dropped hers beside it and quickly filled him in on their day's work so far: Nadia Baidoo's brief stay at the hostel, her abrupt departure and the sad story of her life up to the moment she was arrested and taken to Long Fleet. He could see it had affected them both and when he looked again at Nadia's photograph stuck up on the board, he decided that what he thought was the usual and understandable shock in her eyes might actually have been a deeper emotion, a thorough and inescapable grief.

'We were just discussing whether she needs to be considered a suspect,' Murray said.

Ferreira glared at her. 'Or a potential victim.'

'Of who?' Zigic asked.

'She accused Joshua Ainsworth of attacking her. He lost his job.' Ferreira shrugged as if the theory was so solid she didn't need to back it up further.

'So, you're thinking revenge?'

'I am,' Murray nodded. 'By her on him.'

'No,' Ferreira said sharply. 'Because women who get attacked *never* go after their attackers. We know this.'

'I had a quick poke through the stuff she left at her last home,' Murray said, gesturing towards the cardboard boxes. 'Found two pairs of size nine shoes.' She looked pointedly at Ferreira. 'Which means we have a size match for the footprints forensics found at Ainsworth's house.'

'It's a really common shoe size,' Ferreira said.

'Not for a woman.'

Zigic opened one of the boxes, seeing carefully folded jeans and jumpers inside, a few paperbacks and scented candles in glass pots, a small make-up bag with a broken zip.

On the top was a single photograph in a glittery frame – Nadia Baidoo and an older woman, presumably her mother, sitting in a punt on the Cam. They were both smiling, faces pressed close together, holding flutes of champagne up to the camera. Just in shot behind Lola's shoulder was a pink balloon with 'Birthday Girl' printed on it.

It wasn't much to leave behind you, he thought. Two boxes. Not enough that you would feel you had to go back for it.

He sat down on the edge of the desk.

'For now, she's a person of interest,' he said. 'She can give us a perspective on Ainsworth that nobody else has been able to, so we need to find her.'

'Aren't you curious why she's disappeared off the face of the earth?' Ferreira asked. 'Nadia left the safety of Haven House, where they were trying really hard to help her, with nothing but a few quid and a phone she's got turned off.' She stood with her feet planted wide, a picture of defiance. 'She had no family here, no boyfriend. Her friends all abandoned her while she was grieving for her mother, so I doubt she's decided to reconnect with any of them. Even her church – where she was a regular – haven't heard from her.'

'I agree it's worrying,' Zigic said gently. 'But we both know there are lots of terrible ways for a young woman in Nadia's situation to fall between the cracks.' He watched her face harden. 'The more likely explanation for her disappearance, given everything we've been told, is that Nadia might have killed herself.'

Ferreira threw herself into her chair with a pained grunt.

'We discussed that in the car,' Murray told him.

'Mel, you need to call Missing Persons. Get in touch with Cambridge and see if they know anything about her.'

'She's not got anything on her record since she was released from Long Fleet,' Ferreira said. 'I already checked.'

'Which is why you need to get in touch with them directly and see if they know her as a rough sleeper or something like that.'

'A sex worker?' Ferreira asked. 'That's what you're thinking, isn't it?'

'Coming out of a facility,' he said. 'We know the options aren't good if she's going it alone.'

'That bloke Mr Daya mentioned seeing her with,' Murray said. 'He's the catalyst here. Nadia's withdrawn and quiet and then suddenly she's out having coffee with some guy. And *then* a couple of days later she's gone.' Murray shook her head brusquely. 'You tell me that doesn't sound like a procurer. He's seen her weakness and charmed her away from the only people who can help her get back on her feet.'

'Have we got a description?' Zigic asked.

'No. Mr Daya only saw him from the back.'

Zigic rubbed his cheeks, feeling the peaks and troughs of this conversation like so many pinpricks. He wasn't convinced Nadia Baidoo was a viable suspect, wasn't even entirely sure she'd be able to tell them anything that would lead them to Joshua Ainsworth's killer either.

He'd attacked her and been sacked and she'd been released.

Beyond those bare bones, what more was there to know?

Right now they needed to focus on the staff members Ainsworth had informed on. Follow up on the violence between him and Jack Saunders.

'There is more to this,' Ferreira said, in a low firm voice.

Murray looked thoughtful. 'Maybe she went off with someone she met in Long Fleet.'

'One of the guards, you mean?' Zigic asked, getting a soft snort of derision from Ferreira.

'I was thinking more like one of the other women,' Murray suggested. 'You know what prison friendships are like.'

'Not built to last.'

'But it takes them awhile to realise that.' Murray nodded towards the board. 'Other thing about prison relationships ... if you want revenge they're the best kind of help you can get.'

'They weren't in prison,' Ferreira said wearily. 'These aren't hardened criminals we're talking about, okay? She was a waitress who got arrested because her paperwork wasn't right. What makes you think a year in Long Fleet could turn her into Liam Neeson?'

'Mel, do you think your empathy might be getting in the way here?' Murray asked, her face set in an expression of concern that Zigic expected to be wiped off it imminently by Ferreira's response.

259

Instead Ferreira took a deep breath, sucked her bottom lip into her mouth.

'Okay. Maybe, yeah,' she admitted. 'But we have to keep in mind how massively unlikely it is that Nadia went from victim to murderer in a matter of weeks. We all know how rarely victims find the strength to stand up to their abusers, right? Getting to a place where they're capable of murder is a whole other level.'

'Unless she found someone to do it for her,' Zigic suggested.

Ferreira sneered. 'You old romantic.'

She knew, he thought.

She knew exactly what Adams had dragged him into. Knew and didn't approve.

'Let's wait to see if Missing Persons come back with anything,' he said, wanting to go into his office and close the door, just sit in silence with these racing thoughts for a few minutes. 'And it might be an idea to take this lot up to forensics.' He tapped one of the boxes of clothes. 'Get a DNA sample and see if it hits anything. Fingerprints. Whatever Kate can find.'

'I'll go,' Murray said, stacking the boxes and heading out.

Ferreira was watching him now, on her feet again, an expression like she was trying to burn her way through his eyeballs. She took a couple of slow and deliberate steps towards him.

'Did you make any progress?' she asked.

'What?'

'You were out all day, you must have got somewhere with it.'

The phone on his desk started to ring.

'I've got to get this, Mel.'

He went into his office, closed the door behind him. Through the partition window he could see her still looking as he went behind his desk and answered the phone.

'Don't tell her anything,' Adams said, on the other end.

Zigic swore at him.

'That's exactly what I am, yeah. But we're not involving anyone else in this mess. Like I told you, step away if you need to but you don't get to tag someone else in.'

CHAPTER FORTY-FOUR

The rest of the day shift were gone, the unlucky souls scheduled for Friday night in now and settled around the office as Ferreira waited for Patrick Sutherland to arrive. This was always a strange time, everyone waiting for something to kick off as the evening wore on, the sense of potential mayhem only increased by the hot weather and long days.

Most of her fellow officers were doing the same thing she was, catching up on paperwork, trying to clear their desks before a more urgent task dragged them away. Billy was still in his office. She'd told him to go home without her but he insisted he had a lot of catching up to do.

Earlier she'd overheard him on the phone to Sadie Ryan's mother, defeated-looking as the woman filled him in about the after-effects of her daughter's suicide attempt. The physical damage not as bad as her doctors feared but the psychological still emerging. Sadie was out of hospital now and they'd left Peterborough for her grandmother's place in Kent, couldn't face knowing they were in the same city as Lee Walton and his apparent legions of supporters who were harassing them via social media.

When she'd gone in to borrow his lighter, Billy was staring at the wall, every furious thought visible as it passed across his eyes.

Ferreira forced her attention back to the reports on the ex-Long Fleet staff that Parr, Weller and Bloom had turned in. They'd tracked down all of them bar one, who had taken a job as a long-distance lorry driver and was currently somewhere in Europe. All had alibis of varying strength, which would be picked at until hopefully one fell apart. A couple had minor offences on their records but nothing to suggest a capability for murder. Not that it always worked that way.

Several had mentioned Jack Saunders attacking Joshua Ainsworth and as she read through the reports, she began to realise that the group seemed to regard him as leader of some kind. Definitely the alpha male when they'd been working at Long Fleet, maybe because he'd been a copper doing the job they'd all dreamed of but couldn't achieve. It held a certain mystique for a particular kind of person, the sort who frequently ended up in security.

She'd checked his service record, found that a few minor complaints had been made against him by suspects but none upheld. The usual accusations of undue force that everyone collected whether they were deserved or not.

Saunders's alibi wasn't as secure as he'd made out when they spoke to him. Keri Bloom had talked to a few of the people he worked with, ones who were there at the bowling alley the night Ainsworth was murdered. Saunders was present but the party started to break up around nine when it moved to a nearby pub and nobody could say exactly what time he left.

If he'd lied about that and failed to mention punching Ainsworth in the face, she had to wonder what else he was hiding.

Reception called at ten past seven – Patrick Sutherland had arrived.

Ferreira picked up the file of random mugshots she'd selected and went down to fetch him.

He looked ill at ease, even though the reception area was empty. Or maybe it was just the usual end-of-week malaise that hit people as their last long shift finished. His dark brown hair was mussed, shirt crumpled at the elbows, and when he tried a smile on her, it barely reached his heavy-hanging eyes.

'Do you usually work such long hours?' he asked, as they entered the stairwell.

'When we've got a big case on, yes,' she told him.

'You can't get that many murders in Peterborough.'

'We get more than we'd like.' She opened the door to Interview Room 1 and showed him in ahead of her.

His tiredness abruptly gave way to a nervous energy that sent him around the perimeter of the room.

'Mr Hammond would kill me if he knew I was here,' Sutherland said with an uneasy smile. 'Or sack me and then sue me for breach of contract.'

'This is purely an informal thing,' Ferreira assured him, knowing that was the only way she could hope to get him to talk. 'Nothing you say here will get back to Hammond.'

She sat down and a moment later he took the hint and joined her, sliding into the seat opposite.

'So these are protestors you want me to look at?' he asked, nodding towards the file under her hands.

'We've been seeing some worrying discussion in private groups online about Josh's death, and now we need to identify any of the participants who might have been involved in the protest at the gates or hanging around near staff members' homes.' She slid the file over to him but didn't remove her hand. 'Do you live in Long Fleet village?'

'No, Deeping St James,' he said, with the subtle note of pride she was accustomed to hearing from people who lived in the historic almost-town just north of Peterborough. 'I know a lot of the staff like the village because it's convenient, but I need to get away at the end of my shift or I feel like I'm not really free of the place.'

'I know what you mean,' she said, drawing her hand away. 'There are some jobs where it's best if people can't follow you home.'

Walton popped into her head for a moment, the breadth of him and the crackle of bad energy he carried.

'Are you okay?' Sutherland asked.

'Yep, fine.' She brushed her hand back over her hair. 'Long week, not enough sleep.'

'Do your neighbours know what you do?' he asked.

'I've managed to pretty much avoid talking to any of them,' she said. 'How about yours?'

'God, no. They think I'm a GP in town.'

'You don't think they'd like you as much if they knew you were at Long Fleet?'

'I suspect a lot of them wouldn't approve of Long Fleet's business. We're a nice little liberal enclave after all. That's why I moved there.' He pointed at the file. 'Shall I shut up and get on with this? Let you start your weekend.'

'Whenever you're ready.'

He took his time over each photograph, giving them more consideration than she felt they needed. But people tended to in this situation, wanted to show they were taking it seriously, fulfilling their side of the social contract they had made with the police.

You either recognised a face or you didn't, she thought. It was a split-second thing and it couldn't be changed by extra exposure. In fact, she was sure the longer you looked the more likely you were to convince yourself you'd seen them before.

Which was part of the reason eyewitness reports were such bad evidence.

'How well do you know Jack Saunders?' Ferreira asked, as he was turning over an image.

His hand slowed. 'I can't talk about that, I'm sorry.'

'This is just between us, Patrick,' she said. 'No tapes, no statement. I'm just asking you to give me some background on Saunders. We've heard he assaulted Josh after he was sacked.'

'Yes, I heard that too,' Sutherland admitted. 'But I don't know anything about it.'

'Saunders is still maintaining that he was unfairly dismissed.'

Sutherland shook his head, turned another page, giving that photo less attention. 'Saunders can deny it all he likes. The evidence was there. He was caught on camera, for God's sake.'

His fingers curled away from the file and Ferreira saw the flicker of fear cross his face.

'It was you, wasn't it?' she asked.

He pressed his mouth into a firm line.

'You were the one who got that footage inside Long Fleet.'

'I don't know what you're talking about,' he said weakly, unable to meet her gaze. 'My understanding is that an anonymous whistle-blower did it.'

Ferreira settled back in her seat, letting the silence develop, watching him sit perfectly still, staring through the photograph in front of him. She could hear the quickness of his breaths, smell the stale coffee on each exhalation and the mint he'd tried to freshen them with.

'Look, as far as I'm concerned the person who got that footage out is a hero,' she said. 'I thought it might be Josh's doing but the woman who handled it told us he wasn't responsible.'

Sutherland risked a quick glance at her. 'Please, don't make me say it.'

'It's important I know, so I can disregard it as a factor in Josh's murder,' she told him. 'It goes no further than this room if it isn't a factor. You can just nod if that's easier.'

He closed his eyes, nodded shortly.

'Does Hammond know it was you?'

Another nod.

It wasn't vital intelligence for the investigation but she felt better for knowing. One small mystery cleared up.

'I'm surprised Hammond kept you on after that.'

'He was brought in to clean up the place,' he said. 'Letting me go would have been punishment for telling the truth. And he couldn't prove it. He just put two and two together. Hammond isn't stupid.'

Why did that sound like a warning? she wondered. Was it simply that Sutherland and the rest of the Long Fleet staff were so terrified of breaking their contracts that every time they considered the potential fallout this fear clutched at their throats?

'Do you think Saunders murdered Josh?' he asked.

'He's made accusations about Josh's behaviour inside the facility,' Ferreira told him. 'Accusations that Hammond had enough faith in that he told Josh to resign.'

Sutherland closed the file with a sigh. 'This is what you wanted to talk to me about.'

'No tapes,' Ferreira reminded him. 'No camera. You're not here and we're not talking.'

But he was getting to his feet. 'You don't understand what it's like at Long Fleet. If I talk to you and you take *anything* that I've said to Hammond or anyone else, it'll come back on me.'

'This is a murder investigation.' Ferreira stood, moved between him and the door. 'Do you really think the NDA you signed is more important than finding out who killed Josh?'

'We are subject to the Official Secrets Act,' Sutherland said helplessly. 'Even telling you that probably puts me in contravention of it.'

So that was where the fear came from. She was shocked but she realised this might be the last chance she got to speak to Patrick Sutherland, and she couldn't let herself get sidetracked.

'Is the allegation true?' she asked.

He turned away from her on the spot, fingers running through his hair. 'I *can't* talk to you. If Hammond found out I'd come here … I don't even want to think about it.'

'You were there, Patrick. Did you examine Nadia Baidoo?'

Sutherland rubbed the back of his neck, staring down at the floor, muttering to himself. 'I never should have come here. I wanted to help but I shouldn't have risked it. What was I thinking?'

'Someone must have verified her story,' Ferreira said, taking another quick step as he made for the door. 'It can't have been Josh. That just leaves you.'

He reached for the handle.

Ferreira got there first. 'Nadia's disappeared, Patrick.'

'I'm very sorry, but I can't help you.'

They were inches away from one another; she could see how powerless he felt, the regret making him look nauseated and weak.

'Did Josh attack Nadia?'

'I can't –' He closed his hand over hers and opened the door, darted out into the corridor.

Ferreira followed, matching his fast stride as he aimed for the stairwell.

'I know you're scared,' she said. 'But you've made the right choice before. You were so brave to go into Long Fleet with that hidden camera.'

He ran down the stairs. She stayed at his heel.

'This is no different to what you did then,' she said. 'I just need you to tell me the truth.'

He wrenched open the stairwell door and came to an immediate halt when he realised he couldn't get through the one into reception. He looked at Ferreira's pass.

'Please,' he said. 'Please, can you let me out now?'

'Hammond isn't sure whether Josh attacked Nadia,' she said.

Sutherland let out a low groan, pressed his hand against the door. 'Of course he's sure. He wouldn't have forced Josh to leave if he wasn't.'

Ferreira tapped her key card on the reader and the door opened.

Sutherland bolted out through reception but still she stayed with him, following him down the front steps that he took two at a time.

'Did Nadia talk to you?' she asked. 'Did she tell you anything that might help us find her?'

'I've already said *way* too much.' Sutherland fumbled his keys out of his pocket, dropped them and scooped them up quickly. 'You know what happened now.'

'We need to find Nadia.'

The locks popped on a nearby SUV and he veered towards it.

'I can't help you. Okay, you've had everything I know.' He got into the car but Ferreira grabbed the door before he could close it.

'Nadia could be in danger,' she said. 'Don't you care?'

'I'm sorry.' He hauled the door shut and pulled out of the space.

Ferreira watched him leave, walking back to the steps where Billy was standing smoking.

'It's really unpleasant watching your girlfriend chasing after a younger, more attractive man,' he said, holding out his cigarette to her.

She took a quick drag. 'He's terrified.'

'Of you?' Billy grinned. 'He should be.'

DAY FIVE

SATURDAY AUGUST 11TH

CHAPTER FORTY-FIVE

She woke from a dream she couldn't remember, her heart racing and the vague but fierce sensation of being chased driving her up from the pillow and out of the tangle of sheets, temporarily stricken by not knowing where she was.

Then she saw the heavy chrome lamp on the bedside table and the familiar ink-blue walls and the chair in the corner of Billy's bedroom where she'd thrown her clothes last night when they got home from dinner. She sat back down again, brushing her hair away from her face, looking down at her bare feet on the runner, waiting for her heartbeat to calm itself.

The smell of bacon wafted in from the kitchen, along with a song she recognised, an Afro-Cuban band she liked and Billy insisted was weird and dated, although this was the second time she'd caught him listening to the playlist she'd made on the tablet he kept on the kitchen windowsill. They argued about music a lot, his taste running old and predictable, seventies classics he was too young for and the modern imitators of it. He said her taste was pretentious, which only meant he'd stopped paying attention to what was new sometime around graduating.

So much about him tended towards the conventional: the flash suits and the flash car, the dark and heavy decor in his flat, which she still struggled to imagine him furnishing. There was something comic about the idea of him in John Lewis going through fabric swatches, poring over them as he tried to match the particular mahogany-brown leather of the sofa to a specific teal for the walls. How long had he agonised over that wool rug in the centre of the living room?

Or maybe one of his exes was responsible for the look of the place? Maybe before her some other woman had nested in this flat, picked out the towels she now dried off with and the sheets they fucked on.

The thought provoked a vague pique in her and she decided she didn't want to examine why.

Her mobile chimed as a text came in from Zigic.

He wanted to go and talk to Ruth Garner again, suggested that she might be more forthcoming about Nadia Baidoo than Sutherland had been. That away from Long Fleet she could give up the information they both thought she'd been holding back when they interviewed her there.

She texted back: *What time?*

Half an hour. He replied instantly.

She told him to pick her up. Then asked for forty-five minutes, wanting to eat whatever smelled so good.

There was a pot of coffee on the breakfast bar and she poured a cup before Billy noticed her behind him.

'I was going to surprise you with breakfast in bed, but now you're up ...'

'French toast?' she asked.

'With bacon and bananas. There's maple syrup in the fridge.'

He looked pleased with himself this morning and she wondered if it was because she hadn't brought up last night the obvious question of what he and Zigic were working on. Instead she'd let him suffer through a perfectly nice dinner and then a film and then sex where he applied himself with a degree of conviction that only confirmed her suspicion that he was up to something.

She wondered if he thought she'd been too busy to notice yesterday's absence and Zigic's ragged nerves, or if he simply hoped that by staying quiet about it, he could avoid having his judgement scrutinised.

Ferreira sat down at the breakfast bar, watching him plating up their food in his boxers and T-shirt and striped apron, giving it all the care and attention he'd learned from *MasterChef*.

He put her plate down in front of her with a flourish, then settled onto the next stool.

'What are you doing today?' he asked.

'Ziggy wants to go speak to one of the Long Fleet nurses,' she said, pouring maple syrup over everything. 'Doubt we'll be more than an hour or so. What about you?'

'Gym, maybe. If you're heading out.'

'You'll need the gym after this.' Ferreira shoved a forkful of bacon and French toast into her mouth, let out a groan of pleasure. 'Totally filthy.'

'Just how you like it.'

They talked about nothing while they ate: a new box set he wanted to try, whether she needed anything picking up since he was going out, that her toothpaste was running low and what about that coffee, was it strong enough, should they switch? All achingly normal and domesticated and she wasn't sure how they'd come to this point, when exactly he'd morphed into someone who monitored her toothpaste situation.

It felt like a lifetime since that first encounter, when she'd handcuffed him to the radiator in the living room and fucked him on the floor. And now look at us, she thought.

Playing nice while he's lying his head off, just like an old married couple.

'There's a film on at the arts cinema in Stamford,' he said, reaching across to top up her coffee. 'Some French crime thing. If you fancy it?'

'What are you doing with Ziggy?'

'What do you mean?'

'Sneaking off together,' she said. 'In and out of each other's offices every two minutes. Since when are the pair of you so matey?'

'This is embarrassing.' He sipped his coffee. 'But I've developed a crush on him.'

'For fu—'

'Swarthy good looks, those cheekbones … he's a big, gorgeous bastard and you know it.'

'This isn't a joke,' Ferreira snapped.

'No, it isn't,' he said, chastened. 'How would you feel about inviting him in for a threesome?'

He was smiling but she could see the discomfort in his eyes, the desperation under each attempt at deflection.

'Billy, do not lie to me,' she said. 'What have you dragged him into?'

'He's a big boy, Mel. I didn't have to drag him.'

'You're working Walton.'

He looked away, spiked the last piece of French toast on his plate and slowly wiped it through a smear of syrup. 'The less you know about it the better, believe me; we're just trying to protect you.'

She felt a hot flare of anger up her face. How dare they do this? Go behind her back and investigate Walton when she was the one he was harassing. She'd been the one to bring his girlfriend in, obliterating the alibis that had kept him on the streets through all the years they'd failed to nail him. He was her case as much as anyone's. Her mess to clear up.

'Tell me everything,' she said. 'Right now.'

'I'm sorry, but I'm not going to do that.'

He still couldn't look at her and abruptly she realised he was scared.

'What the hell have you got yourselves into?' she asked, hearing a tremble in her voice.

He didn't answer.

Zigic was sensible, she told herself. He was smart and deeply moralistic and wouldn't dream of venturing into the kinds of dark places Billy might go. He would be a brake on Billy's worst excesses. This couldn't be bad. Not *really* bad.

But the fear was on him, she could smell it now, a sharpness to his sweat that hadn't been there a minute ago. And she felt it infecting her too, sending a sick ache through her stomach.

'I've got a right to know,' she said. 'I'm the one he's coming after.'

Billy put his fork down very deliberately on the plate.

'It might be nothing. Can you just, please, give me a couple of days to work out where we are with it?'

'Is it another case?' she asked and immediately answered herself. 'Of course it's a case. Don't you think I might actually be of some use in this? I am a detective after all.'

'Mel, please.' He slipped off the stool, paced to the far end of the galley kitchen, seemed to need the distance. 'If we're wrong this is going to get really, badly, fucking ugly. I'm just trying to protect you.'

'I don't need protecting,' she told him. 'I need to know what the hell you're doing.'

He walked out of the kitchen, didn't seem to know where to go next, and she caught up with him in the living room, standing with the sofa between them like a rampart.

'If you don't tell me, Ziggy will,' she said.

'He'll tell you the same thing I did.'

She rolled her eyes. 'Made a sacred pact, did you? Pinky-promised to lie to me?'

'No one's lying to you,' he said, voice rising, hands coming down hard on the back of the sofa. 'Why can't you let me take care of this for you?'

He actually believed it, she realised, hearing the petulant edge come into his voice. He thought she needed protecting and that he was the one to do it. After everything she'd gone through, the scars she had, the violence she'd survived.

She went back into the bedroom, stripped off, thinking about this impulse in him that she didn't appreciate. Thinking of how he'd been before they got together, the copper who found himself inexorably attracted to the family members of victims, vulnerable women on the periphery of terrible crimes. Not the ones you would have expected. Looks didn't seem to come into it. He gravitated towards fragility, a certain brittleness that required the most careful handling.

As she went to pull on her jeans, she stopped, looking down at the faded scars on the backs of her legs.

That was when it started. A few months out of hospital, still raw and despairing, avoiding mirrors and showering in the dark so she wouldn't have to confront those dozens of imperfections blasted across her skin.

And out of nowhere he'd called her, asked if she wanted to go for a drink, catch up on the station gossip she was missing while she was out of rotation. It felt natural because they'd slept together a handful of times before and always got on when they found themselves thrown together on a case. It kept feeling natural as the drinks became sex, became more frequent sex, and then something they both had to admit was dating.

But now she was wondering, what exactly about her did he find so irresistible?

Did he seriously think she was one of those fragile women, just waiting for him to come along and save her? Was he such a poor judge of character?

Ferreira grabbed her phone and her bag and stormed out of the flat, slamming the door on his entreaties.

Chapter Forty-Six

They'd been in the car for twenty minutes before Zigic cracked, unable to bear the negative energy boiling off Ferreira, the freighted silence buzzing between them under the hum of the air conditioning.

'Everything okay?' he asked.

'We had a fight,' she said.

He wasn't going to pursue this line of conversation. It was too fraught. The danger was always lurking that he would tell her exactly what he thought of Adams and then where would they be?

'Billy told me what you're doing,' she said, staring across at him, eyes wide and unblinking. 'With Walton's case.'

Zigic said nothing, almost certain that she was fishing. She knew they were looking into potential new charges, knew the two of them had been out all day yesterday doing *something*, but he doubted Adams had come clean about it. He was too worried about the repercussions. There was a dubious kind of machismo in play with him, Zigic thought, keeping Ferreira and Murray out of the proceedings, as if the little women needed protecting.

Or maybe not machismo exactly. Adams would probably consider it chivalrous.

But Zigic didn't want anyone else to jeopardise their career over this.

'Why are you angry about it?' he asked instead.

'You know why.'

'No, I don't,' he said, slowing down to let a pheasant cross the road ahead of them. 'Did you want to be more involved?'

She let out a snort of laughter.

'You're going to play innocent, are you?'

'Mel, I don't know what to tell you.' He shrugged. 'We're looking into a potential case but honestly, I don't think it's going to go anywhere. As much as your boyfriend would like it to stick.'

He spotted the low bulk of Long Fleet Immigration Removal Centre in the distance and accelerated towards it, as if he could leave this conversation behind them.

He hated lying to her and she knew that.

'Billy's scared,' she said. 'And if he feels that way then you're doing something really stupid.'

Zigic didn't answer, told himself it was only a couple more days, then this whole ugly mess would come to a head and everything would be out in the open, one way or another.

She muttered something under her breath and turned away, watching the fields whipping by.

At the edge of the village, he slowed again, passing the green where the crime scene tape was still tacked up over Joshua Ainsworth's front door. A couple were unloading their car in front of number 8, another weekend rental beginning, and he wondered if they were horrified to find themselves next to a crime scene or secretly thrilled. The husband was talking to the postman, pointing at number 6, and he guessed they'd be getting the full story already.

He turned down the lane where Ruth Garner lived. The houses here were wider spaced and set further back from the road. Simple red-brick cottages in pairs and a few detached places in among them, with caravans on driveways and cars parked on the road. Her house was the last on the lane, with a large garden that gave on to pastureland, where a couple of horses stood huddled under the only tree to get out of the morning sun.

'You lead,' he said, as they got out of the car.

'Because I actually know who we're talking about,' Ferreira said sharply.

He let it go. He should have been working the case with her so he supposed he'd earned the jibe.

She knocked on the front door and when there was no answer, they headed off around the side of the house.

They found Ruth Garner sitting on a bench in the back garden, drinking a cup of tea, the remnants of her breakfast being fought over by a few birds that scattered as their footsteps rang out across the uneven paving.

She started when she saw them.

'Sorry,' Ferreira said. 'We did knock.'

'I shouldn't be talking to you,' Ruth said, gathering up her plate and mug and going into the kitchen.

But she didn't shut them out, so they followed her inside. Stood until she offered them a seat, her good manners overcoming her discomfort.

'You know I can't tell you anything else,' she said, leaning back against the butler's sink, arms wrapped around her abdomen. 'My contract – I just can't.'

'We're only looking for some background,' Ferreira said smoothly. 'Nothing you say's going to get back to Hammond or the company.'

Ruth still look wary.

'Do you remember a former inmate called Nadia Baidoo?' Ferreira went on. 'She was released about seven weeks ago.'

'I was on sabbatical seven weeks ago, I already told you that.'

'Nadia was brought to Long Fleet June last year,' Ferreira said, bringing out a photograph of the young woman. 'Did you have any contact with her between that time and your sabbatical?'

Reluctantly Ruth came over to the table, picked the photograph up and gave it a quick glance before putting it down again and returning to her post against the sink.

'I remember Nadia, yes,' she said. 'Nice girl, very quiet, very patient. I remember being surprised that she was in there because I thought she was English when I first met her. But then I found out she'd been over here since was she small so she is English really, in any way that matters.' She shook her head. 'Not the way that matters at Long Fleet, obviously.'

'Did she have medical problems?' Ferreira asked.

'I can't discuss that with you, sorry.'

'She was coming into the medical bay, though?'

279

Ruth nodded.

'Who treated her?'

'All of us at various times.'

'But who predominantly?'

'Well, Patrick and Joshua, of course,' Ruth said with a shrug. 'Look, I'm sorry but why are you asking about Nadia?'

'Did Nadia ever mention a boyfriend to you?' Ferreira said, ignoring the question.

Ruth was silent for a moment, as if weighing the possibility of insisting on getting her own answer first.

'No, she didn't.'

'What about family?'

'We didn't really have those kinds of conversations,' Ruth said. 'But I know her mother was the only family she had in England and she'd passed away. The rest of her family were in Ghana, but I got the impression she wasn't very close to them.'

'Who was Nadia close to at Long Fleet?' she asked.

'I couldn't tell you that, sorry.'

'Because of your contract?'

'No, because I don't know,' Ruth said, getting testy now.

They were drawing closer, Zigic thought. He saw the shift in her body language, how she hunched her shoulders and spread her weight between her feet as if she was steeling herself for where she assumed the conversation was heading.

'We really don't see very much of any given client,' Ruth explained. 'They come in with a problem and we treat them and send them off again. We're not therapists, we don't discuss their personal lives.'

'But you discussed some deeply personal things with the women whose complaints you reported,' Ferreira said, opening her hands up. 'You clearly have a very good idea of what goes on in the rest of the building.'

Ruth brushed away some hair that wasn't really there.

'I feel like there's something you want to ask me,' she said. 'So why don't you just say it?'

'Did you know Nadia accused Joshua of attacking her?'

'No.'

But she wasn't shocked, Zigic saw. So either she was lying or there had been gossip about it, which had reached her ears and which she'd decided not to tell them before.

'There must have been talk about it?'

'Not that I heard.'

'Nadia accused Joshua of attacking her and then he was told to resign,' Ferreira said, trying and failing to catch Ruth's eye. 'Do you seriously expect us to believe something like that never got talked about?'

'All I heard was that Josh left with stress,' Ruth said carefully. 'I was away and when I came back he was gone and I was told he resigned.'

'Dr Sutherland was there when it happened,' Ferreira said. 'There are guards who were there. None of these people talked about it? At all?'

'No,' she said firmly. 'I don't know why. Maybe they didn't know either. Maybe Hammond wanted to keep it all quiet and he made sure nobody outside of admin found out about it.'

She believed the accusation, Zigic saw.

'I still don't understand why we're talking about Nadia,' Ruth said, picking up a damp cloth from the draining board and laying it over the tap.

Ferreira waited until she was facing them again before she replied.

'Because Nadia has disappeared,' she said. 'She was released from Long Fleet seven weeks ago and she disappeared a few days later.'

Ruth straightened sharply, her hand going to her throat.

'You think she murdered Josh?'

Another flicker of annoyance crossed Ferreira's face because it was the obvious and logical assumption and not the one she wanted to be true.

'Why would Nadia murder Josh?' she asked.

Ruth's hands made incoherent gestures in the air in front of her chest. 'I don't know. Revenge maybe.'

'Revenge for attacking her?' Ferreira suggested and got a small, doubtful nod in return. 'Ruth, given that you've obviously reconsidered your opinion of Josh, is there anything further you'd like to tell us?'

'I haven't reconsidered,' she said sadly. 'I don't know what to think any more.'

A shutter came down in front of her face but Ferreira pressed on regardless, hoping there was some way of reaching through it. She tried to impress upon her how much danger the young woman could be in and how important it was they talked to her. Ruth was looking at her the whole time but Zigic wasn't sure she saw Ferreira any more, and though she murmured and nodded here and there, she didn't really speak again.

Zigic left his card and asked her to call them if she thought of anything, walked out of the house dogged by frustration.

His phone rang as he got in the car.

'Is this Detective Inspector Zigic?' a man with a broad fen accent asked.

'It is.'

'You said I were to ring you if there were owt else I could tell you about young Josh,' he said. 'Well, I've got summat here I reckon you'll want'a see.'

'What is it, Mr Edwards?'

But he'd hung up.

CHAPTER FORTY-SEVEN

'Let's just open it,' Ferreira said excitedly, holding the letter Josh Ainsworth's neighbour, Mr Edwards, had signed for on her lap. Ainsworth's name printed on the front of it, nothing else to give away the contents.

'We need to preserve any evidence on it,' Zigic told her, again. 'I know you know this, Mel.'

'There might not be any forensic evidence.' She turned it over in her hands, the evidence bag crinkling, as if something new might have appeared on the plain white envelope in the minute since she last did that. 'We should open it.'

Zigic glanced away from the road and plucked it from her grasp, tucked it into the side pocket of the car door.

'Anything that was sent to Ainsworth special delivery is too important to mess about with,' he said. 'Forensics are opening it.'

She huffed lightly, folded her arms. 'You could stick your foot down, at least.'

He accelerated along the narrow fenland road, a group of cyclists up ahead all wearing the same Team Sky jerseys. He slowed as he approached them, staying well back but getting some disgusted looks from the riders at the rear all the same. When the road was clear he overtook.

'What happened with Patrick Sutherland yesterday?' he asked. 'You never did tell me.'

'Not much to tell,' she said. 'Sutherland's so terrified of breaching his contract I'm not even sure you could torture anything helpful out of him. I mean, he bolted pretty much as soon as he realised why I'd got him in there.'

'You didn't get anything out of him, then?'

'I got to see him without Long Fleet's watchful eye on his back,' she said thoughtfully. 'That was useful.'

It didn't sound very useful, but Ferreira's approach was different to his own; more psychologically based, she'd claim. More gut-driven, he'd say. If she was left to her own devices she'd bring suspects to the interview room over and over again, grind them down with the same questions and statements until they cracked. But that wasn't how you built a case. It was how you got a confession.

Momentarily Neal Cooper popped into Zigic's head and he pushed the image of the broken-down man aside. He was a problem for Monday morning.

'I did find out one very interesting thing,' she said. 'Sutherland was behind the hidden camera footage.'

'I still don't think that's as interesting as you do,' he told her, his attention drawn away from the road to a field where a couple of metal detectorists were working their way up and down the dusty furrows. 'Did he know about the accusation against Ainsworth?'

'Yeah, I'm fairly sure he knew all about it,' Ferreira said, reaching into her bag. 'Somebody examined Nadia afterwards and he was the only other doctor available at that time. Stands to reason he knows exactly what happened.'

'So he risks his job smuggling in a hidden camera, but he won't tell you anything about what happened to Nadia?' Zigic asked.

She swiped lip balm over her mouth. 'That was what I told him. But no. Honestly, I got the impression he feels like he dodged a bullet with the initial whistle-blowing and now he's going to toe the line at any cost, as long as he keeps his job.'

'Some moral crusader he is.'

She let out a thoughtful murmur. 'I think we need to stop considering it an "allegation of assault", you know. Sutherland got all wound up when I suggested Hammond didn't believe it. And if he did examine Nadia …'

'He knows it definitely happened,' Zigic said. 'You think he might have something to do with the murder?'

'What's his motive?' Ferreira asked.

He shrugged. 'He's putting his neck on the line reporting abuses at Long Fleet. Josh Ainsworth was doing the same. So Sutherland feels like the two of them are fighting the good fight.'

'Then he finds out Ainsworth isn't quite as upstanding as he thinks and kills him over it?'

'It's possible,' Zigic insisted.

'But unlikely.'

'You had no problem with an ideologically driven motive for the Paggetts,' he reminded her. 'Now we know about the secret footage, we have to put Sutherland in the same bracket as them. Except he actually *did* something to back up his beliefs. If anything that makes the motive even more viable for him than it did for them.'

'I got the feeling you never bought that as a motive for the Paggetts murdering Ainsworth though,' she said.

'I thought it was a stretch,' he admitted. 'If it wasn't for them mouthing off about kidnapping someone, I wouldn't have even considered it a possibility.'

He pulled off the parkway, heading for the entrance to Thorpe Road Station, quietly pleased that he'd distracted Ferreira from continuing the discussion he'd endured on the way to Long Fleet.

'You want me to push Sutherland some more?' she asked, as they got out of the car.

'Check his alibi,' Zigic said.

They headed up the steps and in through reception.

'The problem I keep coming back to,' Ferreira said, as she opened the stairwell door, 'is we have a staff of – we don't even know how many – at Long Fleet, right? And any one of them could have some personal grievance against Ainsworth, and as long as we can't talk to them, we'll never know about it.'

He'd been thinking the same thing. Right from the moment they first drove through Long Fleet's gates. The nameless, faceless employees who were each and every one of them suspects until they could be reasonably disregarded.

'Hammond is never going to allow us to question them all,' he said, following her up the stairs.

'Maybe we just need to find another way to identify them,' Ferreira suggested. 'We could use the sacked staff members we have to get some names.'

'Or HMRC?'

Ferreira stopped at the top of the stairs, sheepish-looking. 'Yeah, I already thought of that. I didn't want to say anything because you seemed so spooked about getting in Riggott's bad books.'

'And?'

'They're employed centrally through Securitect,' she said. 'There's no way to know who's at Long Fleet and who's just doing property maintenance on their care homes or whatever.'

'It was a good idea but we might not need to worry about identifying them.' He held up the plain white envelope in its clear bag. 'Maybe the murderer's in here.'

Ferreira rolled her eyes at his jokey optimism and shoved through the door into the lab.

There was only one person on today. Budget issues and holidays cutting them down to the wire. If something major happened, extra bodies would be pulled in from home but for now it was just Kate Jenkins's right-hand man, Elliot, sitting in her office, reading a fat science fiction book with a heavily cracked spine.

'Finally, something interesting,' he said, swinging his feet off the desk and coming out to meet them. When he saw the envelope Zigic was brandishing, his face fell. 'That doesn't seem particularly interesting.'

'It was sent special delivery to our murder victim,' Zigic told him.

'Well, that's a bit better.'

Elliot put on a pair of gloves and removed the envelope from the evidence bag. 'You're hoping for fingerprints?'

'We're more about what's inside it,' Ferreira said, leaning on the counter, physically straining towards Elliot as he opened the envelope, looking like she might rip it from his hands if he didn't hurry up.

'Ooh.' He flattened out the single sheet for them to see. 'It's a paternity test.'

'A positive paternity test.' Ferreira turned to Zigic, eyes lit up. 'Why the hell would Ainsworth be running a paternity test?'

He spotted the name of a lab on the letterhead, nothing but a couple of lines of text below it.

'Clue's in the name,' Elliot said lightly.

'Is there anything to suggest who the parties involved might be?' Zigic asked.

Elliot shook his head. 'He'd have sent in samples but I don't suppose a small lab like this is going to be sending them back. Why would he need them? He got his answer.'

'Maybe the lab still has the samples,' Ferreira said, snapping upright, her phone already in her hand. She keyed in the phone number from the letterhead and walked away from the counter.

'If we can get the samples back, you can run them, right?'

'Your chain of evidence is going to be sketchy,' Elliot warned him. 'But, yes, theoretically we can do that.'

Ferreira was speaking, uninterrupted but still impatient, clearly leaving a message.

Saturday morning, Zigic thought, it was unlikely anyone would be at work at some private lab.

'No point examining this, right?' Elliot asked, already folding the paper back into the envelope.

Zigic took it back from him. 'We'll see about the samples.'

'I *almost* got something to do anyway,' Elliot said, deflated.

He returned to Jenkins's office and they went down to CID, Ferreira already throwing out potential candidates for the mother.

'Portia Collingwood, it has to be,' she said. 'That's been an on and off thing for years and she *was* there the night he died.'

'Why would she kill him over a paternity test?' Zigic asked, going to the coffee machine and pouring them a cup each. 'Especially one they didn't even know the results of.'

'Yeah, okay.' Ferreira was circling her desk, agitated but energised. 'You get murdered over a paternity test once the results are back, right?'

'Not necessarily,' Zigic said, putting her coffee down. 'Running an actual test suggests dispute over paternity –'

'Which suggests an affair that has recently come out into the open.'

'Alistair Collingwood has an alibi,' he reminded her.

'You're assuming this is the only relationship Josh Ainsworth was involved in.' She picked up a marker pen and wrote 'PATERNITY TEST' in big letters on the board. 'We've been through Ainsworth's phone records and it's all pretty boring. No major unidentified players in there so if he was having another affair, he wasn't arranging it by phone.'

'Someone he worked with?' Zigic asked.

'What, Ruth Garner?'

'She's got a kid.'

Ferreira paused to pull a face at him and went back to pacing. 'That can't be our minimum threshold for suspicion – "She's got a kid."'

Zigic's brow furrowed. 'Nadia Baidoo?'

'We don't know the nature of the assault,' Ferreira said tentatively. 'But if he raped her, then, yeah, we've got to think that's a possibility.'

'Meaning they were in contact just before his murder?' he asked. 'How else would he have got a sample of the baby's DNA?'

'The bloke Mr Daya saw Nadia having coffee with before she left Haven House?' Ferreira said, then immediately answered herself. 'No way. He reckoned she looked happy. She'd hardly be happy running into the man who attacked her.'

Zigic wished she'd sit down for a moment, stop thinking with her mouth and actually consider the new evidence they had on their hands.

Because the more she paced, throwing out that chaotic energy, the less he was able to concentrate on the slim thread of an idea, which was looping around in the back of his head.

'Does the timeline even work for it being Nadia's baby?' Ferreira asked, swerving away to the board. 'She was taken into Long Fleet June last year. But the assault was barely two months ago. There's no baby to DNA test.'

'The assault she *reported* was barely two months ago,' Zigic said. 'We need to get in touch with Hammond again and find out if she was pregnant when she left Long Fleet.'

'I talked to the manager at the hostel and he never mentioned Nadia being pregnant.' Ferreira stuck her hands on her hips. 'There's no way he wouldn't have told me that.'

'We should check with local maternity units,' Zigic said. 'Just in case.'

Ferreira made a note and stuck it to Keri Bloom's desk for Monday morning, straightened up, sucking her teeth.

'We need those fucking samples.'

'It's the weekend, Mel. Some people have them off, remember.'

'They must have an emergency number.' She slipped into her seat and started tapping at her keyboard. 'All of those DNA tests going out to peoples' houses ... how don't we see murders about this on a weekly basis?'

'I guess most people keep the results to themselves,' Zigic said, swivelling to consider the board. 'But looking at how close this has come to Ainsworth's return from his holiday, it can't be coincidence.'

'No,' Ferreira agreed. 'The lab's website promises a forty-eight-hour turnaround so Ainsworth sent the test in within a couple of days of coming home.'

'We need to pin down exactly what he was doing between landing and getting killed,' Zigic said, looking at the yawning chasm those days presented.

Without Ainsworth's devices they'd found it nearly impossible to ascertain what he'd been doing with himself in the days just before his death. His neighbour wasn't nosy enough and Portia Collingwood apparently didn't go in for conversation, simply turned up at his door for sex and left when she'd had it.

Somebody must know, Zigic thought.

He hadn't locked himself away for four days straight, had he?

At some point he'd met the mother of this child, been given a swab of DNA to send in with his own. Meaning she wanted him to be the father of her child. For financial or emotional reasons, they wouldn't know until they identified her.

Or was it Ainsworth who wanted to prove his paternity? Claim the rights he was due under law.

And where was the other man in all of this?

Nervously waiting for them to knock on his door and start asking questions he would have no good answers to?

DAY SIX

SUNDAY AUGUST 12TH

CHAPTER FORTY-EIGHT

Ferreira lay on the sofa, flicking through a magazine from the Sunday paper. There was nothing much in it but she couldn't seem to hold her attention on anything more substantial than photographs and snippets of anodyne text. The book she was reading was splayed on the coffee table exactly where she'd left it last night, and even television felt like too much of an effort. She'd scrolled through the channels, settling on one thing for a few minutes before switching again, couldn't find anything she wanted to watch among the programmes she'd saved on Billy's planner.

No matter what she tried to concentrate on, her brain kept circling back to Billy and Zigic and what they were doing about Walton.

Last night she and Billy had gone out to the little cinema in Stamford he liked and watched some French film she knew he didn't want to see but which she would normally have enjoyed. All through it she was aware of him glancing over and checking on her, hardly seeming to watch the screen. And then, afterwards in the cellar bar with all the other couples who looked just like them, he'd been too close and attentive, as if he thought Walton was in there somewhere, waiting to pounce.

They'd played nice with each other. Been kind. Talked about the film and the setting, about taking a couple of days in Paris between Christmas and New Year even though they both knew it would be impossible in that dead time that seemed to send people for each other's throats. But they'd pretended all the same, taking comfort in the pretence of normality.

Later in the darkened confines of the car, speeding down the A1, he reached across for her hand, 'I don't want to lose you, Mel.'

Out of nowhere she'd felt tears welling up and all she could do was squeeze his hand and let her silence stand in for the gratitude she couldn't express.

He was doing something stupid and probably dangerous and almost definitely reckless for her, and she decided she would hold on to that. Stop and think about it every time she wanted to fly at him.

Because she realised now that she would do the same for him if it came down to it, and how would she feel to have the gesture thrown back in her face?

He returned from the kitchen with a cold bottle of beer and handed it to her.

'Where's yours?' she asked.

'I've got to nip out for a bit,' he said. 'Hour. Two, tops. You going to be alright?'

She bit back the urge to ask him if she needed to barricade the door while he was gone or which kitchen knife he thought would be best to defend herself with.

Instead she smiled. 'I'll be fine.'

When the front door closed she took a long drink of beer, washing away all the questions she'd wanted to ask him. She went to Netflix and found a big, dumb action film she'd seen a dozen times before, put it on and let it melt her brain.

As the film's 'all is lost' moment approached, her mobile rang – Lee Walton's ex-girlfriend.

The sight of her name on the screen set Ferreira's heart racing and for a moment she considered not answering it, knowing it wouldn't be anything good, nothing she could actually help with. But she owed Dani an ear at the very least.

'Dani, what's up?'

'Lee's out,' she said, her voice shaking. 'Why didn't you tell me? What are you playing at leaving it down to my mum to call me?'

'You're not supposed to be in contact with your family,' Ferreira reminded her. 'We discussed this, remember? If they know where you are, then Lee can find you.'

'How am I supposed to not talk to my mum?' she demanded.

In the background Ferreira could hear the regular beeping of a supermarket checkout. Was Dani seriously making this call in the middle of her food shop?

'Good thing I *am* still talking to Mum,' she said. 'You obviously weren't going to tell me he's innocent.'

'He's not innocent! You know that.'

' I –'

'He got out on a technicality,' Ferreira said, as slowly and calmly as she could manage. 'He's still guilty. You always knew he was.'

'No, you twisted everything and made me think he was. You lot have always had it in for him.'

'He's a serial rapist, Dani.'

'No, you tricked me,' she snapped. 'He warned me. He kept telling me what you what were like and it was true. You fitted him up. I saw the news – I just bloody googled it – he's in the paper!'

Ferreira took a deep breath, tried to find the right words to make her understand when all she wanted to do was scream at the woman to think clearly for once in her life.

'I knew he never did it,' Dani said, as the tannoy in the background blared incoherently.

'Listen to me, Lee *is* guilty. He's only out because someone at the lab misrepresented their qualifications. It doesn't change what you know about him. It doesn't change that you gave him false alibis for the times he was out raping women. Or that those women still identified him.'

'They were lying.'

'You think all of them were lying?' Ferreira asked, incredulous. 'All of those women decided to tell exactly the same lie?'

'You probably told them to lie and say it was him so you could put him away,' Dani's voice was going higher and tighter. 'You made me leave my home and come to this bloody place –'

'We're trying to protect you.'

'Why would I need protecting if Lee was locked up? You knew he was going to be released and you just didn't want us to be together.'

She was babbling now, breathless and near hysterical.

'Lee beat you,' Ferreira reminded her, remembering the tearful conversation they'd had, the visit to the hospital Ferreira had made, seeing Dani lying in bed with Lee at her side, remembered how pathetically grateful the woman had looked for the few kind words he threw her. All spoken for the police's benefit, a way of showing them how completely he owned her and how cheaply her compliance was bought.

'I can't believe I let you do this to me,' Dani said wretchedly, a cry from the gut. 'He loves me.'

'He put you in the fucking hospital,' Ferreira said. 'More than once.'

'You're just jealous.'

'For Christ's sake, Dani, please. Would you –'

Dani ended the call.

Ferreira swore at the dead screen and the action frozen on the television and the sheer, unfathomable stupidity and weirdness of other people's abusive, shitty relationships.

She took a couple of deep, calming breaths and when that didn't work, she drained the last of her beer, then called Dani back.

The phone only rang twice, long enough for her to know that the call had been seen and rejected.

Dani would be phoning Lee now, she guessed. Begging his forgiveness and telling him she couldn't live without him, blaming everything on Ferreira and the rest of them. And Walton would lap it up, say whatever he needed to in order to get Dani and his son back home, which would be very little. He'd probably just whistle to her like a whipped dog.

Dani had been abused and manipulated and was unable to think for herself. But she'd been given another chance, an opportunity to start her life afresh away from him, make a safe home for her son, and she was going to throw it all away. How could she do that to her child?

At the back of Ferreira's mind, a hard voice, the voice of self-preservation, said, 'So, let her come home to him, it'll get him off your back.'

She didn't want to listen to it.

Her job was as often about protecting people from themselves as much as from others. But sometimes you failed in the face of their overwhelming urge towards self-destruction.

There was absolutely nothing she could do to stop Dani coming home.

All she could do, all any of them seemed able to do where Walton was concerned, was wait for him to react in his entirely predictable way and then clean up the mess he'd leave behind.

Chapter Forty-Nine

Zigic spotted Adams's car parked at the bottom of Station Road where the narrow lane became a farm track, heading into open countryside and Ferry Meadows beyond it. Adams had wanted to come to the house but Zigic told him he had Anna's family around, insisted they meet here. Now he was regretting it.

It felt so inescapably illicit. Would look deeply suspect to any of the neighbours who might see him ambling down the road, trying to be nonchalant. If he saw himself heading for that swanky black Audi, he'd probably think he was buying coke.

And that would be less dangerous, less stupid than what he was actually up to.

He got into the passenger side, found Adams had left a padded envelope waiting for him on the dashboard, nothing written on it, sealed and taped for extra protection. An unnecessary precaution given that the chain of evidence was not a factor here.

Zigic stared at the envelope, sitting there so innocuously. It was the kind that Anna received little handmade decorative objects from Etsy in. But this one held a sample of DNA on a scrap of fabric from the cardigan of a murdered girl. A scrap that had been safely filed away in police evidence up until this morning.

'Don't ask how I got it,' Adams said. 'Best you don't know.'

'Attempting to give me plausible deniability would be a thoughtful gesture if I wasn't taking it for an illegal off-site DNA test,' Zigic said, unable to tear his eyes from it but unwilling to actually take hold of the thing.

There was still a chance to back away.

Adams held out a piece of paper with a mobile number on it. 'Forty-eight-hour turnaround; it's as quick as I could get.'

'You could have given them it yourself,' Zigic said, reluctantly taking the slip of paper. 'It's your contact we're using.'

Adams smiled, both of them aware of why he was insisting Zigic take it in. Both their hands would be dirtied, no going back, no turning on each other. They would stand or fall together.

He could walk away, he thought. Leave the envelope untouched, nothing to tie him to this, not even a single stray fingerprint. Adams would be pissed off but he'd continue alone and get whatever result or punishment was at the end of the process. If he was right Walton would go down and Ferreira would be safe and everyone would breathe a sigh of relief. If he was wrong no one would be any the wiser.

Zigic thought of Tessa Darby's mother, bereaved and retraumatised by their visit; Sadie Ryan in hiding after her suicide attempt, her family terrified she would try again. All the victims waiting to see if Lee Walton would come for his revenge.

This was an ugly way of getting justice, he thought bitterly.

Taking a deep breath, he picked up the envelope. It was almost weightless, so light and insubstantial it seemed impossible that it held the potential to end both of their careers and maybe even land them in prison.

There would be no compromised lab to spring them, either.

But he had it in his hand now and as much as his head was pounding and his gut screaming at him to be smart about this, he knew he would be no kind of copper if he didn't follow through on what they'd started.

'How much does he want?'

'*She* doesn't need paying,' Adams said. 'She owes me a favour.'

Zigic climbed out of the car, unwilling to hear any more of this, and walked back up the lane, fighting the fear that told him to fling the envelope over the hedgerow and into the field opposite his house, let it sit there and rot safely back into the earth. Instead he went upstairs and placed it inside an evidence bag, then tucked it away at the back of his wardrobe, ready to be retrieved later this afternoon when Anna's family were gone and he could slip out to meet Adams's contact.

Through the bedroom window he could see Anna sitting next to her mother at the table, Emily in her lap. The three of them were staying safely under the broad canvas umbrella while her father added another layer of sun damage to the leathery finish of his arms and face, standing at the barbecue, turning the sausages the Healeys had brought from their local butcher, who was *so much better* than the one they used.

Everything about Mr and Mrs Healeys' life was superior to the one he could provide for his family, even down to the quality of the meat in their sausages. Zigic had tried one, didn't detect any significant difference and knew the boys would have eaten anything, as long as it was smothered in brown sauce for Stefan and red for Milan.

He watched them chase around the large nut tree in the middle of the garden, smiling at how happy Milan seemed today, like a little boy again, instead of the proto-adult he'd been lately, weighed down with burdens he refused to share. He was laughing and shouting, dodging away from Stefan and getting the broad trunk of the old tree between them, feinting and fooling Stefan into going the wrong way until he saw his baby brother's face begin to redden and his frustration rise, and then he let his movements drag until Stefan tagged him.

It was the school, Zigic thought, with a plunging sensation that drove him away from the window and onto the foot of the bed.

They'd been full of it on Friday evening when he got home. He'd expected that from Stefan, who went wild about anything new he came across, but Milan was just as excited. He'd tried to hide it, too aware of the mood in the house and its cause to openly come out and say he wanted to go there.

Instead when Zigic asked him what he thought, he beamed and said, 'It's just like Hogwarts.'

And that was it.

Milan wanted to go and if Zigic somehow stopped that happening, then he knew Milan would never forgive him. Even if the bullying didn't continue next term and he was fine at the new secondary school he was due to attend. Because what kind of monster would stand in the way of their child going to Hogwarts?

The school wanted an answer by Tuesday.

Anna was going to say yes no matter what he thought.

They were lucky to get two places at such short notice, she'd told him. An unfortunate side effect of the economic downturn, the headmistress said. They'd lost quite a few pupils between terms so they had openings. For the right kind of people.

Zigic cursed himself for his stubbornness. Told himself all his arguments were petty and egotistical, kept repeating it to himself because that was the only way he could force himself to believe it. Anna knew best. The boys would be happy there. It didn't matter that her parents were paying. It was a kindness. It was what you did for family. He didn't have to let it eat him up inside. Once he saw how happy the boys were there, he'd feel nothing but relief and gratitude.

If he held on to those thoughts, drilled them into his brain, then maybe he could convince Anna he believed them too and everything would go back to normal between them?

But he couldn't do it today.

Not with her parents here, poised to gloat over his acquiescence.

Tomorrow, he told himself, his gaze straying to the wardrobe. He could almost feel the presence of the envelope like some toxic substance he'd brought into his home, slowly polluting everything around it.

If the worst happened, he thought, if it went as badly as it could, at least his boys would be safely tucked away in a nice school. At least Mr and Mrs Healey's money could insulate his family from the effects of his bad judgement.

Day Seven

MONDAY AUGUST 13TH

CHAPTER FIFTY

Monday morning. The big briefing.

The office was packed and pungent with the scent of shea butter and aftersun, everyone slightly damp and rumpled from the weekend, which had been too hot for rest and recuperation but just right for drinking heavily and falling asleep in the garden without any sunscreen on. Ferreira counted five instances of serious burns, including one civilian support officer who'd apparently nodded off with his arm thrown across his eyes, leaving a fat strip of white skin between two expanses of furious redness and freckles that probably needed a dermatologist.

Most of the weekend shift were still in place too, working on an attempted murder that had hit in the early hours of Saturday morning: gunshots fired at a house in the middle of a nice village on the side of the A1, blood found in the drawing room but no sign of the victim so far. The gun was legally owned, the man who fired it insisting it was a burglar whose description he couldn't give them.

At the front of the office, DI Greta Kitson had just wrapped up her briefing and Adams took over, giving the most basic rundown of the cases that had stalled. The minor tasks to be done and old ground to retread. Nobody looked very happy about getting those jobs, but it's what police work frequently boiled down to. Watch that CCTV footage for the fifth time, combine that information with your third reread of every single interview transcript, then try to find some new angle in it all and decide who best to throw it at in the hopes of scaring them into letting slip something fresh.

It was often the way cases got cracked, but everyone resented doing it because nobody joined the police to do paperwork. They all wanted to corner the bad guy in a dark alley and take him down hand to hand.

Until they actually found themselves in that position.

Ferreira's fingertips went to the back of her calf, the first time it had itched in months and she straightened again, knowing it was a psychological itch and she didn't need to scratch it.

'Marseilles police have lost George Batty,' Adams said, eliciting a few groans. 'But they tell us Batty was seen hanging around a lorry park on the edge of the city, trying to find an English driver who'd give him a lift.'

'Where was he heading?' someone piped up.

'If we knew that, do you think my face would look like this?' Adams asked. 'Hopefully the stupid bastard's trying to get home. But we still need to nail down the remaining eyewitness statements.'

Ferreira tuned him out, her attention on Ainsworth's board and the timeline of his murder, starting at a point two years before he was killed, the point where he'd reported multiple guards for sexual assault and coercion of Long Fleet inmates.

Zigic thought it was unfeasibly far back to go. That nobody would wait two years for revenge and so far the list of sacked staff members had returned nothing but strong alibis and insistence of innocence.

But she was wondering if they'd gone far enough.

The paternity test wasn't a coincidence. It couldn't be.

And Zigic was right that it was strange timing. Paternity tests suggested wrangling over money or responsibility, deep and complicated splits in relationships, love triangles and abandoned children, and all those big, ugly emotions that could so easily escalate into the kind of murder Ainsworth had suffered.

If the results were known.

But how did the mere act of collecting samples and sending them off lead to a murder?

Ferreira took her tobacco out of her drawer and started to roll herself a cigarette, her fingers moving with practised certainty as her eyes stayed on the timeline, looking at how tight the window around Ainsworth's murder was.

On Wednesday, he flew home from Uganda. Taking travel and rest time into account, he must have gathered the DNA samples on Thursday or Friday. Saturday he was murdered.

Ferreira was convinced all the explanation they needed would be on his missing phone. This must have been argued out and organised while he was away and since the records of his texts revealed nothing she could only assume it had been done through a messaging app. The information stored on his phone and impossible to recover without the actual handset.

They were never going to find his devices though, she suspected. The killer had taken them from his house, probably destroyed them or at least hidden them very well.

She rolled her finished cigarette between her fingers, listening as Zigic stepped up and took over.

'On Saturday morning Joshua Ainsworth's neighbour took delivery of a letter that revealed that Ainsworth had used a private lab to run a paternity test.'

A murmur of interest ran around the room. Even the uninvolved officers' attention was piqued.

'The test came back positive so we now need to ask ourselves what bearing this has on his murder,' Zigic said. 'From what we can work out, the samples will have been collected in the two days immediately after Ainsworth returned from his holiday.'

He tapped the board next to Portia Collingwood's name.

'Mrs Collingwood was involved with Ainsworth, she has a daughter. So she's potentially the mother in this little triangle.' He pointed at Bloom. 'Keri, I want you to speak to her again. She probably won't just admit it to you and her alibi looks sound, but at the very least we should see if she can fill in some of the blanks around the days leading up to Ainsworth's death.'

'What about her husband?' Bloom asked. 'Surely, the man who believes he's the father is a major suspect?'

'He was out of the country,' Zigic reminded her. 'But Collingwood was very eager to hide her affair with Ainsworth, so use that to lean on her.'

'What about the samples he sent in,' Parr asked. 'If we get those we can work back from them, right?'

'Mel?'

'I called the emergency line Saturday and they told me the company had destroyed the samples already,' she told him. 'They do it at the end of the week, so we missed it by like twelve hours.'

A collective groan. Another piece of evidence whipped away from them.

Zigic ran down the rest of the jobs for the day, all resources now turned towards working out where Ainsworth had been on the Thursday and Friday before he was killed. They would go through his phone records again, chase down those calls and ask the tough questions. Re-examine his financials to try and find some pattern in his movements that might give them another suspect.

'We can't just assume Collingwood is the woman we're looking for,' he cautioned them. 'Ainsworth could easily have been involved with someone else we've yet to identify. We need to know who that woman is.'

Ferreira wondered what result Joshua Ainsworth was hoping for when he sent that sample away.

Did he want to be a daddy?

And where was the mother in all this?

'Mel?' Zigic asked from the front of the room. 'You look like you've just had an epiphany.'

'The paternity test,' she said slowly. 'Why haven't we heard anything from the mother? Ainsworth's murder has been all over the local news. It made the nationals a couple of times. She obviously gave him her and the child's DNA samples last Thursday or Friday so we know they're in contact. Why's she not come forward?'

'Maybe she's innocent and hoping we don't find out about her,' Bloom suggested.

'We should make a public appeal,' Ferreira said. 'Draw this woman out.'

'Do we really want to give that information away right now?' Zigic asked.

'Don't think we have a choice, do we?'

Zigic glanced towards the door where the media liaison officer was standing.

'Can you prepare a statement please, Nicola? We'll park it until the six o'clock though.' He turned back to Ferreira. 'Call Ainsworth's brother first and get in touch with his parents again; there's no point giving this information away if one of them knows who she is.'

'Will do,' she said. 'And Nadia?'

Zigic glanced back across his shoulder at the board where Nadia Baidoo's photograph was stuck up.

'One other potential line we have is this young woman,' he said. 'Nadia Baidoo levelled what we now believe is a credible accusation of assault against Joshua Ainsworth. This accusation led to his leaving Long Fleet. Soon after, she was given leave to remain and released.' He looked at his team. 'Nadia has now disappeared.'

'She did it then,' Weller said confidently. 'Revenge killing, right?'

'Nadia Baidoo is in a vulnerable state,' Ferreira said coldly, staring at him across the room. 'She has no money, no contacts on the outside and no family. She doesn't have a driver's licence or a car. So, how do you suppose she managed to get to Long Fleet and murder Josh Ainsworth without leaving any kind of trail?'

Weller shrugged, muttered, 'Taxi?'

'You can add that to your tasks for today then,' she said. 'Call all the local taxi firms and see if anyone went out to Long Fleet on Saturday night.'

His jaw tightened and slowly he turned back to his desk. 'Yes, boss.'

CHAPTER FIFTY-ONE

Adams knocked and came into Zigic's office without waiting for a reply.

'How did the drop go?'

'Don't call it that. You make it sound even worse than it is.' Zigic looked through the internal window, sure that it was obvious to every single officer out there that they were doing something wrong. 'I gave her it, she took it, said it'll be Tuesday or Wednesday before she can get back to me.'

It sounded simple when recounted like that. But it had been nerve-racking, haunted at each step by the knowledge that this was highly illegal and because it was one of Riggott's cases they were attempting to expose, they couldn't rely on him to step in and protect them if they got caught out.

Zigic had sat in his car, tucked away at the furthest edge of a cinema car park, praying that the sample didn't match and this whole shabby exercise would be rendered pointless and forgettable. There were other ways to take down Walton, he insisted to himself, but none sprang to mind.

'How did talking to Mel go?' he asked.

Adams leaned back against the internal window, arms folded, trying and failing to look relaxed. 'She knows we're up to something.'

'Yeah, I gathered that.'

'I said I'd tell her everything in a few days; it seemed to calm her down a bit,'

Zigic seriously doubted Adams was reading the situation correctly, misinterpreting the calm before the storm as actual calm.

'In the meantime,' Adams went on, 'there's someone we should go and talk to.'

'I've got a murder investigation getting heated up here,' Zigic told him. 'I can't keep running out on it every two minutes.'

'It's Cooper's solicitor. I told her we were looking at the case again and she wants to chat.'

'I bet she does,' Zigic said. 'You're gifting her a civil suit for false imprisonment, you do realise that?'

Adams shrugged. 'He probably was falsely imprisoned. Why wouldn't we want to straighten that out for him?'

'Oh, *there*'s your moral centre, hiding just behind your naked self-interest.'

'You're way too far into this to keep playing the puritan with me, Ziggy.' Adams smirked. 'So, you might as well come along and make sure I don't say anything I shouldn't to the very smart lady.'

Reluctantly Zigic went, pausing as he passed through the office to give out words of encouragement to Bloom and Weller and answer a question for Parr. On the front steps they passed Ferreira.

'More secret boy stuff?' she asked, around her cigarette.

Adams went up to her, hand on her waist, face close to her ear and Zigic couldn't hear what he said but he saw the smile Ferreira plastered on her face as she nodded, and then how quickly it fell away once Adams turned his back, replaced by an unnerving blankness.

They drove to an office block in the city centre, tucked between the marketplace and the cathedral precincts, a chunk of relentless brutalism that was all concrete and smoked glass. Cater & Baxter took up a full third of the building but there were huge 'OFFICES TO LET' signs in the lower windows, and Zigic wondered what had happened to the firms that had been there last time he'd visited; an engineering company and an accountants, he thought, gone or reduced or relocated out of the centre.

'Who did you speak to here?' he asked, as they got out of the car.

311

'Moira Baxter.'

Zigic stopped in the middle of the gateway. Moira Baxter was one of the leading criminal defence barristers in the area, the kind who got footballers off their drink-driving offences and finessed members of the local gentry into non-custodial sentences when they turned their shotguns on walkers who dared to use the footpaths crossing their land. She'd also been the first QC to question Zigic in court, and he still had occasional nightmares featuring her merciless stare and cut-glass accent.

'Hold on,' he said. 'She must have been a big deal twenty years ago. Why was she representing Neal Cooper?'

'Apparently his mum was her cleaner, and she went to bits when he was accused so Ms Baxter stepped in and took the case pro bono.' Adams headed for the main doors. 'I suppose she was eager to get Mrs Cooper's full attention back on her toilet bowl.'

Inside a receptionist took their names and checked their IDs, the process conducted with a saccharine smile and an over-bright tone, before he showed them to a softly furnished holding pen on the third floor.

Moira Baxter kept them waiting for fifteen minutes but had the grace to apologise about it as she saw them into her office.

They took their seats and she went around the other side of her cantilevered desk, smoothing her linen shift dress under her as she sat.

'Detective Inspector, is it now?' She smiled slightly. 'Well, I can't say I'm surprised. You handled yourself admirably for a first-timer.'

He gave the barest nod of thanks, even as a small thrill went through him. Immediately followed by a quick poke of shame for being so easily flattered.

'And you're looking into Neal's case again?' she asked. 'May I ask, why now?'

'Information has come to light that suggests another suspect may have been responsible for Tessa Darby's death,' Adams said.

Baxter kept her eyes fixed on Zigic. 'Chief Superintendent Riggott is due to retire next year, I gather,' she said, steepling her fingers under her chin. 'How does he feel about you opening up one of his most significant convictions to fresh scrutiny?'

Zigic heard Adams shift uncomfortably in his chair and resisted the urge to do the same, as she held her steady gaze on him.

'Getting to the truth is more important than any one detective's feelings,' Zigic said.

This time the pleasure lifted her whole face, just for a split second.

'An admirable sentiment,' she said. 'So, what can you tell me about this new suspect?'

'Nothing as yet,' Zigic said slowly, watching her for a reaction she was too experienced to let him see. 'The investigation is still in its early stages, but we'll be happy to keep you up to speed as developments occur.'

He was overpromising and Baxter would know that but she didn't challenge him and, he realised, she wouldn't. Because patience and cooperation here would hand her a significant scalp. If Neal Cooper was falsely convicted it would mean a splashy case and a big payout, with the bonus for her of tainting the final months of Riggott's long and distinguished career. Zigic wondered what history there was between them. As high-flying contemporaries on opposite sides of the legal divide in a small city, there would definitely be something.

'So, what do you want from me?' Baxter asked, settling back in her chair.

'We'd like to know why Neal confessed?'

'I think you already know the answer to that, Inspector.' She propped her elbow on the arm of the chair, rested her chin on it.

'We assume the confession was a result of confusion and his obsession with Tessa,' Adams said.

Zigic heard a note of genuine hope in his voice, saw Baxter register it too and immediately disregard his input.

'From the very beginning Neal told me he didn't kill Ms Darby,' Baxter said firmly. 'And while I don't always believe my clients when they protest their innocence, I believed Neal implicitly. I wouldn't have represented him otherwise. At every point in the process he maintained his innocence. During every interview he was put through, his story never changed.' A new fire entered her eyes. 'I could see how desperate Riggott was getting. As the weeks passed it became clear to me that he didn't have any other suspects and that he was under pressure to charge someone. Pressure he clearly wasn't up to handling.'

Zigic felt the knot of anxiety in his stomach writhe and tighten. He could see Riggott behaving just as she suggested, knew how he would have snapped and raged, that vein pulsing in his forehead as he tried to rally his team, the frustration seething as he took every dressing-down from above and every grilling from the press.

He'd never handled pressure well, not for as long as Zigic had worked under him. Didn't seem able to feed off it like the best coppers could. Maybe that was why he went up the management structure so quickly; the higher he went the less damage he could do.

'The penultimate interview Riggott conducted with Neal ran late; it was almost midnight by the time he finished with the boy, and I had to insist on ending it even then because Neal was exhausted and I could see very clearly that Riggott was trying to grind him down to the point where he'd say anything to make it stop.' She pursed her lips. 'In all honesty, Neal was not the sharpest young man you'd meet, and there was a sustained attempt to use that weakness against him.'

Zigic thought of how Adams went after Neal Cooper at his home. Using the same tactics Riggott had, playing the game his mentor had taught him.

Baxter took a deep breath.

'Neal spent the night in custody,' she said. 'And when I went in to see him the next morning, he told me he wanted to confess.'

There it was.

The knot in his stomach began to throb, so hard he was sure he could feel it beating against the back of his abdominal muscles.

'What reason did he give for changing his mind?' Zigic asked.

'He said he'd been lying because he was scared of going to prison.' She drew her knuckles along her jawline, eyes temporarily losing focus. 'I told him I knew he was innocent but he wouldn't listen to me; he insisted on going back in and making a full confession.'

'And there was no way you could stop him?'

She shook her head. 'When I pressed him he got angry and told me to leave. But I decided the best course of action was to stay and try to get him the best deal I could.' A grim smile twisted her mouth. 'The one thing he was very clear about wanting me to do was to make sure he served his sentence in a young offenders' institution.'

'Where did he get that idea from?' Zigic asked.

Baxter opened her hands wide. 'He hadn't mentioned prison at all up to that point. He was so convinced his innocence would keep him safe. He had absolute and total trust in the system, Inspector Zigic. He was like a child that way; he thought the police protected good people like him and that they wouldn't do anything to harm him. DCS Riggott exploited that trust to manipulate Neal into confessing.'

Zigic thought of Riggott going down to the basement once Baxter had left Thorpe Wood Station, being let into Neal Cooper's cell, let into his soft and vulnerable head. No solicitor to protect him, no recording equipment to capture what precisely Riggott had said.

But Zigic knew him well enough to guess at it.

Keep lying and we'll send you to a category A prison; confess and we'll make recommendations of leniency. You're only sixteen, you can go to a young offenders' institution; they're just like college, you'll be safe there. We've got you Neal, the choice now is how much it hurts.

A few minutes later, interview over, back in the car, Adams asked, 'Do you believe her?'

'You don't?'

He squirmed in the driver's seat. 'She's got her own agenda here. I don't think we should take what she says as gospel.'

Adams had pushed for this, tried to shrug off the weight that would come down on them if Riggott was found to have acted inappropriately. He'd made this happen almost single-handedly, and now the evidence was in front of him, he was scared where it would lead them.

There was a reckoning coming. A conversation none of them would survive completely clean.

'Baxter isn't the only person who knows what Riggott did in that cell,' Zigic said. 'You want verification? Let's get it.'

Chapter Fifty-Two

They were almost back at the station when DC Wahlia called, his voice coming through the speakerphone fast and tight, sending them down the parkway and onto Oundle Road, heading for an address on the more sedate side of the sprawling Orton estates. To a modest detached house at the bottom of a quiet cul-de-sac where most of the neighbours were at work and those at home were more the type to peer through their slatted wooden blinds than to come out and shout encouragement at the two women trying to tear each other's heads off in the front garden of a corner house.

A pair of uniformed officers were already on the scene, trying to separate the women. But Wendy Darby was too determined to be held. Her maternal fury driving her on, trying to shake off a man fifty pounds heavier and five inches taller, sending her feet flying towards Jackie Walton, who was doing more shouting than fighting and letting herself be gently removed to a safe distance.

Zigic was out of the car before it stopped moving, running over and between the two women, into Wendy Darby's eyeline.

She didn't see him, trying to twist free of the big hands holding her firm.

'You know what he is, Jackie!' she shouted.

'Wendy, this isn't helping,' Zigic said, gently, taking a step towards her.

He could smell the alcohol on her breath, guessed the PC holding her didn't know who she was or what she was doing here, maybe hadn't even realised that the Mrs Walton they were dragging her away from was the same one whose son they'd spent thousands of man-hours tracking. He'd smelled gin on Wendy Darby's breath at 11 a.m. and assumed she was the person in the wrong.

'How long did you know, Jackie?' she shouted. 'How long have you been lying for him?'

'She's unhinged,' Jackie Walton said desperately, addressing the group of police and the neighbours.

'You were my best friend,' Wendy choked out. 'You came to my house and you sat with me, and all the time you knew Lee killed my girl. How could you do that? What is wrong with you?'

Her hair was plastered to her face, her eyes watery and red. She looked like she'd spent every minute since they went to speak to her at the garden centre in a state of pure hell.

Zigic felt the guilt like a knife between his ribs.

Hoped Adams felt it too.

His attention was on Jackie Walton though, and all Zigic could hear was her demanding Wendy be arrested, putting on a more refined accent than she usually used, scandalised and indignant at what was happening. But the tremble was real, as was the way she held her arms clasped around her body.

Her eyes met Zigic's and she changed tack.

'You need to take her to hospital,' she said to him. 'She's clearly not in her right mind. I think she needs sedating before she hurts herself.' She turned to the PC standing beside her. 'Really, please. I'm worried about her. She needs help.'

'Expert on psychology are you now?' Adams asked. 'Shame you didn't spot that your son was a serial rapist a bit sooner.'

'She knew!' Wendy shouted.

Zigic tried to dip into her eyeline again but her gaze was locked on Adams and Jackie Walton, so intensely focused that she managed to drag herself and the PC a full two steps closer to them, until she was virtually toe to toe with Zigic.

'She told me years ago she was worried about him,' Wendy said. 'Always hanging around his little cousins, disappearing into the garage with them ...'

The PC hauled her back again.

'Shut up!' Jackie cried.

'You knew what he was and you did *nothing*. Not even when it was your own family he was hurting.'

'This is your fault,' Jackie Walton said, stabbing a finger at Adams, her attempt at decorum forgotten. 'You fitted my boy up and now look what I'm having to put up with. This mad bitch coming around reeking of supermarket gin, accusing me of all sorts.'

'Not all sorts,' Adams said, leaning towards her. 'Just one thing – covering for Lee when he killed Tessa.'

Jackie Walton's face flushed a deep crimson. 'This is harassment. I'm going to get my lawyer onto you. This is a gross abuse of police power. My Lee was found innocent and you've got no right to keep coming after him like this.'

'Get in touch with your lawyer,' Adams said. 'Something tells me Lee's going to need her again in the very near future.'

She stammered around a reply and backed away, stepping into a flower bed filled with bright orange marigolds, crushing a plant underfoot.

The fight drained from Wendy just as abruptly and Zigic noticed the relief on the PC's face. He started to walk her towards the patrol car and she let herself be taken and eased into the back with no resistance.

'I want to press charges,' Jackie Walton said in a wobbly voice, arms still folded, chin down. 'She attacked me, she made me feel unsafe.'

'Yeah?' Adams asked. 'Do you really want to come down to Thorpe Wood and make a statement? We can put you in the same interview room where Lee denied raping all of those women you know he actually attacked. Would you enjoy that, Jackie? Seeing where your boy did some of his finest lying?'

Without another word she turned away and retreated inside her house, the front door closing very softly.

Zigic told the PC to take Wendy Darby out of the patrol car and put her in the back of Adams's instead, thinking the least they could do now was see her home safely and with the dignity she deserved. She moved with the same exhausted compliance and Zigic hoped she felt better for coming here and confronting Jackie Walton, her former best friend.

The thought of her sitting in Wendy's house, bringing her tea and passing her hankies as she cried for her dead daughter, sitting there knowing there was a possibility her own son was responsible ...

How had she done it, he wondered. What feats of denial had Jackie Walton performed over the years to allow herself to keep hugging him and saying, 'I love you, son'?

As he stooped to get into the car, a movement in the living-room window stopped him; Lee Walton, standing staring back at him.

He'd been in the house the whole time. Had seen everything. And now he knew they were onto him for Tessa Darby's murder.

CHAPTER FIFTY-THREE

'I don't understand,' Greg Ainsworth said. 'Why wouldn't Josh have told me about something this important?'

Ferreira was wondering the same thing. They clearly weren't the closest of brothers but something as significant as this … surely, Ainsworth would have needed to unburden to someone.

'Maybe he didn't expect the child to be his,' she suggested.

'Still, it's huge news.' In the background she could hear cartoons playing and a relentless tinny drumming as one of his boys bashed away at what sounded like an upturned saucepan. 'Finn, please stop doing that, Daddy's on the phone.'

'Do you have any idea who the mother might be?' Ferreira asked. 'Did Josh mention anyone he'd been seeing recently?'

'Apart from Portia?' he asked.

'We're speaking to her again.'

'It wasn't necessarily a relationship, was it?' he said tentatively. 'It might have been a one-night stand.'

Ferreira had been thinking the same thing, knew that if that was the case they were relying on the woman coming forward at a time when she had absolutely nothing to gain by helping them. All she'd be doing was potentially putting herself in the frame for murder.

'You don't think that's why he was killed?' Greg carried on, horrified. 'If he'd been sleeping with someone who already had a boyfriend and they found out?'

'It's a possibility,' Ferreira admitted. 'But until we can identify the woman, it's very difficult for us to understand if it has anything to do with his death.'

The banging at Greg's end intensified, accompanied by a high, atonal singing, and then a dog started to bark and he sighed heavily. A sliding door opened and closed and the sound was muffled as he went outside.

'Was the test positive?' he asked. 'Was Josh the father?'

'It's a positive match, yes.'

He let out a small groan, sounding genuinely upset. 'Well, what happens now? We must have some rights, right? The baby is our family too. Mum and Dad are going to want to know about this. They'll want to be involved.'

Ferreira didn't know what to tell him, felt out of her depth.

'I mean, if the woman *is* involved, if she goes to prison or whatever, what's going to happen to the baby?' he asked. 'Will we be able to adopt or something? I'll have to talk to my wife but I'm sure she won't want her niece or nephew going into care.' The panic was rising in his voice, sending him babbling, and she felt a sharp stab of sympathy for this sweet-natured man and his protective instincts. 'I don't understand how you can't know who she is. There must be records somewhere.'

'We don't have Josh's phone,' she explained. 'It's pretty much impossible to find out who she is if we can't access his communications. Not unless somebody can tell us who she is. What about your parents? Is there any chance Josh talked to them about it?'

'No, if Mum knew about this I'd have known about it two minutes later.'

She promised Greg that she would contact him if they found the mother, knowing she could do nothing more than encourage the woman to contact them herself.

Unless she was the killer.

Ferreira ended the call, thinking about how the woman must have given Joshua Ainsworth the DNA samples, that she must have wanted him to be the father because why do it otherwise?

What did she want from him? Financial support or something more significant?

He clearly hadn't believed he was the father, or why even take the test?

Unless the DNA test was because there was another candidate for paternity, she thought, as she unpeeled the lid of her avocado and quinoa salad.

That was definitely the kind of thing that could lead to murder. And it might explain how the mere fact of the test had escalated into violence before the results were through.

A love triangle rumbling along, suspicion and accusation. A relationship already in the process of ending and then the question of who the daddy was to push it over the edge.

Everyone was assuming the child was a baby but what if this was something that had been going on for years? A man having raised a child as his own, then beginning to suspect it wasn't ...

Portia Collingwood was the obvious suspect but Ferreira found the idea of her as the mystery mother didn't quite sit right. It was a long-term affair, seemingly mutually satisfying as a standing arrangement. No reason for that to change. Not that they knew of, anyway.

They'd found no evidence of another relationship but nothing to disprove it either.

If it was someone he worked with there might not be a lot of evidence. Someone he didn't need to call and text regularly because they were together all day.

She thought of Ruth Garner. Wondered how many other female members of staff at Long Fleet might be in the frame. If only they could speak to them.

She called his parents and got his father, who immediately passed the phone over to Mrs Ainsworth. Ferreira could hear her hastily finishing another call as she came to the landline.

'Love you, bye. Bye. Yes, I'll call you back. Bye. Bye-bye.' She picked up the handset and in a slightly different voice, said, 'Greg just called me. Why don't you know who this woman is?'

Ferreira went through the same conversation she'd had with Josh's brother, but a prolonged and more circuitous version this time as if his mother wanted to talk about Josh just for the sake of talking.

Ten minutes later Ferreira ended the call no wiser than she'd been before it.

She finished her salad, trying to tune out the inane conversation Bloom and Weller were having as they ate their own lunches. She thought they'd hit rock bottom during last month's obsession with *Love Island*, but now she realised this was their default setting. Perhaps the minimum requirements for detective-level officers needed to be raised quite significantly.

Had she and Bobby sounded like that? she wondered.

Did Zigic spend years sitting in his office thinking, Shut up, you stupid children?

She rolled a cigarette and found herself in the stairwell, turning the wrong way and heading up to the old Hate Crimes office.

The room was mothballed but open, the air stale-smelling already, a faint mustiness cut with the sharp tang of the plastic covers that had been put over the furniture. She heaved the window open and sat down on the sill as she lit her cigarette.

An unknown number flashed up on her phone and she answered.

'Hi, Sergeant Ferreira?' A man's voice, hesitant but lifted by the need to be heard above the music playing in the background. 'You were asking about Nadia Baidoo? I'm the manager at Beckett Burgers in Cambridge. I think you talked to my number two, last week?'

'That's right,' Ferreira said, remembering the frustrating conversation they'd had with the assistant manager who seemed to feel her authority didn't extend to accessing staff records. 'Has Nadia been back?'

'No, but I thought you might want to know. Someone got in touch with me about her last month. She'd given us as a reference.'

Ferreira shook her head in bemusement. Wondering if Nadia was naïve or ballsy as hell to give the place where she was snatched by immigration as a reference.

'Where was this?' she asked.

'In Peterborough.'

She felt the excitement beginning to stir.

He gave her the name of a boutique in the old arcade, the phone number and the name of the person who called. 'I gave Nadia a good reference,' he said. 'I hope she got the job.'

Ferreira immediately called the boutique, waited to be put on with the owner, who she'd seen when she'd been shopping there for a new winter coat last year. She remembered a petite woman with jet-black hair and severe eyebrows and a penchant for leopard print that verged on mania.

'Nadia, yeah,' she said, in an Essex drawl. 'Don't know what happened with her. She ghosted us after a couple of shifts. She was good and all, had a strong look, you know? I like that in my staff, gives the customers something to compete with.'

'Do you have an address for her?' Ferreira asked.

'Yeah, gimme a minute, I'll call you back.'

She waited, looking out across the front of the station, nervous energy sparking in her chest, already thinking about what she would ask Nadia, about where this new development was going to take them.

Below her she saw Zigic and Adams getting out of the car. Adams full of energy as he bounded up the station steps; Zigic, coming up behind him, was hard-faced and squared off with tension or anger.

She sat down again and waited for her phone to ring.

CHAPTER FIFTY-FOUR

Zigic had left Wendy Darby curled up on her sofa, under a blanket, because by the time he got her home she was shivering despite the heat. The adrenaline had worn off and the crash that came afterwards had all but knocked her flat. She couldn't get out of the car when Adams pulled into her driveway, and Zigic had coaxed her out, holding her hands, which trembled against his, and then caught her around the waist and walked her slowly up the short path, noticing for the first time that she was wearing odd shoes. The colour was the same but the style slightly different, and he wondered how incoherent with despair and rage she must have been when she left the house, so focused on what she had to say to Jackie Walton that she hadn't noticed what she was putting on her feet.

Zigic saw her to the sofa and went to make her a cup of tea, debated emptying out the half bottle of gin, which sat on the worktop, but decided she would need the comfort of it later, no matter how unhelpful he thought it was.

Adams paced the kitchen as the kettle came to a boil.

'Did you see Walton?' he said, voice pitched at a whisper.

'I saw him.'

'I'm surprised he didn't come out and get involved.'

'Why don't you go back to the station,' Zigic suggested, opening the cupboards in search of biscuits. 'I'll call a taxi.'

'No, you're alright. I'll wait for you in the car.'

Wendy Darby stared straight through Zigic as he placed her tea and a plate of biscuits on the coffee table. He felt impotent in the face of her grief, could hardly bear the knowledge that they'd brought her to this point.

It had been bad enough when they broke the news, but seeing how wild she'd been with Jackie Walton and just how deep that betrayal went was heartbreaking.

He sat down in an armchair, looked at the photographs of Tessa lined up along the mantelpiece, more of them on the bookshelves and hung in clusters behind the sofa. He wondered where her father was. The file had mentioned him briefly, but he'd never been a suspect so Riggott's interest in him had ended almost instantly. Had he died or had Tessa's murder ended the marriage like so many murders did?

Twenty years was a long time to bear this burden alone.

'Wendy, it's best you don't approach Jackie again,' he said gently. 'We've talked her out of pressing charges but that might not work next time.'

She didn't reply, didn't stir at all.

'I know you're going through a lot right now and if you need to talk to someone, we can help with that.'

He regretted the words immediately, knew there was no one he could send to be with her, no family liaison he could assign for an off-book case.

Again she didn't respond and all the thin assurances and hopeful sentiments that were rattling around his head smeared together into a meaningless blur. He was doing this for himself, he realised. Was sitting here so he could feel like he'd at least tried to undo some of the damage he'd done. It was a sad and selfish manoeuvre and recognising it only made him feel smaller still.

'Is there anyone I can call for you?' he asked.

She closed her eyes.

'If you need anything you can ring me, okay?' he said, taking out a card and placing it on the table. 'Any time, Wendy. Just call.'

He wanted her to snap to her feet. Rant and rave at him, show some spark of defiance so he'd know they hadn't completely destroyed her.

But she didn't and he left the house, hating himself but hating Adams more because he'd started all of this.

And then in the car, driving back to Thorpe Wood, Adams had finally broken the silence.

'Look, I don't like this either, Ziggy. But we're short on options so we're going to have to do some things which don't sit well.'

At the solicitor's office he'd seemed ready to dump the whole case rather than accept once and for all that Riggott had manipulated Cooper into confessing. That worry had been shelved but Zigic thought he needed reminding that he wasn't in control of this and that their actions had consequences.

Bring it home to him, right here and now in the station.

'Colleen, can we have a word, please?' Zigic asked, as he approached her desk. 'In my office if you wouldn't mind.'

He saw Adams cut a quick glance at Murray and her giving him a questioning look in response, but they both followed. She sat down, Adams positioning himself against the defunct filing cabinets.

'You ready to tell me what you're playing at, Billy?' Murray asked him.

'You know what we're doing, Col.'

'Not the details,' she said. 'Not the specific case.'

'Tessa Darby,' Zigic told her.

A brief ripple of unease crossed her face, before she rearranged herself in her seat, leaning back and smoothing her blouse down.

'You worked the case,' Zigic said. 'Under Riggott.'

She nodded but she was looking at Adams. 'You're playing a dangerous game, mate. This why you've been keeping me out of the loop?'

'We were just trying to protect you,' he said. 'You and Mel.'

'Bollocks. You just never wanted someone who'd tell you what a massive mistake you're making.' She jabbed her fingertip into the arm of the chair. 'That case was solid. We got a confession.'

'Did you know Lee Walton was at the same college as Tessa?' Zigic asked, seeing from her reaction that she didn't. 'And that their mothers were best friends at the time?'

'Cooper didn't do it,' Adams told her.

'Then why did he bloody confess?' She threw her arms wide, looked incredulously between them. 'Christ Almighty, is this what you've been doing? I thought you actually had something on Walton.'

'Cooper's solicitor believes the confession was coerced,' Zigic said.

Her eyes darkened and narrowed and she leaned forward in her chair again.

'No, that never happened.'

'Come on, Col,' Adams said, moving into the seat next to her. 'You know what Riggott was like. You worked closely with him on that case –'

'Yeah, I did. Which means you're accusing me of misconduct as well.'

'No one's saying that.' Zigic tried to keep his voice even but he could feel Murray's annoyance coming across the table, the defensiveness in it that only made him more convinced that the accusation against Riggott was true. 'But isn't it possible that the pressure of multiple interviews might have encouraged Cooper to confess?'

'We all tell them same thing,' Adams said. 'It's standard procedure – confess and you'll get a lighter sentence. If Riggott said that –'

'He didn't say that,' she snapped. 'I was in every single one of those interviews and he never said it.'

'What about the chats that weren't recorded?' Zigic asked.

She glared at him.

'Col, we're getting close to nailing Walton for Tessa Darby's murder,' Adams said, sounding too certain for the evidence they had, but Zigic was sure he believed it, and he could see Murray getting dragged along too, the hard line of her mouth softening, something hopeful coming into her eyes. 'He's rattled, right? You know how Walton was, we never managed to put him on the back foot, not once. Not even when we had him in court. But this has got to him. He did it, Col. I'm sure of it.'

'You can't build a case on "rattled",' she said, retreating in her chair again. 'Is that all you've got? He looks a bit stressed and Cooper's solicitor saying the confession was bent?'

Zigic didn't want to tell her. She went way back with Riggott, had been brought in and trained up by him. Plucked out of uniform where her talents had been underused and her potential ignored. Word was they were close outside of work too, though Zigic had never noticed her getting special treatment. The station gossip mill suggested Riggott was the person who picked her up after her divorce laid her flat.

As big as this case was and as emotionally involved as Murray had become with the victims, Zigic felt certain her loyalty to Riggott wouldn't be swayed.

Surely Adams saw that. 'We've got a DNA sample,' he said.

Zigic winced.

'Where from?' Murray asked, eyes widening. 'What have you done?'

'Don't worry about that,' Adams said, but she clearly was worried. 'We'll have a result tomorrow. And if it comes back as a match for Walton, we're going to go to Riggott and ask him to reopen the case.'

'You're dreaming,' she said, letting out a humourless laugh. 'Are you crazy?'

'We need you to come in on this, Col. You were on the original case; we need you to back us up on Cooper's confession.'

For ten seconds that felt like five minutes, she didn't answer and Zigic could hear her breathing becoming shallow and faster, a phone ringing out on the floor and a sudden high peel of laughter from Bloom, which cut through the room like a blade. Murray was going to storm out of here and straight into Riggott's office.

This was it.

'Col, please,' Adams said, a plaintive whine in his voice. 'We can't get Walton without you.'

She sucked her bottom lip into her mouth, blew it out again.

'For your sake I hope you're wrong about this.' She stood, looking down at Zigic. 'Because if you're right and you upend that conviction, Riggott is going to be your enemy for life.'

She left his office, Adams on her heels, and Zigic watched as he drew her next door into his, obviously planning on softening her up some more.

Or changing the story, he realised. Putting the responsibility and the blame on him for when the shit hit the fan.

Ferreira came into the office without knocking. Saw the look on his face and rapped on the frame. She was smiling. Grinning so wide it must have been painful.

'I've found Nadia Baidoo.'

CHAPTER FIFTY-FIVE

It was a housing development at the edge of Deeping St James, a couple of decades old, established enough for the trees planted around it to have grown and hints of neglect to emerge here and there. Large detached places at the front, neat rows of terraces designed to look like workers' cottages further in, buff brick and slate roofs, peaked porches and short driveways edged with flower beds. A nice spot, quiet and self-contained. The kind of place where the neighbours would say hello in passing but not pry too far, Ferreira thought, hoping she was wrong.

The house they wanted was an end-of-terrace tucked away in a corner. There was no car in the driveway, the windows were all semi-shaded by wooden blinds, but the upstairs ones were open and she felt sure that Nadia Baidoo would be in.

Hoped Patrick Sutherland was too.

The desire to confront him was an almost physical thing now, a stirring of adrenaline and indignation through her blood. When she thought of how carefully he'd evaded her questions about Nadia – the pitch-perfect performance he'd given of a man conflicted, scared for his job, unwilling to fully believe the worst of his former colleague.

He'd duped her.

First at Long Fleet and then at Thorpe Wood Station.

She felt owed the pleasure of turning up unexpected at his door to expose him. Wanted to see his face drop.

'How did he think we wouldn't find out about Nadia?' Zigic asked angrily.

Ferreira held her tongue, remembering how dismissive he'd been of her determination to track Nadia down. And maybe she hadn't anticipated it playing out like this, more concerned for the young woman's safety than anything else, but if she hadn't pursued that instinct, they wouldn't be here now and Patrick Sutherland would still be nothing more than a witness on the periphery of the investigation.

'Surely someone from Long Fleet knew about them,' Zigic said.

'He told me he doesn't have anything to do with any of them outside work. He lives miles away, so the likelihood of bumping into someone who'd recognise her is minimal.'

'But still ...'

'I guess he knew he was safe as long as we never had a reason to turn up at his house.' She smiled bitterly. 'That's why he put himself out coming to the station the other evening. He didn't want us here. I should have seen it.'

'Nobody could have seen that,' Zigic said reassuringly.

She knocked on the front door, watching through its small glass panel for movement in the darkened hallway beyond. A figure came out of a room at the back of the house, and they could obviously see her more clearly than she could see them because she slowed and stopped near the foot of the stairs, as if wondering whether not answering was an option.

Ferreira cocked her head to listen for the back door slamming, primed to give chase if necessary.

But finally the figure moved again and the door opened.

Nadia Baidoo. Taller than Ferreira expected from her photograph, almost six foot and willowy despite the baggy T-shirt she was wearing over a pair of leggings. Younger-looking than she expected too. She could have passed for fourteen right then, with her hair wrapped up in a silk scarf and her eyes flicking nervously between them before she settled on Zigic.

'Is there something I can help you with?'

Her accent was local, vaguely estuary, and Ferreira was momentarily surprised before catching herself. How many times had she snapped at someone for praising her 'excellent English' or being surprised by her accent? In her head Nadia had sounded Ghanaian. A stupid and lazy assumption she'd made despite knowing the young woman had come here as a child.

'Detective Inspector Zigic,' he said. 'This is Sergeant Ferreira. Do you think we could come in, please?'

'I haven't done anything wrong.'

'We'd just like to ask you a few questions,' Ferreira said. 'I'm sure you'd prefer to do that here rather than ...'

Nadia caught her meaning and stepped back to let them in, closed the door and showed them into a large room that went right through the house, sofas at the front, dining table in the middle, kitchen tucked down the back overlooking the garden. There was an unmistakable smell of newness in the room, discernible even under the sharp scent of polish. A mingling of emulsion and new fabric and as they moved to the seating area, Ferreira noticed how plumply perfect the sofa cushions were, as if they had never been sat on before.

Zigic took one end of the sofa, Ferreira the other.

Nadia stood over them, hands clasped in front of her, one foot on top of the other, and she looked so absurdly girlish that Ferreira was glad Patrick Sutherland was out because she wasn't sure she'd be able to keep her hands off him. Even if they hadn't met in Long Fleet, if that terrible unequal power dynamic didn't exist, this relationship would look wrong.

Creepy, she mentally corrected herself.

There was twelve years between Nadia and Sutherland but it might as well have been twenty.

'Do you want tea or something?' Nadia asked.

'We're fine, thanks,' Ferreira said, showing her an open and neutral face, wanting her to feel like she could talk to them. 'How are you, Nadia?'

'I'm okay,' she said warily, moving to a pale armchair that sat too low to the ground for her height.

Ferreira reached into her handbag and took out the photograph they'd found in the boxes from Cambridge, the one of Nadia with her mother.

'I thought you might want this back,' Ferreira said, passing it to her across the coffee table.

Nadia let out a small sob as she took it, hiding her mouth with her hand. Tears sprang up in her eyes. 'I thought I'd lost this.'

'Mrs Loewe kept it for you,' Ferreira told her. 'She kept all your things. I think she was hoping you'd go back home when you could.'

'This is the only photo I have of Mum,' Nadia said, touching her fingertips gently to the image. 'I had loads on my phone but they took it when they arrested me, and when I asked for it back, they told me it got lost somewhere.'

'Are they saved to your laptop?' Ferreira asked.

She nodded.

'We've got that at the station.'

The relief was there and gone in an instant, smothered by fear. 'Can you send me it?'

'We'll sign it over to you,' Ferreira said, seeing how desperate Nadia was not to be taken in again.

They'd anticipated this. Prepared for it. In the car on the way over, they discussed Nadia Baidoo's vulnerability and the importance of handling her carefully. Neither wanted to retraumatise her. But Zigic had insisted she was a suspect as well as a victim, and at some point they were going to have to take her in.

He'd agreed that an initial informal conversation here might make it less difficult on her, but Ferreira was aware of all the more serious questions they would have to ask her soon.

'How are you coping?' she asked. 'Being out of Long Fleet?'

Nadia flinched at the name of the place. 'It's better here. The village is nice.'

No mention of Sutherland and it occurred to Ferreira that Nadia perhaps thought they were unaware that this was his house.

'Why didn't you go back to Cambridge?'

'There's nothing there for me,' Nadia said, curling up a little tighter in the chair, her eyes still fixed on the photograph she held against her knee.

'What about your friends?'

335

'They're not my friends any more,' she said sadly. 'People like that, they're your friends as long as you're the same as them, but when something happens, when you – when your life gets difficult, it's like they think the bad stuff is catching and they run away from you as fast as they can.'

Ferreira thought about what Mrs Loewe had told her, how Nadia was left to her grief for months. No visits, no calls. It was understandable that she felt like this. And maybe she'd said the same to Sutherland and he'd seen the opportunity to snatch her up out of her isolation. No mother to disapprove of him, no girlfriends to wrinkle their noses and say, 'But he's so *old*, babe.'

'Mrs Loewe tried to find you,' Ferreira told her. 'She's been really worried about you.'

Nadia chewed on her bottom lip thoughtfully, but didn't reply, and Ferreira wondered whether things had been so warm at that house as they'd been led to believe. Mrs Loewe hadn't looked very hard for her after all.

'The people at Haven House are worried too,' Ferreira said. 'Why did you leave there so suddenly?'

'They told me I could stay as long as I wanted to.' Still Nadia wouldn't look at either of them.

Ferreira glanced towards Zigic, saw how troubled he was by her behaviour, how he strained as he sat there, wanting to do *something* but not knowing what he could do. For all his talk of Nadia being a suspect, Ferreira could see the father rising up in him, the nurturing instinct that was never far from the surface.

'They were going to help you get sorted, weren't they?' Ferreira asked. 'Find you somewhere to live, get your paperwork all straightened out.'

'What's wrong with my paperwork?' Nadia said, looking up sharply. 'I was given permission to stay. You can't just take it away from me. I haven't done anything wrong. I've just been here, I've been studying. What have I done?'

'We're not here about your paperwork,' Zigic said, putting out a calming hand. 'There's no problem with it, okay?'

Nadia nodded, a little of her defiance bleeding away.

But it remained in the air between them, a certain heaviness. They were fighting against what they needed to do as police officers, trying to be people first, feeling their way through the impossible contradictions of those two positions.

The longer the three of them sat here the more unavoidably obvious it became that Nadia knew why they were here, too. The anxiety was coming off her in waves, written in the stiff line of her jaw and the way she held a defensive arm across her body, every muscle straining against the urge to run, right down to her toes, which gripped the seat pad.

'How did you get here, Nadia?' Ferreira asked.

'I don't understand.' Her voice was tremulous. 'You mean, how did I get here from Peterborough?'

'Why are you living with Dr Sutherland?'

She hesitated and Ferreira realised that Sutherland hadn't considered the possibility of them finding her and asking these questions. Wouldn't he have warned her? Given her an explanation to pass onto them?

'I needed a place to stay,' she said, as if it was that simple.

'You had somewhere. Haven house.' Ferreira watched a shutter come down in front of Nadia's face, but her fingers twitched against the photo frame and her toes flexed against the chair. 'Did you call Dr Sutherland while you were there?'

Abruptly Nadia got to her feet. 'I need some water.'

Ferreira followed her to the kitchen at the back of the room, watched her take down a glass from a wooden shelf, hand trembling as she turned the tap. She concentrated on filling the glass, eyes downcast, lips pursed.

'Why did you have Dr Sutherland's phone number?'

'I didn't,' she said quietly, bringing the glass to her mouth. 'He came to find me.'

Ferreira glanced quickly at Zigic, saw the shock on his face.

'Why did he do that?'

'He was worried about me. He wanted to know if I had somewhere to go.'

'A lot of women leave Long Fleet with nowhere to go,' Ferreira said, bracing her hand against the worktop. 'But you're the only one living in his house.'

'It isn't against the rules.' Nadia turned to face her, spine straightening. 'I'm not in Long Fleet any more. I can do what I want.'

'And is *this* what you want?'

'I didn't have anywhere to go,' Nadia said softly.

It wasn't an answer but an explanation and Ferreira could see the terrible logic of it. How Sutherland might have framed it for Nadia, how inevitable it must have felt given her circumstances.

'Are you two in a relationship?' she asked.

Nadia nodded.

'Were you sleeping together when you were in Long Fleet?'

'No,' she replied, almost before Ferreira had finished speaking.

And Ferreira didn't believe it. Couldn't. She saw the shame in Nadia's eyes, so deep and profound that it stunned her.

Nadia moved away, heading to the chair in the front window again. As Ferreira turned to follow her, she noticed a spatter of dark stains in the pale grout between the limestone floor tiles near the back door. They could have been a dozen different things, she told herself as she squatted down, but she knew what an old wine stain looked like, how it was more purple than this, how curry sauce bled its oily orange spices as it aged, how jam held its colour and coffee went weak and washed out.

Blood looked like this. Only ever blood.

Zigic was questioning Nadia now, asking her about Sutherland and how he'd talked her into coming here. Repeating the same questions Ferreira had asked but at more length because he was distracting her rather than seeking new information.

Ferreira scrutinised the skirting boards near the door, seeing that the wall there had been repainted recently, several thick coats with the roller's stipple marks visible. Done in haste, she thought. In desperation.

The back door was uPVC, would have washed clean easily enough. She opened it and saw the telltale scuff marks where somebody had levered the double-glazed glass panel out of the unit. There was more dried blood on the brickwork near the handle, drips and tracks that had a bleached-out quality, but blood was persistent and mortar more porous than brick.

She played it through in her head: someone breaks in, cutting themselves in the process, and bleeds all over the door and into the kitchen.

But it wasn't that, she realised, as she turned a slow circle, her eyes on the ground, and found spots of what could be blood on the paving slabs. They were bleeding *before* they even reached the door.

Maybe a first attempt gone wrong, she thought.

Except no, there they were, more spots almost hidden in the gravel path that ran through the centre of the lawn. Stray drips dried on the flowers of a drift of white ox-eye daisies almost a metre away, as if the burglar had tried to shake the pain out of his hand. She kept walking, the trail getting light and sparser until she reached the back fence.

The bed in front of it was planted with low, dark-leaved creepers, viciously barbed like a trap. No more than knee high.

They would prick you wickedly but she wasn't convinced they would draw so much blood.

If the burglar came over the fence, they might damage their legs but not their hands. It was barely one and a half metres high, not a drop into the unknown. You would lower yourself down.

Reach up and drag yourself over.

She leaned closer, peering at the top of the fence.

'Gotcha.'

The entire stretch of fence was lined with gripper rods, their spikes short but thick and vicious-looking, designed to rip open the hands of anyone who tried to climb into the garden.

She thought of the mysterious injuries on Joshua Ainsworth's fingers, the regularly spaced punctures torn ragged but semi-healed by the time he died. Pictured him grabbing for the top of the fence to haul himself over and ripping his hands open.

But not stopping.

Something propelled him, bleeding, along the path and through the back door and into that house.

CHAPTER FIFTY-SIX

They called a car to take Nadia into Thorpe Wood Station, called a solicitor too, knowing that she would need representation before they formally questioned her. Zigic found the business card he'd been given by the woman they ran into at Long Fleet. She'd said to get in touch if they needed anything, and he figured this was something she could help with.

It was beyond the basic requirements of his job at this point, possibly at odds with best practice for a detective, finding good legal advice for a suspect when an uninterested duty solicitor would make his life easier. But he wanted to do this right.

Forensics turned up at the same time as the patrol car and he saw the fear in Nadia's eyes as she was walked out of the house, tripping over her feet, her gaze magnetised to the bright red van.

Whatever had happened in that house she knew about it.

How far she was involved and in what capacity remained to be seen.

Zigic called over the two extra uniforms he'd requested and briefed them on the door-to-door: anything unusual noticed in the street late last week, any strange activity sighted at the Sutherland house on the night Joshua Ainsworth was killed.

Ferreira was already next door, standing on the front step talking to Sutherland's neighbour, who kept gesturing behind herself into the house. Ferreira was nodding, making notes. She looked like she was happy about what she was hearing and sure enough, a couple of minutes later, she returned with a spring in her step.

'Break-in mid-morning on Thursday,' she said.

'Broad daylight?' Zigic asked, amazed at Josh Ainsworth's gall. 'Could she give you a description?'

'She didn't actually see it,' Ferreira told him. 'She went out at nine to hang some washing out, came back a couple of hours later and saw that the glass had been removed from the back door. She came over here and knocked to see if everything was okay but didn't get an answer.'

'Ainsworth waited until the house was empty then?'

'I guess.' But she didn't sound entirely convinced. 'Apparently they had a window fitter in the next morning and she went around again to see what had happened – she said they don't get much trouble here so she was worried if it was the beginning of a spate of break-ins, but I think she's probably just nosy.'

'Lucky for us.'

'Nadia told her they hadn't taken anything but then the neighbour started warning her about checking they hadn't got into her bank statements and stuff because of ID fraud and to make sure they hadn't taken her spare keys, but she said Nadia didn't want to talk.'

'What did she know about Nadia?' Zigic asked.

'Not much. As far as she's concerned, Nadia moved in a few weeks ago and they're a nice quiet couple who don't annoy her, so ...'

'Perfect neighbours.'

'Yeah.'

'Did she hear any movement on Saturday night?'

'She was having an "adult sleepover" at her boyfriend's place.' Ferreira rolled her eyes. 'She actually called it that.'

'Probably wasn't comfortable using the term "booty call" to a copper,' Zigic suggested, earning a wry grin.

'Or using it at all in 2018.'

'You'll be old one day, Mel.'

'By the time I'm old everyone'll be sleeping with sex robots and it'll be called genital interfacing.'

He shook his head at her and headed into the house. They walked through to the back garden where Kate Jenkins stood by the rear fence, suited up, her kit box open.

'Have you had a look yet?' Ferreira asked. 'It has to be how Ainsworth injured himself, right?'

Jenkins twisted her long red hair up and pinned it. 'Mel, I know you need this to be right and it certainly does look like a good match for his injuries, but I need to do the actual science stuff before I can say that, okay?'

'The spacing of the wounds looks identical.'

'It does,' Kate agreed. 'But this won't be the only house in the area that's using these grips as an anti-burglar device. Not to mention the fact that Ainsworth might have come in contact with another set in a perfectly innocent way.'

'Is there blood on them?' Zigic asked her.

'There's something that might be blood,' she said carefully. 'But I'm looking at the effort they made to cover up evidence inside the house and I'm wondering why they left these here.'

'They didn't know he came in over the fence.' Ferreira was committed to the theory now and Zigic found he agreed with her thinking. 'He's hardly bleeding until he gets to the back door. I struggled to follow the track down here and I'm –'

'A bloodhound?' Kate asked with a grin.

'I was going to say a highly trained detective with excellent instincts and sharp eyesight.'

'So modest,' Zigic said.

'My point is, if they were panicking – and they should have been – it's logical that they concentrated on getting rid of any evidence in the house. Anyone might have seen the blood in there. But by the time you get to the centre of the lawn, there's almost nothing to see so they failed to follow it to the source.'

Zigic had looked for blood as they came up the garden, hadn't seen anything but an occasional rusty spot on the buff-coloured gravel, a spatter on some white flowers that might have been a common horticultural affliction for all he knew.

'What about in the house?' he asked. 'Anything jump out at you?'

'I'm in the garden, Ziggy,' Kate said, taking a pair of pliers from her toolkit. 'Go and harass Elliot, he's in charge inside today.'

They headed in, found the downstairs empty still but Elliot's stuff was set by the back door and they kept well away from it, not wanting to disturb anything.

Ferreira wandered over to the sitting area, gestured at the sofa and the chairs. 'I'm sure all of this is new.'

'It's got that new upholstery smell,' he agreed. 'You think it got that messy in here?'

'They've redecorated for some reason,' she said. 'Either Sutherland wanted to make the place all nice and fresh for Nadia, or ...'

'Everything got covered in blood and had to be chucked out?' She nodded. 'We'll pull his financials, look for a recent shopping spree.'

'Skip hire,' Ferreira suggested. 'Or a van rental. Getting furniture out of the house takes organising.'

Zigic folded his arms, worried they were running ahead of themselves. Yes, the walls had clearly been repainted recently enough that he could still smell the faint hint of volatile chemicals and the furniture did look brand new, but would Ainsworth's bleeding hands have necessitated such a thorough overhaul?

'How much was he bleeding, realistically?'

'It doesn't have to be gushing out all over the place,' Ferreira said with a shrug. 'A couple of spots of a murdered man's blood in a house is enough to get a conviction.'

That was hope more than experience, he thought.

'Ainsworth breaking in here doesn't mean they murdered him,' he told her, putting some warning into his voice.

'No, but it makes it far more likely that they did.' She leaned over the sofa, peering behind the back. 'For all we know Ainsworth broke in while they were at home and one of them killed him and then took him back to his own place so it'd look like a robbery.'

He put up a cautioning hand. 'Now, hold on a minute, Mel.'

'I'm just thinking out loud.'

'We still don't even know if it's Ainsworth's blood,' he said firmly. 'And there's no way Ainsworth was murdered here on Thursday morning – the post-mortem puts the time of death late Saturday night, early Sunday morning, so you need to disregard that option right away.'

Ferreira sat down on the arm of the sofa and stood immediately as it tipped. She pointed at it. 'I'm not heavy, that's a cheap sofa.'

Zigic pressed on. 'The neighbour told you the break-in happened Thursday morning, which means Sutherland was likely at work at the time.'

'And Nadia was *very* likely at home.'

'And how does Ainsworth know she's here?'

Ferreira considered it for a moment but couldn't come up with an answer.

'Okay, we need to nail that down,' she conceded. 'But let's say Sutherland was home and Ainsworth came here to get to him, the question still stands – why does he want to get at Sutherland?' She placed herself at the centre of the geometric-print rug. 'Well, somebody must have backed up Nadia's allegation against Ainsworth, right? And given that Nadia is living with Sutherland now, I think he'd be the most likely suspect.'

'So you think this is Ainsworth wanting revenge on Sutherland for getting him sacked?' Zigic asked, hearing how right it sounded as he spoke.

'Revenge is always a good motive.' She gave him a dark smile. 'But a spot of light vandalism isn't much of a revenge.'

'This would make a lot more sense if we knew that Ainsworth knew that Nadia was here,' he said. 'Breaking in to go after her … there's logic. *That* feasibly leads to Ainsworth's murder.'

'Maybe he did know she's here,' Ferreira said. 'Sutherland thinks nobody from work knows what he's up to because he's living fifteen minutes away from Long Fleet, but it's not the other end of the world, is it? And unless he's got Nadia under house arrest, there's a chance they've been seen together.'

'That's speculative.'

'We have gaps,' Ferreira said, exasperated. 'We need to speculate or we won't know how to fill them.'

'With evidence?' he suggested drily. 'That's the traditional method.'

'Okay.' She pushed her hair back off her face, a quick flicker of irritation showing. 'If it is Ainsworth's blood, then we have him breaking into the house of his former colleague and the woman

344

he attacked at Long Fleet. Two people he has reason to want to damage. And who have ample reason to want to damage him.'

'They'd have to know he was responsible for the break-in for it to become a reason to murder him.' Zigic glanced out of the front window, saw the uniforms at neighbouring houses, one bending to put a note through a letter box, the other speaking to a young woman with a baby on her hip. 'Nadia must have been home when he broke in.'

Ferreira nodded gravely.

'What did he do to her?'

'I dread to think.' Zigic looked around the achingly ordinary living room, wondering what it had witnessed, what they had worked so hard to strip out of it. 'They both must know what happened here. This clean-up job is too major to handle alone.'

'The question is which one of them then killed him?'

Zigic rubbed his beard, already knowing what she thought, seeing how she'd shaped the conversation towards this point. 'You think it was Sutherland.'

'Do you really believe Nadia is physically capable?'

'I think that if I was her and I was here alone and Ainsworth broke in, I'd be terrified enough to do just about anything to stop him getting near me again.'

'That's motivation,' Ferreira said. 'It isn't capability.'

'We need to bring Sutherland in.'

'Long Fleet, then?'

He nodded. 'Long Fleet.'

CHAPTER FIFTY-SEVEN

The problem started at the main gate.

It was the same guard who'd let them in last time, a tall, dark-haired guy with a deep tan and gym-toned body, the one she'd tried to draw into conversation before and been given nothing but murmurs and grunts.

'You're not on my list,' he said.

Zigic had his ID out, holding it up in the open window, but the guard didn't look at it. Didn't need to anyway. He wasn't looking at his monitor either or the tablet he'd checked to let them in the other day. Word had obviously come down that they weren't to be admitted.

'We don't need an appointment,' Zigic said tersely. 'We're investigating the murder of one of your colleagues.'

'Former colleague,' the guard said under his breath but loud enough to be certain they'd hear it.

'Call Hammond and tell him we're here to see him.'

'Sorry, sir, but I can't do that. We don't take appointments at the gate; that's the responsibility of Mr Hammond's assistant.'

'Call Catherine Field, then.'

'She doesn't take appointments at the gate either, sir. There's a process, as I'm sure you can appreciate. And I don't have any say in it. I just open up when I'm supposed to and keep the gate shut when I'm not.'

Zigic hit the button to close the window, his profile set hard.

'Are you going to ram the barrier?' Ferreira asked, only half joking.

'Only as a last resort.' He took out his mobile and called Catherine Field, waited, tapping his foot lightly against the accelerator pedal, his hand tight on the steering wheel, until she answered. 'Mrs Field, DI Zigic, we'd like a word with you, please. If you could call down to the gate and have the guard let us in.'

Ferreira heard her refuse, in a long-winded and icily polite fashion.

'Well, that's very unfortunate. Because we've just found evidence of a serious crime at the house of one of your employees,' he said. 'We also found one of your former inmates living there.'

Silence at her end.

'Now, we need further information about the situation and there are two options here. We can run a request through this afternoon's press briefing and see if the public can help.' He smiled at Ferreira. 'Or we could come in and have a chat with Mr Hammond. Which would you prefer?'

He hit speaker and Catherine Field's voice came through clear and tremulous.

'Bear with me one moment, please.'

Five minutes later they were shown into Hammond's office.

He looked harassed, shirtsleeves rolled back and his tie recently reknotted, slightly askew, his blond hair lying wrong on his head as if he'd tried to smooth it back hastily and without the benefit of a mirror. There was a half-eaten sandwich on his desk and a pot of tea, the same lapsang souchong that had turned Ferreira's stomach the last time they'd been here.

Not even the most perfunctory attempt at a welcome today.

'I don't appreciate being ambushed like this, Inspector,' he said. 'I've cooperated with your investigation to the best of my abilities and to have you come here now threatening to leak classified information to the press really is beyond the pale.'

'And we don't appreciate being lied to, Mr Hammond,' Zigic told him. 'Which is exactly what you've being doing since the very first moment we came here.'

'I strongly resent that –'

'You knew Joshua Ainsworth was told to resign over a serious assault and you lied to protect your reputation and the reputation of this facility. Now we find the woman he assaulted is involved in a relationship with a member of your staff. A relationship that clearly began while she was interned here.'

Hammond looked genuinely troubled. Field would have told him what they'd alleged so they'd lost the element of surprise, but Ferreira would bet the first he'd heard of it was within the last few minutes.

'I can assure you we were not aware of this relationship,' Hammond said. 'Which member of staff are you referring to?'

'Patrick Sutherland,' Zigic said.

Hammond ran a nervous hand down his tie. 'This is rather a shock, excuse me.'

'Are *any* of your staff safe to be working with vulnerable women?' Ferreira asked.

He didn't answer, only looked at her with an expression of mild outrage that she guessed would have been stronger if he had had any way to refute the allegation behind the question.

'Ainsworth and Sutherland were supposed to be your morally upstanding whistle-blowers, right? And now we have one of them assaulting Nadia Baidoo and the other one picking her off like a wounded gazelle almost the second she stepped out of the prison gate.'

'We're not a prison,' he said reflexively.

'But you have rules about relationships between inmates and staff, I assume?'

'Nadia Baidoo is no longer a resident,' Hammond said. 'I can fully appreciate how troubling this looks though and I will be suspending Dr Sutherland with immediate effect, until we have carried out a full and thorough investigation into this alleged relationship.'

'Judging by the physical evidence we found at Sutherland's house, you might not get a chance to suspend him,' Zigic said.

'You should have security bring him out to us,' Ferreira suggested. 'Much quieter if we take him in from here than wait until he gets home. You never know who's filming arrests these days.'

Hammond folded his fist into his palm, pressed his knuckles against his mouth. The panic was back, a haunted look coming into his eye; it was clear he was picturing the press circus descending on Long Fleet. The vans and cameras parked up on the verge, reporters filming outside the gates, speaking to the protestors. The eyes of the country drawn to a place that was supposed to operate behind a discreet veil. He would be thinking of the calls to his bosses' office, the fears of the shareholders and how long he could hold on to this job from inside the eye of a media storm.

He was already sweating, a fine, shining layer across his forehead and top lip, slightly greasy-looking. The camera was going to hate him, Ferreira thought. It would turn him shifty and grubby, magnify his complicity until people started to ask, 'Well, why would he look the other way on all those abuses? Was he doing the same thing as those doctors?'

Across his shoulder, through the gleaming picture window, she could see three women in dark green tabards working in the vegetable garden, hoeing the weeds from between the lines of salad leaves, the sun across the backs of their necks, each of them eyes down and forlorn-looking. She wondered if they were being paid to do it, knew the inmates were put to work here for a few pounds a day, but would management make gardening a reward rather than a job? Be good and we'll let you go outside?

Hammond wet his lips. 'This serious crime ...'

'Ainsworth's murder,' Zigic said. 'What else would it be?'

Wearily Hammond reached for the phone, pressed a button and was immediately answered.

'Catherine, have Dr Sutherland brought to my office, please.'

CHAPTER FIFTY-EIGHT

Sutherland was indignant at first, protesting his innocence in the hallway outside Hammond's office, accusing them of trying to intimidate him into breaking his NDA by arresting him for a crime he *obviously* had no part in.

He kept it up as Ferreira cautioned him, speaking over her, addressing himself to Hammond more than either of them, as if he genuinely believed his job was in greater jeopardy than his liberty. Hammond watched him with his arms folded and his skin darkening in increments until it was a deep and livid puce and finally he snapped.

'You are the absolute worst kind of hypocrite, Sutherland.'

Then he stalked back into his office and slammed the door.

'No Securitect legal team for you, Patrick,' Zigic told him.

As they pulled out of the main gates, Sutherland changed tack, asking how they could possibly think this of him in a subdued, almost fully defeated tone.

'I'm a good person,' he said. 'I don't know how you think I'd be capable of hurting anyone. Never mind actual murder.'

Neither of them answered him. Let him talk because he was giving himself away, showing them the line of defence he would put up once he was in the interview room. The longer he spoke the more they could refine their approach in questioning.

Zigic hadn't expected him to break down and admit everything. Occasionally they got lucky and a murderer's guilt did half of their job for them, but even a week on from Ainsworth's death, Sutherland appeared to be stuck in denial and self-protection.

Maybe because he was innocent.

But Zigic felt sure he was guilty of *something*. Actually doing the deed or helping Nadia cover up her own crime. And that should be telling on him.

After a few minutes of silence, Sutherland spoke again.

'I love Nadia,' he said, his voice thickening. 'And she loves me. This is a *real* relationship. However it might look to you and whatever you might think of me for how it started. We do love each other.'

In the passenger seat Ferreira made a nearly imperceptible gagging noise and Zigic knew she wouldn't believe Sutherland. He still wasn't sure, wouldn't be until they'd laid out everything in front of Sutherland and seen how he reacted to the evidence against him.

Assuming Kate Jenkins and her team could find it.

Sutherland fell silent as they reached the edge of the city and he let himself be walked into Thorpe Wood Station without resistance, only a split-second hesitation as he stepped across the threshold, like a man approaching his execution.

'I want my solicitor,' he said.

Ferreira nodded. 'We'll call him.'

Zigic left her to process Sutherland and went up to the main office to debrief the rest of the team on what they'd found at the house and get them started on taking apart Patrick Sutherland's life. Financials and phone records, the uniformed officers stationed on his road to be kept check on, updates immediately given and forensics to call.

He took that job himself. Rang Kate as he rearranged Joshua Ainsworth's board to reflect their new line of enquiry.

'Anything you can tell me yet?'

'You left here barely an hour ago,' she said, sounding exasperated, but he could hear the familiar thrill of discovery underneath it. 'There's not much sign of blood throughout the rest of the house. Basically, what we can plot from the placement of the residue we've found is someone coming in the back door and going upstairs into the bathroom.'

'To look for bandages, maybe?' he suggested. 'That would be your first move if you'd ripped your hands open.'

'Makes sense,' Kate said. 'There's residue on the bathroom cabinet and in the grout on the tiled floor up there. It's a bugger to get out of grout. They should have refinished the floor if they wanted to hide it.'

'What about after the bathroom?' he asked. 'Is there any sign of him entering the other rooms?'

'Nothing.'

He thought about it for a moment. 'He was a doctor. If he bandaged his hands up properly, we wouldn't expect to see blood anywhere else, would we?'

'Probably not?'

'Have you got enough blood to get a DNA match?'

'I've found a few deposits they missed,' Kate said. 'Should be enough for a DNA test.'

'Fingerprints?'

'We've lifted some from the most likely places, so with a bit of a luck we should find a match if it's there to be found.'

He'd hoped for more, felt himself deflate a little at the idea of going in to question Sutherland with such a scant arsenal.

'We're going to talk to Sutherland soon.'

'Subtle hint there,' Kate said lightly. 'We're actually nearly done, so I should be able to put something together for you before close of play.'

'Thanks, Kate – before you go, we need every scrap of paper-work you can find. Receipts, delivery notes, all that stuff.'

'Wow, Ziggy.' He could almost hear her eyes rolling and winced at himself. 'I've been on sabbatical not meth. I think I know you need the paperwork.'

'Sorry.'

'You can apologise in the form of baked goods or not at all.'

Ferreira returned from seeing to Patrick Sutherland, went straight to her desk and started to roll a cigarette.

'You call his solicitor?' Zigic asked.

'On his way.'

He filled her in on what Kate had reported, watched her lose some of her fighting edge as she took the information on board and realised it didn't give them much to work with.

'Where was Nadia while he was hanging around in the bathroom, bandaging his hands?' she asked.

'Maybe she was out,' Zigic suggested. 'You've got to hope for her sake that she was, and this leisurely medical session in the bathroom makes me think Ainsworth was alone in the house at the time.'

'That's something anyway.'

'It makes it far less likely that either of them knew Ainsworth was on the warpath though,' Zigic pointed out. 'Which means their motives evaporate.'

'No, it means *this* motive evaporates. Everything else is still in play.' She started hunting for a lighter among the debris on her desk. 'I think we've got enough to take a preliminary run at him.'

'Maybe we should start with Nadia,' Zigic said unenthusiastically.

Ferreira appeared reluctant and he felt the same resistance. Didn't want to subject Nadia Baidoo to questioning yet. Speaking to victims of sexual violence was always a harrowing experience, but at least you got to feel you were on the side of right, helping them through, trying to bring them justice. With Nadia she was potentially victim and suspect, and the thought of having to switch between modes with her sent a sick feeling into the pit of his stomach.

'Sutherland's the weak link,' Ferreira said slowly, as if she was still working through the reasoning for herself. 'Nadia's been locked up for months, she's still got that guarded mindset in place. And she expects bad things to happen to her, it's put her in lockdown. Sutherland is indignant. I think we should use that against him.'

Her reasoning was sound enough if he didn't examine it too closely. Anything to delay what they were going to put Nadia through.

'He's going to expect us to want to talk about Ainsworth's murder,' Zigic said. 'So, we ask him about the break-in instead.'

'Wrong-foot him.' Ferreira nodded. 'Get his story down, then take it apart when we have something more concrete from Kate.'

'Establish he's a liar and then go from there,' Zigic said.

'He has to lie about it, doesn't he?' She shrugged. 'Unless he wants to actually admit Ainsworth broke into his house and give us a motive for murder.'

CHAPTER FIFTY-NINE

Patrick Sutherland was on his feet when they entered the interview room, hands pressed together in a pleading gesture aimed at the wall, his back turned to his solicitor. It was rare to open the door onto silence but this time they had, and Zigic wondered if Sutherland had so little to say to his legal advisor because he was guilty or because he was innocent. The guilty often began this process stoically enough, thinking the less they said the less chance of incriminating themselves. But the innocent were frequently stunned into silence, all mental energy diverted to why this was happening to them and what was going to be thrown at them and how the hell they would manage to convince the two strangers coming in of their absolute unsuitability for the role they'd been cast into.

'Take a seat please, Patrick.' Zigic waved him into the chair opposite and Sutherland complied.

His solicitor was a young man Zigic had encountered before and wasn't worried about. He was with a small local firm, worked as a duty solicitor with the minimum level of professionalism required, took his wage and apparently spent most of it on handmade shoes and nice suits and discreet cufflinks.

He wondered how Sutherland had come to settle on Ben Lawton as the right man for the job. Wondered if he'd found himself in legal trouble before, the kind that got tidied away without the involvement of the police. Or if like most seemingly respectable people having their first brush with criminality, he'd just called someone from the firm who handled his last house sale.

He hoped it was the latter. Rather than a personal link, which might cause Lawton to dig deeper into his repertoire.

While Ferreira set up the recording equipment Zigic stared at Sutherland, watching him becoming more uncomfortable by the second. Less than an hour in custody and already his hair was pulled about, his lips cracked and dark sweat patches had appeared under the arms of his blue linen shirt.

When he stated his name for the recording, he spoke slightly too loud, trying to sound confident but merely giving the impression of barely contained anger.

Zigic had expected more composure from the man. Given the pressures of his job and the added weight of carrying it out somewhere like Long Fleet.

For a few long seconds nobody spoke and Zigic could see how the silence unnerved Sutherland, how desperate he was to fill it with something. There was a story in him, Zigic thought. Excuses and explanations he was desperate to try on them, but he had just enough willpower left in him to hold steady.

'So, Patrick, why don't you tell us about your break-in?'

Sutherland blinked at him. 'What?'

'It's my understanding that we're here to discuss the murder of Joshua Ainsworth,' Lawton said, seeming just as perplexed as his client.

'We'll get to that,' Zigic said. 'On the morning of Thursday August 2nd, your house was broken into, Patrick.'

'We were burgled, yes.' Sutherland's forehead creased. 'I don't see what that has to do with anything.'

'Where were you during the break-in?'

'At work.'

'And how did you find out about it?'

'Nadia called me,' he said.

'Was she home at the time?'

'No,' he said quickly. 'She'd gone out for a walk. She likes to go out as much as possible. After being locked up for so long, it's good for her to get used to being able to go where she wants again.'

Ferreira made a note of that. They would check with the neighbours, see if anyone had noticed her coming and going, if she had a routine Ainsworth might have exploited to get in the house while it was empty.

'What was taken?' she asked and when Sutherland didn't answer, said, 'A burglary typically involves the theft of items from a house. What did they take?'

'Nothing, as far as we could tell.'

'You must have something worth stealing,' she said. 'I noticed your TV was still there and Nadia's laptop. Or are they new?'

He shrugged. 'I suppose the burglars didn't think they were worth anything. TVs are so cheap now.'

'It seems strange that someone would go to all the trouble of breaking into your house in broad daylight and not take anything,' Ferreira said. 'Paperwork, spare keys, credit cards, they didn't take any of that?'

'I don't think so.'

'Did you check?'

He hesitated for a second, seemed to be considering it when it really wasn't a question that required consideration. 'I did, eventually. I was more concerned with calming Nadia down. She'd never been through that before and it upset her quite badly.'

'Lucky she was out,' Ferreira said.

Sutherland nodded.

'Did they make much of a mess?'

'Not really.' He seemed to think that was enough of an answer but got the hint and continued. 'They took the glass out of the back door, they didn't even smash their way in. I suppose we should be thankful they were so considerate.'

'Most burglars completely ransack a place,' Ferreira told him. 'Some will vandalise it after they've done looking for whatever it is they want. Especially if they don't actually find anything worth taking.'

'Your place looks spotless,' Zigic added. 'You've redecorated, right?'

'I bought some new furniture a few weeks ago,' Sutherland said. 'Look, is this really relevant?'

'You'd rather talk about something else?' Ferreira asked. 'What would you like to talk about, Patrick?'

His eyes widened, frustration drawn in every line on his face and the way he splayed his fingertips on the tabletop. 'Well, since you've dragged me in here over Josh's murder, I rather expected we'd talk about that.'

'We are talking about Josh's murder,' Zigic told him. 'Because we both know it was Josh who broke into your house.'

An incredulous laugh huffed out of Sutherland. 'That's ridiculous.'

'Those spikes on your garden fence.' Ferreira opened up a photograph of them on the tablet she'd brought in with her, turned it to face Sutherland. She gave him a moment to look at them and then swiped the screen. 'And the injuries on Josh's hands. Perfect match.'

'Just because the wounds match it doesn't mean they were created by this particular length of – what are they – nails?' Ben Lawton said. 'That could have happened anywhere.'

'This particular stretch of carpet grip has blood on,' Ferreira said, still looking at Sutherland. 'The same blood our forensic team found in your kitchen and in your bathroom.'

'It must have been the person who broke in,' Sutherland said hesitantly. 'I mean, I didn't put them on the fence. I suppose the previous owner did it. This is the first time I've even seen them.'

'It's not an uncommon way for homeowners to try and deter burglars,' Lawton added helpfully. 'Can you prove it was Joshua Ainsworth's blood?'

'Even if it is we thought it was just a regular burglary,' Sutherland said. 'Me and Nadia were both out. How would we know who broke in?'

He had them and Zigic was annoyed how quickly they'd got here. They'd come in underprepared, both wanting to avoid the inevitable next step of questioning Nadia, which was the job they

358

should have done first, gritting their teeth and accepting the discomfort of it.

'Why did you lie to me when I asked you about Nadia?' Ferreira asked, trying to drag the interview back onto useful ground.

Lawton started to intervene but Sutherland spoke over him, and Zigic noticed annoyance flash briefly across the solicitor's face.

'I knew how bad it looked,' Sutherland said.

'But Nadia has her leave to remain, she isn't in Long Fleet any more,' Ferreira said innocently. 'She's free to do what she wants. Why would you think that looked bad?'

'After everything that's happened at Long Fleet and my involvement in reporting abusive staff members, I thought you'd think I was a hypocrite.'

Ferreira smiled thinly. 'And why would my opinion matter?'

'I'm not like those men,' Sutherland said. 'And you can't help who you fall in love with.'

It was a non-answer and Zigic wasn't even sure he believed it himself. That shame had come from somewhere and he was sure Ferreira's good opinion was of little to interest to the man. Unless he figured she would see the relationship as evidence of some deeper moral failing and was worried it might lead her to see him as a murder suspect.

'You love Nadia.'

He nodded. 'I do.'

'Enough to kill Joshua Ainsworth for her?'

'I didn't kill Josh,' he said resolutely. 'And why would I need to kill him for her? What world do you live in where that kind of thing happens?'

'Josh broke into your house looking for Nadia,' Ferreira said, fixing her gaze on him. 'He attacked her in Long Fleet and he got sacked for it. He must have been furious with her. And you. He would have wanted to punish you both for exposing him. Josh Ainsworth, the good guy, the whistle-blower, one of the very few men in Long Fleet with clean hands.' She brought her palm down on the table. 'He must have been furious with you two.'

'This is all completely unsupported,' Lawton said.

But Sutherland was trapped, couldn't seem to drag his eyes off Ferreira.

'And Nadia must have been absolutely terrified,' she said. 'We spoke to her earlier and I can see it, Patrick. I can see how traumatised she is.' Her voice went low and emotional, her hand to her heart. 'Look, I'm just a copper but I felt for her. I can only imagine how you must feel. Seeing the woman you love so scared.'

'I think you should present something more substantial than feelings,' Lawton said, his tone firmer now, impatience showing.

'I mean, why else would Josh break in except to get to Nadia?' she asked.

'We didn't know it was him,' Sutherland said again, less forcefully this time.

'And she got lucky that time, she was out.' Ferreira shook her head as if she couldn't bear to think about the alternative. 'But what about the next time Josh came for her?'

'These are just feelings with question marks at the end of them,' Ben Lawton said, bringing his hand down on the table between them and inserting himself across Sutherland's eyeline. 'Mr Sutherland is happy to answer your questions. *Real* questions, DS Ferreira. But you quite clearly have no compelling reason to keep him here.'

'We've got hours to keep him here yet,' Zigic told Lawton.

He gestured to Ferreira.

'Interview suspended 6:22 p.m.'

Chapter Sixty

Half an hour later, Nadia Baidoo was in an interview room, her solicitor seated next to her. Ms Hussain was clearly ill at ease with the situation as the recording devices began to roll.

'Nadia wishes to make a statement,' she said stiffly. 'We appreciate that you will have questions for her, but in the first instance, she would like to correct some misinformation she believes you have about her and Dr Ainsworth.'

The room was stuffy, the air thick and stale, smelling of all the bodies that had been in here before them already today: fear, sweat and aftershave, hot feet and a trace of absurdly tropical aftersun lotion. The lighting over the table was blown and the only sun that made it in through the high, narrow window was diffused by the dirt on the reinforced glass, making the room oddly gloomy, everything rendered slightly insubstantial by it.

Nadia looked smaller, hunched over behind the table, her face tight like she was in physical pain. She took a sip of water before she began and even swallowing seemed to give her some trouble.

Zigic felt a bolt of sympathy for her. He was dreading what she was about to say, knowing that if she admitted killing Ainsworth after he had attacked her, he was going to have to charge her and he would hate himself a little for doing that.

'Take your time,' Ferreira said gently.

'I've lied about Dr Ainsworth,' Nadia said, shooting her a quick and haunted glance. 'In Long Fleet. I said terrible things about him and they weren't true.'

She paused and Zigic noticed Ms Hussein was watching her carefully. She looked troubled and that concerned him too.

Whatever advice she'd given, Nadia had obviously decided to speak in spite of it.

'Before I was arrested I didn't know I was in the UK illegally. I didn't understand my status. I was a student. I was working and paying my taxes. I was paying for my home. I thought I was safe.' She blinked slowly. 'And then I was in Long Fleet and it was hell. I was so scared I hardly slept, I was like a zombie from the sleep deprivation. It's like a blur now. I don't know what I was more afraid of: being sent to Ghana or being kept in there for ever.'

Nadia stared at a point in the centre of the table, her shoulders rounded, hunched slightly forward as if projecting herself into the story she was telling.

'Everyone was scared. All of the time. Some of the women starved themselves until they couldn't even walk or speak. Some of them cut themselves. I didn't understand that but a lady told me it was so they wouldn't get sent away. They believed that if they could convince people that they had mental health problems, they'd have to be allowed to stay. But it didn't work because they'd still disappear. We'd hear the doors open in the middle of the night and the next morning they'd be gone. You didn't even get to say goodbye to them.'

She swallowed hard and inclined her head towards the wall, as if she didn't want them to see the look in her eyes when she spoke again.

'We were hopeless. We were ... used.' Her jaw worked at nothing for a few seconds as she steeled herself. 'You can't understand it until you're there. You have to make a decision. One of the other women, she told me to find someone who'd protect me. She told me that if I chose one man, then maybe the others would leave me alone.' She turned to Zigic, eyes hot with rage. 'Do you understand what I'm saying? It's one man or all of them?'

Zigic nodded because he couldn't bring himself to speak.

She looked to Ferreira and Zigic noticed Mel's posture now, chin dipped and her hands cupped together in front of her mouth. Closed off and defensive and she knew better than that, knew how important it was to hold yourself open and receptive in here as people unburdened themselves.

He knew where this was bubbling up from in her: Walton.

This was why Adams was prepared to risk so much on his hunch, Zigic realised. Because if she was like this now, then how bad was she in the early hours of the morning, laying awake and wondering if Walton was outside waiting for her?

Nadia gathered herself again, smothered the rage, chewed up all the other words she could have used but decided not to for whatever reason. Because she thought they reflected badly on her or because they were still too raw to share with strangers he didn't know.

'I did like Patrick,' she said. 'I was lucky because he liked me too. But *I* made the decision.' She looked again to Ferreira, desperate for understanding. 'It was better, right? To be in control of what was going to happen to me?'

'You did what you had to,' Ferreira said, her voice low and throaty. 'But you never should have been put in that situation.'

'None of you should,' Ms Hussein said. Her face clouded over and she looked down into her lap. She obviously wasn't surprised by what she was hearing, just unhappy about it.

Zigic could see her adding this to the mental inventory of Long Fleet's crimes she carried around. He hadn't expected the interview to take this turn when he called her, but he found he was relieved she was here rather than some duty solicitor.

'Patrick knew all about my case,' Nadia said pensively. 'I didn't understand it and my solicitor told me right from the beginning that there wasn't much point arguing because I didn't have any good reason to stay in England. Mum was the one who couldn't go back to Ghana. I'd be safe there.' She smiled bitterly at the idea, shook her head. 'One day Patrick told me they were preparing to deport me. He said it was going to be very soon.' She took a deep breath. 'I cried. All day and all night. I couldn't eat. I decided I'd kill myself before I let them send me there. And then I understood why the other women went on hunger strike. They can't send you back if you do that. So that's what I did. Within a few days I already felt like I was dying and they took me into the medical bay. Patrick was upset with me. He kept telling me not to give up but what else was I supposed to do? It was better being in there on a drip than being deported.'

She reached for her water again, took a tiny sip, her hand trembling.

'He told me there was a way I could stay here.' Nadia shrank slightly into her chair, drawing back from the table and away from Ms Hussein. 'He said he'd tell me exactly what I needed to say because he knew how the system worked, and you couldn't get around it unless you understood it inside out. He told me to make a report that Dr Ainsworth attacked me, then I'd be allowed to stay.'

'But he didn't?' Zigic asked, as gently as he could. 'Dr Ainsworth didn't attack you?'

'No.' The planes of her faces sharpened, pain and shame along every angle. 'I didn't want to do it. Believe me, I kept telling Patrick it was wrong. Dr Ainsworth was a good man. He was the only man we trusted.'

'Why did you trust him?'

'Because he was a homosexual,' Nadia said.

'He wasn't,' Zigic told her.

She considered it, frowning, eyes scanning the tabletop as she tried to fit the new information into her conception of Ainsworth.

'Then he was a very good man,' she said sadly.

Zigic winced internally, thinking of how low the bar was set for Nadia. That she could conceive of no other reason for a man not to take advantage of his power over her and the other women in Long Fleet than that he was gay.

'Nadia, I need you to be very clear about what you're saying,' he told her. 'Are you saying that Dr Ainsworth didn't attack you?'

'Yes,' she said.

'You don't have the power to charge Nadia for events that took place within Long Fleet's walls,' Ms Hussein said, her voice firm, eyes boring into him. 'Nadia has come clean now because she wanted to set the record straight about Joshua Ainsworth in case it has any bearing on your investigation.'

364

'I deserve to be punished for what I did,' Nadia said.

Ms Hussein put a steadying hand on her arm. 'What happens in Long Fleet is an internal matter for them.'

She was right, Zigic realised. The complaint had been dealt with internally. The police were never involved. Nadia had been morally in the wrong but legally there was nothing they could charge her with, no reported crime it related to.

And yet he found himself wishing there was.

It was a horrible, discomforting feeling, wishing that on someone who had suffered so much. He understood why she had done it – she'd made sure they understood, a cynical voice in the back of his head noted – but there was nothing to justify lying like that.

Already he was thinking of the damage it would do if it got out. A single high-profile false accusation could derail any number of other assault cases, feeding into the hateful and pervasive misinformation about women who falsely accused men for their own ends. Nobody would remember why she did it, or consider Patrick Sutherland's Svengali-like role in the whole affair; all that would stick was the idea that women lie.

He thought about how far the accusation against Ainsworth had derailed the investigation. How they'd allowed it to, by believing it.

Because why wouldn't they? Everything they knew about Long Fleet before and during this case supported the likelihood of it being true. And wasn't there something tempting about the whistle-blower who turned in all the other offenders to take the heat off himself? Some twisted logic to it.

Sutherland did the same, he reminded himself. The theory was correct but the guilty party wrong.

'I'm sure you have lots of questions for Nadia but after that rather harrowing conversation, I think we need a break.' Ms Hussein stood up, smoothing her hand down the front of her tailored linen dress. 'If you wouldn't mind, Inspector?'

'Fine,' he said, still slightly shell-shocked by the revelation.

Ferreira ended the recording and Ms Hussein asked if she could speak to them for a moment outside.

She walked a few paces away from the door and back again, and Zigic realised she was building up to something, but he wasn't particularly in the mood to listen to justifications or applications for more lenient treatment. A good solicitor would know that, he thought. She would wait until some of the heat had drained from the moment.

She came back and leaned against the wall, exhausted-looking.

'I can see that neither of you is very impressed with Nadia right now,' she said, tucking her hands into the small of her back. 'But I'd like to remind you that she is a vulnerable young adult and that she was under significant mental duress in Long Fleet.' Ms Hussein glanced at Ferreira. 'I also think it's reasonable to say that she is still under a serious degree of duress from Patrick Sutherland.'

Zigic folded his arms. 'What do you want from us, Ms Hussein?'

'I know you're a good guy,' she said smoothly. 'You wouldn't have called me to represent Nadia otherwise. So I'm relying on your moral compass here.'

'Nadia is staying in custody,' he said. 'We might not be able to charge her with false reporting but she's still a suspect in a murder inquiry.'

Ms Hussein nodded. 'I've discussed the matter with Nadia already and I can tell you she is completely innocent of any involvement.'

'It's not really your place to call that,' Zigic told her.

She shifted where she stood into a more offensive posture, before realising and clasping her hands in front of her.

'Nadia chose to come clean to you today against my advice,' she said gravely. 'She is a decent, honest young woman who has made a terrible decision under circumstances you and I will likely never find ourselves in.'

'And is she going to come clean about Ainsworth's murder?' Ferreira asked impatiently.

'She is,' Ms Hussein said.

Zigic heard the unvoiced 'but'.

Ferreira voiced it. 'She wants something in return?'

'I'd like to be able to tell her that you'll inform the CPS that she has cooperated with you from the moment you first spoke to her.' She held a finger up. 'Which she has. Nadia has been scrupulously honest with you and she will continue to be.'

'It kind of depends what she knows,' Ferreira said. 'And if the evidence backs her up. She's hardly a reliable witness right now.'

Zigic felt a prickle of unease, listening to them talk. Deals made in corridors and promises for support that might not be justified – he didn't like working this way, thought that it undermined the whole process. Sometimes it was necessary and he would swallow his principles and do what had to be done. But he wasn't convinced it was necessary in this case.

Ms Hussein obviously read his reluctance. She stepped back very slightly.

'Why don't you take some time to consider it, Inspector,' she suggested. 'I think Nadia has been through enough for one day, don't you?'

Ms Hussein returned to the interview room briefly to say goodbye to Nadia before she was taken back down to the cells for the night. Then she left as well, taking the corridor at a brisk clip, as if she had plenty still to do this evening. Zigic suspected she would arrive fully prepared tomorrow for the next round, knew she wasn't someone to underestimate.

For a moment they lingered in the corridor. Neither of them was quite ready to return to the bustle of the office after what they'd heard.

Ferreira drew her fingers back through her hair, blew out a long slow breath.

'You were right.' The admission looked painful to make after days of arguing with him over Nadia's innocence. 'She lied about the whole thing.'

'It's a bit more complicated than that though, isn't it?' He sat down on the cold radiator. 'Nadia was desperate for a way out and Sutherland took advantage of that desperation to manipulate her into bringing a false charge.'

'She didn't have to do it.'

'Didn't she?' Zigic asked. 'What would you have done in her situation?'

'Took a guard hostage, fought my way out.'

She forced a smile and he managed an unconvincing chuckle in return.

'Why do you think Sutherland wanted her to make the accusation?' Ferreira asked. 'Assuming we can even believe that part of the story.'

'He says he loves her. Maybe he just wanted to make sure she wasn't deported.'

'Okay, let's assume that's right,' she said. 'Why Ainsworth in particular? Why not one of the guards? Sutherland and Ainsworth were supposed to be fairly friendly. What changed?'

Zigic considered it, feeling the hard ridges of the radiator cutting into his palms. 'A guard would have been a much easier sell.'

'Right. Ainsworth was Hammond's golden boy from what we've heard. Even with a theoretically pretty credible report from Sutherland, he still didn't entirely believe Josh was guilty.' She spread her hands in a questioning shrug. 'So why did Sutherland make life difficult for himself by trying to frame the most trustworthy member of Hammond's staff?'

'It's got to be something personal,' Zigic said.

'We need to talk to Hammond.'

He checked his watch. Half past seven.

'Find Hammond's home address, let's see if he's any more forthcoming away from Long Fleet.'

Chapter Sixty-One

'I'm not usually a "first one up against the wall come the revolution" type,' Ferreira said, as they pulled up outside James Hammond's home. 'But fucking seriously?'

'Private-sector money.' Zigic shrugged.

But it rankled him a little, too, seeing what keeping vulnerable women locked up in small cells for indefinite periods of time got you. A large stone cottage, five broad windows wide, with a thatched roof and four chimneys. His and hers Mercedes parked in the green oak garage and something sportier with a decal he couldn't place, occupying the third bay. The houses around it were much the same. This was the village you moved to when you didn't want mere middle-income earners as neighbours.

Ferreira stalked away from him along the pea gravel drive and by the time he caught up to her, she was banging on the front door with the side of her fist. Giving it the attitude of a bust rather than a request for assistance.

'Best I lead, I think,' he said.

She cocked her head at him. 'Don't trust my manners?'

'He doesn't like you.'

'I'd worry if he did,' she said, stepping back to allow him to fill the space on the doorstep between two deep red acers in lead planters.

James Hammond answered the door and even off duty he had a whiff of the managerial about him, dressed in chinos and a pink polo shirt, a cut-glass tumbler of Scotch in his hand.

'You shouldn't have come to my house,' he said, making no attempt to hide his annoyance. 'This is Long Fleet business and it belongs at Long Fleet. Make an appointment and I'll see you tomorrow.'

He moved to close the door on them and Zigic shoved his forearm against the wood, holding it open.

'We're sorry to have to visit you like this, but it's a matter of urgency and we'll try not to keep you from your evening.'

Reluctantly Hammond let the door swing open again, but didn't invite them in.

'Do you really want to do this on your driveway?' Zigic asked.

'Fine.' Hammond huffed, reached for a set of keys from a bowl on a console table and began to lead them towards the garage, up a set of exterior steps and into a large room, which covered the span of the building. It was set up like an artist's studio, blank but primed canvases leaned up against the brilliant white walls, shelves of painting materials and brushes in tall ceramic pots. The works in progress were vibrant abstracts, impasto finishes and deep surfaces all bisected with spidery fault lines.

'Your work?' Zigic asked.

'My daughter's,' Hammond said, full of pride. 'She's the artist.'

There was a faded orange-velvet chesterfield pushed up against one wall and Hammond waved them towards it. They sat as he pulled over a stool to sit on, awkward with his glass held in both hands between his thighs.

'Have you charged Sutherland yet?' he asked.

'We still trying to figure out exactly what happened,' Zigic told him. 'But during questioning Nadia Baidoo told us that the accusation she brought against Josh was false.'

'I bloody knew it,' Hammond said bitterly. 'I was sure he wasn't like that.'

But you still sacked him, Zigic thought.

'Why did she lie?' Hammond asked.

'She didn't want to be deported.'

Hammond nodded. 'The usual ploy then.'

'You didn't deport the other women who reported attacks?' Ferreira asked.

'It was case-dependent,' Hammond said firmly.

'And Nadia's case wouldn't have been compelling without the attack?'

'I can't recall the details at the present moment.' He sipped his Scotch. 'But she wouldn't have been given leave to remain simply because she made an accusation against a member of staff, no. That would create a dangerous precedent. It would be tantamount to giving in to blackmail.'

Zigic didn't believe him. From what they knew of Nadia's case, her asylum status was based on her position as a dependant and the moment she reached eighteen and was no longer reliant on her mother, the law would have considered her safe to return to Ghana.

Hammond wasn't going to admit that though and it had little bearing on their case anyway.

'Can you remember who examined her after she was attacked?' Zigic asked.

'It would have been Sutherland,' Hammond said, virtually spitting out his name. 'Josh was the alleged perpetrator so Sutherland would have done the examination. There wasn't anyone else.'

'Nadia claims Sutherland concocted the allegation.'

'Because he wanted to get her out of custody for his own use.'

Zigic winced at Hammond's choice of words, apposite but brutal, and wondered if it was a comment on Sutherland or if Hammond's role made it impossible to see those women as anything more than units on a balance sheet.

'We assume that's why,' Ferreira said. 'Sutherland collected her from the hostel within a few days of her release. He seemed to have it all figured out.'

'The sly bastard,' Hammond muttered.

'The question we have now,' Zigic said, 'which we're hoping you might be able to assist us with, is why Sutherland chose Ainsworth as the target of the allegation.'

Hammond scratched his eyebrow, bemused-looking. 'That is rather an odd one. Are you certain he made that choice? Mightn't she have decided for herself?'

'Nadia maintains that it was very much Sutherland's call.'

'And you believe her?' Hammond asked. 'Even knowing that she's a liar.'

'Within the context of the rest of her statement, yes, we do believe her.' Zigic shifted his weight and felt something that might have been horsehair poke into his backside, shifted again. 'Sutherland and Ainsworth were supposed to be quite friendly. They'd worked together to report abusers in the past. We're struggling to understand what might have caused Sutherland to turn on Ainsworth.'

Hammond looked pensively into his glass. 'You do appreciate the position I'm in here, Inspector. I've worked damned hard to clean up Long Fleet. I've spent two years doing everything I can to improve the lot of our ladies; I've tried to make their time with us as comfortable and as safe as possible.'

Zigic was sure he could hear Ferreira's teeth grinding.

'And in all of that time,' Hammond said, 'there's not been a single credible report of abuse by any staff member.' He pointed at them. 'Not. One.'

'You've done an admirable job,' Zigic told him. 'And we understand how badly this could reflect on you when it comes out. Which is why I think it's in everyone's best interest to build a solid case against Patrick Sutherland.'

'If he's responsible,' Hammond added hopefully.

'*If*, yes,' Zigic conceded. 'The stronger the case we put in front of him and his solicitor the higher the probability of a confession and the less likely you are to find yourself at the centre of a media circus.'

'So we need to know what went on between Sutherland and Ainsworth,' Ferreira interrupted, the frustration sharpening her tone. 'Where did the break occur?'

Hammond threw back the last mouthful of his drink and rose from the paint-spattered wooden stool. He made his way over to a chaotic workbench, filled with sketch pads and pencils, old Coke cans and water bottles.

Zigic glanced at Ferreira and she shrugged one shoulder, seemingly as uncertain about where this was going as he was.

Under the workbench Hammond rummaged around in a plastic box and came up with a half bottle of vodka.

'There was an incident,' he said, his back still turned to them as he poured another drink. 'Earlier this year. A woman was admitted – I forget the details – but about six weeks after she came in, Josh found out she was pregnant.'

'How pregnant?' Ferreira asked.

'Four to six weeks, Josh said.' Hammond replaced the cap on the bottle and took his time returning it to the box under the bench. 'It was so close that there was no way to say for certain if she'd fallen pregnant before she came to us or not.'

'But Josh thought it happened in Long Fleet?' Zigic asked.

Hammond turned around, nodding. 'He asked the woman about it but she wouldn't tell him anything. Not who the father was, not when it happened.'

'She must have said something.'

'She wouldn't.'

'Did you speak to her?' Ferreira asked.

'That isn't part of my job,' Hammond replied. 'But I did in this instance. Mainly, because we'd been doing so well that I was – and I'm not ashamed to admit this – I was bloody angry that something like that might have happened again on my watch.' He sighed. 'But she wouldn't talk to me. She sat there shaking, she could hardly even look at me.'

'She was scared of you,' Ferreira said.

Zigic nudged her gently. There was no point rubbing it in.

'Who did Josh think the father was?' he asked.

'At first he didn't want to speculate.' Hammond came back to his stool, lowered himself down slowly as if he considered it untrustworthy. 'I'm not sure he had anyone in mind at that point. But he kept pressing the young woman to talk, he was monitoring her more closely – he didn't need to, the pregnancy was progressing perfectly well – but he used that as an excuse to speak to her.' Hammond took a mouthful of vodka and winced slightly at the rawness. 'Eventually he came to me again and told me he thought there was something amiss with Sutherland.'

'Why did he think that?'

Hammond grimaced. 'He couldn't give me a straight answer. That was the problem. If he could have shown me evidence. Or if she would have just spoken up, I could have done something. Honestly, I didn't even believe him at the time. I thought he'd got so accustomed to looking for abuse that he'd started to see it where it didn't exist.'

'Why didn't you mention this to us sooner?' Ferreira demanded. 'You must have realised it might have been significant.'

'Until you came for Sutherland this afternoon, I'd forgotten all about it,' he said, sounding wounded. 'Josh had concerns that didn't stand up to scrutiny and I put it out of my mind and got on with my job.'

It sounded unlikely but Zigic suspected it was the truth. When you dealt with so many people on a daily basis, your mind had a way of wiping them out, freeing space up for the next group and all of their problems and demands. He could only guess at the stress Hammond was under, the money involved, the scrutiny from his bosses.

'Did Sutherland know Josh suspected him of abusing the woman?' he asked.

Hammond looked queasy suddenly. 'I spoke to him about it, yes.'

'You directly accused him?'

'Indirectly,' Hammond said. 'But he must have been aware that the idea came from Josh.'

'How was their working relationship after that?'

'As far as I know they carried on much the same as before. But there was rarely any reason for me to visit the medical bay, so they might have been at each other's throats for all I know.'

Zigic thought of how obscure Josh's working life had remained throughout the investigation. They hadn't been allowed into the main body of Long Fleet, hadn't see his office, had spoken to only Sutherland and the nurse, Ruth Garner, who hadn't mentioned any ructions between her co-workers.

All they'd heard was 'stress' and 'moral discomfort' from the people who knew him best. No mention of a feud. Nothing that could have led them to Sutherland quicker. Hammond was helping now because they had him on the back foot, leveraging him with the threat of media intrusion, but without that threat would he even be telling them this?

'What happened to the woman?' Ferreira asked finally.

'She was deported.' Hammond's gaze dropped to the floor between his feet.

'You do remember something about her case then,' Ferreira said, and Zigic heard speculation behind the reproach in her voice. 'Where was she deported to?'

Hammond frowned. 'I'm afraid I can't give you any more information about her. There are rules governing privacy –'

'This is a murder investigation,' Ferreira snapped. 'And whatever happened to this woman plays directly into it.'

'It isn't a matter of whether I want to tell you or not,' Hammond said, calmer than Zigic expected him to be. 'I simply can't share her information with you.'

'We need to speak to this woman,' he said.

Hammond looked worried, his hand going up in a gesture of surrender or mollification. 'Inspector, please. I want to help you however I can but this is just something I can't do.'

'Then what can you do?' Ferreira asked.

'I'll send you the report I have on Nadia Baidoo's attack,' he said, looking to Zigic, hope in his eyes. 'Sutherland claimed he witnessed Josh attack her. And you know that isn't true now because she's told you the truth.' The hope was morphing into desperation. 'If you can put Sutherland's lies about it to him, then surely he'll have to come clean?'

It wasn't exactly what they needed but it was as much as they would get from him, Zigic realised, and it was more than he expected from the man as they approached his house.

Showing Sutherland his own lies, there in black and white, might just be enough to upend him.

Chapter Sixty-Two

'So, let me get this straight,' Billy said, topping up her glass with red wine. 'Ainsworth knew Sutherland got some woman pregnant inside Long Fleet and then Sutherland convinced Nadia Baidoo to accuse him of assault so he'd be sacked.'

Ferreira took a sip, placed the glass on the worktop next to the chopping board where she was slicing garlic. 'That's about it, yeah.'

'But Sutherland was a whistle-blower?'

'What better way to look clean than to expose everyone else who's dirty?' She scraped the garlic into the pan. 'Sutherland wanted to keep up his shitty behaviour, he needed rid of Ainsworth. Because he was watching him from that point, I guess.'

'You can't prove any of this though,' he said. 'Ainsworth's dead, Hammond won't go on record and you have no idea where the woman is.'

'We don't even know *who* she is,' Ferreira told him. 'I called Ruby Garrick – she runs the Asylum Assist charity – and asked her to put the feelers out, see if anyone she knows is aware of a woman who was deported earlier this year while she was pregnant.'

'That's got to be a fair few women,' Billy said, reaching over to turn down the heat under the pan. 'The garlic's going to catch.'

'Maybe, but I can't think of any other way we can track her down without a name or a location. Happy to take suggestions from my senior officer if he has any, though.'

Billy pulled a face. 'He doesn't have any. Sorry.'

She emptied a tin of anchovies into the pan, where they fizzed and hissed, blooming that salty ocean scent into her face; the smell that always took her back to her childhood, her mother cooking this on the temperamental two-ring hob in the caravan, sending her to school the next day reeking of it.

'You probably won't need her anyway,' he said. 'I read Ziggy's report –'

'You actually read those reports?' she asked, grinning.

'Diligently. It looks like Nadia's going to turn on Sutherland.'

'Not the grand romance he thinks it is, hey?'

'Her solicitor's obviously on the right track. Give evidence against him, hope the CPS don't prosecute.' He picked an olive out of the jar and tossed it into his mouth. 'What I don't get – yes, she needed him to help her get released – but why did she go and live with him after that? She was free. She could have gone back to her old life.'

'I don't think she had much of a life,' Ferreira said grimly. 'She's a kid, Billy. She was eighteen when she was picked up. Her mum had only been dead a few months and she was struggling to deal with it. I think Sutherland saw that she was lost and adrift and he took advantage of the fact that she didn't have anywhere else to go.'

'There's always other options.'

'You know what coercive control is, don't you? We investigate that now, DCI Adams.'

'But is that what you're looking at with her?' he asked. 'I'm not disputing that she was in a very tough situation with limited options. But I think you might need to step back slightly and at least consider the possibility that she might be a bit tougher than you're giving her credit for.'

'You think she killed Ainsworth?' Ferreira asked.

He shrugged. 'I don't know. But I wouldn't rule it out just because I feel sorry for her. And I *do* feel sorry for her, Mel. Poor fucking kid shouldn't have had to go through any of that.'

Ferreira sloshed some wine from her glass into the pan and put the lid on.

'This wants to simmer for a bit.'

They went out onto the balcony. It was barely large enough for a cafe table and a pair of chairs, and even though it was at the back of the block, you could still hear the traffic noise on Thorpe Road, but the view over the Mere was nice enough and it felt good to be outside for no other reason than to enjoy it.

She rolled a cigarette and lit up.

'What about you and Ziggy?' she asked. 'Making progress?'

'Mel ...'

'I know you have. Because he's scared shitless and you're full of yourself. Dead giveaway.'

He lit his own cigarette, scrunched down in the chair and rested his feet against the railings, like he was trying to disappear into himself.

'We should know one way or the other tomorrow,' he said. 'Maybe Wednesday.'

'What are you waiting for?' she asked, trying to figure the timescale. 'A DNA test?'

'You're talking yourself into being an accessory after the fact here.'

She took another deep drag on her roll-up, wondering if things were really so serious or if he was just trying to scare her off.

In the living room her mobile started to ring and she went in to see if it was something she could ignore.

Dani.

She wasn't in the mood for another argument with the woman about whether Lee Walton was guilty or not and whether she'd been manipulated into giving evidence against him and whether that had ruined her life and the relationship they'd had that she thought was perfect despite the high rate of broken bones and black eyes it entailed.

Ferreira thought about diverting it to voicemail, just like Dani had done to her yesterday afternoon. But if Dani was calling, it was probably important.

'What's up, Dani?'

'Nothing's up with her,' Lee Walton said. 'Not now she's back home where she belongs.'

Ferreira looked at the screen again, checking that it was definitely Dani's mobile he was calling on.

'And she's very apologetic, very eager to be forgiven,' he said, the menace thick in his voice, and Ferreira knew he wanted her to hear it, for her to understand the implications. 'But then I don't blame Dani. She's not the sharpest, she'll say anything you tell her to if you she thinks it's the safest option.'

'Well, you'd know, Lee.'

Billy stepped through the sliding door, a questioning look on his face.

Ferreira put her finger up to stop him as he came closer, seeing the stirring of anger in his eyes.

'Threaten her with prison,' Walton said. 'Threaten to have my boy took into care – course she's going to give you bastards whatever you want.' He snorted. 'But you won't get her like that again. She's wise to you now.'

Billy mouthed at her: 'Speaker.'

'That what you called to tell me?' she asked. 'You've smacked some sense into Dani?'

'Put your boyfriend on.'

'You know where he is if you want to speak to him,' Ferreira said. 'Just walk into the station any time you like.'

She could hear the agitation in Walton's breath, could see Billy getting wound up now too, as if the men were face to face.

'Is he there?' Walton asked. 'I don't think he's left you alone. He's got you at his place now, hasn't he?'

The muscles across her abdomen tensed and she turned towards the open doors, certain he was out there. Hidden in the trees, the Mere at his back. His favourite hunting ground.

'It's almost like he thinks you're in danger.'

Billy gave her an urgent look and reluctantly she hit the speakerphone, holding the phone between them.

'How's your mum, Lee?' Billy asked.

Ferreira blinked at him, trying to decode such a stupid, random question.

'You want to stay away from my family,' Walton snarled, all control gone. 'This is harassment. I'm an innocent man and you need to fucking think of that before you start going around talking shit about me and my mum.' He gulped the words. 'Sending that mad bitch around my mum's house shouting the odds, embarrassing her in front of her neighbours. That's libel, that is. It's slander.'

'Wendy was in an emotional state,' Billy said, his voice level but pleasure lighting up his face at hearing how uncomfortable Walton was. 'Maybe your mum told you, Lee. Wendy seems to think you might have killed her Tessa.'

'I never touched her,' Walton barked.

'How many times have I heard you say that?' Billy asked, eyes fixed on the screen, boring into it like he could actually see Walton. 'And it was always a lie. You touched Tessa alright. You followed –'

'I'll have your fucking job,' Walton said, voice ragged, unrecognisable. 'I'm telling you right now, you keep harassing me and my family over this, I'm pressing charges. I'm not having it. It's not fair. I did my time and you need to stay out of my fucking life.'

'No, Lee, it doesn't work like that,' Billy said, relishing every word. 'We just go where the evidence points us. And it points straight to you. All of it. We're coming for you, Lee.'

'I'll fucking dest—'

Billy reached out and killed the call.

But Ferreira could hear the rest of the threat like a ringing in her ears. *'I'll fucking destroy you.'*

'Fuck. Me. Have you ever heard him that rattled?' Billy shoved his hands back through his hair. 'You remember what he was like during the interviews? He barely blinked, cool as you like and lying his head off all the time. We've got him this time, Mel. We've fucking got him and he knows it.'

Ferreira dropped onto the sofa, getting out of his way as he paced around the room, trying to walk off the furious energy surging through him, all the adrenaline he'd raised to throw at Lee Walton but not needed.

Numbly she wondered what Walton was doing with his excess adrenaline but there was really only one option.

He'd be throwing it into Dani's face.

Billy had wound him up and set him loose and Dani was the one who'd suffer.

Day Eight

Tuesday August 14th

CHAPTER SIXTY-THREE

The morning briefing was just beginning when DCS Riggott appeared in the doorway of the main office, hands hanging in loose fists by his sides, all the colour drained from his face. Silence fell across the room, all heads swivelling in his direction, everyone wondering who was for it. Racking their brains to see if it was them.

'Detective Chief Inspector Adams,' Riggott shouted.

Zigic felt the air go out of his lungs, heard Ferreira swear under her breath as Adams turned away from the conversation he was having with DI Kitson. Whatever defiance he'd pulled together across the last few days evaporated when he saw Riggott's expression.

'My office, right fucking now,' Riggott snapped. He pointed at Zigic and Ferreira. 'You two as well.'

Murray was already in there, sitting on the small leather sofa pushed against the far wall. She'd told him everything, Zigic realised. He tried to catch Adams's eye but he wasn't looking at anyone but Riggott, his face showing a studied blankness that Zigic doubted he'd be able to maintain for very long. They'd both been preparing for this for days but now it was actually happening, Adams looked lost, overwhelmed in the face of his mentor's rage.

The room was full of the acrid reek of too-strong coffee, clashing with the sickly-sweet vapour residue from Rigott's e-cigarette. The air was close and stifling.

Adams went to sit down.

'Who told you to sit?' Riggott said. 'On your feet.'

He snatched the chair away and hurled it across the office into the window, which cracked but held. The chair hung there for a second or two before it clattered to the ground, ripping the blind off its fixings with an almighty crash.

'This was all me,' Adams said quickly. 'They shouldn't be here.'

'Aye, very fucking noble,' Riggott spat. He looked at Zigic. 'I'd have thought you'd have had a sight more sense than to listen to this wee cunt.'

Zigic said nothing. He should have had more sense but nothing Riggott could say would change the fact that he and Adams were probably correct.

'We were right to look again at Tessa Darby's murder,' Adams said, sounding like he was pulling the words up from somewhere deep and bruised. 'The original investigation had no idea what Lee Walton is capable of, it's understandable he wasn't pursued.'

Riggott gave him an incredulous smile. 'Sure, that's very big of you, son.'

'I'm just trying to say –'

'That you know better than me?' he demanded, storming over to Adams and stabbing a finger into his chest. 'That your superior fucking coppering skills are more reliable than a confession?'

Adams's cheeks flushed. 'Not all confessions are reliable.'

'You want to say that again?' Riggott asked, swaying slightly as if shaping up to deliver a blow.

'Neal Cooper obviously isn't the full ticket.' Adams said, stepping backwards, away from the blast of Riggott's stare. When he spoke again his voice was weakened and apologetic. 'Cooper probably believed he did it. At the time.'

'Fucking priceless.' Riggott slammed his palm hard against the wall next to Adams's head. 'I'm sure you've got a pair of balls down there, Billy. Get them out if you're going to. Let's see if they're as big as you're claiming.'

'I don't think his confession was valid.'

'You're still dancing around it.' Riggott shook his head, playing up the bravado but Zigic could see how badly this had stung him and that he wanted Adams to feel it too, the pain of betrayal, was going to force him to lay it out fully and suffer through every second. 'Say it!'

Adams cleared his throat.

'We think Cooper felt intimidated into a confession,' Zigic said.

Riggott dragged his eyes off Adams. 'By who?'

'By the process.'

'You saying Colleen scared him?' He waved in her direction and she curved slightly tighter in on herself.

'We're saying he thought he'd be found guilty and he confessed to try and get a reduced sentence,' Adams said. 'It happens. We all know that. People make that choice all the time. Especially people like Cooper who aren't very smart and do whatever their solicitor advises.'

It was a small lie and Zigic hoped it was enough. This was a horrible situation and no copper ever wanted to find themselves in it. Actively trying to overturn a superior's conviction.

Riggott stalked around the desk, kicked his own chair aside, muttering about Moira Baxter under his breath.

'Walton's rattled,' Adams said, attempting to move things on. 'The victim's mother was best friends with his mother, okay? Word's got back to him that we're looking into the case again and he's losing his shit.'

Riggott just stared at him, like he was trying to taking him apart cell by cell. The depth of contempt on his face was painful to see, and Zigic could only imagine how Adams felt, standing in the office where he'd been shaped as a copper.

'Tessa Darby is a perfect fit for Walton's victim profile,' Adams said.

Riggott nodded. 'That's mighty compelling. I'm sure the CPS will be able to build a solid case on it. Twenty years later. With a conviction already made and a sentence served. And what about this DNA sample you stole?' he asked. 'Or bribed some stupid bastard to give you.'

'I stole it,' Adams said, too fast.

Riggott gave him a pitying look. 'Son, I know how to get hold of a twenty-year-old DNA sample and it's a fucking bribe. You're a bit late protecting the stupid cunt who gave you it. Casualty number one, there.' He jabbed his finger at Adams. 'On you, that.'

'We'll have the result in the next twenty-four hours,' Zigic said. 'Maybe we should see how it comes back before –'

'Before what? How much more fucking damage are you intending on doing?'

His attention was all on Zigic now and the heat of it was severe enough to send a trickle of sweat down his back.

'If it comes back as a match for Walton, I think we need to reopen the case.' He heard the trepidation shaking his voice.

'Walton's too dangerous to be out on the streets,' Adams said. 'Are we really going to ignore a chance to put him away for life just because it's embarrassing admitting we made a mistake accepting Cooper's confession?' He took a step closer to Riggott's desk. 'I am sincerely sorry that we went behind your back on this, but the stakes were too high to ignore a solid opportunity to send him down again.'

Riggott rubbed his temples, skin creasing into those well-worn worry lines, dragging at the bags under his eyes. He looked old and exhausted now, not the man he was, not even the one he'd been last year. The recent forensics scandal had taken more out of him than Zigic had realised. The loss of convictions, all those countless hours slogging away on cases brought to nothing, more wearing than the PR fallout. Although he'd focused on that publicly, Zigic knew bad PR wasn't the thing that would have kept him awake at night.

So close to retirement this would feel like one last kick in the balls to see him off.

If retirement was actually the end of the matter. There was every chance Riggott would be investigated about the confession, that he would lose his pension and the security it had promised, maybe worse than that too. Charges weren't out of the question.

'Alright,' he said finally, dragging his spine straight once again. 'We continue on the quiet for now. But you keep me informed.' He glared at Adams but there was no heat in it any more, the ferocity spent rather than exorcised. 'Out. Out, now, go on.'

They started to leave.

'Not you, Mel.'

Chapter Sixty-Four

Riggott pointed at the sofa and Ferreira went to sit down, feeling a stirring of anxiety. He'd never been the kind of boss to sugar-coat anything; he gave out praise and bollockings in exactly the same manner, rarely enquired after people's spouses or kids or asked how their holidays were. She couldn't remember having any kind of personal conversation with him during the ten years she'd served under his command.

She had never once in all that time sat on this sofa.

It was firmer than it looked. Underused, she supposed.

He sat down against the opposite arm, elbows on his knees, said, 'Why didn't you come to me when Walton first approached you?'

'I can handle Walton,' she said, but she no longer believed it. For the last few days she'd found herself reliving that moment in the garage under her building, remembering how small and weak he'd made her feel, how hard it had been to breathe when he was in her face. And every night as she tried to sleep, she'd run through the terrible possibilities of him catching her unawares. All the ways she was vulnerable and all the places she no longer felt safe. She wasn't prepared to admit that to Riggott though, was still struggling to admit it to herself. 'He's just trying to scare me.'

'You should be scared of him,' Riggott told her, voice low and serious. 'You know what he's capable of.'

She gritted her teeth. 'I know what I'm capable of too.'

'Well, I admire your attitude but that's the kind of thinking that gets police officers damaged.'

'Dani's gone back to him,' she said. 'He's got no reason to hassle me any more.'

'Do you think that's going to stop him?' Riggott asked, incredulous. 'You know better than that. You don't take your eye off an animal like Walton, you don't go thinking you're safe because he's slipped into the shadows.'

'I'm not getting complacent,' she said defiantly. 'I know exactly what he is.'

Riggott nodded. 'Alright. I'm going to have a patrol car outside your place. He comes near you again and we'll haul him in.'

She felt her face flush with a sudden shame and anger at him for thinking – just like Billy – that she couldn't look after herself.

'That's not necessary,' she said, forcing her voice to stay even.

'I'm not asking your permission, Sergeant.'

'There's no law against him being there. What are you going to pull him in on?'

'Whatever I fucking want to,' Riggott said firmly. 'He needs teaching that we take care of our own. A few nights in the cells should put it through his thick skull.'

'I'm staying with Billy.'

No reaction to the news but she guessed it wasn't news to him. Station gossip eventually percolated up to the higher echelons.

'Way Adams is running around all over the place playing the fucking maverick, you don't want to be relying on him to look after you.'

'I'm not,' she snapped. 'He's no tougher than I am.'

Riggott made a placating gesture. 'Alright, Mel, this isn't a gender equality issue. It's a sheer fucking scale of the ugly bastard issue. I wouldn't fancy Billy's chances against him either.' He gave her a short nod. 'The car's going to be there.'

'How long for?'

He got up and went around behind his desk, yanking his e-cigarette from its charger. 'Until we get the result of that fucking DNA test.'

She left his office, thinking of the tacit admission in the statement. He knew what result they were going to get, or he was pretty sure about it anyway, which meant he *had* coerced a confession out of Neal Cooper. Probably in the full expectation that he was guilty, driven by his instincts and whatever scant evidence they'd dragged together in the case. But she knew he, like so many of his team, the ones he picked and shaped because they mirrored him so closely, were gut-driven detectives. And that was their main failing, trusting their guts that step too far.

Ferreira knew she'd done exactly the same thing with Joshua Ainsworth's murder and it seemed to be paying off now. But as guilty as Nadia Baidoo and Patrick Sutherland currently looked, there was the small matter of the paternity test.

A piece of grit too sharp to ignore.

She grabbed her tobacco and went downstairs for a smoke, tucking herself away around the corner of the building in a spot of shade where nobody else went, needing a few moments alone to decompress.

The first drag took some of the edge off and as she leaned back against the wall with her eyes closed, she realised that the weight that she'd been carrying for days now had lifted slightly. Knowing that the case Zigic and Adams had been working was viable, that Walton could feasibly be back in custody very soon, she could finally admit to herself how deep her fear of him ran.

Because she'd seen what he was capable of and she hadn't felt confident in her ability to deal with him alone if it came down to it. Despite what she'd said to Riggott.

Would a patrol car outside deter him? She wasn't entirely sure it would but maybe now that Walton could feel the net drawing closed around him, he'd think twice before approaching her again. If he had any sense of self-preservation, it would work.

But what about Dani, she thought, and her son.

Dani had gone back to him of her own free will but the boy had no say in it. How old was he now? Nine or ten, big enough to try and get between them when Walton decided to lash out at Dani. Big enough for Walton to think it was high time the boy was reminded of his place in the pecking order.

The poor kid wouldn't stand a chance.

'Now you definitely are hiding,' Adams said, coming around the corner.

He looked hollowed out. Face slack, movements smaller and more contained than usual as he lit up and slumped against the wall next to her.

'So, that was rough,' she said. 'You okay?'

'I was half expecting him to hit me so, yeah, went better than it might have.'

'You should have told me what you were doing,' she said, unable to stop herself now everything was out in the open.

'I know. I'm sorry.' He scuffed at the ground with his toe. 'I didn't want Riggott to take it out on you as well.' He smiled faintly. 'I thought, if I lose my job over this, at least Mel can keep me in the style I'm accustomed to.'

She found a smile for him.

'You okay?' he asked. 'What did Riggott want with you?'

She explained about the patrol car and he accepted it without a murmur. She wondered if he felt as intimidated by Walton as she did, if maybe he doubted his own presence would be a deterrent to the man.

'I was thinking about Dani and her son,' she said. 'Do you think I should get in touch with social services?'

'After that shit last night, yeah, probably a good idea,' he agreed, thoughtful-looking. 'I've got a mate there owes me a favour. Let me call him and see about getting someone to keep an eye on them.'

'Thanks.' She grabbed his hand and squeezed it quickly.

He fluttered his eyelashes. 'Oh, my God, public display of affection at work. Be still my boyish heart.'

'Fuck off then,' she said, grinning as she dropped his hand.

They went back up to the office, Adams walking past Colleen as if she didn't even exist. Ferreira felt a prick of sympathy for her, was sure she'd gone to Riggott with the best of intentions, wanting to keep Adams from getting himself into any deeper trouble. But it was going to take awhile for that rift to heal. She would talk to him later about it, try and get him to make the first move with Colleen. They'd worked together too long to fall out over this.

Ferreira moved to the board where Ainsworth's murder was plotted out, Zigic already standing there, Bloom, Parr and Weller all arranged facing him. He'd started the briefing without her but it hardly mattered. They were getting close now and she was increasingly convinced that the most significant part of their day would be questioning Nadia Baidoo again.

'Forensics,' Zigic said, uncapping the marker pen and beginning to write on the board. 'Blood-type match for Joshua Ainsworth on the carpet grip removed from Sutherland's garden fence and several deposits inside the house.' He wrote fast and almost illegibly and Ferreira knew she'd have to rub it all out once he was done and print in the same words. 'We also have Ainsworth's fingerprints in the kitchen, up the banister and in the bathroom.'

'But nowhere else?' Parr asked.

'He bandaged his hands up,' Bloom said, looking at Zigic. 'Maybe he kind of came to his senses while he was doing that, realised how much evidence he was leaving behind and gave up on whatever else he'd gone there for.'

'What he was doing there can wait for now,' Zigic said. 'The important thing is we can prove he was in Sutherland's house. Now,' he took a breath. 'We just need to prove that they knew he'd been there.'

'Nothing from door-to-door yet.' Parr reached for a can of energy drink. 'I noticed a couple of places had CCTV cameras though, so I was going to head back and see if we can get the footage.'

'Any of them pointing directly at Sutherland's place?'

'No, sir.'

'Any on the entrance to the close?'

He frowned. 'No, sir. It's a long shot I know.'

'Get hold of them,' Zigic told him. 'Check everything.'

Weller waved a vague finger towards the suspects column. 'Are we forgetting the rest of them, then?'

'Right now we're concentrating on Patrick Sutherland and Nadia Baidoo,' Zigic said firmly. 'We'll be questioning both of them today and I'd like us to have a comprehensive, preferably irrefutable, bundle of evidence when we head in there.' He clapped his hands smartly. 'Crack on then.'

CHAPTER SIXTY-FIVE

A few minutes after ten a call came up from reception.

'Lady down here for you, Mel.'

'Who is it?'

'She won't give me her name.'

The woman from their paternity test? Ferreira wondered, as she hurried down the stairs. Someone naïve enough to believe she could hold on to her privacy and untroubled life by simply refusing to say her name.

When she saw the woman, Ferreira realised she hadn't been brought out by the public appeal, which ran on yesterday's local news.

She was around sixty, tall and slim in baggy combats and trainers and a Momentum T-shirt in the same Soviet red as the clip-in streaks that stood in striking contrast to the perfect, silvery whiteness of the rest of her shoulder-length hair. She had a severe face and a steady gaze, which settled on Ferreira as she walked up to her. In a moment she felt the woman take her measure and relax slightly, as if deciding that, yes, she could talk to this policewoman.

'Ruby Garrick called me,' she said. 'You want to know about a woman from Long Fleet.'

'We should discuss this upstairs,' Ferreira told her and immediately the tension returned to the woman's face.

'I'm not going to talk to you here,' she said.

Ferreira nodded. 'Okay.'

'There's a pub up the road.'

'Bit early for the pub.'

'They serve coffee,' the woman said, starting out of the door.

Ferreira followed, knowing she probably should have insisted. This woman could be a fantasist or dangerous, although she didn't look like either. She looked like a seasoned protestor, someone who'd already spent time in police stations under circumstances that hadn't been pleasant, and wouldn't step into one of her own volition without a very good reason.

As they walked up the road, the woman moving at a swift rate, Ferreira considered trying to get her talking there but decided against it. She might spook otherwise and if she had information she was too important to let slip for the sake of a couple of minutes.

She texted Zigic as she walked, letting him know where she was going.

The Woodman was a new-old chain place on the edge of the golf course, and a few athletes were already in when they arrived, tucking into bacon rolls or full English breakfasts before they set out. There were a couple of suits working at laptops, earbuds in, paperwork out, and a pair of elderly ladies drinking what looked like mimosas with their eggs Benedict. They spoke quietly but laughed loudly and Ferreira half wished she could nab a seat nearby and eavesdrop.

'What are you having?' she asked.

'I'll buy my own.'

They ordered coffees and went to a seat as far away from the other customers as possible, a small table next to a painted fireplace filled with electric candles. The woman took the straight-backed wooden chair, leaving Ferreira the lower leather wing chair.

It was an interesting move, she thought, but would gain the woman nothing.

'Judy,' the woman said finally.

Ferreira doubted it was her real name and she would need more if the woman had the right kind of information, but she'd leave it at that for now.

'Mel,' she said. 'How are you involved with Long Fleet?'

'I'm not involved with them. I help run a charity for refugee women who've been unfairly incarcerated. We try to get them legal help, make sure their families know where they are and can keep in touch with them.' She was getting angry just describing the work and Ferreira could only guess at the horrors she heard. 'A lot of women are essentially kidnapped from their homes or workplaces without anyone being informed where they've been taken. We try to give them a link to the outside world. Get their stories out, engage their local MPs, the press, anyone who can help with their asylum applications.'

'That must be frustrating work.'

'Don't pretend you care,' Judy said, shooting her a withering look.

'I've spent the last seven years workings hate crimes,' Ferreira told her. 'I see what happens to women on the margins of society, I know how vulnerable they are. Believe me, I have nothing but sympathy for the women in Long Fleet.'

'But you work for the people who oppress them.'

'Not everyone in the police force is an oppressor.'

'No,' Judy said, the sneer turning into a contemptuous smile. 'Just enough of them to make life difficult for anyone with the wrong name or the wrong skin colour.'

She wanted to argue with the woman but knew there was no point.

'The woman you're looking for,' Judy said. 'Why do you want to speak to her?'

'As I told Ruby, we've been given a tip-off that she fell pregnant while she was locked up and we'd like to speak to her about how that happened. I'm assuming it wasn't consensual.'

'How can it be consensual in that place?' Judy snapped. 'He might not have pinned her down but only because he didn't need to. Long Fleet had already done it for him, locking her up, taking away her hope and her self-esteem. He *groomed* her into thinking it was what she wanted.'

'Does she still think that?' Ferreira asked.

'No,' Judy said quietly. 'Once she was deported she began to understand what happened.'

The same as with Nadia Baidoo, Ferreira thought. Sutherland using his access and his position of trust within Long Fleet to get to the most vulnerable women, using kindness and charm rather than force, but was it any different, really? Was he any better than the guards he'd helped to get rid of?

She wondered how he saw himself. Not as a sexual predator, of course not. He could point to more blatant ones and distinguish himself from them too easily to see how similar he was. When he said he loved Nadia, he sounded like he believed it. Maybe he thought the same about this woman. Or had wanted to convince himself that he did, that there was a deeper and more meaningful connection in play.

'Do you know who's responsible?' Judy asked her.

'We have an idea,' Ferreira said. 'But from what we could gather she wouldn't tell anyone while she was in Long Fleet, so we need to speak to her to be certain who we should bring in. Do you know who he is?'

Judy shook her head. 'Dorcus wouldn't tell me who was responsible. I strongly advised her to make a formal complaint. Involve her solicitor, insist she brought the police in even if you didn't actually do anything.'

'We would have taken her seriously,' Ferreira said.

A waitress came over with their coffees and for a moment that killed the conversation, both of them waiting for her to finish straightening the chairs at a nearby table and turning a small vase of flowers to the correct angle before she returned to the bar.

Judy dumped three sugars into her coffee, stirred it slowly.

'Honestly, I think Dorcus was hoping it would all go away if she just kept her head down and didn't whip up any trouble. That's how she handled being locked up. Went into her cocoon.' She blew on her coffee and took a small sip. 'I explained to her that a complaint was her best chance of being given permission to stay. Long Fleet are nothing if not risk averse. They'd have done it just to keep her quiet.'

'But they deported her instead?'

'Because that's the most effective way to silence someone, isn't it?' Judy said. 'Send them off thousands of miles away.' She crossed her legs and cupped her hands around her knee. 'Dorcus was terrified of being sent back with a baby on the way. She's a very religious young woman from a very traditional family. She knew they wouldn't forgive her for getting pregnant, no matter how it happened.'

'Have you spoken to her since she was deported?' Ferreira asked.

'Yes, a few times. I try to keep in touch with the women we lose. I don't want them to think they've been forgotten.'

'Did she have the baby?'

'Of course she did,' Judy said sadly. 'I advised her to terminate the pregnancy while she was in Long Fleet. Given her circumstances it seemed the wisest course of action. But she wouldn't hear of it.' She smiled slightly. 'She had a beautiful little boy.'

Judy's hand strayed to her pocket but stayed outside it.

'Do you have a photo?' Ferreira asked. 'I'd love to see it.'

Judy stared at her for a few seconds, as if trying to decide if this was genuine interest or some sneaky police trick.

Eventually she took her mobile out and scanned through the photos, then held the phone out to Ferreira, making it clear she wouldn't let her take it.

The baby was chubby and cute, swaddled tightly in a brightly patterned blanket. He was smiling although one of his eyes was swollen and gummed shut.

'Nasty case of conjunctivitis, bless him,' Ferreira said.

'Oh, that's cleared up now,' Judy told her, putting the phone away. 'She had a visit from a doctor friend of hers, he took some medication over. She was having a hell of a time getting something for it over there.'

'A doctor from your charity?'

'No,' Judy said slowly, seeming uncomfortable. 'Actually, he worked at Long Fleet.'

Judy couldn't look at her now and Ferreira was angry with herself for letting the woman dictate the terms of their conversation. She should have hauled her up to an interview room, made her do this on the record.

'Which doctor?' she asked sharply.

'Joshua Ainsworth.'

Ferreira took a deep breath, feeling the anger climbing up her spine one vertebra at a time, building and burning as it reached her skull.

'You knew he'd been murdered and you said nothing,' she snapped. 'Didn't it occur to you that this might have been important information?'

'How could it be?' Judy said weakly. 'Dorcus is in Kampala. He was killed at home. I assumed it was a break-in.'

Ferreira bit down on the reply she wanted to give – to remind this woman that she wasn't a police officer, that she knew nothing about the case, was in no position to assume anything. Instead she reached deep inside herself and found a small and neglected reservoir of near calm.

'Was Dorcus happy to see Ainsworth?'

'He isn't the man who got her pregnant,' Judy said, in a withering tone she didn't deserve to be throwing around. 'He was always very kind to Dorcus. She trusted him. She saw him as a friend. I mean, if they weren't friends why else would he have gone over to visit her?'

Ferreira knew why.

'I'm going to need to speak to Dorcus,' she said.

Chapter Sixty-Six

Zigic didn't like it. Some woman who wouldn't give her real name, wouldn't go any further into the station than the reception area. Someone who obviously had an axe to grind with Long Fleet. That wasn't the kind of informer you wanted to build a case on.

'I don't know about this,' he said. 'It sounds like "Judy" has a vested interest in stirring up bad press for Long Fleet and she's seen this case as an opportunity to do it.'

Ferreira rolled her eyes at him. 'You think she picked this story out of her arse?'

He wrinkled his nose.

'Look, we went through Ruby Garrick because we hoped one of her group might be able to put us onto a contact for Dorcus and she's done that.' Ferreira opened a bottle of juice but didn't drink it. 'What kind of person did you think we'd end up talking to? They're protestors. None of them were going to be big fans of the police. Shit, if you didn't want to dirty your hands dealing with unsavoury elements, then maybe this wasn't a good job choice.'

He gave her a warning look but she met it.

The last couple of days had eroded whatever slim moral high ground he'd carved out for himself over the length of their working relationship. Getting dragged into an off-book investigation with Adams had seen to that. Hiding it from Mel had only made it worse.

Dimly, he realised that was why he was being so picky about Ferreira's new contact. He was trying to claw back some semblance of moral certainty. For himself, not for anyone else. He wanted to be the kind of copper who did things the right way again.

'She knew Josh had been in Kampala visiting Dorcus, yeah?' Ferreira said, visibly restraining herself. 'We never made that public. So she's obviously got *some* insider knowledge.'

'We didn't go public but other people knew about it.'

'If she manages to get Dorcus to talk to us, then we'll know, won't we?' She took a drink of orange juice and put the bottle back down on the desk, next to the remains of a breakfast bagel. 'But this is all starting to make sense now.'

'The DNA test is from Dorcus's baby?' Zigic asked. 'That's your theory?'

'Ainsworth suspected Patrick Sutherland of grooming Dorcus and getting her pregnant,' she said. 'Now she's given birth – literally, a couple of months ago – and Ainsworth goes over to Uganda bearing medication and, I'm guessing, some swabs to take a sample from the baby.'

'And what about Dorcus? Do you think she knew what he was doing?'

'I'm going to ask her that,' Ferreira said shortly. 'But don't you think the timing of the break-in at Sutherland's place is interesting when you put it in context?' She went over to the board and slammed her knuckles against it. 'Wednesday, Ainsworth comes home from Kampala. Thursday, he breaks into Sutherland's house, apparently stealing nothing and not going any further than the bathroom.' She looked expectantly at him.

'Where you'd probably find something with DNA on, okay.'

'Friday, the samples go in the post and Saturday, he's dead.'

Zigic folded his arms. It all flowed on very neatly but that didn't mean her theory was right.

'This would sort of make sense *if* Sutherland knew Ainsworth broke into his house.'

'We only have his word for it that he didn't know it was Ainsworth,' she said irritably. 'And does he strike you as a particularly honest person?'

'We'll put it to him.'

'Okay, great,' she said. 'Let's go.'

'I want to speak to Nadia first,' he told her. 'Her solicitor is due in about half an hour. There's no point questioning Sutherland until we find out what she's prepared to give us.'

'Ziggy,' Adams called across the room and he was grateful for the momentary respite.

There was CCTV footage paused on Adams's computer screen and he had the dry-eyed, rumpled look of someone who'd spent the better part of the morning skimming through low-quality images in search of someone who wasn't there.

'What's this?' Zigic asked. 'You're not still on Walton?'

'I am, but no, this is that idiot who did a runner the other week. Got a tip-off that he's come back into the country through Dover but nobody thought to pick him up. By the time they decided his stupid face matched the picture on their wanted list, he was gone.' Adams stretched his neck, eliciting a small but sickening crunch that made him wince. 'Yeah, that's the one.'

'What's the problem?' Zigic asked, already wanting out of the office, his mind halfway to the interview room.

'Just keeping you in the loop,' Adams said, perching on the corner of his desk. 'Social services just visited the Waltons and were refused admission. Threats were made. Evidently, the gentleman carrying out the visit believed the threats were valid as they're now adding little Robbie Walton to a register.'

He looked very pleased with himself about it.

'And you did that?' Zigic asked.

'Well, it was Mel's idea to have someone keep an eye on the kid.' He crossed his arms. 'Given how Walton's losing his shit right now, I think a bit of backup from social's a good thing, don't you?'

Zigic thought it was antagonistic and part of him suspected that was the whole point of Adams's sending someone over there, but he wanted to believe Adams was better than that.

Zigic walked out of the office, pushing away all thoughts of Walton and that ongoing fiasco.

He needed to focus on Nadia Baidoo.

CHAPTER SIXTY-SEVEN

Ferreira rolled a cigarette and took it downstairs out onto the station steps, switching her phone back on.

There was a missed call from Dani. The sight of it sent an ache through her chest and gut, knowing it would most likely be Walton calling on Dani's phone, wanting another chance to taunt or threaten her.

She lit up and took a deep drag before she called Dani back.

She answered immediately.

'Why are you doing this to me?' she asked in a furious whisper.

For a moment Ferreira was stunned into silence, wondering what Dani could possibly mean.

'Doing what?'

'You know what. Social services have just been round here. We've never had any trouble with them before. We're good parents.'

Ferreira was surprised an underfunded and overworked social services team had gone around to the Waltons' this quickly. Even with Billy calling in a favour. Or maybe she was doing them a disservice. The facts of the case were worrying enough to catch the attention of even the most harassed social worker.

'Dani, you're in danger. Your son is in danger. That's why social services are visiting you.'

'*You* did this to me.'

'They're not worried about what *you*'ll do to Robbie,' Ferreira pointed out. 'It's what Lee's going to do. And as long as you're with him, you'll both be vulnerable.'

There was a long pause and Ferreira hoped Dani was considering what she'd said, but she could hear how light and fast her breathing had become, could feel her waiting and listening. Could almost taste the fear coming down the line.

'I can get you somewhere safe right now,' she said. 'Just say yes and I'll come and fetch you myself. You don't have to live like this.'

'Lee's furious,' she said finally. 'This is harassment. He's a good dad. He'd never hurt Robbie.'

'He's hurting Robbie every time he sees his mum getting beat up by his father.'

In the background a door slammed and she heard Walton bellowing, calling for his mum. She thought of the four of them thrown together in the mother's house, hoped the woman was a calming influence but guessed she wasn't. She'd raised him. She was probably just as terrified of Lee as Dani was.

'If he finds out you set them on us …'

'What, Dani?' Ferreira demanded. 'What's he going to do?'

'You need to watch yourself.' It should have been a threat but it sounded more like a genuine warning and she wondered why Dani could give that advice but not take it. 'And you better not call me any more.'

She rang off and Ferreira swore into the air.

It was inevitable, she told herself, as she relit her dead cigarette. Sending social services around was always going to antagonise Walton. She knew that when she thought of it and when she'd discussed it with Billy. But Walton's overreaction was exactly why it was necessary to call them in.

You didn't back down from a bully.

You didn't give them what they wanted out of fear for their response.

Upstairs she found Zigic ready and waiting to go. 'Ms Hussein's here. You ready to start?'

'Totally.'

The solicitor was in the corridor when they got there, standing at the interview-room door as if she wouldn't let them enter until she'd said her piece. Ferreira admired her tenacity, thought that if she was ever in trouble this is what she'd want from a solicitor, even as she felt slightly annoyed by the liberties she was taking.

'Good morning,' Ms Hussein said brusquely. 'I've impressed upon Nadia the importance of being completely open and honest with you today. She understands that you're her best hope now, please don't let her down.'

Zigic looked uncomfortable with her approach but he opened the door for her and ushered her in. Ms Hussein went to take a seat and next to her Nadia seemed very small and very young, dishevelled from her night in the cells, her hair crushed on one side and her skin dry and greyed under the strip light.

Ferreira set up the tapes, hoping Nadia would give them what they needed so they could do their best for her. For all her lies, she was a victim and she deserved whatever protection they could give her.

'We'd like to talk about the break-in,' Zigic said. 'Can you tell us what happened, please, Nadia?'

She glanced at Ms Hussein, received an encouraging look.

'I was in the kitchen washing up,' she began, her voice weaker than it had been yesterday, parched and thinner. 'I saw somebody come over the back fence and I panicked because I thought they must be going to try and break in. So I went to lock the back door and when I got a better look at the man, I realised it was Dr Ainsworth.' She reached for the water bottle in front of her, tried to open it and couldn't. Ms Hussein took it from her and unscrewed the lid, handed it back to her for her to drink. 'I didn't know what to do. I ran upstairs and hid in the wardrobe.'

'Did he see you?'

'I don't know,' she said. 'He screamed when he came over the fence but I didn't wait to see why or what he would do. I just ran and hid. I thought he was going to kill me.'

There was a tremble in her voice, impossible to fake.

'Why did you think he wanted to hurt you?' Zigic asked.

'Because of what I said about him.'

'Did you know he'd lost his job over it?'

She looked down into her lap. 'Patrick told me he resigned. He said it was nothing to do with me but I'm not an idiot, I knew it was. I didn't think that would happen when I said it. I didn't think about it at all, I was so desperate to get out of there.'

Ms Hussein put her hand on Nadia's arm. 'It's okay, just answer the detective's questions, you don't need to explain yourself.'

Zigic frowned, but didn't pursue the line. 'What happened when he got into the house?'

'I heard him in the kitchen, he was swearing and talking to himself,' she said. 'Then he came upstairs and I thought I was going to die. I closed my eyes and prayed he wouldn't find me.' She wrapped her arms around herself. 'I heard him in the bathroom, I think he must have been looking for something to stop the bleeding because after he was gone there was blood on the floor.'

So far her story tallied with what they had from forensics, but this was where the evidence fell away and they needed her statement.

'Where did he go after the bathroom?' Zigic asked tentatively. 'Did he find you?'

She shook her head.

'You need to speak,' Ms Hussein told her before Ferreira could. 'It's for the tapes.'

'Sorry,' she nodded to them. 'No, he didn't find me. He went back downstairs and I spent a really long time trying to work out whether he was still in the house. I couldn't hear him any more but I daren't move in case he was waiting for me down there. I don't know how long I waited but eventually I got out of the wardrobe and went down and found the house was empty. I called Patrick then and he came home.'

'Did you tell Patrick who had broken in?'

'Yes. He wanted to call the police but then I told him it was Dr Ainsworth and he said we shouldn't call you.' She folded her hands together on the tabletop. She'd painted her nails a bright coral pink at one point, but the varnish was chipped now and picked at. 'He said he'd speak to Dr Ainsworth and tell him to leave us alone.'

Was that how it happened? It sounded too perfect, Ferreira thought. The kind of line a solicitor might encourage a client to add to a story or the kind of thing you'd come up with during the long hours after midnight, waiting in a cell to have your say.

It fitted though.

She could imagine Sutherland going around to Ainsworth's place and warning him off. Ainsworth having none of it. An argument turning into a fight turning into a murder.

But why have that conversation so late? You only went into someone's home under cover of darkness for nefarious reasons.

'And when did he go to speak to Dr Ainsworth?' Zigic asked, a hint of reticence in his voice.

'Patrick wanted to go right then,' Nadia said. 'He was upset and angry and I begged him not to leave me on my own.'

'And did he go?'

'No, he stayed with me. He tidied the house up and called someone to come and fix the back door, then he found some cardboard to cover it up with overnight. He was trying to make everything like it was. He kept talking to me the whole time, not about what had happened. He was making plans for what we'd do at the weekend. He was trying to distract me so I'd calm down.'

She frowned but Ferreira saw the affection in her eyes. It surprised her but of course Nadia had feelings for Patrick Sutherland. He'd groomed her, charmed her, sprung her from Long Fleet and brought her to his home. Twenty years old, vulnerable and alone, how could you not feel a little love for the person who did that for you?

'By the time he'd finished tidying up, he seemed a lot calmer as well,' Nadia said, her face clouding over. 'He was fine until we went to bed.'

Ferreira felt a uneasy sensation creep across the back of her neck.

'Patrick went for a shower and when he got out he couldn't find his hairbrush.' She looked between them, absolutely perplexed. 'He was using this voice he has when he's trying to sound reasonable, but I can tell he's really irritated by something. He asked me if I'd moved it and I said I hadn't. Then he asked if I'd used it, and –' She gestured at her curls. 'Of course I hadn't. I don't know why he was so wound up about it.'

'Was it there before the break-in?'

She considered this briefly. 'I think so. It was there before Patrick went to work because I remember him brushing his hair while I was in the shower.'

Ferreira bit down on the satisfied smile she felt tugging at her face.

Ainsworth *had* broken into Sutherland's house for DNA to test against Dorcus's baby. That was why he only went as far as the bathroom. He knew what he wanted and where he'd find it. He probably had no idea Nadia was even in the house. No idea she was with Sutherland at all maybe.

She glanced at Zigic but his profile was set straight and hard as he looked at Nadia.

'Was anything else taken?' he asked.

'Nothing,' she said. 'Just Patrick's hairbrush.'

'How did he act the next day?' Ferreira asked.

Nadia inclined her head towards her, twisting her mouth into a thoughtful shape. 'He was quieter than usual. I didn't want him to go into work but he said he couldn't let them down. They were short-staffed since Dr Ainsworth left and they were having trouble getting a decent locum. He was very stressed out at work.' Spoken like a wife describing her long-suffering husband. 'I was worried that Dr Ainsworth might come back again but Patrick said he wouldn't. He was very certain.'

'Why do you think that was?'

'He said, "He got what he came for."' Her gaze drifted across the tabletop, as if she was still trying to understand the comment. 'But I was still scared. I made sure everywhere was locked and closed all the blinds. I just sat on the sofa and waited for Patrick to come home.'

Zigic took a deep breath, resigned-sounding, but Ferreira knew he was readying himself for the next part. It felt like they were close to something but there was always the fear in the moments before you levelled your most important questions that they would result in answers you didn't want.

'On the Saturday night,' Zigic said slowly. 'Saturday the 4th, what did you and Patrick do?'

Again Nadia looked to Ms Hussein before she would answer and again the solicitor gave a reassuring little nod. It was beginning to look like prompting and Ferreira wondered if Zigic was thinking the same thing, how malleable Nadia would seem in a witness box. How a jury wouldn't trust her testimony if it appeared to be directed like this.

'Patrick was very quiet on Saturday,' she said, sliding her hand nervously up the sleeve of her T-shirt and gripping her shoulder, looking defensive. 'I wanted to go out but he wanted to stay at home, but then he didn't want to do anything there either. He spent a long time in the bathroom with the door locked and I don't think he was doing anything, he just didn't want to be with me.' She was troubled by the thought, hurt in her eyes as she recalled it. 'We had dinner and watched a film and then Patrick said we should have an early night.'

'What time was this?' Zigic asked.

She shrugged. 'Around ten, I think. I remember thinking it was too early to go to bed and I wanted to watch a couple of episodes of *How to Get Away with Murder*.'

Ms Hussein's nostrils flared in alarm and Nadia realised what she'd said.

'It's just a show.' She looked desperately between them. 'It's not like a how-to guide.'

'Great show,' Ferreira said reassuringly. 'So addictive.'

Nadia calmed slightly and went on. 'So, we went up and Patrick brought me my sleeping pill and I went to bed.'

'Do you usually take a sleeping pill?' Ferreira asked, already suspecting the answer by the matter-of-fact way Nadia mentioned it.

'I've been taking them ever since I got out,' she said. 'I can't sleep without them.'

'And does Patrick usually decide when you're going to take one?'

Nadia's shoulders rounded even further, like she wanted to fold herself up. 'No, he isn't like that. He's not controlling.'

'But he insisted that night?'

'Yes,' she nodded. 'And I didn't think it was *that* weird because I wasn't feeling great, and he was trying to look after me and make sure I got enough sleep, so I thought, he's a doctor, I should probably listen to him.' Her brow furrowed. 'I fell asleep and that was it.'

'Did Patrick leave the house that night?' Ferreira asked.

'I don't know.'

'Did you hear anything? His car leaving maybe?'

'I was knocked out,' she said. 'They're really strong pills.'

'What about the next morning? What time did you get up?'

'My alarm's set for eight.'

'And was Patrick at home?'

'Yes, he was in bed with me.'

'How did he seem to you?'

'Normal,' Nadia said. 'He didn't wake up when my alarm went off but he doesn't always, so I left him in bed and went down to make breakfast.'

Ferreira was trying to keep the frustration out of her voice, trying to hold a steady pace to her questions but she was failing.

'Did you see anything to suggest that Patrick left the house on Saturday night?' she asked.

'No, I'm sorry.'

'Did he mention Dr Ainsworth to you?'

'No.'

'He didn't express an intention to go and speak to him?'

'Only that one time after the break-in,' she said shakily.

Zigic was looking at Ms Hussein now, his hands clasped tightly on the tabletop, a bare thrum of annoyance coming off him. She'd suggested Nadia had vital information, used it to ensure her client was treated more gently, tried to leverage a recommendation of leniency out of them.

Nadia did have useful information but there was no way Ms Hussein could know the significance of Ainsworth stealing a hairbrush. And as it stood Nadia wouldn't need their goodwill to help her avoid a prosecution because she appeared to know absolutely nothing about Sutherland's movements on the night of the murder.

Had Nadia changed her story overnight? Ferreira wondered. Come up with this sleeping pill excuse so she could claim ignorance of Patrick's behaviour and sidestep being an accessory after the fact?

'How did you feel when you heard Dr Ainsworth had been murdered?' Zigic asked, voice stony.

'I was very sad,' she said. 'He was a good man.'

'Did it occur to you that Patrick might have been responsible? She blinked, her eyes shining. 'He promised me he wouldn't go there. If he promised me then why would he go?'

'Patrick expressed an intention to scare Dr Ainsworth off.' Zigic's shoulders squared angrily. 'Then, on the night of the murder he drugs you and packs you off to bed. You're an intelligent young woman, Nadia, that must have struck you as a suspicious chain of events.'

'Nadia has explained the situation to the best of her capability and recollection,' Ms Hussein said in a warning tone. 'I'm sorry she couldn't give you what you need but the fact remains that she has cooperated fully and you have absolutely no reason to keep her in custody any longer.'

'Interview suspended 12:14 p.m.,' Zigic said, then pointed at Ms Hussein. 'Outside, please.'

They went into the corridor, Zigic moving in that slightly stiff way Ferreira knew meant he was fuming and trying to hide it.

'You have nothing to charge her with,' Ms Hussein said the second the door was closed. 'You may as well release her now and I can try and get her into a decent hostel while we still have some of the day left.'

'Nadia's hiding something,' Zigic said as if he hadn't heard her. 'Yesterday you implied that she had information about Ainsworth's murder.'

'No, you assumed I implied that,' she countered. 'I simply assured you that Nadia would cooperate to the best of her ability, which she has done.' She patted the bun at the nape of her neck. 'And I'd say she *has* given you pertinent information. Does Patrick Sutherland have an alibi now? No, he does not. Has Nadia's sighting of Ainsworth breaking into the house given Sutherland a motive for murder? Why, yes it has.'

'We're going to need to talk to Nadia again,' Ferreira said. 'Things are moving very fast right now and there's a good chance she can help us still.'

'Which she can do from a hostel.'

'She's staying here,' Zigic said, in a tone that killed further debate. 'We'll call you when you're needed, Ms Hussein.'

CHAPTER SIXTY-EIGHT

'She's good,' Zigic said bitterly. 'I'll give her that.'

'Are you regretting calling her?' Ferreira asked.

'Yes!' He shook his head immediately. 'No, I suppose not. She's just doing her best for the girl. I can't blame her for that.'

They were standing at the board, nothing new on it since they'd gone into the interview room but Nadia had given them something at least. Not what they wanted, a firm statement against Patrick Sutherland, but it was a start.

'So, I *was* right about Ainsworth going for a DNA sample,' Ferreira said, sounding slightly smug about it but he guessed she deserved to feel that way. She turned to him, an urgent look on her face. 'Do you think the hairbrush is still at Ainsworth's house?'

'Was it in with the stuff from forensics?' he asked.

'No, but why would they take a hairbrush they will have thought belonged to Ainsworth? They already had his DNA.' She called over to Murray. 'Colleen, are you busy?'

'It's nothing that won't wait.' She spun away from her desk. 'You want me to go and see if I can find this hairbrush, then?'

'If you could.'

Murray grabbed her bag and her keys. 'Do you know what it looks like?'

'Bristles, handle,' Ferreira suggested.

Murray pulled a face of fake amusement. 'I'll go down and ask Ms Baidoo for a description, will I?'

'That's probably a good idea,' Zigic said.

'And I'm guessing it won't just be in the bathroom?'

'Check his office,' Ferreira said. 'He seemed to like keeping stuff in box files and since he was clearly trying to build some kind of case against Sutherland my guess is he'll have separated it out somewhere.'

'Got it.' Murray traced a salute at her and left the office.

'You think that's what he was doing?' Zigic asked, dropping into Murray's vacated seat. 'Trying to gather enough evidence to go after Sutherland?'

'Why else would he want to prove it?' Ferreira was writing on the board now, adding what they'd got from Nadia. 'Sutherland cost him his job on a trumped-up assault charge; it makes total sense that Ainsworth was looking to get his own back on him. Find the evidence that Sutherland was grooming and exploiting inmates, get the DNA match for Dorcus's baby, then he takes it to Hammond and he has to sack Sutherland.'

'Not come to us?'

'I don't think this was about getting Sutherland banged up,' she said, tapping the marker pen against her knuckles. 'Ainsworth had his reputation shredded, I think he wanted to do the same to Sutherland.'

Zigic considered it, idly picking a couple of jelly babies from the open jar on Murray's desk. Joshua Ainsworth seemed like a highly moralistic man, someone who put his ideals before everything, taking a job that paid less than he could have earned elsewhere, which was more stressful and drew down the kind of hassle that you didn't suffer working in A & E or a GP surgery. He was at Long Fleet because he believed it was the best place for him to do good and being *that* man was clearly important to him.

Wasn't it natural that he'd want to regain his untarnished reputation?

Natural too that Patrick Sutherland would want to protect his own good name. And the access Long Fleet gave him to vulnerable women who would be susceptible to the gentle manner and easy charms which he used to groom them.

Nadia Baidoo was in love with him. Believed in him. Trusted him.

Did she want to protect him now just like he'd protected her?

'Do you buy the sleeping pill story?' Zigic asked.

Ferreira grimaced. 'I don't know. It's *really* convenient from a self-preservation point of view, but I was surprised she didn't cover for Sutherland given how she was going on about him.'

'She didn't drop him in it either,' he said. 'Basically, we can't charge her with anything and until we find some compelling evidence to place Sutherland at Ainsworth's house, we can't charge him either. They're both safe from us.'

'But you still think one of them's responsible, right?' Ferreira asked, her tone making it clear that she did.

'I'm not sure the break-in is a motive,' he admitted, eyeing the names on the board behind her.

Names which they'd drifted away from but hadn't fully ruled out. The girlfriend, the protestors, all the guards who'd lost their jobs thanks to Joshua Ainsworth.

He felt like they had the right people in custody, that they had most of the pieces they needed to prove guilt, but still that vital something was missing.

Kate Jenkins had been in touch to say she was starting work on Sutherland's car. There had been some delay getting it released from the car park at Long Fleet, but it was in the station garage now and he knew she would be giving it her fullest attention.

They were well overdue something useful on the forensics front.

'Do you want anything from the canteen?' he asked, hauling himself up.

Ferreira shook her head. 'Oh, actually, some chocolate.'

'I meant proper food.'

'And a Coke, please.'

'You're going to rot all your teeth right out of your head,' he told her as he left the office.

Downstairs he got what was going to pass for Mel's lunch from the machine, grabbed himself a chicken sandwich and a smoothie, thinking about Nadia hiding in the wardrobe as Joshua Ainsworth came up the stairs. Tried to imagine how that had felt, knowing what she'd done to him, how much he must hate her.

And then how Sutherland had felt when she told him about it.

Even without his own selfish motives he would have wanted to protect her, Zigic thought. Assuming Sutherland *did* love her.

He wasn't sure he believed that either. Was finding he believed nothing Sutherland said. The man was clearly an arch manipulator. Seemed to have even drawn Ferreira in for a while there and, God knows, she had a cynical streak half a mile wide.

They would have to be careful with him. Go in with a plan and not deviate from it.

Back in the office Ferreira was at Bloom's desk, both of them standing looking at something on the screen, expressions giving nothing away.

'Come and see this,' Ferreira said. 'Keri, tell him what you've been up to.'

'I just thought I'd check through Sutherland's record again,' she said, vaguely apologetic about it.

Because it hadn't been her job, Zigic thought, and she probably felt like she was stepping on someone's toes.

'What did you find?' he asked.

'Five days ago we've got a ticket on his number plate for jumping a red light in Werrington. So I pulled the image from the camera,' she said, moving aside so he could see the photo she'd found, blown up on her screen. 'It's not brilliantly clear, sorry.'

It wasn't, but it didn't need to be. Even with the pixels breaking apart Zigic could see that Patrick Sutherland was in the passenger seat. Nadia Baidoo driving.

'That changes things a bit,' he said.

'Just because she can drive, it doesn't mean she drove to Ainsworth's place and killed him.' Ferreira took her chocolate from his hand and ripped it open. 'We weren't ruling her out just because she couldn't drive.'

'No, but we were adjusting our likelihoods based quite heavily on the fact that we didn't think she could get to his house,' Zigic pointed out.

They'd come a long way in a little over a week, made more progress than he'd expected them to, but the finish line still wasn't quite in reach.

If anything it felt further away now than it had this morning. The path to it split suddenly. Nadia Baidoo down one lane, Patrick Sutherland the other.

And he didn't know which way to go.

CHAPTER SIXTY-NINE

Sutherland was on his feet when they entered Interview 1, staring up at the high window as the guard in the corner watched him with indifference.

His solicitor, Ben Lawton, sat in the seat against the wall, typing something out on his mobile, thumbs skipping fast across the screen. He made a show of switching it off as they approached the table, and slipped it into his jacket pocket.

'How's Nadia?' Sutherland asked.

'She's fine,' Zigic told him.

'I hope you haven't questioned her without a solicitor.'

'Why would she need a solicitor?' Zigic asked innocently.

Sutherland spread his hands wide. 'She's a vulnerable young woman who's been grossly mistreated by people in positions of authority.'

'People?' Ferreira said. 'Plural?'

He looked at her, flustered. 'The whole system. Everything she's been through. The last police officers she saw snatched her out of her life and locked her up. Do you think being here is going to be easy for her?'

Ferreira sat down at the table and set up the recording equipment, looking at him the whole time, her voice neutral and even when she prompted him to state his name for the record. He said nothing the first time.

'Dr Sutherland, for the record, please state your name.'

He took a couple of grudging steps towards the table, leaned in. 'Patrick Sutherland. I don't know why you're doing this. I already told you everything I know.'

'Sit down, Patrick,' Lawton said in an undertone, so low it seemed that Sutherland didn't hear him because he retreated from the table again.

Zigic leaned against the wall, wanting to keep Sutherland on his feet. Suspects were always less stable when they were standing; once seated they began to compose themselves, took their time in answering, considered their responses more carefully. So much easier to trip him up like this.

'We've spoken to Nadia,' he said. 'And her account of the break-in on Thursday August 2nd doesn't tally with what you've told us.'

'Perhaps Ms Baidoo's recollection is flawed,' Lawton suggested smoothly.

'I very much doubt she's misremembering seeing Joshua Ainsworth coming over Patrick's garden fence and forcing his way into the house.' Zigic turned back to Sutherland. 'And I doubt she's misremembering you losing your temper and saying you'd go and warn Ainsworth to stay away from her.'

'You only have her word for all of this,' Lawton said.

'You've lied to us on record, Patrick. This is your one and only chance to come clean about what happened between you and Joshua Ainsworth.'

Sutherland exhaled sharply, his shoulders slumping as he did it, chin dropping onto his chest. He looked thoroughly beaten, shirt a mess of creases and rumples, sweat-stained under the arms, hair greasy and chaotic, the previously rakish waves now seedily plastered to his skull.

He threw his hands out in a gesture of surrender. 'I was trying to protect her.'

'From what?'

'From herself.' He drew his head up again, slowly, like it was too heavy for his neck. 'But I can't, can I? Not for ever.' He shoved his fingers back through his hair. 'She was doing so well. I actually thought she might get over it, given enough time and care. Maybe I was naïve to think I could fix her, but ... that's what love is, isn't it? Fixing each other.'

It wasn't, Zigic thought. But of course Sutherland would see it that way, this man who sought out women who were weakened and scared, who would look to him with fear and adoration and meet every small effort he made for them with disproportionate gratitude. It was skin-crawling, seeing how his mind worked.

'She *was* getting better,' Sutherland said, a hint of pride in his voice before his eyes hardened. 'Then Josh came to the house. He tore the place apart looking for Nadia.'

'It didn't look torn apart,' Zigic said.

'I cleared everything up. I didn't want Nadia to have to see a single trace of his presence there.'

'You missed quite a bit of his blood,' Zigic told him, letting some of the pleasure he felt show.

Sutherland went on as if he hadn't spoken.

'Thank God, she saw him before he saw her and went to hide.' He shuddered. 'I don't even want to think about what he would have done to her if he'd found her.'

'Why didn't you tell us about this the first time we asked you?'

'Because of Nadia,' he said, as if it was obvious. 'I didn't want her to have to suffer through explaining everything he'd done to her. And it's my house, I didn't think it was anyone's business if we had a break-in. There's no legal requirement to report a crime.'

'But there's a moral one,' Ferreira told him. 'Because your one unreported crime could keep us from solving other linked ones.'

'I wanted to call you,' Sutherland said earnestly.

He took a seat at the table finally and Zigic saw an admission in the move: Sutherland needed to concentrate now. He was opposite the empty seat but directing his story across the table to Ferreira.

'I was scared,' he told her. 'I'm ashamed to admit it but I was scared for Nadia and for me. I knew that calling you would expose our relationship and I wasn't ready to deal with that yet. But I was more afraid of Josh and what he'd do to Nadia. I told her we'd have to call you and she begged me not to.' He pursed his lips. 'She was convinced that any contact with the law would have her leave to remain revoked. And I tried to explain to her that it only happened to people who'd committed crimes, not victims of them. But she was just so … terrified. She wasn't thinking straight. That level of fear … it's impossible for any of us to understand, I think.'

Zigic slid into the free seat. Sutherland gave him the merest flicker of acknowledgement before turning back to Ferreira.

'Nadia was trapped,' he said, his hands locking together on the tabletop. 'Between her fear of being deported and her fear of Josh coming back.'

'It must have been very difficult for her,' Ferreira said softly, giving him an earnest look now. 'And you.'

'She wasn't in her right mind.' Sutherland shook his head helplessly. 'You have to understand, Nadia has PTSD. She was and is incapable of rational thought where Josh is concerned.' He closed his eyes, pressed his fingers to his mouth. 'It was self-defence. She was in fear for her life.'

'What are you saying, Patrick?' Ferreira asked. 'What did Nadia do?'

'Saturday night,' he said, looking queasy as he forced out the words. 'I woke up and realised I was alone in bed. I thought maybe she couldn't sleep and had gone downstairs to watch TV – she was having trouble sleeping but she won't take pills because of the side-effects.'

Zigic felt a cold, tumbling sensation in his stomach. Something in the pitch of Sutherland's voice and the inward-turned expression on his face, led to an indefinable, entirely illogical feeling that this was the truth coming out of the mouth of this well-practised liar.

Nadia had claimed to be a long-term user of sleeping pills. Sutherland, as a doctor, would know how easily they could test her blood for their presence.

So why say she wasn't taking them if she was?

'She wasn't downstairs,' Sutherland said. 'She wasn't anywhere in the house. I panicked. Of course. She never went out of the house at night.'

'Did you go and look for her?' Ferreira asked. 'Call her mobile?'

'I was getting dressed to go out when she came in.' He rubbed the back of his neck, eyes averted but Zigic could see the tension running up the line of his jaw. 'She was covered in blood.'

Ferreira glanced at Zigic quickly and he saw his own doubts reflected back at him.

'Was she hurt?'

'It wasn't her blood,' he said, almost whispering. 'She said she couldn't stand it any more. The waiting.' He looked desperately between the two of them. 'It isn't her fault. You know what he did to her. You see that, don't you? She's so damaged. So traumatised. I don't think she really understood what she'd done until the next day. She came home so ... numb. It was like she was in a trance.'

Zigic sat back in his chair, watching Sutherland's eyes lose focus just like Nadia's did when she recounted her time in Long Fleet, like everyone's did when they dredged up the really bad stuff.

Next to him Ferreira was leaning forwards, forearms on the table, palms flat, her fingertips inches away from Sutherland's hands. The same short distance between them there had been at the first interview. He'd picked up on the charge between them at the time, sensed it remerging now, but he wasn't sure if it was real or a ploy.

Ferreira came in here convinced Nadia was innocent but she was too good a detective to ignore what they were hearing now. Not the words that could so easily be a lie, but the emotional undertow, that stripped throat quality to Sutherland's voice, the loss in it.

'What did Nadia say?' she asked. 'Did she tell you what she'd done?'

'She didn't mean to do it,' he said defiantly. 'It was self-defence. If there's any justice in the world, people will see that. I'll make them see it. Nadia is the victim here.'

'She is,' Ferreira agreed.

'She couldn't defend herself against Josh when he attacked her that first time, but she wasn't going to let it happen again.'

'Except,' she said, her fingertips drumming the table lightly, 'Josh didn't attack Nadia.'

Confusion clouded Sutherland's face.

'Nadia told us herself. Josh never touched her.'

He groaned into his hands. 'No, she's just saying that now because she doesn't want you to think she has a motive to kill him. I examined her myself, I know *exactly* what Josh did to her.'

'What you *told* Nadia to say Josh did to her,' Ferreira said, but there was the bum note of doubt again in her voice. 'You told Nadia to fabricate an allegation to increase her chances of avoiding being deported.'

He shook his head sadly. 'I didn't tell her to do any such thing. Josh attacked her. And yes, when she told me about it I pleaded with her to report it to Hammond because it was important that he know what kind of man he was employing to work with vulnerable women. And yes, of course I didn't want her to get deported. Nothing had happened between us then but I already had feelings for her. I didn't want to lose her.' Sutherland's face hardened. 'But I did not say it would improve her case. Being attacked doesn't improve anyone's chance of staying in the country. Obviously. Think about it, do you really believe the Home Office could be swayed that easily?'

'Then why was she allowed to stay?' Zigic asked.

'I don't know the intricacies of her case,' Sutherland said impatiently. 'I'm just a doctor, I'm not involved in those decisions. My guess is she just got lucky. It happens sometimes. She's been here since she was a child. Maybe someone took pity on her.'

It sounded unlikely but without verification from Hammond they couldn't judge whether it was true or not, and Zigic suspected they'd got as much from the governor as they were going to. Despite the promise he'd made them at his house, he hadn't even come through with the report into the alleged attack. He was clearly hoping this would quietly resolve itself without his input. A hope which was looking more likely by the minute.

'You don't know what that place does to people,' Sutherland said, all the energy drained out of him. 'It *breaks* them. And it isn't like a real prison but it creates a lot of the same behaviours in people that a prison does. They get ... closed off and anxious, the slightest thing can trigger disproportionate emotional responses. And that's just what the day-to-day reality of being locked up does.' He rubbed his mouth. 'But what happened to Nadia, the violence of what Josh did to her, that is something else altogether.'

'She doesn't seem like a violent person,' Ferreira said.

'She's not,' Sutherland replied sharply. 'She's not dangerous, she'd never hurt someone for no reason. But when Josh came to the house something shifted in her. She was never going to feel safe as long as he could just jump the back fence and get to her.'

Zigic thought of Lee Walton and the effect he was having on Ferreira. As accustomed to violence as she was, as trained in dealing with dangerous people. He thought of the way Walton was dictating her movements and limiting her life, how his mere presence had dragged them all into a situation that could ruin them.

How would someone like Nadia Baidoo deal with that pressure?

Alone and scared, traumatised already.

It was horribly credible.

'Nadia needs help,' Sutherland said desperately. 'The level of trauma she's been through, you couldn't even say she was fully mentally capable of knowing right from wrong. She has PTSD. Any doctor talking to her for five minutes will tell you that.'

For a moment nobody spoke and Zigic could hear a voice in the corridor, muffled but pitched at anger, and then the creak of Lawton's chair as he shifted his weight slightly.

'I think now might be a good moment to take a break,' he said.

Ferreira gave Zigic a questioning glance and he nodded, letting them have it.

He needed a break too, needed to step back and consider this mess in front of them.

CHAPTER SEVENTY

They were silent all the way back to the office and when Ferreira rolled a cigarette, wanting to get a few minutes peace to consider what they'd just heard, Zigic said he'd come down with her. 'For some air.'

She'd walked into that interview room convinced that Patrick Sutherland was guilty, and despite Zigic's insistence on keeping an open mind, she was sure he had felt the same way. It had just seemed too unlikely that Nadia had it in her to kill Joshua Ainsworth. From everything they'd been told about her by the people who knew her, from her build and personality and the typical behaviour of women who'd suffered violence. Even knowing that Joshua Ainsworth hadn't assaulted her in Long Fleet hadn't changed Ferreira's opinion. Because, yes, she'd lied about that but at Sutherland's insistence, and with a broader motivation linked to her desperation to escape the place. It didn't mean she wasn't scared of Ainsworth, only that she had a slightly different reason to fear him.

But now, now she felt that certainty had been whipped away.

Outside, tucked around the side of the station, she lit her cigarette, watching the play of doubt across Zigic's face.

'I wasn't imagining it, was I?' he asked. 'Sutherland's story sounds right.'

'We know he's a liar,' she said.

'And we know Nadia is too.' He shoved his hands into pockets. 'And he knows we know that now, so what if he's using that to try and lay the blame on her?'

'What if she's doing the same to him?' Ferreira suggested. 'If either of them's physically capable, it's Sutherland.'

'But it doesn't take much strength to bludgeon someone who's already down.'

'Look, we had this conversation at the scene,' she reminded him. 'You didn't think a woman could put Ainsworth down with enough force to break that table.'

'Kate did say it was flimsy.'

He walked away a few steps, eyes on the ground that was littered with dead cigarette butts and scraps of rubbish blown in on the wind and trapped in the lee of the building. He looked like he was searching for something but it was inside his head and she wasn't sure he'd find it like that.

'Sutherland's a manipulator,' Ferreira said, needing to say it out loud because she'd found herself beginning to believe him as he gave his version of events. 'What if he's playing us?'

Zigic stopped dead, turned sharply. 'It all hinges on the sleeping pills, doesn't it? Sutherland claims Nadia wasn't taking them, she says she was on them every night and that he gave her one on the night of the murder.'

'So he could sneak out without her knowing what he was doing.'

'Right,' he nodded. 'So that's the one point where we can definitely prove whose story is true and who's lying.'

'Let's get a blood test then,' Ferreira said. 'If they find traces of medication in Nadia's bloodstream, we'll know she's taken the pills recently.'

'It'll still be in her hair if she's been on them long term, won't it?'

'That's going to take more time.'

'We need an answer,' he said. 'It takes as long as it takes.'

When they returned to the office he called Parr, who was still hunting for CCTV at the houses around Sutherland's, told him to go in and bring back whatever medication he could find. Then he called for the station nurse to organise drawing Nadia's blood and asked DC Bloom to sort out the paperwork.

As he was giving her the details Ferreira's phone chimed. A text from Judy telling her that Dorcus was ready to talk to them.

They made the Skype call from Zigic's office, the pair of them seated on the visitors' side of his desk with the blinds drawn at the internal window, wanting Dorcus to feel that she had some semblance of privacy for this conversation. It wasn't going to be easy for her, they thought, and as far as possible they wanted her not to regard this as a police matter.

Ferreira used the email address Judy had texted her and they waited as it rang.

Judy said Dorcus was back with her family, living with a grandmother who had taken her in and was helping with the new baby. Considering the alternatives it seemed as good an outcome as anyone could hope for. When Dorcus answered she was in a pink-painted bedroom, a neatly made bed behind her, clothes stacked on a chair nearby.

She didn't look much older than Nadia Baidoo, early twenties at most, with a full and pretty face, her brows high and arched, above a pair of cat-eye glasses. She'd put on a slick of brilliant red lipstick that perfectly matched the patterned scarf holding back her hair. She looked more together than Ferreira had expected someone who'd recently been deported to be, and as relieved as she was for Dorcus, it only made her feel worse about what they were doing.

Dorcus held her soundly sleeping baby against her chest. Already much bigger than in the photograph Judy had shown Ferreira and here, where the light was better, she could see that the baby had a white father.

'Hello, Dorcus,' she said. 'I'm Mel. This is Dushan. Thank you so much for agreeing to speak to us.'

She wasn't quite prepared for this conversation herself, felt the weight on her, the need to be delicate but also to get the information they needed from Dorcus.

'Good afternoon,' Dorcus said, eyes lowered. 'Judy said you want to talk to me about Dr Ainsworth.'

'If you're okay with that.'

'I am sorry to hear that he has been killed,' she said, stroking her son's head gently. 'He was a very kind man. He did not deserve to die in such a manner.'

'He came to see you recently, didn't he?' Ferreira asked.

'Yes.'

'Did you stay in touch with him after you were deported?'

The question felt crass, but Dorcus seemed unfazed.

'No, he found me on Facebook,' she said. 'He told me he was coming to Kampala for a holiday. He asked me about the city. He had not been here before.' She smiled slightly. 'He did not know anybody in Kampala. Only me.'

'And he came to see you when he arrived?'

'Yes, he brought medicine for Joseph's eyes.'

'Are they better now?' Ferreira asked.

'Much better, yes.' She looked down at him, taking hold of his tiny hand and stroking his fingers.

Dorcus seemed happy despite everything, and Ferreira struggled to imagine how she could possibly feel that way. Given what she'd gone through, how she'd managed to come to terms with falling pregnant while she was locked up and then being deported in the middle of the night. Ferreira felt angry on her behalf, wondered how Dorcus had found this calm within herself.

She noticed the small gold cross she wore and supposed maybe that helped.

'Did Dr Ainsworth tell you he'd left Long Fleet?'

The contented expression on Dorcus's face faltered momentarily, as she lifted her eyes towards the camera, but then she returned to her baby, cradling his head and rocking him from side to side.

'He told me this, yes.'

'And did he tell you why?'

Her face turned grave. 'At Long Fleet the good people are punished for helping. This is why he left. He was made to leave for telling the truth.'

'He wanted to tell the truth about what happened to you, didn't he?' Ferreira asked, watching Dorcus carefully for any sign that she needed to pull back, but she only nodded.

'I did not want to make trouble. If anyone made trouble they were the first to be sent away,' she said. 'But they took me anyway.'

'Did Dr Ainsworth know who attacked you?'

Dorcus lowered her eyes again, her face becoming pensive. 'I was not attacked.'

'We were told you fell pregnant in Long Fleet,' Ferreira said. 'Was that not true?'

'I was blessed with my boy there, yes. But I was not attacked. Dr Ainsworth said it is the same thing though. When a man has power a woman does not, there is no reason for him to be violent. His power *is* his violence.' She pursed her lips. 'Judy told me this too, but I did not believe her. My nana, she said, "Never believe the words of a man who wants you."' Dorcus smiled wanly. 'I believed Patrick. He said he loved me and he would make sure I was not sent away.'

Zigic let out a low breath next to her.

The same story as with Nadia, except Sutherland's ploy worked in her case.

'How was he planning on stopping your deportation?' Zigic asked.

'He said there were medical troubles he could make it seem like I had. If I had some of these things wrong with me, I could not be deported.'

Ferreira was sure that wasn't true, but could imagine being convinced by the lie in Dorcus's situation. When you were desperate it would sound logical enough to hang your hopes on.

'Patrick said he couldn't live without me.' There was something like scorn in Dorcus's voice now and Ferreira wondered if it was directed at Sutherland or herself for believing him. 'He called me his "ebony queen".' She rolled her eyes. 'Those are not the words of a man in love, are they?'

Ferreira shook her head, momentarily tangled in the sheets of the English Lit student she'd dated at uni, listening to all the words he knew for the colour of her skin. She'd been young enough to enjoy the intensity of his attention then, only ended it when he lifted his head from between her thighs and told her she tasted different to English women.

'Dr Ainsworth was suspicious of Patrick's behaviour when you were still in Long Fleet, wasn't he?' Zigic asked. 'He wanted you to speak to the governor.'

'Patrick said if Mr Hammond found out about our relationship, they would deport me immediately. I trusted Patrick to help me. So, I said nothing.'

'What about when Dr Ainsworth came to visit you last month? Did you tell him about Patrick then?'

'I will never be able to go back to England,' she said despondently. 'But Joseph will, one day. He is half an English boy, they won't be able to tell him no and lock him up.' She smiled down at the boy, radiant as she watched him sleeping. 'Dr Ainsworth knew already. At Long Fleet he asked me if it was Patrick and I would not say. I should have said then. The other women needed to be kept safe from him but I did not understand that when it was happening. Because he didn't hurt me, I thought what we were doing was not bad. But it is. It is wrong that Patrick lies to women and gives them false hope to get what he wants from them.'

'Dr Sutherland has been suspended,' Ferreira told her. 'He won't be working as a doctor any more.'

They'd agreed not to share his suspected role in Ainsworth's death but she thought Dorcus deserved to know this much, to have the guilt she felt lightened slightly by the knowledge that he wouldn't be going back there.

'Dorcus, did you give Dr Ainsworth permission to take a DNA sample from your son?'

'Yes. And from me also. He said he would use it to prove what Dr Sutherland did, so he would lose his job and not be able to be a doctor any more.' She looked directly into the camera, a new fierceness in her eyes. 'I am glad he has lost his job.'

Her baby stirred, wriggling against her chest, his small fist fighting the air, alerted by the strain in her voice and the shift in her posture as she leaned closer to the camera. A second later he began to wail. She cooed and shushed him, but he only got louder.

'Dorcus, we should let you go,' Ferreira said. 'You've been a great help –'

'Tell him that.' Her voice rose over the crying. 'Please tell Dr Sutherland that I helped you.'

432

Ferreira smiled. 'I'll tell him we wouldn't have caught him without your help. I'll make sure he knows you did this to him.'

Dorcus nodded and reached forward and the call ended.

'Is it less bad that Sutherland groomed her rather than physically attacked her?' Zigic asked, looking troubled as he stared at the dead screen.

'I guess that's a matter for the individual,' Ferreira told him. 'From our perspective though – being a cold-hearted bitch for a minute – how can we use this against Sutherland?'

Zigic propped his chin on his fist, still a little dazed.

'I'm not sure we can. It's the same behaviour he exhibited with Nadia and we know he doesn't feel any shame about it.' Zigic shrugged. 'Maybe if Nadia found out he'd gone through the same routine with another woman before her, she'd get jealous and turn on him but she's already turned on him.'

'You're back to thinking he's responsible,' Ferreira said, hearing the subtle shift in his tone.

'I'm thinking about the hairbrush.' He stroked his beard absent-mindedly. 'Josh only needed a hair or two for the DNA sample, so why take the whole brush?'

'Maybe he was just being overly cautious,' she suggested. 'I guess he didn't fancy breaking in a second time if the initial test failed because of contamination or something.'

'Or did he want Sutherland to know it was missing?' Zigic asked.

'Why bait him like that?' She shook her head. 'No, Ainsworth had no way of knowing Sutherland would find out he was responsible for the break-in, so this doesn't read as baiting to me. It makes much more sense than he was being thorough taking the whole thing and he just expected Sutherland to think he lost it.'

Zigic's phone started ringing and he asked her to give him a minute.

Ferreira went back out into the main office, ate the rest of the now slightly melted chocolate bar she'd left on her desk.

She kept thinking about Sutherland and Dorcus, what kind of man he was to exploit his power over her and how they could turn that against him. But it felt like an impossible task. She had a terrible feeling he was going to get away with this. If they couldn't definitively prove his guilt, and it came down to his word against Nadia's in front of a jury, she knew which way they'd rule.

And meanwhile, what would he do?

He'd be another Lee Walton, accused but evading justice. Still free to practise medicine, still with his life all ahead of him to keep using and abusing women from behind the protective façade of his good job and his nice hair.

Chapter Seventy-One

Now it was a matter of pulling everything together.

Ferreira was desperate to drag Sutherland back to the interview room, storm in there and take his story apart, but they needed to be thorough, Zigic insisted. Sutherland had proven to be a tricky customer and while they had enough compelling evidence to prove he was a liar, they still didn't have the silver bullet he wanted.

Murray had returned from Joshua Ainsworth's house with the hairbrush he'd stolen from Sutherland's place. She took it up to forensics, waited while they retrieved enough strands to run a DNA test and dusted it for prints, came back down with it in an evidence bag.

Zigic looked for Bloom, wanting her to chase forensics, but there had been a sudden shift in Adams's attempted murder case and he'd commandeered her and Weller into the manhunt.

The board with Adams's missing suspect George Batty's mugshot stuck at the top of it had been moved to a position of greater prominence and a list of known associates was being examined, as they tried to work out where to deploy their limited resources for his return to Peterborough. Wanting to pick him up and get him into custody before the embarrassment of losing him the first time deepened any further.

Joshua Ainsworth had been shunted aside in the process and as Zigic was looking at the board, considering yet another ill-advised coffee, Kate Jenkins called.

'Blood in the car,' she said. 'Type match for Ainsworth. The usual provisos but hopefully that helps you.'

'It does, thanks, Kate.'

Buzzing from the caffeine and the elation of *finally* having some forensic evidence to tie Sutherland directly to Ainsworth's dead body, he added her initial findings to the board, Ferreira looking on.

'Doesn't tell us which one of them drove over there, though,' she said.

'It's blood in the car. You should be much happier than that.'

'I'll be happier when we have the results of Nadia's tests and we know which one of them is lying to us about the sleeping pills.'

'Did you get an ETA on the results?' he asked.

'Twenty-four to forty-eight hours. The usual.'

'They can do it quicker.'

'I know they can,' Ferreira said. 'And I told them that, but apparently they're short-staffed and they've got a lot on and that's how long we've got to wait.'

Zigic let out a low growl of frustration. It felt like each incremental move forward was being countered by a heavy backward drag. Logically he knew they were doing well, that the case had actually progressed quite swiftly, even with his attention divided between Ainsworth and Lee Walton, but it felt like he'd been pulling double shifts for the last few days. Sleeping badly, eating badly, the disagreement with Anna rumbling away in the back of his mind, disturbing his equilibrium and making it impossible for him to rest when he was at home.

It was because they were so close. He knew that. His mind and body were preparing for the inevitable collapse, which came after closure.

And he couldn't afford that collapse, because while the tests they needed on Nadia Baidoo were going to take up to forty-eight hours, the one they were all waiting for – but not acknowledging since this morning's bollocking from Riggott – the one that would prove Lee Walton's guilt or innocence, was due today.

Either he was guilty and everything kicked off.

Or he was innocent and they were back to square one.

'Okay.' Zigic rubbed his face, hoping some of the blood he brought to the surface might redistribute itself into his brain. 'What about a urine test? That's quicker. We can have her urine tested in an hour, right?'

'We can, but it'll only tell us if she's taken anything within the last day or two.'

He swore.

'Let's just go up there and take a run at him,' Ferreira said, her body already turning towards the door. 'He's getting seriously stressed out, we need to push him as hard as we can.'

She had a point and it was tempting but Zigic shook his head, walked over to the coffee machine and poured another cup, ignoring the palpitations fluttering in his chest.

'I really don't enjoy being the voice of reason but I can see you vibrating from here,' Ferreira said. 'For God's sake, have a chamomile tea or something.'

He put the mug down, the sound shooting through his head.

'Or maybe a nap,' Ferreira suggested in a tone so reasonable he wondered if there was something wrong with her.

'If you think I'm going to close my eyes while you're desperate to go and interview Sutherland again, you've got another thing coming.'

A stronger tremor shuddered across his chest and for a second he thought he was actually having a heart attack until his phone chimed and he realised he'd put it in his shirt pocket. He took it out: a message from Parr.

Important incoming.

'What is it?' Ferreira asked.

He dialled Parr's number and he picked up after two rings.

'What's "important incoming"?' Zigic demanded.

Parr turned down the music playing far too loud in his car. 'Sorry, sir. Shouldn't have been so cryptic, should I?'

He sounded hyper, a thrill in his voice Zigic didn't think he'd ever heard before.

'What have you got for us?'

As he started to answer Zigic switched the phone to speaker, watched an expression of dark delight spread over Ferreira's face, felt his own smile become a little twisted as Parr finished explaining himself.

'I'll be fifteen minutes,' he said.

'We'll be waiting.' Zigic ended the call. 'I think that's worth a fifteen-minute delay, don't you?'

CHAPTER SEVENTY-TWO

Back to Interview 1.

Sutherland had been fed and watered, but didn't look any more lively for it. Even his solicitor seemed slightly less crisp second time round. He'd brought a massive cup of coffee in with him, the smell of it deep and rich in the close confines of the small white room. Strong, but not strong enough to cover the sharp, sour odour rising from Patrick Sutherland's body.

Zigic fixed his face in a neutral expression as Ferreira set up the tapes, aware of Ben Lawton watching him, trying to get a steer on where this would go, what they'd returned with and how it was going to affect his client. Sutherland kept his eyes down, arms folded on the desk, nervously picking at the buttoned cuff of his shirt, which he'd made some attempt to straighten out. As if that could give him an air of respectability at this late stage.

'The good news is we've found out why Josh broke into your house.' Zigic opened the folder he'd brought with him and took out the paternity test results, pushed them across the table to Lawton. 'The day before Josh was killed he sent off this paternity test to a private lab. As you can see the results came back positive.'

Sutherland should have been shocked.

But he wasn't. Didn't even attempt to fake it. He already knew about the test.

Zigic removed a photograph from the folder and pushed that across the table too.

'Do you recognise this hairbrush, Patrick?'

He gave it a cursory glance. 'No.'

'This is yours,' Zigic told him. 'It still has some of your hairs, not to mention your fingerprints, on it.'

The photograph was clear and precise, taken under aggressive lighting, the dust still faintly visible through the plastic, and the strands of his dark, wavy hair that were snagged in the bristles.

'Your hairbrush was recovered from Joshua Sutherland's house. Hidden in a plastic bag in a shoebox at the back of his wardrobe. Did you look for it after you killed him?'

Lawton put a hand on Sutherland's arm, as if to silence him. But Sutherland had already gone mute.

'You took the time to find his phone and his iPad because you thought stealing them would convince us that it was a burglary gone wrong.'

Sutherland only looked back at him, mouth pressed tightly shut, palms pressed tightly together. Zigic could see the vein at his temple pulsing.

'This was what Josh broke into your house for,' Zigic said, pointing at the brush. 'And you knew it was missing. Nadia told us you went crazy looking for it but you couldn't find it.' Sutherland's jaw clenched even tighter. 'The *second* you realised it was missing you knew what Josh was planning, right?'

Lawton cleared his throat. 'This paternity test is from some shady online DNA testing firm, let's not read too much into it.'

'They're an accredited lab with an excellent reputation,' Zigic told him. 'You thought you'd got away with it, didn't you, Patrick? Dorcus was deported, nobody was going to see that suspiciously light-skinned baby of yours she was carrying.'

Sutherland was sweating right through his shirt.

Another photo came out of the file, screen-grabbed during their conversation with Dorcus.

'Your son,' Zigic said, pushing it slowly across the table into Sutherland's eyeline. 'She named him Joseph.'

He expected Sutherland to deny it but he didn't seem capable of speech. Tentatively he reached out and his fingertips crept over the edge of the photo, drawing it slightly closer to himself.

'You groomed Dorcus, just like you groomed Nadia,' Zigic said. 'Played on her fear of being deported and her isolation. Told her you loved her. Told her you'd move heaven and earth to make sure she'd be able to stay in the UK. All so she'd sleep with you.'

Lawton cleared his throat noisily. 'This would be an internal matter for Long Fleet management, I presume.'

Had Sutherland already flagged this possibility with him? Zigic wondered. It seemed unlikely that Lawton would be aware of the specifics of Long Fleet's procedures otherwise. Or maybe they'd discussed a potential charge in relation to Nadia Baidoo and that was how he'd planned to head it off.

Sutherland's attention was still fully fixed on the photograph, mouth hanging open slightly.

'Josh broke into your house to get a DNA sample,' Zigic said. 'He needed it to prove paternity of Dorcus's baby so he could expose you for what you are. A predator.'

'All of that may well be true,' Lawton said, a stirring of unease in his tone. 'But Patrick was completely unaware of Ainsworth's plan or his intentions. It isn't a motive if my client was ignorant of it.'

'I already told you what happened to Josh,' Sutherland said, dragging his gaze up to Zigic with an effort that looked monumental. 'Nadia crept out of the house while I was asleep. When she came home she was covered in blood. She was shaking. I thought she was hurt. I wanted to take her to hospital but when I suggested it, she broke down and admitted what she'd done to Josh. I undressed her and put her in the shower and then I burned her clothes and her shoes.'

His voice was toneless and he sat perfectly still as he spoke in those short sentences that were maybe as much as he could manage, as he felt the world shifting under him. Or maybe he thought they sounded more honest for their simplicity.

They didn't though. It was the speech pattern of a caught liar and Zigic knew it only too well.

Sutherland kept going.

'I know it was wrong of me to do that,' he said. 'I destroyed evidence. But I was only trying to protect her. I knew she'd acted in self-defence. Or she believed she did. I was scared for her. I didn't want to lose her.' He passed a hand in front of his face. 'I'm not denying helping her. I'm an accessory to murder. But that's all I am. I didn't kill Josh.'

Zigic knew that manoeuvre as well. Admit the smaller crime in an attempt to claim innocence of the larger one.

'And that's how Josh's blood got in your car?' he asked.

'Yes.'

'Did you attempt to clean the interior of the car afterwards?'

He hung his head. 'Yes.'

'You destroyed more evidence?'

'Yes.'

'When did you clean the car?'

Sutherland paused and Zigic saw him fumbling for an answer. He wasn't expecting them to ask for more details. Thought he'd given them enough already.

'I always wash the car on Sunday afternoon, I did it then.'

'In full sight of your neighbours?'

'I didn't think it would look strange because I always do it then.'

'But you're not usually cleaning large deposits of blood from the upholstery,' Zigic commented. 'How did you clean it?'

'Is this really relevant?' Lawton asked, seeing that Sutherland was struggling. 'Patrick has told you everything you need to know. Maybe you should be talking to Ms Baidoo now since she's the guilty party.'

'There wasn't *that* much blood in the car,' Sutherland said finally, his brain dredging up an answer by going to the truth for once. 'I just used the regular cleaning fluid I always use. I don't know why it matters.'

He had cleaned it, Kate Jenkins had told them as much. But he hadn't done a very good job, hadn't got right into all the nooks and crannies where she knew to search for evidence, because people always missed the same places.

441

'What time did Nadia get home?'

'I don't know. It was the early hours of the morning.'

'Was it light?'

'No.'

'And you cleaned her up and put her to bed, is that right?'

'Yes,' Sutherland said, getting testy now, not wanting to repeat himself because maybe he was smart enough to know that lies fell apart in the repetition of them.

'Did you go to bed at the same time?'

'Yes.'

'So when did you burn her clothes?' Zigic asked.

Another fumble, another slightly too long delay in answering a question about a moment that should have been seared into his memory.

'The next day. I went outside and burned them in the garden incinerator with some old newspapers and things so it wouldn't look suspicious.'

'Your neighbours can't have liked that,' Zigic said. 'Setting a fire while they'll have wanted to be enjoying their gardens over the weekend.'

'I did it early. Before eight. Nobody was up at that time.'

Zigic nodded, as if he was convinced. 'Yeah, nobody wants to be up that early at the weekend.'

He lifted up the cardboard file and took out the tablet he'd been keeping, half hidden, underneath it, tapped the screen. A video player opened, a clip paused, ready to run.

'There's one other thing we'd like you to explain for us, please, Patrick.' Zigic positioned the screen between Sutherland and his solicitor. 'At 12:45 a.m. on the morning of Sunday August 5th – that's around an hour after Joshua Ainsworth was murdered, so you're clear – one of your neighbours was searching for her dog. It slips its lead quite a lot apparently.'

Lawton's manicured fingers twitched.

Zigic noted the action with a slight smile, reached out and set the video playing. The neighbour had recorded with sound and despite the hour the image was clear enough to make out the number plate of Patrick Sutherland's vehicle parked up in his front drive.

The woman hadn't been interested in that though, panned over it in a split second as she focused on what she'd really thought worth filming: Patrick Sutherland, barefoot and naked except for a pair of tight white boxer briefs, getting out of his car.

Her supressed giggle was absurdly light in the interview room. Beyond it the sound of Sutherland closing the car door with exaggerated care, not wanting to wake the neighbours and create a potential time frame when they might later be questioned. Then a metallic noise as he dropped his car keys. An appreciative murmur broke out of the woman as he bent to retrieve them and Zigic wondered how Sutherland hadn't heard her.

Was the blood still rushing in his ears? Could he hear nothing but his own heartbeat and the breaths, which refused to come slow and calm again even an hour after he'd beaten Joshua Ainsworth to death?

On screen Sutherland let himself into his house and closed that door almost silently. There were no lights on in the windows, only the porch light burning and he turned it off as soon as he was inside. It was too late though, he'd been caught perfectly framed under it: slack-faced and wide-eyed. Guilty.

Zigic tapped the screen and stopped the video.

Sutherland was balled up tight in his chair, fists punched into his underarms. He was staring at the tablet like he was trying to make it combust with the force of his mind.

'Where were your clothes, Patrick?'

Sutherland's voice came out at a croak. 'No comment.'

'What happened to your shoes?'

'No comment.'

They had him. He was falling apart in front of their eyes, but one more 'no comment' and his solicitor was going to call for a break and they would risk losing the momentum they'd worked so hard to build. Patrick Sutherland was stripped of his charm and looks, all poise gone, all intelligence spent. They had him reduced to his true self now, the liar, the predator, the man who'd groomed a woman right out of Long Fleet and into his house and then, very nearly, into a prison sentence that should have been his.

One more question to finish him.

Zigic took a breath.

'Why did you leave the porch light on when you left?' he asked, but didn't allow Sutherland space to answer. 'You didn't expect to be sneaking back into your house in your underwear, did you? You didn't actually go to Josh's house intending to kill him. You just wanted to talk, right?'

There were tears in Sutherland's eyes now. Everything falling apart around him, his lies catching up with him, his counter-accusation against Nadia rendered ridiculous.

'Did Josh taunt you?' Zigic asked.

'He –'

'Don't say anything, Patrick,' Lawton snapped.

'Josh beat you and he wanted to rub it in,' Zigic said. 'He let you into his house so he could tell you exactly what he'd done. He wanted you to know he'd beaten you. He was going to ruin your life just like you ruined his. How did that feel, Patrick?'

'I just went round there to talk to him,' Sutherland said, the words so low Zigic almost thought he'd imagined them until he spoke again. 'He started it. He wasn't in control of himself. He was drunk and raving. He went for me.'

'You look fine.'

'He grabbed me,' Sutherland said, finding his voice again, latching onto the only lifeline he could see, the one he'd tried to throw to Nadia: self-defence. 'I didn't have any choice but to fight back.'

Zigic nodded, showed him an understanding face.

'I didn't mean to kill him.'

Ten blows, Zigic thought. Ten times he hit Joshua Ainsworth across the temple with the table leg but that was a distinction for the courtroom. For now all he needed was the admission and he had it.

He leaned back in his chair, watching as Sutherland broke down, burying his face in his hands.

'Okay,' Zigic said, hearing the satisfaction in his voice. 'Interview terminated 5:07 p.m.'

A round of applause greeted them as they returned to the office, whipped up by Adams who strode between the desks in full DCI mode, grinning broadly.

'Very nice work, Ziggy,' he said, clapping him on the shoulder. 'He was a sneaky piece of shit but you weren't having any of it, were you? Nailed him to the fucking table.'

'It was a team effort,' Zigic said, looking around for his team and finding them bundled in with Adams's lot on the opposite side of the office, working his escalating case. 'Great stuff, everyone. Thank you.'

The faces all turned back to their tasks, that brief, uncomfortable interlude over. Much to Zigic's relief.

'What are you doing about Nadia Baidoo then?' Adams asked.

'We don't have anything to charge her with,' Ferreira said.

'She might not have known all the details but she knew Sutherland had done something seriously wrong,' Zigic reminded her. 'She should have come forward the second she knew Ainsworth had been murdered.'

'Not worth making anything out of though, is it?' Adams said, a command decision buried in the seemingly friendly suggestion. 'Given what she's been through. I'd imagine she didn't come forward because she was in an abusive, controlling relationship and she was scared of the consequences of reporting him.'

'I'll write it up and see how it looks,' Zigic told him, still not entirely sure what he thought about Nadia's involvement.

She'd made a false accusation of serious assault. Claimed ignorance of a murder via the handy excuse of sleeping pills they now weren't sure she was taking.

If it got to court he was confident she'd be found guilty of assisting an offender, but he wasn't ready to pass judgement on the young woman yet.

'Bail her,' Adams said, directing the order to Ferreira. 'But make sure the solicitor knows her obligations.'

She headed down to the custody suite to deal with the paperwork.

'Quick drink to celebrate?' Adams asked, gesturing towards his office.

'Not tonight,' Zigic said. 'I've got family stuff.'

He looked wounded by the refusal but Zigic had bigger concerns than professional courtesy.

CHAPTER SEVENTY-THREE

They waited until the kids were in bed, then they went into the living room with their second glasses of the wine from dinner, the curtains drawn against the last of the late evening sun and the lamps lit in the corners, the television on to give some cover to the conversation they were going to have now.

'Okay,' Anna said, taking a seat in the centre of the sofa, perched on the very edge of the cushion. 'Let's talk about it then.'

Zigic sat down opposite her, placing his wine glass on a coaster, knowing what he was going to say but still not quite ready to do it. There was a small core of resistance in him that he couldn't put aside, convictions too long held and firmly set for him to simply ignore.

Anna was just as firm in her decision; he could see it in the tilt of her head and the tension in her toes as they gripped the rug under the coffee table.

'I was reading this article in the paper,' she said. 'About how the numbers of hate crimes in schools have exploded in the last year. These were reported figures from police forces. Not anecdotes from teachers or on social media, these were incidents that were severe enough for the police to be called.' She pressed her fingertips together, flexing her knuckles. 'Muslim girls having their headscarves ripped off, threats of lynchings and jokes about gas chambers. And what about all the things that happened without anyone seeing them? Because you know how insidious racism is, Dushan. You know that better than anyone.'

He looked at the pattern on the rug, the curlicues and flourishes, going exactly where she wanted him to and he couldn't help it.

Back to the school he hated, the trouble starting on day one when a teacher didn't know how to pronounce his surname and her mistake stuck for the rest of the term, despite endless corrections. The stupid cruelty of children which turned Dushan into 'Dustpan'; it was a meaningless insult, he saw that now and maybe understood even then how petty it was, the kind of joke which would only raise a laugh in the narrowest mind. But the laughter kept coming and the viciousness of stupidity knew no end, he'd found. Didn't stop with reasoned argument or physical violence. In fact once he'd resorted to violence, the nickname got thrown around even more by girls who'd realised he wouldn't hit them and by bigger boys who were giving him a reason so they could hit him back.

He'd got good at fighting. Got used to black eyes and busted lips and bruised ribs.

His father told him it was important to stand up for himself, that he learned how to take pain and give it back, because he would meet as many bullies in adult life as in the schoolyard and the sooner he equipped himself to deal with them the better.

They never went to the school to complain.

His mother washed the blood off his shirts and his father would smile as he took hold of his scuffed knuckles: 'You are becoming a man, Dushan.'

He imagined Milan coming home with his face swollen and his knuckles cut from fighting, and the thought of it set his heart aching. He didn't want that kind of childhood for Milan and Stefan. Or Emily, he realised, because girls were no better than boys, less likely to indulge in open violence perhaps, but perfectly capable of making her life hell once they'd fastened on the particular difference that would allow them to target her.

Even in a city as multicultural as Peterborough.

He did want to insulate his children from that.

He wanted the best for them, a childhood that felt as safe as he could make it for as long as he could manage. The world was going to be cruel to them, as it was to everyone, but he wanted them to be prepared for it as well as possible.

And this school would do that.

'Are we just delaying the inevitable though?' he asked, looking up at Anna. 'Say we send them there and it's all lovely and idyllic and there's this great zero tolerance policy on bullying. What about when they leave? They won't know how to handle aggressive people.'

'You're worrying about what's going to happen in seven or eight years' time,' she said stiffly. 'I'm worried what happens next month when Milan goes up to that big new school, and his bullies fall in with an even bigger group of bigoted shits and they all decide to gang up on him.'

'Maybe it won't be like that at secondary,' he said weakly.

'Well, from what I remember of school, everything got worse at secondary. And the teachers get a lot less interested in stepping in because they don't want to risk the bullies turning on them.'

Anna was crying now.

'Why won't you just back me on this?' she asked. 'I'm not suggesting we sell their organs or sign them over to the foreign legion. I just want to keep Milan safe.'

'I know,' he said, going over to her, feeling the ache in his chest that her crying always provoked. 'I'm worried about him too. I don't want the kids to dread school, either.'

'You're not here,' she said. 'You've got no idea how terrified he's been about seeing those little shits again. He packed a bag.' Anna reached for her wine glass so sharply that a few drops sloshed onto the hem of her sundress. 'I found it under his bed – that little suitcase we bought him – he'd packed it full of clothes and books and one of Emily's stuffed toys. And when I found it and asked him why he just started ... wailing. Like he hasn't done since he was a baby.'

Zigic pressed his hand over his mouth, tears in his eyes.

His boy, that scared, but he never said anything, didn't come to him and talk about it. Just held it all in his tiny chest, the fear and the desperation, until running away became the only logical option for him.

He thought of the last time Milan had packed that case, fastidiously folding his summer clothes on the final day of their holiday, and how confidently he'd wheeled it through the airport, his little man, the world traveller, so open-minded and bold.

And now this. One incident robbing him of his self-assurance. 'Why didn't you tell me about this?' he asked.

She wiped her face dry. 'Because I didn't want you to feel like I was emotionally blackmailing you. I *hoped* you'd come to the right decision on your own but you're not going to, are you? So now you know. That's how bad things have been these last few weeks. That's how scared Milan is. And I'm not going to let him live out his childhood in a state of permanent terror.'

Zigic rubbed her shoulders until she stopped sobbing but the feeling of helplessness had settled in his chest, a feeling so strong it was like a physical restraint on every breath he took.

Suddenly all the complaints he had felt petty and futile. So what if he wasn't comfortable taking money from her parents? So what if he didn't like the idea of his children being whisked off into some privileged enclave?

His principles felt like self-indulgence compared to what Milan was going through. The high-minded ideals of someone who wouldn't have to live with the consequences of their actions.

'Okay,' he said, kissing her head. 'This is the right thing to do.'

Anna turned and slipped her arms around him, buried her face in his neck, and he felt the pain in his chest begin to dissipate instantly.

CHAPTER SEVENTY-FOUR

The phone woke her, the ringtone blaring at such an urgent pitch that she was on her feet and looking around for it before she'd fully shaken off the dream she was having.

'It's alright, it's mine,' Billy said, digging it out from between the sofa cushions where her head had been a moment before.

Ferreira sat back down, letting the wooziness clear. She looked at the time on the BBC news channel: it was barely eleven and she'd fallen asleep on the sofa. It had been a long day, she reassured herself, as she picked up the book she'd dropped and put it on the coffee table.

Billy was pacing around the room, nodding. 'Good stuff, Col. You called it. I owe you a fiver.'

He looked wired, his missing suspect George Batty back in town by the sound of it.

'Yeah, wait for me. I'll be ten minutes, tops.'

Ferreira followed him into the bedroom, flopped onto the mattress, watching him dress for action.

'Where did Batty show up?' she asked. 'Not at his mum's?'

'His dealer's. That boy's priorities are all messed up.'

'He'll be docile when you bring him in, anyway.'

'And we get the dealer for harbouring,' Billy said, looking almost obscenely pleased with himself.

She knew the case had been weighing on him, even with the Walton investigation running alongside it. Nobody liked losing a suspect. It felt like a personal affront, the sense of failure only deepening with every day you didn't bring them in.

'You look shattered,' he said.

'Thanks.'

'For Christ's sake, get some sleep.'

'No,' she said, but she stayed where she was, curled up at the foot of the bed. 'I'm going to wait up for you like a dutiful girlfriend.'

He grinned, slapped her backside and walked out of the room.

A couple of seconds later his phone rang again and she heard him stop to answer it in the hallway.

'We'll go for him now,' he said firmly, listened briefly, then lowered his voice. 'I'll meet you there, *don't* go in without me.'

The door opened and closed, slamming hard.

Ferreira looked at the clothes he'd left on the floor, wondering why Murray had called back only to have the same conversation. Or were Weller and Bloom already overstepping the mark? He'd taken them in for extra eyes but they were both eager to stake their claim in the office.

She rolled off the bed and went into the living room, closed the curtains and switched on an extra lamp. She'd stay up for a while yet, have another go at the book she felt like she'd been reading for weeks now. There never seemed to be time for it as much as she was enjoying the story. Long days leaving her brain numb by the evening with not enough mental energy left for anything but the simplest TV programmes. She'd tried reading in bed before work but Billy was a morning person and seemed to consider any book she had in her hand as a rival and would do his damnedest to distract her from it.

She was two chapters in when she heard the noise.

A low whirring coming from the hallway.

Some distant part of her brain that barely registered knew what it was, drove her up and towards the door as it increased in pitch and speed.

An electric lock pick, entry tool of choice for cat burglars and stalkers.

Ferreira dashed into the kitchen and grabbed a knife from the block. Her vision already swimming, her heart already hammering against her ribs.

She held the knife low by her side, gripping the handle so hard it hurt. She wanted to run but there was nowhere to go. She wanted to hide but she knew he'd find her.

The door opened and she felt everything beyond the room fall away into nothingness. There was only her held breath and the cold metal in her palm and the sound of his footsteps coming closer, barely four paces between the front door and the kitchen, and without meaning to she was moving to meet him, her wrist angling, turning the blade, and then they were face to face and she slashed up through the air between them, slicing open Walton's bare arm from elbow to shoulder.

She saw the cut, white then red, then his fist coming at her faster than she could duck away from it. She heard bone break and she was temporarily blind, her head snapping back so hard it rattled her brain against her skull.

The knife dropped from her hand and she dropped down after it. Blood on the floor. Hers and his.

And then she was moving again. His hand knotted in her hair, dragging her out of the kitchen. She made a desperate snatch at the knife, her fingertips grazing it but he was too strong, pulling her clear too quickly.

'You wanted my fucking attention,' he said. 'Now you've got it.'

Every hair on her head was screaming, her broken nose pulsing, but the pain was floating just beyond her. Not felt yet. There was too much adrenaline in her blood screaming at her to get up and fight, grab something, anything, stop this.

Stop it right now.

He kept moving, hauling her into the living room, the rug rucking up under her feet as she twisted and kicked.

Ferreira stuck her hand out and grabbed the leg of the console table, toppling its contents, the landline phone and a pair of lamps and an ammonite on a brass rod scattering across the floor. She snatched hold of a lamp and struck out blindly with it, catching him across the side of the kneecap.

Walton grunted in pain and let go of her hair.

Her vision swimming, she quickly scrambled back onto her feet again. She yanked the lamp out of the wall, held it ready to hit him again. Her throat was filling with blood she spat out onto the floor.

'There's a patrol car outside,' she said. 'Two officers, on their way up here right now.'

Walton shook his head. 'One officer asleep, the other one on her phone.'

'I called them the second I heard you breaking in, you stupid bastard.'

'No, you didn't. You're too arrogant to do that. You're like all the rest of them. Think you're invincible, swanning about, making shit for people, abusing your power. You think you can do whatever you want. Until you run into someone like me.' He threw his chin up at her, coming closer. 'Look at you, you're terrified.'

Ferreira backed away and he lashed out again. She threw the lamp up, blocking the blow.

The second one caught her. No real power to it.

She could feel him holding back, knew then that he was going to make this last. Whatever he did to her. He wasn't worried about being disturbed, wasn't bothered what happened to him after this.

Her breath caught in her throat. She couldn't exhale, couldn't even blink away the cloudiness across her eyes.

He was going to kill her.

'There it is,' he said. 'The look they all get when they know it's over.'

Her hands tightened around the lamp.

'Still got some fight in you?' He nodded. 'Good. I reckoned you'd be a challenge.'

Where was Billy?

Why tonight? Why had that stupid kid come home tonight and walked straight into a surveillance operation and taken him away from her?

She would kill him for leaving her like this.

'You should have told your fucking boyfriend to stay away from my family,' Walton said as if he knew what she was thinking. 'I warned you. And him. You've brought this on yourself.' He took another step towards her and she took two more back. 'Everything that happens tonight, it's on you.'

Keep him talking, she thought, seeing how fast the blood was running out of his cut arm, pooling on the floor by his feet.

'You don't think some of it's your own fault, Lee?'

'I just wanted to make a fresh start,' he growled.

Another step towards her. The sound of his blood drumming onto the wooden floor, the beats coming faster.

Ferreira took another two back, shuffling. Out the corner of her eye she saw her bag, thrown down behind the sofa when she came home.

'You got a fresh start.' One more step. 'You got your family back.'

Walton's eyes darkened and he lurched towards her, faltered and grabbed at the corner of the sofa, bloodying the leather, splashing the cushions.

'You sent social services,' he said, drawing himself up again, huge and square, his face flushing. 'They were going to take my boy away from me.'

He pushed away from the sofa and Ferreira threw the lamp at his head, dropping onto her haunches and snatching up her bag. He lunged towards her and she kicked out, catching him in the face as he fell, sending him sprawling onto his back.

She reached into her bag, watching him right himself. Up onto one knee. Then two. Then on his feet again as her fingers fumbled blindly and finally closed around a slim metal canister.

Walton dived at her and she sprayed the CS gas in his face. He roared in pain, eyes streaming, nose burning, but he kept coming. Hit her again, full-fisted.

Her lip burst open. A raw, sharp pain that made her cry out.

His hands fumbled for her throat and she felt the weight of him pressing on her, crushing her pelvis and ribs, his fingers tightening around her windpipe.

She jabbed the canister into the knife wound down his arm and he screamed, snatching his arm back. She hit the button again, spraying it directly into his open mouth.

Walton collapsed onto his side and she shoved him away onto his back. She could hardly see now, the gas tearing up her eyes too, burning and raw in her throat, stinging her split lip. She forced herself up onto her knees, bent over him as he bucked and thrashed, trying to wipe his face clean. He caught her a glancing blow to the face and she reeled back, no thoughts in her brain beyond the single notion of stopping him rising again.

She pinched his nose shut and emptied the gas canister into his mouth.

He rolled onto his front, trying to spit it out, his eyes swollen shut. The agitation was sending the blood pumping out of his wounded arm even faster.

Ferreira inched away from him, heart hammering, knowing she should stop this, call an ambulance, call the patrol car that was parked downstairs. She should do the right thing.

She *would* do it.

She had no choice.

CHAPTER SEVENTY-FIVE

Mrs Walton's house was all lit up when Zigic arrived. The only one in the cul-de-sac still awake at half past eleven, but he supposed things were more fraught there than at the neighbours. Harder to sleep when your son was a killer, when your boyfriend was waiting for the slightest reason to hit you, when you knew a murder you'd got away with twenty years ago was poised to come back and snatch away your new and undeserved liberty.

Zigic got out of his car and looked at the curtained windows warmly lit against the soft pink glow that hung over Orton Wistow, the scent of the bagel factory's late shift on the air and an acrid hint of cat spray coming from the bushes nearby. Movement at a bedroom window across the road drew his eye; someone who'd heard his car and wanted to see who was about at this hour.

He should have been at home.

Would have been if he'd resisted checking his texts and seeing the results of the DNA test they'd run on Tessa Darby's cardigan. Or if he'd kept it to himself rather than calling Adams to pass along the news.

He hadn't expected him to swing into action right away. This could have waited until tomorrow. Should by all rights have waited until they'd rerun the DNA test legally and with the blessing of DCS Riggott, who they needed to reopen the case.

Tomorrow was going to involve a lot of finessed paperwork, he assumed.

Adams wanted Walton too badly to pause and think any of the details through, though. And Zigic understood the urge. They'd taken a gamble on this case, pissed off Riggott, risked their reputations and careers. Of course Adams wanted to move swiftly to prove they'd been right, that it was all worth it.

Adams's car pulled into the close, a patrol vehicle with its lights strobing but no siren sounding behind him.

Zigic rolled his eyes. Adams wanted this to be a spectacle and the neighbours were already stirring. Lights going on, curtains and blinds opening, windows and doors following, obscured faces watching as the cars pulled up and Adams and the uniforms got out.

'You two, go round the back,' Adams said. 'And watch yourself, yeah? He's got some bulk.'

Zigic waited until they were through the gate before he spoke.

'This is stupidly premature,' he said, voice low. 'Don't you think we should have waited until we had proper, legally viable evidence?'

Adams shrugged. 'We're here now, just try to enjoy yourself.'

'And what pretext are you going to arrest him on?'

Adams knocked on the front door. 'Relax, we're just taking him in for questioning.'

'At nearly midnight?'

'Why not?'

Adams knocked again, harder this time. 'Police, open up.'

'Sure you don't want to bash the door in?' Zigic asked and immediately regretted it because he wasn't sure if Adams would see it as a legitimate suggestion rather than sarcasm.

'They're obviously up,' Adams said, going to the front window where the curtains were tightly drawn, not a sliver of the room beyond visible. 'If he thinks he can hide in there and wait for us to go away –'

'Sir!' PC Hobbs emerged from the side gate. 'You should see this.'

'You go,' Adams said. 'I'm not having Walton give us the slip.'

Zigic went down the narrow path past recycling boxes filled with cartons and old magazines, following Hobbs into the small

458

back garden where a paddling pool sat deflated at the centre of the handkerchief-sized lawn.

'There,' Hobbs said, hanging back.

Zigic looked in through the window, the view partly obscured by a set of half-closed wooden blinds, but the blood stood out vividly against the white tiled floor. He could see distinct footprints going in circles around the glass table.

He tried the door, found it locked. But it was flimsy and old, soft wood badly tended, and it gave on the second blow.

He could feel it in the air, recent violence. The stillness after desperate breaths and ignored entreaties. He moved through into the hallway following the bloody footprints and the fingermarks on the walls and the staircase.

The living room was empty. A mug of tea on the table next to a magazine open to a partially filled crossword puzzle and a packet of biscuits. A careful hand had gathered the scattered crumbs into a neat pile to be cleared away later.

The television was showing a film, some old comedy from the eighties.

Zigic started up the stairs, hardly breathing, fully braced for what he already sensed he would find. Hobbs followed behind him, heavier-footed and muttering what sounded like a prayer.

The bathroom door was open, the room lit. Blood on the sink and the towels left on the floor.

At his back he heard the telltale rasp of Hobbs flicking his baton out.

Zigic opened a bedroom door, the room empty.

He kept moving. Opened the next door to the master bedroom, and stopped at the threshold.

'Call an ambulance,' he told Hobbs. 'Tell them we've got multiple casualties.'

Mrs Walton lay across the bed, her face turned away from him, and for a few seconds Zigic thought she was still alive. He went closer, checking for a pulse he realised wasn't coming, seeing the red marks on her neck, the span of Lee Walton's hands and the strength of the rage that had crushed the life out of her.

As he was straightening again, he saw a pair of feet poking out beyond the foot of the bed.

Dani, left where she'd fallen in the narrow gap between the bed and the wall.

'Where's the kid?' Adams asked from the doorway.

He walked away, shouting at Hobbs to search downstairs.

'And get the garage opened up!' he snapped. 'If we're lucky, Walton'll be hanging in there.'

Zigic could already hear sirens at distance but they were too late for Mrs Walton and for Dani. Her face was beaten beyond recognition, skull fractured in several places.

'Dani, can you hear me?'

He inched forward, the space too tight, his feet too big, and it felt like a transgression against the dead but he needed to be sure.

He reached for her wrist, seeing her pink-painted fingernails still intact, no blood or skin cells under them. She hadn't put up a fight. Too scared or too quickly overpowered to defend herself.

No pulse.

Gently he laid her hand back on the floor.

The detective part of him was analysing the trauma, the ferocity on display. It saw the purple three-kilo hand weight that Walton had used to bludgeon his girlfriend to death, and its twin sitting just under the bed, lined up with the rest of the set, lightly dusted and long forgotten. Read the sudden flaring of Walton's temper against Dani and then his mother coming to intervene. Maybe not too fast because she was already used to hearing him rage and didn't realise at first how much more serious this argument was. Maybe because she was scared to get between them. By the time she came it was too late. Then Walton had turned on her. Put his hands round her throat to silence her and kept them there.

This was always a possibility, the cold and rational part of Zigic said. The moment Dani returned to Walton she was in danger of an escalation of the abuses he'd already committed against her.

But the better part of him knew they had hastened this violence. Pursuing Walton so openly rather than working the case quietly. If they'd done things right – if Adams hadn't let his ego run rampant – the first Walton would have known of it was when they came to arrest him.

Instead they'd goaded him, backed him into a corner, started to unpick his family around him. Did it deliberately because they thought an unbalanced Walton would be easier to deal with in the interview room. They'd wanted to break him and never properly considered how dangerous he would become with nothing to lose.

'Found the boy,' Adams said quietly, standing in the hallway, staring at the floor.

'Dead?'

'Smothered, by the look of it.'

'We should get out of here before we make any more of a mess,' Zigic said, walking numbly towards him and shepherding him down the stairs and out of the front door.

Adams fumbled a cigarette out of the packet, fingers trembling. 'This isn't on us. Whatever we did. Walton made that choice.'

He was right. Technically.

But Zigic felt the guilt tight around his chest, the pressure of it building behind his eyes. They'd failed to protect Dani and her son and Mrs Walton. Like their predecessors had failed to protect every one of his victims after Tessa Darby, by screwing up her murder investigation and letting an innocent man confess his way into a twelve-year jail term, leaving Walton free.

And if he'd checked his messages an hour or two earlier, they might have got here before all of this happened and the family would still be alive.

His heart ached with the knowledge and he knew it would never fully go away, the guilt would be there for ever, a gnawing black thing in his chest; every time he was with his own family he would think of what happened here and how he could have prevented it.

Adams walked over to the driveway, the garage door up, the strip light on.

'Fuck.'

Zigic forced himself to move, look inside.

No Walton hanging from the rafters, no car in there either.

'Where the hell is he?'

Adams dropped his cigarette in a shower of sparks. 'Mel.'

CHAPTER SEVENTY-SIX

She thought she'd dream about him, but she didn't. Slept for ten blissful hours, knocked out by the painkillers the doctor in A&E gave her after he reset her nose, a quick, practised flick of his hand that hurt more than the initial break. He had the grace to apologise for it though.

The pills were wearing off now and she found the packet on the side table but nothing to take them with. Carefully she got up, swung her legs out of bed and stood. There was a dull ache along her jaw where Walton had punched her and when she probed with her tongue, she found two teeth at the bottom were loose. The only thing that could make this worse was a trip to the dentist and she prayed it wouldn't come to that. The teeth were at the back, she figured she could live without them.

She trudged into the kitchen, found Billy unpacking two bags of food from M&S.

'Go back to bed,' he said. 'I'll bring your breakfast in.'

'I'm good.' She filled a glass with water and swallowed a pill. Her throat was raw and dry and she heard the residual burn in her voice, the after-effects of the CS gas she'd inhaled. 'I thought you'd gone to work.'

'They can do without me for the day.' He eyed her warily. 'You're not planning on going in, are you?'

'I just want to get this over with.'

'Riggott won't be expecting you today.'

'What else am I going to do?' she asked. 'I can't go anywhere nice looking like this.'

'You look fine.'

'For someone who took a battering.'

'Can you eat?' he asked, taking a bag of pastries out.

'I'm not really hungry.'

'I'll make you a smoothie. You shouldn't be taking those pills on an empty stomach.'

He was putting a brave face on, working at this carefree display as if he hadn't walked into a massacre last night. She wondered at his ability to compartmentalise.

Zigic was taking it hard. She'd seen that last night when they found her in A & E. Zigic looking about ready to collapse, face slack, eyes dark, and as Billy explained what they'd found at the Walton house in an oddly neutral voice, she could see Zigic turning further in on himself.

If he'd been in charge of the cold case, it wouldn't have happened, she thought. He would have been more delicate, more circumspect. Ziggy never would have started pitting people against one another to see what happened.

She felt the guilt spread heavily across her own shoulders. Dani and her son, Walton's mother, all dead because he knew he was heading back to prison and couldn't stand the idea that their lives would continue without him.

And then he'd come for her.

She wished he'd made her the first stop on his spree. Or that Dani had just listened to her when she told her not to come back to Peterborough.

She watched Billy pouring fruit into the blender, concentrating on it like it was a far more complex task than it was.

She wanted to tell him how badly he'd fucked up, but she guessed he already knew. Last night he'd been all apologies for leaving her at home alone right when she needed him, for bringing Walton to their door. There were endless apologies and promises but she wasn't the person who needed them. The people who did were all dead.

The blender whirred into life, painfully loud in her tiny kitchen. She closed her eyes, seeing again the blood on the floor and the chemical burns across Walton's face. Her own injuries throbbing harder now, the pain carrying the remembered fear through her bloodstream once again, flooding her with adrenaline she had no use for.

'I'm going to get dressed.'

In the bedroom she searched through her clothes for something suitable, but there was no proper outfit for this. Or if there was it wasn't here. Seeing the gaps on the rails, she realised how much of herself she'd moved into Billy's place.

Eventually she would have to go back and collect some of it. But the thought of walking back through that door was unbearable. She wasn't sure she would ever be ready to do it.

She pulled on a pair of jeans and a light T-shirt, stuffed her feet into a worn pair of trainers and laced them with her head swimming.

Dutifully she returned to the kitchen and drank the smoothie he'd made her, only distantly aware of the taste of banana and mango and honey running dulled over her tongue. A side effect of the painkillers, she told herself. Nothing more than that.

Billy kept up a monologue as she sat at the breakfast bar, his voice bright, saying nothing. Did he think she needed this relentless, upbeat talk? Or was he doing it for himself? Trying to keep his own dark thoughts at bay?

Last night as he drove her home from the hospital, he asked what happened. She'd told him already while Zigic was there but he thought she was holding back, wanted to ask if Walton's attack had gone further than she'd said, but he couldn't quite bring himself to shape the words.

In the end she said them for him, assured him that she'd already told him everything.

'I'm going to sell the flat,' he said, as he washed out the blender.

'You don't have to do that on my account.'

'I've been thinking about it for a while.' He put the jug on the drainer, turned back to her. 'It's too small and with you being over so much … it feels like the right time.'

'In this market?'

'It'll sell,' he said. 'You could let this place go as well. Pool our resources.'

'You are all about the romance,' Ferreira said, giving him a smile that made her jaw feel freshly traumatised.

'Will you think about it?'

She nodded. 'But let me get this out of the way first, okay?'

'Do you want me to drive you in?'

'Yeah. I'm probably not safe with this much codeine in me.'

At the station she managed to avoid going into the main office, heard the focused quiet of people conscientiously cleaning up after a murder that needed minimal investigation. Forensics to be collected and collated, the grim business of the post-mortems that would happen this morning. Eyewitness reports and statements from PCs Green and Sands, who would be facing disciplinary action for managing to miss Walton as he went into the building through the entrance they were supposed to be watching.

When Ferreira had made it down to them, bleeding and battered, they didn't notice her until she hammered on the roof of the patrol car.

Riggott's secretary winced when she saw her face. 'You can go straight in. He's expecting you.'

'I should see the other fella, right?' Riggott said, rising from his desk and going to close the door behind her. He peered at her, not quite so sharp without his reading glasses. 'You must have strong fucking bones, girl. Fella that size laying into you and you're in pretty good shape still.'

'Is there a commendation for that?' she asked.

'Ought to be.' He smiled briefly, then took her elbow and steered her towards the sofa. 'No messing now, how are you feeling?'

An involuntary sigh forced its way out of her. Something about the earnest expression from him knocked her flat. She'd intended to come in here all calm and poised, show him what she was made of, that she was tough enough to go through *that* and walk into work the next morning like usual.

As much as she pitied Billy for needing Riggott's approval, she realised she felt the same way. Too many years working under his guidance, too many secrets shared and disasters averted; he'd made her what she was and even though she rarely stopped to consider what that meant, it swam up at her now. How much she owed him and how much she had to lose.

Her eyes started watering and she willed down the emotion.

'Alright, girl.' He patted her back lightly. 'None of us get away from it easy, believe me.'

'Fucking painkillers,' she said.

'Aye, they'll do that to you.' He went to his desk and fetched a box of tissues she couldn't believe he actually kept in his drawer. 'Getting a faceful of CS gas isn't much fun either.'

She exhaled slowly, dragged herself together again.

'You need me to make a statement?'

'We'll do that later. First up, I want you to tell me what happened. Not just last night, from the first time you saw him outside your flat.'

Ferreira went through it with him, from the moment she'd caught Walton standing under the street light across the road, staring up into her window, through the threats in the parking area and the ones on the phone, up to the second she realised that the whirring sound was someone – him – breaking into Billy's flat.

'He punched me in the face,' she said. 'I cut him with a kitchen knife.' She gestured high up on her own arm. 'He dragged me into the living room. We fought – I threw a lamp at him. He hit me again. I got the CS spray out of my bag and used that. He hit me in the jaw, then when I was down he tried to choke me. I gassed him again. Close range.' She took a deep breath, could still somehow taste it. 'He was losing a lot of blood. Eventually he just passed out.'

Riggott's brows knitted together. 'We've got the preliminary report on Walton's death,' he said.

She wasn't expecting that, didn't think it would be a priority given how he died. But she'd been naïve.

'You caught his brachial artery,' Riggott said.

'Okay. That explains why he was bleeding so much then.'

'The pathologist has it down as a fairly minor wound. Long but shallow.' She heard the warning in his tone. 'He put the bleed-out time around twenty to thirty minutes.'

Ferreira said nothing.

'Your injuries won't be considered consistent with an attack of that duration.'

He chose his words carefully and made sure that she realised where he was going with this, giving her one of his meaningful looks.

'I'm going to assume you were knocked unconscious,' he said slowly. 'I *think* what must have happened is that after you sprayed him in the face, he lashed out and hit you in the jaw there.' He gestured towards her swollen face. 'And that blow knocked you out cold. By the time you came around he was already dead. You did your duty as a police officer and immediately checked for a pulse but couldn't find one, at which point you rushed downstairs to the officers guarding the building and raised the alarm.'

Ferreira nodded.

'Is that what happened?'

'Absolutely,' she said, remembering how she'd watched the pool of blood around Walton growing larger, minute after minute, spreading under the sofa and reaching towards her no matter how many times she backed away from it. Watched his protests become weaker, his breathing more laboured, thinking of all the women he'd watched as they suffered, all the pain he'd caused, the lives he'd ruined. She'd watched his skin flush then pale and then, when she was sure all the fight was gone out of him, she put two fingers to his throat and waited until his pulse slowed and weakened and finally stopped.

She met Riggott's flinty gaze.

'That's exactly what happened.'

ACKNOWLEDGEMENTS

My deepest gratitude first and foremost to Alison Hennessey for her wisdom and guidance as Zigic and Ferreira returned from their brief hiatus. She has always been their fiercest champion and without her continued support they might have detected their last in 2017. All authors should be so blessed.

Gushing thanks as well to Marigold, Ros, Lilidh, Lindeth and Sara Helen for everything they've done over the last year in shepherding this book to its final form and then taking it out into the world. The team at Raven really is special, passionate about good writing and dedicated to producing beautiful books, they are a continuing delight to work with.

Thanks to my agent Phil Patterson and the team at Marjacq for all their hard graft behind the scenes.

Thanks, as well, to Jay Stringer, Nick Quantrill and Luca Veste, for vital moments of distraction and occasional lapses in good sense.

As always I owe thanks to all the lovely reviewers and critics who have supported the series, and to all of the festival organisers who have been kind enough to let me on their stages, sincerest thanks.

Final thanks to my amazing family, for absolutely everything else.

NOTE ON THE TYPE

The text of this book is set in Linotype Sabon, a typeface named after the type founder, Jacques Sabon. It was designed by Jan Tschichold and jointly developed by Linotype, Monotype and Stempel in response to a need for a typeface to be available in identical form for mechanical hot metal composition and hand composition using foundry type.

Tschichold based his design for Sabon roman on a font engraved by Garamond, and Sabon italic on a font by Granjon. It was first used in 1966 and has proved an enduring modern classic.